THE LANTERN CLUB

THE LANTERN CLUB

Pete Bostock

Book Guild Publishing
Sussex, England

First published in Great Britain in 2009 by
The Book Guild Ltd
Pavilion View
19 New Road
Brighton, BN1 1UF

Typesetting in Baskerville by
Keyboard Services, Luton, Bedfordshire

Printed in Great Britain by
CPI Antony Rowe

A catalogue record for this book is available from
The British Library

ISBN 978 1 84624 327 1

Contents

A Paler Shade of Green

From the busy street, I came through the heavy swing doors into the club, glad to escape the thoughtless jostle of the shoppers. Buster Howes was in the bar and I tried in vain to hurry through to the lounge. Not that I didn't like the man, but when he was in drink, which was often, he could be a bit of an embarrassment and now, as he glanced across the bar towards me, it was evident from his owlish grin that he was already well into his stride.

'Have one with me,' he shouted, and, 'How's The Detail lately?'

I winced at the question as, still grinning foolishly, he clapped a Thespian hand over his mouth, knowing as well as I did, that Details were not to be discussed anywhere but in the upstairs room. But I went over to sit with him, knowing well that if I didn't, then I would either have to shout back or else leave the bar, and, as I said, I did like the man. He had courage and loyalty and, when he was sober, good conversation.

'Have a drink,' he slurred and, to save argument, I accepted.

'How's Doreen?' I asked.

'Fine. She's fine.' Buster always averred that his wife was fine. It always seemed that she was, too. A big-chested blonde who thought the world of him, she, too, drank, supposedly in secret. But there was never less of a mystery, for although no one could actually remember ever having seen her the worse for drink, yet it was almost as rare to meet her when she was cold sober. Whenever your

1

paths happened to cross, she would greet you happily –
whatever the time of day.

Doreen and Buster loved each other. And they both
drank.

'And how's your Janice, nowadays?' he enquired in turn.
I lifted my glass in answer and, in so doing, my eye fell
on his tie – tiny gold lanterns on a dark-green background
– one of only three such ties in existence. As it always
did when I saw any one of them, my mind took its usual
course. How long had it been now? I lied to myself. For
I knew exactly how long it had been. It had been four
years and two months since the Lantern Club had been
started in the upstairs room here.

The building belonged to the Social Club, here in
Fawkley, and a few associate members, myself among them,
had first mooted the idea of a splinter section in answer
to the cricket supporters in the place, of whom there
seemed to be a great deal too many. Any one of them,
in response to polite enquiry health-wise, always managed,
during the season, to make irritating reference to the
game, their remarks being limited to just the one phrase:
'Heard the latest score, then?'

As often happens, the whole thing began as a joke, but
by the end of the season we would just about be at the
end of our tether at such a strain on the precepts of
common courtesy. Buster alone would come out of it
happily. 'Thirty-eight million and one for two,' he might
reply, or, 'Love, twenty-six, the last I heard.'

Warwick Edwards, now our chairman, had made the
remark that, with summer approaching once again, the
leather-on-willow brigade would, as usual, show us no
mercy, and what could we possibly do about it? For murder
was out of the question. For one thing, it was against the
law. We couldn't have that, Warwick being one of the
town's most respected solicitors.

Kindred spirits had made suggestions and, as remarked, if only in jest to begin with, rules for a new club had been discussed. The thing took root and easily the most popular qualification agreed upon was the one which stated that any member of the Fawkley Social Club could apply for membership and would probably be accepted – unless of course, that member had ever been heard to express even a passing interest in the game known as cricket.

A member's tie was designed – tiny gold lanterns on a dark-green background. Leisurely, then, ideas were bandied about and a committee adopted. Annual outings and other such social activities were suggested and acted upon, and, for a time, this was about the extent of the new club's affairs.

Then, one day, when Buster had had a few too many and was becoming rather boisterous, someone made a remark which was to take the club rather more out of the ordinary. 'Tell you what, Buster,' the man had shouted above the din. 'Give up the booze for a fortnight, give us a bit of peace, and we'll make you the man of the year.' Everyone laughed, and in high spirits, others took up the idea, the upshot being that it was put before the committee for more or less serious discussion.

Nothing was heard for a few days and the matter was all but forgotten. But then, one evening, a single sheet of paper was passed around those members who happened to be in the club at the time, and in the equally light vein in which the idea had first been presented, the heading was 'Highly Secret'. 'Lantern Club members only'. Once again, everyone laughed, never a one of us having the faintest idea of the far-reaching results that would arise from that so lightly presented single sheet of paper. But at the time we laughed at it like schoolboys.

The single idea adopted is the one to be called The Detail.
This will be in the nature of a task, or assignment, which

may be suggested by any member, the said member also having the choice of attempting to carry out the task himself, should he so wish, providing that, in the opinion of your elected committee, the task and the member are suitably matched. (A particular task which may prove easily performed by one member could well prove nigh on impossible for another.) So, as a general precept, a suggested Detail should stretch the abilities and patience of the agent to the full, without being hurtful to anyone else. Illegal activities of any kind are out, of course.

Reward for successful completion of a Detail. Various ideas were mooted on the honour to be bestowed, it finally being decided that such a triumphant applicant will be presented with a special tie, one which will differ only from that of an 'ordinary' member's garment, by having a slightly darker-green background. This subtle difference will make it more unlikely that a non-member of our club will make remark.

We are, affectionately, your committee.

Everyone read the paper carefully, and Ken Sapey, laughing in his turn, had then taken the paper back, returning it to his pocket. A hospital porter, Ken was also a committee member – one of only four. 'That's it then,' he said. 'No social club noticeboard for this one, highly secret as it is.'

'I have a question,' said Kevin Lowe, entering into the spirit of the thing. 'Why should the committee alone decide when a Detail and a member are suitably matched? Tell me that, Ken.' Kevin looked around at the others, proud of his searching observation, and to his obvious delight, there were several grunts of assent.

'Well, as to that,' returned Ken, 'you'll all have to wait until the next general meeting for all the details. But on your particular point, Kev, I can give you the answer straight away, obvious as it should be. You see,' and he lowered his voice now, for effect, 'don't you think that some of these Details might be of a delicate and sensitive nature?' They had all fallen quiet. 'Don't you think,' he went on patiently, 'that there might be certain members who may inadvertently let something slip, to the embarrassment perhaps, of the whole club?'

All eyes turned to Buster. 'Don't look at me,' he spluttered. 'I can keep my mouth shut when I have to.' But in the finish, his laughter was as loud as anyone's.

As, gradually, the idea of the Detail took hold, it was soon appreciated by all, what subtlety and forethought had really gone into that single sheet of paper, whether with serious intent or not. For one thing, it was more than obvious after a moment's thought, that, for certain undertakings, discretion, at the very least, would be vital. This being virtually impossible to be assured for a body of twenty-odd members, no matter how good their intentions, the secrecy clause was thus inserted, the committee members alone being responsible for its application.

Another thing was the modesty in cost, of the honour to be bestowed on those who succeeded. Honour with little expense to the club. And it was only a single sheet of paper after all, flippantly produced and presented, so that if no one took the idea up seriously, then little or nothing was lost.

But the idea was taken up, exceeding all expectations, and the rules soon proved to be both popular and successful. The pros and cons of any suggestion were carefully weighed by the committee before commencement was allowed and no reasons were given in the case of refusal.

* * *

Had every member of the Lantern Club been asked to vote for the person least likely to succeed in his Detail, to win the first dark tie, they would no doubt have voted, so almost to a man, for Buster Howes. And almost every member would have been in error, for Buster, the beer-swilling, loud-mouthed, easygoing gossip, had shown us all a clean pair of heels.

The club was still very much in its infancy, with the rules not yet dry on the paper, when someone, slyly, perhaps even a bit spitefully, had suggested, as a Detail – the very first Detail – a six-week course on a health farm. No alcohol, said the man maliciously, and no bacon sandwiches at mid-morning. Not much of anything in fact. Except abstention. But think of it – the honour – the very first Detail.

Of course, the suggestion had been made well within Buster's hearing and after he'd had a few. Blustering forward, he'd been hustled quickly – and before he could change his mind – into the presence of John Combes, the only committee man in the club at the time and urged to put the idea forward, just as though it had been his own.

No secrecy possible here, many members hoping that expected and speedy failure might take some of the hurricane out of Buster's sails – if only for a time. The committee was quick enough to give the go-ahead, too, even deciding that the course could be paid for out of club funds.

Sober once more, Buster bluffed it out bravely. What was six weeks after all? Six weeks, I thought, was perhaps but an instant on a luxury cruise, but in a dentist's chair, an eternity, and this, I had no doubt, was how Buster would come to measure it during his ordeal.

We waited. In ever growing wonder, we waited and, after it was all over, it was the one topic of conversation

Buster would never open. I well remember the first day he first came in the club after his ordeal and it was easily seen that he'd lost a good twenty pounds in weight and, for a time, the sparkle had gone. And out of all those present I believe every one of them suffered some degree of guilt, someone even avowing that perhaps we'd gone a bit too far. It was hard to judge. Everyone seemed reluctant to open the topic and, for me at least, this only went to prove what a decent bunch they really were. It was thought-provoking, to say the least.

Buster's tie arrived and he was made to put it on, pink-cheeked with embarrassment for once. Then, as time passed and as the talk of this first Detail had died down, Buster's air of lethargy dwindled in its wake and more than once I caught myself unkindly wondering whether he hadn't milked the situation just a little. But I did have the grace to blush for myself a bit.

Whatever the case, the twenty pounds and the beer intake were soon back where Buster thought they should be, and for myself I had a new respect for the man. With little or no persuasion, he'd risen above what most people regarded as his problem, before settling back comfortably into the life he loved. I also thought of Doreen, his wife, in all this, and what part she'd played. The few times I did see her during Buster's sojourn at the place, she appeared to be her usual, happy and self-comforting self, completely, if a little hazily, in accord with Buster's actions.

All this was three years ago. Since then, only two more ties had been won. Three ties in three years. Three ties and a couple of failures – failures without disgrace, far from it, but still failures. Things had changed, rather. Many suggestions had been rejected as not being taxing enough to the individual and different qualities were now in demand, enthusiasm alone not being considered enough. The club, too, was now very comfortable financially and outlooks were broadened. John Combes and Barry Smith, two local businessmen, together with Ken Sapey and Warwick Edwards, still, however, comprised the committee. This was something which hadn't changed and it said something for the four of them that they had been returned yearly without opposition. I'd always had a sneaking desire to put up myself one year, but I knew I wasn't that popular. There it was.

For the rest, I had at least now proposed my own Detail.

I was still looking at Buster's tie. It was newish, for recently, at the cost of a few pounds, he'd decided that the old one, greasy and beer-stained as it was, was no longer in keeping with his station. I looked down at my own tie, which was just that bit paler shade of green. And I remember being rather gratified at how the committee had reacted at my suggested Detail. For they knew me after all – knew me for what I was – a motor-oil salesman without even the assertion of pretensions. A little pompous perhaps, yes, but only in a sorry kind of defiance. You see, I was trying to be honest with myself at last. They weren't very pretty thoughts. No wonder the committee had acted the way they had.

It was the bitter row with Janice which had really brought matters to a head, although, having been toying with the idea for quite a while, I knew that I was merely using the row as an excuse. Conscience was already at work, playing an uncomfortably large part in the whole thing, but I tried to put this firmly aside. Neither did it help much that Janice earned more than I did. It might have helped had she been ungenerous enough to mention it, but she never did. Working at Pellings in some kind of analysis work concerned with the internet, she contributed financially more to the household than ever I cared to admit. Except to myself, and even then, only in moments of self-pity. I expect it was simple guilt at just travelling around the country selling motor oil. Perhaps this was because I enjoyed the job so much. Then there was the horsey set she liked to knock about with. Some of them had real money and didn't have to live in the real world. All sour grapes on my part, of course. Janice had her own horse but she could afford it. It wasn't the money. It was the time. I said she should spend more time with Jamie. She'd come back with the answer, quite reasonably, that our son was nine years old, sensible, and liked being with his friends. And, as I was so concerned, why didn't I get a different job myself, spend more time at home?

She was right, of course; this is what it kept coming round to. Motor oil sold itself, being merely a matter of taking the orders. I was in a rut. A comfortable rut, but a rut just the same. The bickering had gone on. Hardly an ideal background for suggesting a Detail, this unsettled frame of mind. But I could hardly prevent the idea from presenting itself. I'd been passing through Morbury on my rounds at the time.

Morbury is one of those places that I was never sorry to leave. Perhaps I was missing something and, naturally, I am unable to speak for the residents themselves, but for me at any rate, it was the place where Dante might have lived, 'that awful other world', but even he'd had the best of it, I thought, for here, even the sun itself seemed to lack warmth.

As we waited for the lights to change, I studied the cab-driver on my offside. Under cover or not, a cap was jammed firmly on his head, making me wonder, unkindly, if he wore it to bed. I could almost see the red weal on his forehead and his expression was tense as he willed the lights to change. But I was invading his privacy and I turned away, to look instead through the limited view of my nearside window. There was a wall, its honesty hidden by neglect.

It was a windowless, Morbury wall and, over the years, the wind-blown dust had coalesced into sheets of grime and had got itself to work, eating into the mortar and staining the bricks. The healthy terracotta hue should, by now, have disappeared completely from the eye of man. But aided by the coat of the careless passer-by, the ceaseless assault of the wind and rain had managed to loosen this faceless outer skin's hold and it now hung in great strips, like spent wallpaper, or the hide of some great beast, in acceptance of imminent extinction.

The honking of the vehicle behind me made me start. The cab-driver, together with his cap, were almost out of sight. I moved on, looking at the houses for the first time in my many visits to the place. They were each someone's home, but it would have been hard, I thought, to detect any sign of welcome in any one of them.

The decision to stop here for lunch, too, was more than a mere whim. It was a sudden desire to look the place over properly and, like a painter suffering for his art, I chose deliberately to eat in the place most suited to my purpose, with comfort and its relatives pushed firmly aside. But there was little hardship in this choice at least, for all such establishments appeared to present an almost identical aspect, which was that of grimy frontage and questionable odours. I had always had something of a delicate stomach and thus, already full of self-praise, I dined at Tommy's. But if the man himself existed at all, he was not in evidence, the staff being made up of women, stooping of shoulder and tired of eye.

Seated on one of those hard, brown, round-seated chairs

reminiscent of those provided in the old-style dentist's waiting room, I noted without too much enthusiasm that there was a 'Waitress Service'. As I sat there waiting for my meal, I also had time to wonder how often the window cleaner called, and did he do the inside as well? But then, as a seasoned traveller, I had to admit that when the meal did arrive, it was hot, tasty and wholesome. What I could see of it, that is, through the layers of tobacco smoke, some of which, no doubt, were today's. And when I did thankfully emerge from the place, even the dank air of Morbury tasted sweet.

Fed on such a rich harvest and my personal life being at the low ebb that it was, my idea now took on more definite form. I would undertake to live in Morbury at weekends on a more or less regular basis and, to an agreed point, in somewhat unsavoury conditions – perhaps even cohabit – for a specified period.

The projected difficulties were both obvious and enormous at a glance, but as a mere agent I would hope to be leaving the more awkward bits, including financial decisions, to the committee. The main setback, of course, was Janice, and I quailed the first of many quails.

A little uncertainly now, I decided I'd be guided totally by the committee. For my own head was spinning on its way to join my scruples. Not the best of beginnings, perhaps, but if Buster Howes could win a tie ... I hoped I'd got the same kind of courage. In whatever form it was demanded.

I will always recall with pleasure the sharp-eyed glances, the frank interest and the surprise they'd shown as I'd outlined my idea. All had then looked directly at Warwick Edwards, whom, though under constraint to give it first word, would, so to speak, necessarily have the last one.

His well-known sense of humour now masked by his pose, he was tapping his long finger-ends together and looking at the ceiling, as one imagined he did with his clients as he imparted some of his vast and expensive knowledge. But pose or not, the thoughts were obviously tumbling through his mind, for when he did at last speak, and brief though the words were, the matter was put into simple perspective. 'I think we can get round any legal hitches easily enough,' he intoned. 'Any real difficulty is in the question of morals. Can we in conscience justify the ploy?'

During the pause that followed, my mind wandered to Warwick himself – surely a prime case for study. To one who didn't know him at all, and going on his appearance and general bearing, he would just as surely be put down as the archetypal cricket supporter and one who had probably played the game with some success in his 'varsity days'. I also caught myself wondering whether he really did study the scores.

But all eyes were suddenly upon me and, having written down what I had to say, I read it out, short and to the point as it was. The content of it was, that in my undertaking, should it be approved, no real hurt would come to anyone and, should anyone at all suffer, it would be me alone, and this, I respectfully reminded them, was what we were about.

I ended on an even more personal note, stating that whilst Janice had her horse, all I had was my motor oil.

Warwick's lips twisted in humour at that. 'Leave it with us,' he said then. 'We'll give the matter some thought.'

I could tell they were impressed, and I spent the next few days soul-searching. For it was no longer just an idea. I was committed. It was now a tangible prospect. It was all about standards really and I knew beyond doubt that if the positions had been reversed – if Janice had been the one belonging to a female version of the Lantern Club... I shied away from that one. (Why had lanterns been chosen as our emblem, anyway? I could never remember. And it was no good trying to hide behind irrelevancies, either.) So what I did swear to myself, was that I would take every step I could in lessening any discomfort to others. What else could I do? I thought of the few that had already won their ties.

Warwick Edwards, that finger-tapping man of business, with his spare frame and his smooth hair, had climbed the Eiger. The north face. So I couldn't offer to do that, thank goodness. Neither did I need Buster's health farm. Not really. Then I thought of young Harold Stone, the only other tie holder, and shuddered.

I did thank heaven for the secrecy rule, which stated that the agent alone could discard it should the task be one where secrecy was not required. Like the attempt last year made by Bill Thrower to swim the Channel. Bill had to be pulled out after three miles, with cramp. He hadn't won his tie and there were no second prizes. My goodness. I would be the first to invoke the... No, I would not. Jack Billets came to mind. He'd not only disappeared for a time, to come back pale and shaken, but he'd had regular bouts of absence since. Even Buster could find nothing out. It was obviously a good rule. I made up my mind there and then to be kindly to Billets, next time I saw him.

The committee was more generous than ever I could have hoped and Warwick was smiling as he outlined the terms, giving me the distinct impression that lately, suggested Details were getting a bit thin on the ground.

'You're to pose as a workman,' Warwick began, 'the Detail being approved without reservations. Flat-capped and muffler-clad, you're to become involved in what is euphemistically known as a relationship. How far this is taken is up to you,' and here, his smile broadened. 'From the establishment of this, er, liaison, a period of no less than six months will elapse.' I did gasp a bit at that one. 'Any queries from your wife during a number of weekends specified in the conditions will be dealt with in a satisfactory manner. In this respect, we have come to an agreement with your employers.'

To put it mildly, I was impressed, wondering what they'd said to old Stokes at the office. I expect solicitors do start off with an advantage in such situations.

Warwick carried on speaking. 'Naturally, the club will pay all expenses and, on the successful conclusion of your Detail, the club will arrange for a solicitor,' and here, the fingertips came together once more, as the other three members of the committee smiled outright, 'to inform your, er, lady friend of your sudden demise, together with the immediate promise of a cheque in a one-off payment of five thousand pounds, as a direct result of your "will", should the committee deem this action to be appropriate. You will not, at any time, either by inference or direct speech, make any suggestion of a closer relationship such as marriage. That would be against the law. For the rest, it will be a matter for your own judgement. The committee, in reaching these conclusions and in full agreement, obviously wishes you good fortune,' and Warwick was now smiling once more.

There was genuine interest in the atmosphere as they each shook my hand, certain as I was that they were amazed yet, that it was I, the motor-oil salesman with the rounded stomach and the slight air of self-importance, who had thought this one up.

'Don't enjoy yourself too much, now,' Warwick was saying as I passed through the door on my way out, and although he was the last man on earth I knew would indulge himself in sarcasm, I still detected a little dryness in the tone.

I boarded the 1803 passenger in plenty of time for the forty-odd minutes of the journey, nodding to my fellow passengers as I did so. On these occasions, I then always sat back, trying to relax, willing myself to be calm. But I never really made the condition. The train pulled out on time and this was the moment when I always told myself that I was once again committed to the routine.

The journey over, I alighted quickly, eager to get the next part over with for, for some reason, it seemed to me to be one of the more shameful exercises. I had a locker in the Brierley bus depot and making my way there via the subway toilets, I got changed. A large and scruffy-looking kitbag now held my city suit, together with my collapsible suitcase. A dirty blue work shirt was placed on top of the lot and then I climbed the concrete steps to the street. A seven-minute bus ride then brought me to Carson Road, where I began the twenty-minute walk to Garland Close.

For some reason, I always timed these journeys to the minute, always fearful that this time, something would go wrong – that the whole imposture would be exposed in some way. For one thing, my overalls were far too clean. They hadn't in any way been used since the last washing and I often had the almost insane desire to roll about in the street to try and soil them a bit, any humour in the situation escaping me completely.

In the rather vague belief that the exercise would somehow calm my nerves, which by now were as taut as bowstrings, I always walked, the irony being that this always had the completely opposite effect. It was no different today and, as I neared my destination, the sweat ran down my back, making me wonder stupidly if this would at least add authenticity to my role. But perhaps I was cheating not only others, but myself as well. Perhaps I walked merely to put off the inevitable.

My head began to spin. I wondered whether it would do any good to throw myself down after all – pound the pavement with my fists and maybe laugh hysterically. The sweat ran down to my bottom.

The councillors had been wily all right, when they gave the name Garland Close to the place. Probably trying to attract tenants quickly, get the rent started. But whatever image might be conjured up on hearing the name for the first time, it was bound to be the wrong one. It was a street of semi-detached boxes, was Garland Close, like so many other streets around it. No bay windows, no porches, no tiny sign of the architect's skill. But at the time it would be something, of course. Moving into a new house, I mean. 'I'm moving to Garland Close, you know.'

It was as I was clenching my fists, ready to turn in at the gateway of number 15, when a small, fluttering movement in the road caught my eye. A sparrow had been hit by a car. Its wing was broken and I picked up the terrified mite, cradling it in my hand. We went up the front garden path, soulmates together.

Over a period of nineteen weeks, this was my eighth visit to the house, 'coming home' every other weekend, or sometimes every third, in order to break the pattern. Janie would see me come up the path and she would open the door before I had chance to reach it. I always phoned and she was always waiting. Janie – Janice – Jamie. It always gave me a jolt whenever I thought about it. But I wouldn't read anything else into it.

* * *

16

It had been on the fourth weekend of my Detail when I met Janie. In the Lass and Garter. I had alternated between this pub and The Bell, seeing little point in trying to cover too much ground. I was dressed as a workman, although even in the beginning I had baulked at wearing a flat cap.

I'd been lucky, too, in meeting Janie so soon, for had many more weeks gone by the Detail could so easily have finished before it even started, through sheer lack of results. I couldn't keep coming here for ever and, whatever arrangements Warwick had managed to make with Stokes at the office, I couldn't keep up the break in my routine, small as it was, for ever.

But I'd smiled and Janie had smiled back. I'll never forget that moment. Not ever. It was the second when panic had almost set in. It wasn't too late even then. Not too late at all. I could go back and say that I simply couldn't find anyone and that the idea wouldn't be much without that. I would come up with another idea. Go back in failure.

'You're not from round 'ere.' She didn't speak too badly and I'd felt some relief about that. Not that I felt at all superior in any way, the odds being that her morals were better than my own now were, but I don't think I could have borne it if we couldn't converse in at least a reasonable way.

Neither was she a heavy drinker. She went there it seems more for the company of both sexes. But the reason, I think, why I was the most thankful was that she wouldn't take me home with her for several weeks. If the Detail wasn't going to prove worthy of the name, so be it. But any points on this score were dispelled once I saw the inside of the house.

Janie hadn't had an easy time. She hadn't seen her husband for years. He'd just taken off one day, leaving a note that he wouldn't be back and there was no reason to disbelieve her when she said he'd been both work-shy and an incurable womanizer. To make ends almost meet, Janie now worked at Cohen's Clothing, sitting at a sewing machine for hours on end.

I remembered having spun my own well-prepared tale. I worked away for a construction firm, I said, coming to stay at a workmate's home on odd weekends, a few miles from here. On one occasion, we'd arrived at his home only to find that his father, who'd been ill for a while, had died. Having been there a few times, I knew the family fairly well, but in their grief I had excused myself and promptly caught a bus back here. Fred, my workmate, had appreciated the gesture.

There were holes in the story, of course, and I'd searched her face anxiously for signs of suspicion, but she'd appeared quite satisfied with it. And it wasn't that she didn't listen to every word, either. For, to my shame, she seemed rather pathetically interested. My misery couldn't be measured in any way, but it was there, and I tried to comfort myself a little by the fact that it was I alone who was suffering from the charade. But deceit it was, and for this, I could find no real excuse. Strangely, too, I was rather thankful that this was so.

'Ready, Robbie?' There was a boy, about the same age as my own Jamie, and his mother could only go to the pub when he stayed with a school pal. I was, once again, thankful of the situation – that she wasn't in the habit of leaving him to his own devices. For what could I have done? The thought reinforced the fact that I was in an alien world and that I would have to tread carefully. Early doors, I know, for my stomach to start rumbling, but I'd always been a bit sensitive in that area. 'Is that the Rangers' scarf, Robbie?' Whenever I was there, and when Morbury were playing at home, I would take him. The first time I met him, he'd seemed ill at ease, apprehensive even, and saying little. But I soon coaxed him out of his discomfort by bribing him unashamedly.

I couldn't help but compare him with Jamie, of course, and I must say that Robbie came out of it well enough. Just a bit rougher round the edges, perhaps, but, everything considered, I suppose this was to be expected. And I think it was when I was talking to Robbie that my conscience pricked me the most, for I knew I should be spending this time with Jamie. Conscience. I wondered whether or not Warwick and the others had discussed the point. Surely they must have done. There were probably certain members of the club to whom all this would have been child's play – would have been turned down for the Detail simply on these grounds. I ardently hoped so. For I was convinced I was earning points already. Taking three schoolmates, two of whom made a point of ignoring my presence completely, to a match in which I hadn't the smallest iota of interest.

But Robbie himself was OK, and strangely I was more uncomfortable with his mother and this bothered me a great deal. On that first occasion when she finally took me into her bed, I faltered like any gangly youth. With her thin little body pressed up close and her tight little buttocks as hard as tennis balls, I just lay there, stiff in all the wrong places. 'I'm sorry, Janie,' I whispered into the darkness. 'I have a bit of a problem sometimes.'

'Don't worry about it,' she murmured back. 'Don't we all?' and promptly fell asleep.

* * *

19

On rare and treasured occasions, a large and quite undeserved blessing makes an appearance in most people's lives, I believe, and I was granted a boon. This was in the shape of my adopted family's personal habits. The first time I saw the house, I'd expected the worst, and once inside, I glanced around me fearfully, having the sudden hope, unlikely though it could possibly happen, that some kind member of the club committee would appear like a genie, see my trepidation in situ, and drag me off, saying that it was all over.

My main fear, however, quickly proved groundless, for Janie and the boy, together with their apparel, were always spotless – Janie through choice, and Robbie perhaps, through persuasion. In all of this, I soon came to what I saw as the only practical explanation, this being that as there was only a finite amount of energy and time to be spent, what with her having to go out to work and all, she expended what spare energies she had on herself and the boy. It made sense. On the limited diet she could afford, the house itself was too decrepit, too forbidding a challenge, for it to be otherwise. And then I saw what my Detail was really to be after all. It was the house itself.

The problem had grown quietly over the years, gathering strength for the time when its reign might possibly be disputed. Neither was there much to choose from in any of the rooms, but the kitchen was the nucleus – the obvious nerve centre of the whole issue – and here, the logical starting place was the floor.

A nicely polished red clay tiled floor is always a welcoming sight but, if over the years and through lack of care, slopped water is allowed to seep unheeded into the crevices, then it will inevitably respond by becoming somewhat uneven in plane. This is what had happened at 15, Garland Close, and it was always wise to keep this in mind, especially when carrying a hot utensil.

The sparrow was stiff and dead as, in the early-morning light, I took it from the paper-lined shoebox, wondering on the exact moment it had ceased to exist. Then I thought back over the weeks, how, here in the kitchen, surveying for the first time the scene in general, I had tried to determine which were the worst bits and where I might make the best start. I remembered my stomach beginning the first of its rumblings as I'd studied the tiles and marvelling on the time that the family had managed to live with them. And how these problems tend to grow so slowly that this present state of things comes to be regarded as the norm, together with the ever-increasing likelihood of an eventual accident.

Then there was the quiet but ominous hissing sound, constant and invasive, worst when the house was in slumber, pervading the whole place. And there was scant relief in finally tracing its source to the living-room gas fire. For although the irritation could be toned down a good deal by the simple expedient of closing the inner door, the custom of the household in general was, for some reason unspoken, that the door was always left wide open. I never did find out why.

Still in the kitchen, the paintwork was a contradiction in terms, and through it, the grain of the wood was clearly seen. Then there was the lightshade, flyblown and grey with the total acceptance of defeat.

But all these things were a mere setting, a complementary background hardly worthy of the name. For without any doubt at all, the centrepiece of the place had to be the larder door, which, for some reason beyond the ken of man, had been framed by a single row of white tiles. Crazy with the network of old age, the glaze on these strange oddities had all but disappeared and there was no help for any of them. No cure is known for the complaint and they languished there like pale old men craving the sun, brown only in the wrinkles – the etchings of time.

But, at least, they blended well enough into the setting, framing the door as they did in submissive self-effacement, for no matter where the glance was directed, the eye was always drawn back, as in some clever painting, to the focal point – the door itself.

I would catch myself gazing at it for minutes on end and, detecting the presence of an enemy, it would waken from its uneasy slumbers, sullen of mien and with the lethal breath of a basilisk. Even from my first cursory study of it, it became my bitter rival – my evil opponent. Battle was joined and one of us at the least would not survive in our present condition.

Surely, too, I was in good company, for I thought that Turner himself, that master of colour, would, on being asked to attempt a similar hue, have fled the house in shame.

The door was green, like the core of a boil, and when it had been painted on that day long ago, the workman had been in a hurry, due perhaps to the fading light of the day and, cursing the door and his employers both, he could once again be seen assailing the innocent panels, with long, coarse and vicious strokes, his brush as laden as it might be. And as I watched, I noted, without any surprise at all, that the man's features were not at all unlike my own. Quite without warning, he then dropped his brush in the pot and rubbed gently at his stomach, as though in some discomfort. For the years of insult, it seemed as though the door was now trying to exact some kind of revenge – or perhaps it was a cry for help.

The image began to fade and I tried to turn away, but I could not. Rooted to the spot, I still gazed at the door, quite nerveless to do otherwise, and we suffered together.

''Ave you made the tea, then?' The thin figure of Janie was behind me and I jumped visibly.

For a time, the kitchen door ruled my life. For there was no one with whom I could share my revulsion. 'Do you think I could have my tie now, Warwick? You see, there's a certain door. I think it's made me suffer enough.'

'Hm. Have you given thought to the fact that perhaps you're not quite up to your Detail? You *are* looking a bit pale.'

The cold light of morning was the worst, as situated directly opposite the only window in the kitchen, the damned door faced roughly east. It was then that the ravages of neglect were most plainly to be seen, certain painful-looking patches in particular seeming to emanate a plea to the morning sun, on one of its rare visits, to show them special favour, to illuminate them perhaps for a brief moment, in the illusion of lost youth.

Comparative relief might ensue as the day progressed, with the deepening gloom hiding the door's excesses a little as they blended in with their dingy background. Then, in the kindness of twilight, there would be further respite, a thankful but momentary peace, before starting again in horror, as the light from the sixty-watt bulb half lit up the room.

This sudden, shadowless glare was perhaps the unkindest cut of all, and the bile was back like the morning – maybe just a little paler shade of green.

I saw this hour as the Regency period – the door was a raddled Vauxhall buck, pitted with age and disease, the desperate, greasy make-up a mere death mask, accentuating, rather than hiding, the horrors beneath.

Only at bedtime each night, with its black blessing, was there any relief, and strangely I now began to see my role as one approaching empathy, with the door coming to represent all that was wrong with Morbury – the lost hopes, the carelessness, the submission.

* * *

Behind the door was the larder, a fitting partner to its guardian, and the first thing to be seen in this airless and gloomy cell, was a waist-high monolith of concrete, resting horizontally on a row of raw bricks on either side of it. But it wasn't really a fallen giant. It was just a shelf, known as 'the stone', a built-in feature of the house and on which rested the milk, butter and so on, to keep them cool. The designers needn't have bothered, though. The Ice Queen herself would have been content enough in that place. Providing she could have withstood the damp, of course.

But big as 'the stone' was, commanding such attention as it did in such an enclosed space, there was another which vied equally for notice. This was the beer bottle. Brown, empty and greasy with layers of dust, it stood in the exact centre of 'the stone', cap screwed firmly in place – a silent sentinel defying all comers. It isn't that I didn't know what it was. It was a beer bottle. The thing that made me ponder, however, was its station in life – its reason for being there.

Other, less definable articles skulked on the various shelves, as though waiting for signs of mischief. There they loitered, most of them coyly reluctant to reveal their identity, although one small container, a little bolder than its fellows, did proclaim its contents as Bicarbonate of Soda, the common properties of which are known to be white, crystalline and soluble in water. But I was sure that the small brown pebble in the bottom of the box, if put to the test, would easily have defied each one of these claims.

At my sudden, unwonted invasion of their privacy, they all cowered back, but although I sympathized with their nervousness, and knew that even should a tiny handful of antibiotics be hurled in there, they would have screamed for mercy, I bravely picked one up. This happened to be a basin. The only basin.

White with the pallor of ill-health, it had to contain bike grease. Or perhaps it was oven cleaner. 'What is this, Janie?'

'Why, it's dripping, you ninny. To cook with.'

What a ninny I was.

'Would you like me to decorate this kitchen, Janie?' I almost choked on every word. It was like telling the firing squad that it was a bit chilly and would they get on with it. But Robbie had a nasty cold and it was raining anyway.

Janie looked round the room in casual appraisal, as though there might be valid debate on the matter. 'It is a bit since it was done,' she said at last, her eyes coming to rest on the larder door.

I was holding my breath.

'Colour 'as faded a bit,' she conceded. But whether she would have made further comment was now left to conjecture, as at this moment, the front door was heard to open. 'That'll be mum.' Knowing her as I did, I thought the distraction would be complete. But I was wrong. I could hear them talking in the hall and, as they came through, I caught the tail-end of the gossip. '... said 'e'd start on the kitchen.'

Janie's mother was a tidy woman, keen of eye and severe of manner, and on the very few times we'd met, she'd been polite enough, deeming this, I suspected, to be nothing less than her Christian duty. But this was the warmest response I could ever evoke from her. I also had the impression that she'd long despaired of her daughter and subsequently, of course, a similar feeling would be extended to anyone associated with her.

But widow that she was, and thinking little of Janie as she might, she still carried out her maternal duty as she saw it, calling regularly and buying all Robbie's clothes.

On hearing now of my proposal to do the place up a bit, her eyes widened a little, making me wonder if this could be the beginnings of a certain respect. Janie had poured her a cup of tea and this she now studied intently, as though looking for cracks.

'The place could certainly do with it,' she said then, having none of her daughter's doubts on the matter. But there was no kinder comment, judgement being reserved until any results were forthcoming. Quite sensibly, too, I had to admit.

I could picture her own home, lacking any kind of welcome-mat, but clean, and with not a thing out of place.

When Warwick Edwards had climbed the Eiger for his tie, Alan Parkin, the one club member I didn't care for much, but who was subsequently to prove how ill judged my feelings were, was overheard to say that Warwick would have tackled the climb anyway. Whether the statement was taken out of context or not, it was quickly pointed out to Parkin that Warwick had not only insisted on paying his own expenses, but that he'd also been sponsored, raising two thousand pounds – a thousand for charity and an equal amount for the club. Comfortable enough, he was by no means what one would call a rich man.

When Parkin had made his remarks, Buster Howes had also been present and, having had one or two, he treated Parkin to his usual disarming smile, before saying, 'Tell you what, Alan. Give us two grand for your tie, and we'll let you off doing the Eiger.' Parkin had made no reply. He didn't ever appear to be the happiest of men.

I was boiler-suited, and the tools of the trade were scattered about, ready for me to make a start. If 15, Garland Close was my Eiger, then I reckoned that the kitchen door was the north face, and as I sat there, wondering where first to dig in the icepick, the front door was rapped and Janie hurried off to answer it. Her mother had already arrived. It was unusual, this, for her to call so soon after her last visit, making me think that perhaps she couldn't wait to see whether I'd made a start, that it wasn't just talk.

I affected to study the task in hand, whilst she responded by maintaining an uneasy silence. Robbie, who still nursed his cold, was treating it to a few sniffs and, as he read his comic, his grandma stroked his hair.

Muffled voices were heard and then Janie came in followed by Barry Smith. My jaw dropped. 'This man's from the Council. I mean the government,' Janie was saying. 'Asking if we'd mind answering some questions.'

Barry was smiling at everyone, holding out a small plastic wallet containing his photograph. 'Department of the Environment, actually. I wonder if you'd mind? It's just a survey – number of rooms, that sort of thing.'

I just had time to wonder how close this was to breaking the law. It had to be, but Janie was already motioning him to a chair. 'Of course,' she was saying. 'Will you 'ave a cup of tea?'

'Thanks very much. We did shove a note through the door. Earlier in the week. Is this the gentleman of the house?'

At this question, Janie's mother sniffed pettishly, whilst, I just sat there on the floor, playing with a tin of paint-stripper and smiling foolishly. The crafty devils though. Not a word of warning. But there wouldn't be, would there? Note through the door, indeed. But what did I expect, after all? They knew what the Eiger was like, as they also knew the kind of place in which Buster had sojourned.

But they didn't know Garland Close, number 15. Probably not even Morbury. Why, this place could have been a

27

little palace, all nicely tucked away in a sea of comfort. 'Sorry, old man. This won't do. Nice try though.' But apart from the number of rooms in the house, there was something else that Barry Smith didn't know and that was how long that tea had been made. He was just lifting the cup to his lips and as he paused for the merest instant to study the cracks in the vessel, I smiled in spite. But it had barely touched his mouth when his eye fell on the larder door. I gave silent thanks that I hadn't yet done it.

Barry wasn't bad. His gaze hardly faltered as he caught my eye. And I was just beginning to recover from seeing him. 'We were jus' sort of wonderin' whether to decorate,' I said. 'Change of colour, mebbe. Purple, mebbe. I'm startin' in 'ere.'

I'd dropped my aitches nicely and I held his gaze, which was saying something like, 'Rather you than me, too, but I think you may be overdoing the workman bit a little. You don't look too clever. Don't make yourself poorly.'

At least, that's what I hoped it said.

'... Three bedrooms upstairs,' Janie was chanting. 'They've only got two across the road, of course, but you'll already know that,' and Barry had to bestir himself, make some show of writing it all down.

Then, a little later on, as he was making his escape, I made the remark that he hadn't finished his tea. He winced visibly. 'Oh, I didn't, did I? Must get on though. Thanks awfully, everyone. G'bye now.' He dug me in the ribs as he passed out of the front door and I wondered if he'd caught Robbie's cold. I know I had.

It was over. I boarded the train and sat down, nervously fingering the knot of my tie – the one with the pale-green background. I looked out of the window at the dark walls of Morbury Station, wanting the train to start, and, as I did so, my mind drifted back over the weeks, on how I had almost faltered, with the combination of the smell of paint and Janie's cooking leaving memories not to be quickly erased. I hadn't felt too well lately, either. Maybe I was starting with a stomach ulcer.

I thought of Buster and Warwick. And I thought about young, impetuous Harold Stone, with his strange, but privileged upbringing and his high ideals. He'd gone abroad eighteen months ago. Human rights in China. When would we see him again, I wondered? We'd had just the two letters. His tie was waiting for him.

I thought of myself, wondering what the worst kind of suffering really was. It's up to the qualities of the individual, of course, but speaking for myself, I knew that the only thing which had kept me going was the agreed time limit and, even so, it had been a close-run thing. And I hadn't yet finished by any means – my conscience would be bothering me yet awhile. The committee had to be given credit for that, had me pegged just about right, I suppose, and ever afterwards, I could never quite make up my mind whether or not to be flattered by this.

I'd done two downstairs rooms, getting my well-kept hands into the grime and knowing that this particular little piece of Garland Close was now the better for it. There would be rejoicing by all concerned, casual and muted though it might be.

In the spirit of Saint George, I'd gone straight for the jugular – the larder door. I would never have been really able to concentrate properly on anything else otherwise, and the door had now lost its influence over me completely, in whatever guise, now shining with pride and green gloss as it was – a beacon to light the way to number 15.

The living-room gas fire might still be hissing in defiance, but the beer bottle was gone and, the very last time out,

I'd bought Robbie a new ball and boots. I also had the memory of Janie's mum, staring with approbation tinged with disbelief, at the kitchen walls, now mushroom in tone and ablush in unaccustomed splendour, whilst Janie herself dusted the new light bowl. This was every half-hour to start with, although these intervals would, I fancy, soon lengthen in time. Until the novelty wore off altogether.

I'd levelled the kitchen floor so that one could now walk across it in complete safety, whilst the crazy white tiles surrounding the door, were gone, chipped away, and with the gaps plastered and painted.

The living room should have been far less of a challenge, but with the steady increase in my physical ailments, I only just managed to finish it, now almost always sweating in pain.

There were other things. I'd lost weight, and Janice, my wife, from whom I'd started to grow apart, had remarked on it – shown concern. We were starting once again to grow closer together. Neither had the committee been idle, having already arranged with old Stokes, at the office, that I should have a change of route. Bit of a change and all that. How they'd managed that was a real mystery, but I wouldn't be coming to Morbury again. I understood, too, that in about a fortnight, Janie would be getting notice of my 'sudden demise' as the result of an accident, and of her expectations from the insurance company. A little while later, she would receive a cheque for five thousand pounds in a one-off settlement resulting from my 'will'.

I wondered what her mum would make of that.

The train rattled on towards Janice and Jamie. And I thought of Robbie and how, for a while, he might, in his own way, miss me a little. But not for long.

My name, by the way, is Derek Greene. D. Greene.

A PALER SHADE OF GREEN

Dark Green. Funny, that. Anyway, I hoped that the whole episode had in some way made me into a better man – less selfish; that the wish for a simple tie had been the innocent vehicle for bringing me home to my real responsibilities. Judge me if you will. Perhaps I had taken a tortuous sort of path to do it. But life is like that sometimes.

Double the Odds

David Clyde looked around with sudden interest, having the thought that it was rather unusual to see someone actually running in The Mall – shouting, too, which was even more unusual, especially when the noise was coming from a well-dressed businessman. But that's what was happening – waving his arms and shouting, 'Stop that woman.'

But there were several women – several dozens of women, in fact. Which one did he mean? And why did he want her stopped? Was it his wife, to tell her that she hadn't given him the car keys, or was it some stranger whose purse he'd found?

One young lady did hurry past, making for the stairs and smiling apologetically at David as she caught his arm. Very attractive she was, too, wearing a smart maroon suit rather than the usual sweater and jeans. He turned to give her a second look, for she was certainly worth it as she nipped smartly but calmly onto the escalator, going down, with her loose brown curls being the last part of her to disappear.

Then the arm-waver-cum-businessman came up, stopping a middle-aged, military-looking chap near David. 'Did you see her? Which way she went?'

The one with the ramrod back and short, greying hair, grabbed one end of a bristling moustache between finger and thumb. 'I believe I did, sir. Running? Pretty? Made for the stairs, sir.'

'Down or up?'

'Down, I believe. Why, sir? What's the trouble?'

But the arm-waver was gone in pursuit, and, intrigued as he was, David hung about, for there wasn't that much excitement in his life. Neither, just at the moment, was there that much urgency, for he was on his dinner hour. And the girl had been very attractive; what bit he'd seen of her, that is. Having already eaten, he glanced at his watch. Plenty of time. Neither had he long to wait, for now, a dark-suited young man of about David's age appeared in the wake of the older one, his hurried manner indicating an interest as he searched faces, going from one to the other in apology.

Loitering as he was, it was now David's turn for attention. 'Excuse me. Do you happen to have seen...'

'Down the stairs,' David interrupted, and off the young man went, thanking David as he ran.

They were a while. Four and a half minutes to be exact, the two men coming back up the moving stairs together and, curiously now, David was suddenly conscious of a thankful relief that they hadn't got the girl with them. They were talking animatedly together and David now assumed a right to know. 'Did you catch her, gentlemen? What was the trouble?'

The two stopped willingly enough. 'Thief,' said the older man, still a little out of breath. 'We're at the jeweller's on the corner. She was clever. Took a watch to the door. See it better in the daylight, she said. Before I could even think about it. Smartly dressed, you see. It makes all the difference, although we should really know better by now. Then she was off. Had us wasting time having the toilets searched downstairs. Too clever to be caught in there, though.'

'Watch worth much?'

'Four-fifty or thereabouts. That's hundreds, of course,' the jeweller grinned without humour.

David pursed his lips.

'We are insured, of course,' the man said then, and nodding in a friendly way, the pair then made to move off. But the older one turned back quickly again. 'By the way,' he said. 'Did you happen to get a good look at the girl at all? See anything about her I might have missed?' 'Sorry,' David lied, 'I only caught a back view, I'm afraid.'

'Well, thanks anyway. We'd better get back before they empty the shop,' and this time, there was even a touch of humour in the grin. Again, they nodded in farewell and moved off.

As he made for the stairs himself, to take him to the street, David was suddenly struck by the most alarming idea. She had brushed against him. Had she shoved the watch in his pocket? He had heard of such things. Stupid, really. Why would she do that? But as his hand shot to his pocket anyway, he felt real relief at finding it empty. It was as though the incident had unnerved him in some way. And then he knew what it was. It was that glance of hers – the glance that had reduced him, like some witless schoolboy may have been, to lie so readily.

Coming out now into the street, he gazed into the distance for a moment, suddenly wishing that the whole thing could happen again – that time could go back just that tiny bit. Then he'd be ready to ... ready to what? He looked at his watch and knew that he'd have to hurry if he wasn't to be late back for work, to the humdrum life of the building society. And daydreams were all very well, he told himself, but perhaps she hadn't been that pretty, after all.

He saw her through the window of the café. There she was, calmly drinking tea and opening the pot lid to peer

in as he watched. Not for the briefest second did he
hesitate, even though he was now certain that he'd be
late back for work. 'Can I join you at this table?'

At the sudden intrusion, she looked up quickly, but
recovered just as quickly to look meaningly at two other,
empty tables nearby and with her eyebrows raised the
merest fraction. There was not the slightest sign of fear,
of apprehension. Neither did she offer to speak as,
uninvited, he sat down. 'How much is it worth, do you
think? The watch, I mean.'

'Watch?' Her self-possession was quite remarkable, he
thought. As it had to be, of course.

'Yes. The one from Caseys. The one they tried rather
hard to get back just a short while ago.'

'Ah, *that* watch.' Her voice was like velvet, something
of a dark colour, he thought.

'That's the one.' But he was lost, knowing now without
doubt why he had become so deliberately involved. For his
first impression, fleeting as it may have been, was now
certified beyond all thought. She was some beauty. In the
eye of all beholders, surely. His first sight of her, in fact,
had in no way done her justice. The large brown eyes, the
loose curls, the soft, generous mouth. Yes, he was lost, and
it was all he could do to stop himself from staring.

'Are you the police?'

'No.'

She was now smiling softly, idly levelling the sugar in
the bowl with her spoon as she did so. 'Are you going
to turn me in, anyway?'

He tried his most winning smile. 'Now why would I
want to do that? It wasn't my watch. I suppose that makes
me not an upright citizen, doesn't it? What's your name,
by the way?' It all sounded a bit trite, he knew, but for
the present at least, he'd been robbed of whatever wits
he had.

'Jennifer. Jennifer Wentworth.'
'Do people call you Jenny?'
'People call me Jennifer. What do people call you?'
'Well, most of them call me David Clyde.'
'And what are you doing here, David Clyde?'

By the time he left, now certain to be well late back for work, she had agreed to see him again. But now that his wits were returning a little, he quickly put this into perspective, for under the circumstances, it was obvious that she would agree to do so. Simple expediency, of course, and there was no chance at all that she would turn up. But this didn't stop him, as he now hurried along, from dwelling heavily on the business. He tried hard to be honest with himself, readily admitting that he wasn't the most enterprising soul in the world. Confused, he then gave thought to the morals of the thing, and thinking about the law as the next logical step, he thought it was more than likely that he'd broken that already, and after all, he did work in a building society, a place where trust was paramount.

Why am I doing this? he wondered. Wasting time. All rather academic. He then finished up by telling himself that he probably wouldn't even bother to keep the appointment himself, although this conclusion did create a little ball of disappointment, which came to rest unhappily in the pit of his stomach.

Eric Southern raised his brows and looked pointedly at his watch. David went across to him. 'Sorry, Eric. Unavoidable, I'm afraid.' He then gave Southern a brief account of the incident in The Mall, blaming his late arrival back to work on his words with the jeweller. And

Southern seemed satisfied, his eyes gleaming as David described the girl's figure. It was common knowledge that Eric appreciated a well-turned ankle, married though he was. Tittle-tattle was bandied about in the office, but in a place like this, thought David, it would have come as something of a surprise had it been otherwise. It served to lighten the burden of the day, after all, and David would have loved to see Eric's face should he have had the slightest inkling of the meeting in the café. But David quailed at the very thought, grinning to himself as he made his belated way to his window – Eric as a ladies' man with the front half of his hair gone and with his soft, white and rather podgy frame. Still, he thought, Eric's always been OK with me.

'Good afternoon, madam. Can I help you?'

Jennifer looked radiant – even lovelier than he remembered. There was never any real doubt about his going, of course. He was at least ten minutes early – it was more like twenty in actual fact – concealing himself in a doorway, like a burglar, watching the spot. Then there she was, on the corner of Jason's Emporium, well away from The Mall. He watched her greedily for a full minute, drinking in the sight of her.

'You came, then,' he said lamely.

'Of course I came.' The smile was genuine. 'Why wouldn't I?'

Why not indeed? He didn't say it, though. For with her looks and figure, she could rather have, well... He'd always considered himself just about average. At twenty-six, he had a good enough body, played football once a week for the Fawkley Office Workers team. Had a good enough standing in the community and so on, but he then quickly shied away from this one.

'What would you like to do?' was what he did say.
'I'm hungry. What about a hot potato filled with cheese.'
'Sure. Whatever you want.' He looked at her in an even
newer light, having been quite prepared to spend more
than this – had fully expected to do so. She had dressed
like the spring that it was, in a suit of vernal green with
just a touch of white froth at the throat, the picture of
beauty – of innocence. The thought gave him a start.

Jason's Emporium has balustraded walkways, reached
by steps from the street, and here, overlooking the market,
with the ribbon of river beyond, they sat in one of the
alcoves with their modest meal, and a glass of the strong
beer for which the place is famous. Then afterwards, they
rested there in comfort, just watching the light fade and
saying nothing. He was more than content in her silence
– just to be there, but at last, as other lights began to
twinkle over the town, in surrender to the evening, they
looked across at each other, knowing they would have to
move. 'What now?' he asked.

'My place, I think,' she said simply.

'Shall we take a shower?' she had asked, and all he'd
managed in reply was a breathless nod, his mind more
pliant than the softest putty.

She had a flat on the edge of town, near the hospital,
and the twenty-five-minute walk from the emporium had
been made in the same comparative silence they'd enjoyed
for the last hour.

David's thoughts were nothing more than a jumble, a
mess of tangled questions. What did Jennifer really think
of him? What about the watch, with all its implications?
What was he getting himself into? But in this present
comfortable state, he held all these things at arm's length,
refusing to let them even begin to take more serious hold.

Jennifer, too, had spoken little, content, it seemed, as they walked, to enjoy the quiet of the evening. There was a slight chill in the air and stars began to appear – pinpricks of silver, puncturing the velvet of the night sky. She'd taken hold of his hand, making him wish that the walk might last for ever. For he knew how fleeting the whole affair was bound to be.

The flat had turned out to be both roomy and strangely immaculate, without so much as a book out of place. There was the one single ornament, that of a young girl in bronze. She was in the act of pulling a vest over her head, the taut young nipples pointing upwards.

The only other real indulgence towards decoration was a painting on the matt-finished walls, a scenic diorama of the type so often seen in one of those galleries, narrow and long, and in which one only ever seems to see, should one be looking for signs of life, the proprietor himself, lean and bow-tied, and daring the mere passer-by to invade his privacy.

'Shall we take a shower?'

To David, the following hour or so was a time when every detail would be recalled again and again, to be savoured and dwelt on, lingered over, before being put back like a costly wine until next time. Jennifer, in the impeccable setting of the flat, had the kind of figure seen in glossy magazines, those pictures which had been so carefully picked out of hundreds. Her skin had the sheen of health, firm, but with the touch of silk.

They showered together and then lay on the bed, covered by a single sheet. He caressed her gently, his hand coming slowly down her belly to the dark triangle below. She opened her slim thighs willingly but without wantonness, an act of surrender rather than one of passion. Then shortly afterwards, unable to help himself and in the crudest of terms, the end came quickly. But after the briefest of rests after which his heart had slowed down to a more bearable rhythm, he began once more, gently again but firmly, and this time she too, moaning quietly, reached the heights, as he once again reached his.

The flat was on the second floor and there was a tiny balcony. With the windows open, they sat there on a low couch, a blanket round their shoulders against the cool night air.

A cat had appeared from somewhere, Suky, a tortoiseshell, but still a mongrel several times over. She jumped on David's lap, as was her right, purring loudly.

'You like cats, do you?' asked Jennifer.

'Have I any say in the matter?' he laughed back.

'Would you like a drink of some kind, then?' she smiled.

'Nothing, thanks.' He would really have loved one, either hot or cold, but he just didn't want things to move on. He wanted to stay like this. Soon though, he knew the time had arrived. He knew he could have put it off another ... minute? Ten minutes? 'Jennifer.' It came as something of a shock to realize that it was the first time he'd actually used her name.

'Yes, David.' A single lamp burned behind them in the far corner of the room, making the hospital show bright with a hundred lights. But as she turned to look at him, her face was indistinct in the shadow of the couch.

He was now hesitant and uncomfortable, as though he was about to betray a trust. 'It's about the watch,' he said unhappily.

'Of course it is,' she replied. 'And you've a right to know. Though not every right.' She turned her head again, looking into the distance and putting her head back on his shoulder. The faint fragrance of her hair almost intoxicated him and, yet again, he began to feel arousal,

41

his resolve melting like butter. But the die had been cast. 'It's my living, David,' she said, almost making him jump. 'Stealing is my sole source of income. I'm pretty good at it, too.'

She was still gazing across at the twinkling hospital, and she paused, as though expecting him to interrupt, to protest. But he said nothing. He was determined to listen.

'It's a simple enough story,' she went on then. 'Whether morals are supposed to play a large part in it is a thing I don't often care to think about. If I did... Anyway, it all started when I was seventeen, six years ago. Mother had died two years previously, an operation that went wrong. I thought Dad would go crazy, but as time passed he seemed to get over it a little. I was suffering a great deal myself, naturally, but in the early days, distraught as he was, I had everything to do – run the whole house, young as I was – and the work seemed to take my own mind off it a bit.' Beneath David's hand, her shoulders were trembling at the memories. 'Then eventually, things seemed to be getting themselves into some sort of routine. But then it started. As I said, I was seventeen, and that only barely. I would catch Dad looking at me in a strange way. He would colour up and look away. But then he would accidentally come into the bathroom when he knew I was in there. So one day, when he was out at work, I just packed a case and left, leaving him a note, so that he wouldn't report my absence to the authorities.'

Outside, it was now quite dark, and Suky, deciding she'd had enough of his lap for a while, jumped down without so much as a glance of thanks, although David hardly noticed.

'I got a cheap room,' Jennifer went on. 'Incredibly dirty it was, too, but then, I was in no position to pick and choose. Then I got a job as a waitress in a café which wasn't much cleaner than the room, but I wasn't much trained for anything else and I had to earn a living quickly. The life wasn't the best in the world and on average, once I did start work, I got my bottom pinched twice a day. I didn't snap. I just took the decision, and the very next time it happened, I stumbled, dropping a bowl of boiling mulligatawny in the man's lap – a fat youth, really, with a lardy skin. Even as I began to apologize profusely, I thought he was going to burst. At the end of the shift, I told the manager that I wouldn't be back. He was a large, not unkind man, paying me till the end of the week and saying he was surprised I had stuck it for as long as I had, that I deserved something better. I'd been there for less than five weeks. But the next three years were more of the same. Three years, David.'

Her head was still on his shoulder as she stared out at the hospital, reliving the nightmare of it all. It was a while before she spoke again, during which time it didn't even begin to enter his head on whether to judge her one way or the other, or on the path he would have chosen for himself in similar circumstances, as happily, the occasion had never arisen. Being brought up normally by his parents here in Fawkley, his path had, so far, been a smooth one.

'Then one day,' Jennifer now went on, 'I went out, spent money on smart clothes and started stealing. It's so easy and, in all this time, I've made money. I've got insurance against that, too.' She turned to look at him again, putting her hand impishly where he would most have wanted her to put it. His breath started coming in gasps and then there was a loud clatter from the kitchen.

He sprang to his feet, startled, noting absently that the cat was curled up on a chair, close by. At the noise, the animal merely glanced up in casual enquiry and Jennifer was laughing out loud.

'It's all right, David. Really. It's my flatmate. We have a signal. And for you, it means that it's time to go.'

'Flatmate?' he said, stupidly. 'You didn't tell me you had a flatmate.'

'No, David, I didn't. Neither did I tell you that I have a liking for mayonnaise. Now you know both things.'

But he wasn't listening, for panic was setting in. He was being bundled off. Was this it? The brush-off? 'Will I see you again?'

'Of course you will. But you have to go now.'

He could hardly get his jacket on in relief, making arrangements as they walked through to the kitchen. There was no one there and Jennifer made no explanations. 'You'll see her some other time, perhaps,' was all she said. But at least, it was further relief to hear that the mystery person was of the female gender.

Warwick Edwards, honorary chairman of the Lantern Club, didn't think much of the idea at all, and said so, and vague as it had been in the telling, David couldn't say that he much blamed him.

The idea had come to him as he walked home from Jennifer's place. At almost every step, he'd tried to think of ways in which to make the notion more clear, more detailed, if it was to go for possible perusal by the committee.

David had been lucky, catching Warwick in the bar on the first night after his date with Jennifer. 'Can I see you in private for a few minutes, Warwick, do you think?' and, taking their drinks with them, the two had gone up into the sprawling old room they used for general meetings, a room which had changed little or not at all since the place had been a coaching house so many years ago. Comfortable enough, but lacking a crowd, there was a rather gloomy air about this great chamber.

They sat down in two of the battered old chairs and

44

David launched into his tale and his idea for a Detail, telling Warwick briefly of nearly the whole affair concerning Jennifer, though concentrating rather on the more salient details of the robbery. It was at this point that Warwick held up a hand in alarm. 'Stop, David,' he said hurriedly. 'Before you go any further, let me say this. Name me no names. Some of the jewellers in the town are my clients. I am their trusted solicitor. Caseys in The Mall, and the Overton Brothers quite near it are but two of them, so please, David, name no names.'

It had been a close-run thing and David could have kicked himself. Of course. Warwick was solicitor to many in town, as he was to David's own parents. Ever since he had first set eyes on Jennifer, he hadn't really been able to think straight and he had almost made Warwick's position untenable. He let his breath out in late relief and carried on cautiously with his tale, coming to a close by saying that what he wanted was a way in which he could persuade Jennifer to give up this kind of life, return the stolen watch perhaps – settle down to something more normal? Could Warwick perhaps enlarge on the idea in some way? As a detached observer? And was it worth putting in front of the committee?

Warwick Edwards, who besides climbing the Eiger, had seen it all and more, smiled fondly at the younger man. 'You want the lot, David, is that it? The help, the tie, and the girl? Are you sure that's all?'

'Something like that, Warwick, yes,' David smiled back, trying to sound diffident.

The older man now put the tips of his long fingers together, leant back in his chair and gazed up at the ceiling, the very picture of pomposity. David looked at the man, affectionate in his turn, knowing that the pose, whether studied or not, could not have been further from the truth. For Warwick Edwards was the finest man he knew. When he had climbed his mountain to win his tie, he had also raised a thousand pounds for charity in the process, and when he studied the ceiling like he was now doing, David knew that it was usually for someone's good.

It was a while before Warwick's gaze came back to David. 'Look at me and listen carefully, David,' he said now. 'At my hats. I'm wearing three hats.'

'Three hats?'

'Yes.' He now became brisk, businesslike. 'I'm your friend, your solicitor and the chairman of your club. And it's rather difficult to separate the three roles. There are very obvious difficulties in your idea, David. Firstly, the watch. The law on theft is very specific but, of course, you know that. But let me remind you of the Act. It says that a person is guilty of theft if he, or, of course, she, dishonestly appropriates property belonging to another with the intention of permanently depriving the other of it. That's your Jennifer, David. As for yourself, your case is slightly different. As you didn't aid, abet, counsel or procure the commission of the offence, you can't be tried as a principal offender.'

David had now begun to look somewhat uncomfortable. This was, after all, a cold analysis of the facts and, for the moment at least, the romance was being left far behind. But Warwick didn't even pause in his flow.

'But concealing an offence, even though, under this section, prosecution may be instituted only with the consent of the Director of Public Prosecutions – I do go on, do I not, David? But you begin to see how serious it is. However, I won't snitch if you don't,' and at this, he smiled for the first time.

'What next? You say the wench is good in bed. My goodness, David, when did you last have a bad one? And what do you actually know about her? You know she's a thief, and she could, therefore, just as easily be a liar.

She could have been telling the truth, of course. About her past, I mean. Probably is. It's a damned shame how some people are treated, I know. But tread carefully, David. You say she's very particular, that the flat is spotless. Well, if she wasn't fibbing after all, that's probably because she had to live in squalor for so long. In that case, it's a wonder she didn't make you take a bath before you got her between the sheets.'

David's jaw dropped and Warwick laughed. 'I was right, then. She did.' But he quickly became serious again. 'And who is this flatmate, David? Surely she has to be in the thick of it. Did Jennifer ever actually get caught, did she say? Stealing, I mean?'

'Once. And she said she had insurance.'

'Insurance?'

'I'm sure that's what she said...' The utterance of which, of course, meant that he wasn't sure at all. In fact, he wasn't really certain of anything any more, having the thought that Warwick was also wearing a fourth hat, which was that of critic. For the moment though, the solicitor had now fallen quiet again, pondering the facts.

'I'll have to give it more thought, David,' said the older man at last. 'I must be honest, though. I can't really see much in the idea. Not yet, anyway. We legal blokes have a saying which fits your case nicely. Being legal blokes, it's a bit long-winded, but here it is. "There is nothing in a client which is as regularly dishonest as one with an erection, for when push comes to shove, as it usually does, then both guilt and conscience are left far behind." Think about it, David, and we'll talk again. Now let's go down and have another drink.'

Although he was seeing Jennifer on the following evening, which was the Friday, she had also said she would see him

47

during his lunch hour, at The Sidings, a big pub near his place of work, and a relic of the old railway days. It was as though she was eager for his company and he was flattered.

By the time he arrived, the place was already filling up with the lunch-hour trade, but she was already there, at a small table near the window, a white wine in front of her, and beer for him, ready on a mat. This was some girl, he told himself, ignoring the fact that he might be taking these modest actions on her part out of all proportion. If only she...

'Hello, David. I was a bit early. Beer of the house all right?'

'Fine, thanks.' He took a good draught of the cold beer. 'How's Suky?'

She laughed. 'She's fine, too. Missing you, I think.'

They made small talk, easily, and without any sign of the strain he'd feared. The relationship was, after all, still a young one. They couldn't talk intimately of course, not in here. And he suddenly realized that this was what he wanted – to shirk what he knew were his responsibilities – let things drift on as they were. There was, after all, nothing like the good times. He didn't want to have to worry about her past, with all its attendant worries. All daydreams.

'OK for tonight?' he asked. 'Sure you don't want to go anywhere different?' As he said this, he couldn't resist putting his hand under the table and onto her silk-clad knee.

She tapped his hand and pushed it away. 'My place will be fine,' she said in mock primness. 'Unless, of course, you...'

He smiled happily. 'You kidding?'

Had he given it any thought at all, the last person David

would have wanted to see come through the door of the pub was the jeweller from Caseys, but just about the next one in line now did so in the shape of Eric Southern. There was no chance of avoiding him, either. He saw them straight away, weaving his way through the crowd without even calling first at the bar. Not that he wasn't already drooling. 'Hello, David.'

David had to look up, expressing surprise, and Southern just stood there, without either a drink or a chair, and willing David to get him both. But David did neither, hoping that the man would take the hint and excuse himself.

Jennifer was smiling without embarrassment. She'd known enough Erics to last her a lifetime, was fully inured to all their affected charms.

'Aren't you going to introduce me, David?' Eric wasn't the one to give up so easily as that, not seeming too worried about the weakness of his position as he looked round desperately, hoping to grab a chair without leaving his spot.

'Oh, sorry, Eric. Of course. You haven't met Jennifer, have you?' said David, hoping that his tone suggested that he wasn't quite sure. 'Jennifer. This is Eric. Eric. Jennifer.' He wasn't at all certain whether it was polite to introduce one or the other of them first, but then, he began not to care, his annoyance at Eric's stupidity getting the better of his good manners. He just wanted Eric to go.

But Eric was made of much sterner stuff than that, and anyway Jennifer was giving him a smile that would just about melt stone. Eric reacted predictably, beginning to devour her from the ankles up.

'David,' she said then, 'aren't you going to get Eric a drink?'

At this, Eric's eyes shot across to David, but David would have none of it. 'I'd love to, of course, my dear,' he said sweetly, 'but we just don't have the time,' and he was already getting to his feet and pointing to his watch. He cupped a hand under her elbow, steering her to the door. 'Sorry, Eric,' he flung over his shoulder. 'Another time, eh?'

'That's all right, David. Next time, then.' Eric's eyes were still on stalks.

Fifty yards down the road, they clung to each other in paroxysms of laughter, and in this woman David saw nothing unseemly in it. For the merriment was genuine, breaking down a few more barriers between them. 'Did you ever see Bluto in the *Popeye* cartoons, eyeing Olive Oyl?' he spluttered.

'I think I did,' she laughed. 'Poor old Eric,' and they began to giggle once more. Then a tiny cloud appeared in the day, as he thought he detected a note of spite in her laughter. It wasn't much, and she may even have been unaware of it. Or perhaps she was trying to disguise it as the memories came flooding back.

Then it was really back to reality, and she sauntered back with him to work, there to squeeze his hand in farewell. 'Tonight,' she whispered. He hurried to work, walking on air.

Eric was already back at his desk. 'You lucky dog,' he said, as David passed him, and from Eric, David couldn't help but remark to himself that the remark sounded somehow distasteful.

As he dressed carefully for his meeting with Jennifer, David looked round his bedsit in dismay. Working where he did, he could easily have kept his eye open for a far better place than this, but with his lifestyle, casual as it was, he knew that this was the biggest place he could trust himself to keep clean. And the trust had been broken at that. He shuddered as he thought of Jennifer's place. One more stale crumb on his old carpet, and it would have been a case of the two extremes. He promised himself he would go through the place properly on Sunday. Then, as he was still looking around, his eye caught the huge bunch of flowers, and the wine, both looking a bit out of place in the dingy room.

He picked up the bottle to read the label again. 'Cuckoo Hill Viognier, Vin de Pays. Good with fish or chicken.'

'Hm. I wonder what it's like at Cuckoo Hill?' he said to himself, for nothing could really repress this flippant mood of his as he thought of Jennifer. His eye was still going absently down the label, although he knew nothing much of wine, but at six pounds the man behind the counter had said that it was a bargain, this week's steal. Even in his present, happy mood, the word made David wince.

'Prezzies,' he said, as she opened the door. She was dressed in a soft, diaphanous garment the colour of flame, with a wide belt of the same material holding it in at the waist. He looked at her in awe, wondering if he would ever manage to get used to her beauty, or indeed, whether he would know her long enough to get the chance. 'You look gorgeous,' he said, and she smiled, holding the door wide.

He went in, looking round the room almost anxiously. But there was no sign of anyone else and he stood in thought for a moment, unsure of whether he was pleased or not. 'I thought she might be here – that I might meet her. Your flatmate, I mean.'

'Oh, she went out a while ago,' she answered, taking the flowers and going into the kitchen for water. 'She'll be back later,' she was saying as she came back into the room. 'Aren't the flowers lovely?'

What he would have liked to say then, was, 'When?

When will she be back, Jennifer?' But he said nothing of
the kind, knowing that the question would be out of place,
like some badly ad-libbed line in a play, spoiling the
atmosphere – even perhaps creating a certain tension.
And he could never remember being so happy. He wouldn't
spoil this for anything. Strange, too. For in addition to
his pleasure, he could never before recollect feeling so
sensitive to a situation, so aware. But then, he had to
admit that he wasn't much in the habit of giving a great
deal of thought to anything.

She was still looking at the flowers, now in a heavy,
cut-glass vase in the centre of the table. She moved them
again just a fraction. 'They are lovely, David,' she said
again, kissing him lightly on the lips. 'Let's have something
to eat now, shall we?'

It was goulash, lightly flavoured with paprika, and there
was fresh, crispy bread. She opened the wine and, taking
a delicate mouthful, said it was just right. Not a wine
person himself, David enjoyed it well enough, thinking it
had a nutty taste. After they had eaten their fill, he sat
back and, shamefully, felt as though he could have nodded
off. Jennifer got up and began to clear the table, saying,
'Why don't you go and lay on the bed? I'll just wash
these dishes.'

'No shower?'

She smiled,. Almost a dreamy expression. 'Let's not
bother. Not tonight.' And what he wondered vaguely as
he went to the bedroom was what Warwick have said to
that. Quickly and completely disrobed, he got under the
single sheet, then got up again to go to the bathroom.
He came back, looked at himself mischievously in the
dressing-table mirror, and then lay down once more. He
was asleep in under two minutes.

He knew where he was, cracking his eyes open almost
in panic, and looking at his watch. He'd been asleep

twenty minutes, or thereabouts. He could hear movement on the other side of the door, just before it opened. 'Sorry I've been so long,' she said. 'You look comfy.'

'All the better to eat you with,' he answered, laughing.

She came across to him quickly, leaving the one small lamp burning, and on this occasion, he noticed, her eyes were moist-urgent. He began to get up but she pushed him back, straddling him straightaway. 'Foreplay later,' she said hotly.

'If you insist,' he murmured back.

She began slowly, in a steady rhythm, her breath coming in light gasps, and coming at him as she had, he had to control himself – tried to think of other things, such as why she had never mentioned protection of any kind, and how he would like to stay here for ever. In any capacity. Stupidly, an old song came into his head, but he could only think of the first line. That's usually the case with old songs, he said to himself. 'On the good ship Lollipop...' He reached up to cup her breasts, but that was his undoing, shooting up into depths unknown. Then, a bare second later, Jennifer's own breath came out in a whoosh as she collapsed on top of him.

She rolled away from him and he raised himself on a bent elbow, looking anxiously at her face. Then, satisfied with her expression, he caught his own breath for a moment or two before beginning again, kissing her lips and her body as he eased her onto her back, then poking her navel with his tongue and caressing the inside of her thigh. It was like velvet. He raised himself up – slid gently inside her.

David couldn't help but smile. After they were both completely spent, they'd rested for a while before getting dressed. Jennifer had then gone to the kitchen and made cocoa for them both, as though it was the most natural thing in the world. 'You do like cocoa, don't you?' she'd asked.

'Just about my favourite,' he'd answered. Or it was, twenty years ago, he thought.

Suky suddenly appeared again, jumping on his lap somewhat condescendingly. The lights in the hospital had already started coming on, and in the quiet of the evening Jennifer now came to sit beside him, neither of them speaking. There was no embarrassment in the silence. Not with her, and not for the first time, David thought about this.

She stirred at last. 'I'd better wash the cups.'

'No, Jennifer. Leave them just this once,' he said. 'For me?' And reassured, it seemed, that it would be all right, she sat back in compliance, her hand in his. 'Just for you, then.'

Dirty cups and no shower, he thought. And what would Warwick Edwards make of that?

The minutes passed in pleasure until, from somewhere beyond, wicked sprites kept trying to invade his contentment, each of them with a different question. But he refused to let a single one of them take hold. He wanted to keep all these seconds for himself, store them up for later, like a miser. But they kept on until, at last, one of them finally managed to rattle the lock of the outer flat door, and when this closed with a bang, Suky, after digging her claws into his knee just to let him know where he stood, leapt from his lap.

'My flatmate,' said Jennifer, getting up. 'I'll just go through.'

'Do I get to meet her?' he asked.

She smiled over her shoulder. 'We'll see.' Then she closed the door behind her.

It was less than a minute later when the door opened again, and she now had her outdoor coat on. David got quickly to his feet. 'Well, Jennifer? Do I get to see the lady of … Jennifer?' It wasn't Jennifer. He didn't quite know why. Then Jennifer came into the room, too.

'Here you are then, David,' she said. 'My flatmate, my sister, Joan.' She turned to the other girl. 'Joan, this young fellow, the one with his mouth wide open, is David. It's all right, David. You can close up. The dentist's gone home.'

The three of them had sat for ten minutes round the small kitchen table, most of the talking having been done by Jennifer, as the only one who knew the other two. They were twins, of course, the girls, and she had added to the story of her former home life by saying that their father had been about to start in on either or both of them. They had left together, little more than waifs.

But there must have been stern stuff there, thought David, as he listened. For the girls had made decisions. Joan was to try for a degree in art and design, the grounding already being there, whilst Jennifer worked to keep them both. Then they were to change roles, and, for a time, things had worked out.

It was easily told, but David could sense the dangers – the murky undercurrents, the day to day grind, the constant hardships and, probably, the naked fear.

Changing jobs as often as she had, Jennifer had finally landed one with some promise, modelling clothes, at which she'd seemed a natural. The money was good and the owner of the house didn't bother her. He didn't bother any of the girls. He was gay. But when Jennifer had been there for about four months, he moved on, going into some kind of film work. The new owner seemed all right, however. He was a real charmer, too, and finally, she slept with him. Then after a further three weeks, during which he was kindness itself, he asked her to sleep with another man, a big customer. She said she would think about it, going then to the changing rooms to pack a basket full of the most expensive clothes, telling the dresser she'd been ordered to model them somewhere in a hurry, and would she be kind enough to order her a taxi? 'I was learning fast, you see, David,' she said, 'and now I think it's time you went home. We're all tired.'

Rather than consider these last words as a rather brusque dismissal, he found her directness refreshing and without false airs. What he had been told had been done so with an equal frankness – proof, surely, that they'd decided to put further trust in him.

He stood up quickly, ready to go. There were, of course, a hundred other questions, the main one being concerned with himself – where he really stood in all this. It being more than likely that this meeting had been prearranged between the sisters, he would have liked nothing more than to stay – ask his questions now. But they would have to wait – *if* he ever got to know the answers at all. Would he see her tomorrow night?

She also made a half-promise to come and watch him play football in the afternoon.

Morbury Rangers seemed a little off form and the Fawkley Clerks beat them by two goals to one. Even so, David knew that the result might have been even better for the home team. Playing on the right wing as usual, and normally a fairly accurate passer, he'd booted the ball over to Wes Thompson, or anyone else in the goalmouth area a few times, but he'd not been quite on target. He wondered if Tom Beaney, the trainer, standing there on the sidelines, had noticed his unusually indifferent performance.

David knew well what the trouble was. Well before half-time, Jennifer had arrived, smiling and waving. He'd seen her straight away. But about five yards away from her, and separated by about the same number of onlookers, he'd also seen Eric Southern. After half-time, the two were standing together, and although she had still appeared to be watching the match and trying to enjoy it, there was also an obvious distraction in her bearing. As though she wouldn't be at all sorry when the final whistle went.

David knew it was ridiculous. Jennifer could handle Eric all right; he knew that. But that was hardly the point. It was bound to be some kind of strain, and forty-five minutes is a long time. He was responsible for her being here and he'd wanted her to enjoy it. It put him off his game. Under his breath, he cursed Eric roundly.

'Two, one. Good win, lads. Well done.' Back in the changing rooms, Tom Beaney was giving his usual brief version of the match. 'I did think you might have popped another in, though, Wes. And your game wasn't quite up to the mark, either, Dave. Somewhere near pathetic, in fact. Might be because you missed training last Wednesday evening. What do you think?'

I think that on Wednesday evening I was in a far nicer place than this, Tom, was what David thought. 'I'll do better next time, Tom.'

Outside the ground, she was waiting for him. Eric was there, too, keeping her company. 'Good match, David,' he said, as the young man came up to them. Curiously and without obvious reason, he was thinking about Eric's wife. He'd met her on the odd occasion, a pretty but faded woman. He found himself wondering what her home life was like. Where was she at this moment. Sat at home, sewing? Visiting her mother? 'Why don't we all go on for a drink somewhere, David?' Eric was saying.

But wandering thoughts or not, David was ready for him.

'Sorry, Eric. Didn't you tell him, Jennifer? We have to go on somewhere. We're a bit late as it is.'

Jennifer put the back of her hand to her mouth in mock dismay. 'Of course,' she said. 'It had completely slipped my mind. And I'd half promised Eric we'd go, too.'

Eric tried, not too successfully, to look cheerful about it, forcing a smile to his lips. 'Never mind, eh? Maybe next time. Take care now. See you Monday, David.' He turned and walked disconsolately away. They didn't laugh. Not this time.

'Do you think you could ever end up like that, David?' she asked, watching the man almost out of sight.

'What? Married, you mean?'

She dug him in the ribs with her knuckles. 'You know well what I mean. Where are we going, anyway?'

'You OK for a walk?'

'I am, yes. But aren't you tired? After your match, I mean.'

He looked at her beauty. Tired? He knew what he would have liked to do, tired or not. He would have liked to coax her into the bushes yonder and have his wicked way with her. 'Not too tired,' he said. 'I'll manage.'

She looked into his face. 'David,' she laughed, 'don't you ever think of anything else?'

'Of course I do,' he laughed back. 'On occasion.' Then his mood changed a little and he took hold of her hand to pull through the crook of his arm. 'Jennifer?' and this time, he spoke her name in a tone of more serious enquiry.

But almost at the same time, she cut him short. 'No, David,' she said quickly. 'Let's just enjoy the walk for now, eh? Talk tonight? Put things as straight as we might?'

It was uncanny the way she could read what was in his mind. He tightened his hold on her hand a little. 'Of course,' he said, and they made for the river, peaceful in the cool afternoon sun. Then reaching the towpath, they were just able to walk two abreast. It was now like being in two different parts of the country, which, in a way, it was, with the old railway workings on their right, whilst over the river, far on the other side, were the much older, red sandstone crags – wild and rugged and untouched by man.

As they walked, he remarked on various features – the huge circle, still curiously weed-free, where the turntable for turning the locos had been. There were the lines of wagons, their lives' work long finished, with the wheels and the ribbons of steel they stood on, red with decay. Each wagon had its own number, still faintly visible on its battered flank, like a beast waiting for slaughter.

'This is all part of our inheritance, Jennifer,' he said. 'Everyone should see it.'

Way over the river, to their left, they were now coming in sight of the castle, high on the crags, and sorry remains though they were, it was still the usual, romantic sight and Jennifer pointed to it. 'That's prettier,' she said.

'Yes, it is,' he responded. 'Thirteenth century, but then, it wouldn't be so pretty living in it at the time, Jennifer. Not if you think about it for a moment.'

She stopped walking. 'What is it, David? The mood, I mean.'

He stopped beside her and looked into her face, searching for an understanding. Then he looked across at the castle, its edges now blurring in the fading light. 'People in general. They seem to make a mess of so many things,' he said at last. 'I just wanted you to know, Jennifer, that I'm a thoughtful person and one that can be trusted. That's all.'

She nodded slowly and then they walked on, as far as the reach, where the canal had been cut and where the old hoist lay like a giant with a broken arm.

* * *

With its modest frontage, Kathy's Kaff had a nicer interior than might at first have been supposed, with tablecloths and cups and saucers. It was well known for its quiche and, both of them being healthy eaters, they each had a generous helping, filled with smoked eel. They had a large pot of tea and David had a cream cake. When they came out, he said he had to do some shopping and they walked together into the centre of town, where they went their separate ways until later.

It was almost eight o'clock by the time he knocked on her door. She was dressed in a towelling housecoat, blue as the sky and setting off her brown curls to perfection.

'You look ravishing,' he said sincerely. He'd brought wine and she fetched two wafer-thin glasses. It was a Hungarian Chardonnay and David was smiling broadly at the memory of the wine shop.

'It's a cheeky little thing,' the man had said, eyeing David speculatively and taking his hand off his hip only long enough to take the money. 'Gently voluptuous,' he went on and by this David thought he probably still meant the wine, although, by now, he wasn't too sure. 'A witty companion to salmon. And my name's Arnold.' This last remark had to be shouted as David fled the shop. Arnold. I'll remember,' David had flung over his shoulder.

'All right. What is it then?' said Jennifer. 'What's so amusing?' and, between giggles, he told her exactly.

'Oh, Jennifer,' he finished, 'you should have been there.'

By this time, she was laughing as loudly as he was, but at this last remark, she said, 'Ah, yes, David, but don't you think my presence may have cramped Arnold's style a little?'

'You're probably right,' he answered, 'although I wouldn't have counted on it. Arnold seemed very determined.'

Almost in hysterics, they collapsed on the couch together.

They settled down more comfortably and, as Arnold

receded gradually, private thoughts invaded their minds and they stared across at the hospital, now sharply lit against the sombre background of the night sky. There was no sign of the cat and David put his arm round her shoulders.

'Anything to eat?' she asked after a while. He looked at her meaningfully and she shook her head. 'Sorry, David. I've got the creditors in.' He blinked a couple of times at that and she laughed out. 'Come on,' she said, getting up and pulling him gently to the bedroom. 'Let's see if we can't give you something to keep you ticking over. Can't have you seizing up altogether, now can we?'

Later on, back on the couch, they were finishing the wine. 'You know,' he said, looking across at the hospital, 'a good telescope on a tripod would be just the thing for this window. A clear view, straight into the women's ward, or in your case, of course, the men's.'

As earlier in the day, she had dug him in the ribs, she did so again, but with her elbow this time. But soon, it came down between them again, an almost tangible barrier which wouldn't go away – the time for question, for gentle inquisition. 'Jennifer,' and the banter was now a mile away, 'I mean it. I'll help in any way I can. Please don't think I'm carping. I wouldn't dare and, anyway, I haven't the right. But others besides you and Joan have suffered. But please, don't let it sour your life. These last days have been the happiest I can remember and my offer comes with no strings – none at all. But I have to take my head out of the sand. Terrified as I am of knowing, I have to hear what you have to say. You surely know how I feel about you. I have to know whether there's any chance of our having any sort of future together. I have to know tonight, Jennifer.'

Drained, he looked out towards the hospital. Her answer, when it came, was low – thoughtful, the words carefully picked. 'All right, David. Here it is. I like you. I like you a lot. So much so that I can feel the poison draining out of me. But how far it goes, I'm not sure. Not yet. My thoughts are still too muddled. But I did give myself to you. Willingly, too. Unprotected sex, David. That must mean something. Don't you see? I wanted to start giving something back, and you were the one. But I don't fully trust anyone. Not yet. Only Joan. Give me time, David. I won't finish up like Eric's wife.'

'You've never met her, Jennifer.'

'Oh, but I have, David. Many times. Over and over. In all sorts of places and with all kinds of Erics. I would sooner never go with another man. Ever. I've been hurt enough. I'll tell you one thing to please you, though. Joan and me. We've given up the bad life. You've helped with that, David.'

He started to say something, but she interrupted him.

'No, David. In case you're going to say it, we won't give anything back. Society isn't that kind. So it's tit of tat. We didn't ask for the bad life. Oh, people can preach – say *they* would have done things differently. I wonder. Anyway, what's done is done and I'll be looking for a job shortly. I don't quite know what kind. Not yet. That's about it, David, and believe me, I really do hope you're happy with all of this.'

It was at this moment that Suky made an appearance, jumping on his lap, and in a quite absent way he began to play with the cat's ear as he thought deeply of the last few days. 'Happy enough, Jennifer,' he said then, squeezing her hand, a gesture she returned willingly. His mind then came to Warwick Edwards, with his particular kind of wisdom. What would he have said to all this, David wondered?

* * *

His eyes snapped open on the first note of the alarm, his finger shoving the button down before it even got properly started. But although he knew he'd been tossing and turning for the last hour, he didn't get up straight away, just laying there thinking of recent events and knowing he should have felt more settled in his mind. That Jennifer felt the same way he did, he was certain. However she'd put it. And she had made commitments, burying her past. Great. So what was the worry? For worry there was. Something was niggling away at his mind – some seed of irritation.

Angry at himself, he got out of bed, his mood not improving in any way as he looked round the bedsit and thinking how hard he'd worked at it yesterday. It had to be cleaner. But it just didn't look any different. Still bleary-eyed, he shaved, did himself an egg of somewhat doubtful age, and got out of the place. First thing Monday morning never had been his favourite time.

Immersed as he soon became in his work, reminders of his early-morning doubts nevertheless insisted on making their occasional forays into his thoughts, and the note, waiting for him as he got back from his lunch break and surprising as its arrival was, came as almost a relief. He wasn't supposed to be seeing Jennifer till tomorrow – Tuesday – but with all the curious little misgivings coming to unsettle him, he had the sudden urge to see her – to know what she was doing.

Marion Tinge, from accounts, and who had always had an eye for David herself, handed him the note, unable to resist making observation. 'She's quite an eyeful, isn't she, David?'

Unable, in his eagerness, to think of much else, he replied simply, 'Yes, she is, Marion. Thanks for the note,' and turning aside, forced himself to open it calmly. 'Come tonight at seven. J.' was all it said. Nothing if not cryptic, thought David.

'She just can't keep away, can she, David?' Eric said from behind him. David turned round and Eric was positively leering. 'She wouldn't stop to talk, though.'

I wonder why, Eric? thought David, but he just smiled and said nothing. How he got through his afternoon's work, he never knew.

Although it was well before seven o'clock, the door opened straightaway to his knock. He half reached out towards her, but in the next second, he knew it wasn't her at all. He quailed visibly.

'Sit down, David. Jennifer's gone.' Her calm approach to the situation had at least some influence on his raging mind and he sat down without speaking. She sat down opposite him and, sensibly, got straight down to it. 'She got caught this morning.'

The horror sprang to his face, but Joan raised a quick hand. 'No, David, please. Let me finish.' Her quiet poise had its effect and he sank back against the cushions, cursing the butterflies in his stomach. He would listen, however; he would emulate her own calm – out of shame if nothing else.

'You see, David, she was detained by chance, by bad luck. For a past crime.' He warmed towards her as relief overwhelmed him.

'It really was the worst of ill-luck,' Joan was saying, 'getting caught like that. She wasn't even in the shop. Just passing. The store detective must have seen her through the door and recognized her from the past. She made a citizen's arrest. As she had every right to do, of course. She said Jennifer had stolen a necklace from the store, the jewellery department, over three months ago, but they had been unable to catch her. They sent for the police. She made bail, though. I don't know how. But they're pressing ahead with the case. The girl behind the counter at the store confirmed that it was the same girl. Not conclusive proof, of course. But Jennifer's gone, anyway. Done a bunk, David.'

He should have been numb with misery, but he wasn't. For as the minutes had passed, he had begun to hope. Joan had sent for him. This might mean next to nothing, of course, but he now chose to think otherwise. 'What's happening now then, Joan?' he asked, for the decision was undoubtedly hers.

'I have to leave this place, too, David,' she said with more than a note of regret. 'The insurance is up – "double the odds" no longer valid. Shame. Just as we'd decided to give up the life of crime. But there it is. I can prove where I was this morning, of course, but this time we'd be rumbled for sure.' She smiled at him sadly and, wearing this particular expression, David's amazement returned at how alike they were.

But he still knew that this girl wasn't Jennifer and he was strangely thankful for this. For it was Jennifer he loved. He knew that, too.

'Where will you go? I'll help in whatever way I can,' he said then, and he meant it. 'Really help, I mean.'

She walked to the window to look out at the hospital, the scene David had come to know so well and one he would so much miss, although without Jennifer, of course, it would be nothing.

Now, at this offer of help, Joan had come back to him and, for the first time, his sympathy went out to her alone, for, calm as she appeared, her own thoughts must have been in turmoil. She faced him squarely, searching his face. 'Thank you, David,' she said, 'I'll not forget that. But for the time being at any rate, I'll be staying with my young man. He lives near where I work. Near the old warehouses. I'll have to see to the lease of this place, and so on. Quickly, too.'

Young man, she'd said. David thought how refreshingly quaint the term sounded. These girls just never had conformed. And why should they? He wouldn't be surprised to learn that they didn't have a single pair of jeans between them. Then his thoughts returned to her immediate problems and, though in some doubt as to whether or not he had the right to ask, he did so anyway. 'Does he know everything, Joan, or shouldn't I ask?'

'He knows nothing, David. I just don't know how he would react,' and at these words, and just for a second, the joy leapt to his eyes. For didn't this mean that he alone had been entrusted with their secrets. But it only was for a second, his newfound pride taking a bump as he reminded himself of the circumstances of his and Jennifer's first meeting. He almost laughed aloud at the thought.

'What happens to me, Joan?' The fear had returned quickly and, even as he said the words, he felt his throat constrict, as though appalled that he should utter them. Joan, it seemed, decided to tease him a little, anxious though she knew him to be. Test him to the utmost. 'You, David?' she said, as though the thought had never entered her head, 'What should happen to you? What do you mean?'

'You know. Jennifer. And me.' There was bewilderment in his tone and, seeing his face and sensing his misery, she relented quickly, not having the heart to torment him further.

'How much do you think of her, David? Really.' She was now quite as serious as he was.

'Everything,' he replied simply.

'Very well. Here it is, then. She's gone to Chester and as soon as she finds a place, she'll let me know the address. She knows the number to ring. I was to tell you. If you wanted to know.' He was already scribbling his own number. 'I'll ring you then,' she said, as he handed her the number. 'Or *she* will.'

He took both of her hands in his. 'You won't be sorry. Either of you,' he said.

For answer and just for a moment, she tightened her own hands on his, saying, 'I know we won't, David,' and now, for the first time, she was smiling a little.

'Till next time, then.' He was on his way to the door, when he suddenly turned back. 'By the way,' he said. 'Did Jennifer take Suky with her?'

Joan's eyes widened. 'Of course. The cat. I'd forgotten... I don't think she has... Wait.' She walked to the door and opened it. Suky walked in without so much as a glance at either of them. 'Cats do that,' Joan said.

'Does the boy, er, young man, like cats?'

'I don't know.' Her tone was doubtful. 'A lot don't.'

David picked up the animal. 'I'll take Suky with me. One less thing for you to worry about.'

'I'm grateful already,' she said.

He'd arrived with a worry and left with a cat, and as he walked he hugged the unprotesting creature just a little closer to him, for was it not, after all, just a little part of Jennifer?

Upstairs in the Fawkley Social Club, the two men sat in the same old chairs they had occupied on their previous meeting. Three days had gone by since David's farewell to Joan Wentworth and he'd just finished his account, not only of Jennifer's doings, but also of his own actions since. He'd told Warwick Edwards that not only had he now got her new address in Chester, but that in only two more days he would be going himself. To do what, he didn't yet quite know. And back at the building society, he'd pleaded urgent and personal affairs, being unable to say exactly when he would be back. A statement, thought Warwick, which was at best, a little understated.

David had finished by asking his friend if he would do him the kindness of keeping his ears open with regard to himself personally and, when he could, he would ring Warwick from a call-box, for although he didn't say so, he wouldn't wish to involve him further by giving him the girl's address, or indeed, any other relevant information other than what was absolutely necessary. 'Would you do this much for me, Warwick?' he'd finished, and gravely, but without hesitation, Warwick Edwards had inclined his head in assent.

For a few long moments they sat in silence, each of them busy with his own thoughts, until at last – 'What I don't understand,' David remarked, 'was how she managed to get away at all. From the police, I mean.'

'Well, as to that,' Warwick replied, 'and in the knowledge, David, that this conversation never took place at all, let me expound the case a little. The rules on bail are pretty straightforward and, from what we know of your Jennifer's arrest, it sounds to me as though, under the 1984 Act, and assuming the custody officer had no reason to doubt the name and address she gave, that she would, in fact, appear in court to answer bail, that he had reasonable grounds for believing that she would not commit a further offence, and one or two other small points, then providing the arrest wasn't made under a warrant, which we know it wasn't, then she would have to be released, either on bail or without it. There are further details on conditional bail, of course. No need to go into that, however, for it sounds to me like a case of "bail of person not charged at the time, through insufficient evidence until further enquiries have been made". There it is, David. The girl has skipped bail – flown the coop, as we legal blokes say. Bad luck, her getting caught like that, though – just as she'd decided to go straight. Of course, I've never met the girl...' He looked at David searchingly.

'Honestly, Warwick...' David began to protest.

'Oh, I'm not doubting your judgement, David. Really. It's my concern for you, that's all.'

Another short silence ensued until David finally stood up. 'I'd better go. Wish me luck, Warwick?'

'More than that, my boy.' The older man extended a hand.

They made to go downstairs. 'I'm nervous, Warwick,' said David.

'So you should be,' was the reply. 'Special ties, just like special brides, are hard to come by. I'd be nervous myself.'

Harold Stone

He was a dreamer and he came with a dreamer's tale. And there was a rather distant, even mystic air about him. But that Harold Stone was a gentleman, I never had any doubt, being one of those people whom one was never sorry to be seen talking with. He was also above pettiness of any kind – impatient of formality, and thus, he was able to converse on any level. To him, however, it was really the act that mattered, the telling of it being something of a carefully concealed irritation. And if, after some creditable deed, he should be offered some kind of accolade, as indeed was the case, then with his tired smile he would accept it courteously – rather as he would a plaything from an eager child, or half of the last cigarette from an old man.

My own name is Derek Greene and had I been able to tell my own story to all and sundry – how I had suffered – then I would indeed have rejoiced. That was the difference between us.

'My one aim in life was to get through it in as pleasant a manner as possible,' he began. His skin had the pallor of waxen parchment and, as he spoke, I had the further chance of studying him at close hand. I'd hurried upstairs to the big room in order to get my customary seat, close to the speaker, and was able to see quite clearly that he'd aged rather more than the eighteen months or so since I'd last seen him here at the club, before he'd taken himself off to China again, to 'try and help out a bit'.

71

Unbidden, the thoughts came of the time when my own health and my marriage too, had been in danger, the time before the horrors began at last to recede a little. 15, Garland Close, in Morbury, was hardly as far as China, but still... I tried to shake it all off, listen to Stone, but the details came flooding back in eidetic images. I shuddered as though frozen. And then I knew that, somehow, this man would help me in some way.

Stone was now warming to his tale. 'Much to the disgust of my father,' he was now saying, 'my aged aunt left me the money. The lot. She was a direct descendant of the Peach-Carters, and father's half-sister only. And it always annoyed him intensely that she had such lineage – that and the fact that she always seemed to think so much of me, thought so much of one who was so, well ... indolent was the kindest word he ever used. Not that I ever really understood his attitude. He was my father, after all.

'Anyway, having no children of her own, and when the will was read out, leaving me everything, it was the last straw, although what he'd really expected I don't know. And when I bothered to give it some little thought a while afterwards, I supposed it must have been a bit galling for him, getting nothing at all.

'However, he kicked me out. Only verbally, of course. I hadn't lived at home for ages. Poor mother. She said nothing at all, but then she seldom says anything about anything. Except clothes. That's about all I inherited from her, I think, my, er, easygoing ways, shall we say? And the brains from father. It's a terrible combination, you know – intelligence and what? Congenital idleness? For I was completely without substance – a shell – the judge of nothing but taste, the arbiter elegantiarum.'

Stone paused for breath, asking to be excused as he took a mouthful or two of beer and, for some reason, I thought of Alan Parkin, another member of the Lantern

Club, but for whom, for some reason, I had never cared much. But I had sensed, on the instant, a similarity in the two men. What could it be? I looked round quickly but in vain, for Parkin wasn't in. What could it be? Was it perhaps the same distant manner? Or was it the same fine lines around the eyes, premature lines too, and certainly not caused by laughter. Was it possible that Parkin, too, had undergone a difficult childhood? Was it possible...? I pulled myself up short, almost laughing aloud. I was in danger of becoming the little psychologist.

Stone had resumed his tale. 'I went to Cambridge with precisely the same attitude,' he was saying. 'It was the easiest line of resistance, you see, and as there's no policy about subject preferences at Selwyn and as supervision was available for the course I fancied, I opted for that. The subject was the Chinese language, both the classical and the Mandarin forms. Don't ask me what the attraction was. Probably my subconscious was something to do with it, telling me that, with such a difficult subject, there would be little or no disgrace in packing it all in when the going got too tough, as I assumed that it soon would. And China was so remote, you see. Vague, sort of. Like my ambitions.

'There was another possibility behind my choice, I suppose, this being that if I had a flair for anything at all, it was languages. Back at school, everyone took French and German and I found it fairly easy to pick them both up, colloquially anyway, which was as far as I was prepared to go. Just a moment, though, that's not right. Let me be fair with myself – what I should have said was, that this was as far as I was able to go. Innate idleness, the kind from which I seem to suffer at least, is as much an addiction as, say, alcohol. That's what I believe anyway. And less sympathized with. Just think of it. The thought of any sort of effort at all, can make you physically sick.'

73

Stone stopped speaking, now staring into space as though he could still hardly believe what he was saying, that he was merely giving us an account of a nightmare after a cheese supper. But this particular incubus was in no hurry to depart and, having nothing better to do, it now decided to see just how far it could exert its evil. Stone's weakness was upon him and the opportunity could not be missed. Without delay, the poison was now injected, the proof quickly becoming clear on his features and, whatever the dark thoughts now running through his mind, the pose was infectious.

For me at least, the ensuing silence stretched into long seconds, my throat becoming tight, my breathing laboured. In vain, I tried to look round at the others, but I could not. Neither dared I try to clear the constriction in my throat, fearing that if I did so, the others would all conspire to direct their venom towards me alone, accusing me of giving forth with a bawdy song at the graveside, following the vicar's prayers.

Then at last, just as I was about to enter the door of 15 Garland Close in Morbury, never again to be let out, Stone slowly moved his head, raised his eyes to look round the room. My throat began to clear and I breathed more easily. I closed my own eyes for a moment in thankfulness. When I blinked them open, Stone was still looking at us all in turn. There was a dull but censorious gleam in his expression, his eyes a pair of sapphires misted by scorn. It was a challenge to anyone who might be expressing doubt in his statements. I was perspiring freely. And to think I had considered this man to be little more than a nonentity.

'Gentlemen,' he said, 'after what I'm about to say, and should you wish me to do so, I will apologize sincerely and abjectly – crave your forgiveness. But as members of the Lantern Club, with its aims and philosophies, lightly as we may sometimes appear to take them, I'm sure not only will you understand, but also that you will actually welcome, what follows next. I trust, indeed I sincerely hope, that at least some of you were affected in some small way by my, er, experiment just now.

'I tried it for two reasons, the first one being entirely selfish, and for this I ask your indulgence in advance. This was simply to prove to myself that I dare try it, this being the first opportunity I've had for doing so. Again, I hope you'll forgive the liberty, but to forewarn you all was to render the thing useless. I was taught it on my travels by the Chinese, but only in the sketchy way that an Occidental can even begin to take it in. All jesting aside, the Chinese are indeed an inscrutable race and some of the more advanced exponents of the system, the name of which, incidentally, I was never allowed to know, with hundreds, possibly thousands, of years of knowledge behind them, can, with no bother at all, influence quite a large crowd in minutes. The real experts are few, of course.

'I'm not lecturing, gentlemen. It's necessary that you know all this. You see, the method kept me going through the dark days, for it can even more easily be directed inwards – a sort of self-induced hypnosis. Of course, to begin with, one has to have a working knowledge of the language.

'And now to the second reason. First, however, would you kindly indulge me once again by raising your hands, and that without hesitation? The ones who were affected?'

I raised my arm quickly, uncaring that I might well be the only one to do so. But thankfully, three others did the same, one of whom was Ken Sapey, a committee member. The other two were mere acquaintances but that didn't matter.

Stone looked at the four of us gratifyingly and seemingly

quite satisfied with the result. I was also curiously happy for him, to see that as far as I could tell, there was in the others a total lack of scepticism at least, most of them seeming to be in various stages of bemusement.

But there was something wrong. I knew it. Something niggling away at the back of my mind and spoiling the whole thing for me – something about the experiment. I tried to think what it was, but Stone was speaking again.

'Here is the second reason then, and I'm relieved to tell you all that the success of the experiment will help, I think, to verify my story. You see, had no one raised their hand at all, then I would have been much less confident in carrying on with my tale. I know what happened to me over these months, but conveying its complete truth to others is another thing. And why should you believe the whole of my tale, after all? Why should I not embellish my story a little? I am, after all, a comparative stranger to the club.'

I, for one, knew what he meant, for had I been able to recount my own experiences, would they not have sounded little more than a domestic upheaval? For every experience loses something in the telling, no matter how skilfully and sincerely told.

'Fortunately though,' Stone was saying, 'I believe that the four of you who raised your hands gave me some credibility. For rather than garnish the simple truth to gain effect or sympathy, I would sooner retire.'

And his whole manner changed. As sudden as it was welcome, a weight seemed to drop from his shoulders and he smiled at us all, almost apologetically, it seemed, and he looked suddenly very human, very vulnerable. The strain of his past trials, and of talking about them to a bunch of people he scarcely knew, now showed plain in his face. 'I'm sorry if I seem to be perhaps overstating it all a bit,' he said, 'and my modest endeavours in China

76

may not, after all, seem so much to some of you chaps, but... I say, do you mind if we all get a drink?'

I got up, still annoyed that something about the experiment, together with what Stone had said, wouldn't go away.

Buster Howes was at the bar and he was still sober. 'Buster,' I said, 'where have you been? Stone's been talking for a while.' It was something Buster didn't do – miss opening time.

'Nodded off in front of the telly,' he said in an aggrieved tone. 'Me and Doreen both. Here. I've got you a drink.'

Then, for no reason at all, I knew what had been bothering me all this time. 'Buster,' I said, 'do me a favour, will you? Take the drinks to the table. I have to speak to Stone.'

'Done,' he said.

Stone was talking to John Coombes, the committee man. 'Would it be at all possible to butt in, gentlemen?' I said. 'Speak to Stone here? It is important. To me at least.' They had appeared to be talking only casually.

'It's OK, Derek,' said Coombes graciously. 'I'll leave you to it.' He prepared to move away, but I held up a hand. 'No need, John,' I said. 'Please stay.' In his case, as a committee man who already knew my story, my question didn't matter, even though Stone might quiz me about details. And he stayed willingly. 'Stone,' I said, 'may I call you Harold?'

'Certainly,' he said. 'Derek Greene, isn't it? Of the secret story?' He was smiling.

'Let us say rather the one of discretion, shall we?' I smiled back. 'And I assure you, should you be really interested, I'll tell it to you some time. With all the lurid details, too. It's just not for general publication.'

'I'd like that. I really would. Now then. What's your question?'

'Well, it's simply put. You did say, did you not, that those inner thoughts of yours kept you going during the darker days?'

'That is so, yes.'

'Well, I had the visions all right, but unfortunately I experienced exactly the opposite effect to that which was intended. My own thoughts, rather than soothing in any way...'

He was already nodding in understanding. 'Easily explained,' he said. 'I didn't want to prolong the thing too much – tire you all with too much detail – but the fact is, one amongst many, that unless trained to do otherwise, the mind, making its escape from the present, retires to the weakest point – the most accessible retreat. And you, Derek my lad, obviously still have a guilty conscience.'

My mouth dropped open. 'I do?'

'You do.'

In the background, John Coombes was laughing out.

'It's really that simple, is it?' I said.

'It is.' Stone was sincere. 'But listen,' he went on, 'the others are returning to their seats. I'll see you afterwards if you like. Tell you how simple things really are. How's that?'

'That's fine,' I said. 'And thanks. Thanks very much.'

I returned to my seat and lifted my glass to Buster. 'Tell you later, Buster,' I said. But what I would tell him would be very little. You could share many things with Buster, but confidences weren't one of them.

Stone took up his tale again. 'There I was then, at Cambridge, not quite sure of anything, doing my course in a rather desultory way, even though I was quite aware at the same time that many people would have given their eye-teeth for these same chances. Not that I cared about that. And I really don't know how I would have finished up, had I been left to my own devices. I could have drifted, of course. What else was there? Drugs had never appealed to me at all. Too common, I suppose. Too ordinary. Even now, I often think about this period, brief as it was.

'And then I had my stroke of luck – sensed it and grabbed at it. That's what you have to do. Recognize it and grab at it. By chance, I was thrown into the path of four Chinese undergrads. Their elected spokesman was one Yuan and I courted him unashamedly. It doesn't sound much but I knew this is what I had to do. And I quickly knew I was on the right track. For I would never have mastered their language without them. I knew that now. Clever as I imagined myself to be and in my state of health ... well, I would soon have been back at square one.

'Naturally enough, they did seem suspicious of my overtures, and who wouldn't be? But I had some kind of impetus at last, probably my last real chance. I did discover one thing pretty quickly, this being that if one seeks any kind of adherence at all from a Chinese, then the quickest way to do it is to show a willingness to learn his language. They know what a Herculean task it is, of course, but as this was my original aim anyway, this seemed a good omen.

'I began to read hope into my whole situation, although, had I even begun to suspect the size of the undertaking, I might yet have thrown in the towel. It's a difficult language all right. There's no alphabet as such, you see, just thousands of characters, and about four thousand of which need to be mastered for reading anything like. And as for speech, well, that depends to a great extent on tone, the same utterance having up to four different meanings.

'But in my new-found hope, I stuck at it, going at the thing head-on in almost frenetic single-mindedness and, in so doing, my inherent weaknesses began to disappear, or subside into the background at least. It isn't the way to go about anything, of course, but had I paused to think about method, well, I simply dare not. And if the language was difficult, it was almost as confusing trying to keep up with the politics, which were all part of the course. And these changed so quickly.'

Stone paused at this point, looking round the room with an attempt at briskness, but obviously trying to garner his strength. For the strain was showing. Then, appearing to make a quick decision, he carried on.

'I'm sorry to burden you with all the details,' he said, 'but I really see no other way. I know some of you chaps, at least, are familiar with the prevalent conditions of the time and place of which we speak, for I clearly remember discussing it with some of you at the time when I first joined the Lantern Club, which I did as a break from my studies. But not all of you, of course, and so I see no other recourse. In addition, it may well be that my own memory is at fault and so, in reminding you, I also remind myself. So if it all begins to sound like somewhat of a history lesson, then I know you'll bear with me. But, for the present, gentlemen, I've had it. Do you think we could carry on tomorrow? I'd be more than obliged.'

The man had impeccable manners. And he now had an arm raised in my direction. 'What an important fellow I must be, Buster,' I said. 'Stone wants to confer with me again, look. Here.' I fished money quickly from my pocket, slid it across to him. 'Get them in, Buster, and I'll join you in a bit. Will you do that?'

'I will,' he said. 'But I'll want to know every word that was said. In confidence, of course.'

'Of course,' I lied.

Closer up, Stone looked more tired than I'd first thought. 'You've been talking a while, Harold,' I said. 'If you'd sooner leave it until another time...'

'That's all right.' He made a conscious effort to relax and, lacking false airs of any kind, he got straight to the point. 'Glad you're interested in what I had to say. I'm not saying that everyone would have got the same sort of benefit out of the experience as I did, for as I said, it's a rather hit-and-miss business for Westerners. But from what I was able to learn, I gathered that the trick is to channel the thoughts into a problem's origins.'

I tried to look intelligent.

'Listen,' he went on, 'you've heard of Freud. Ever tried to read him?'

'Can't say that I have, no.'

'Well, you know his worldwide reputation. But take out the two little words, guilt and sex, and what are you left with?'

'Tell me.'

'I will. Very little. You see, it's in the interest of so many people – is it not? – to complicate our lives. Politicians, psychoanalysts, and yes,' he said with a grin, 'tax-gatherers. How else would they make a living? Think for a moment of some of the things in which, even as intelligent adults, we place so much credence – superstitions, phobias, cultures. They all evolved from something simply explained, some natural phenomenon perhaps – a sudden death – an eclipse of the sun – a tidal wave... And the ones with an eye for it grabbed at it with both dirty hands. Do you begin to see, Derek? We're still in the hands of the witch doctors.

'Mind you, I think people are beginning to wake up a

81

bit. But for now, Derek, remember. Think simple. Think innocent. And let's talk again.'

On the grounds of his weariness, he declined my offer to join some of us for a drink and, after shaking me warmly by the hand, he departed for home. Whether what he had said made any real sense to me, I couldn't at present say, but at least his beliefs were based on experience and I had no doubt at all of his sincerity. The recent trials he had undergone also seemed to have made him into a passionate man, impatient of his inherent weaknesses with which he was trying so hard to cope. No wonder he was tired.

I thought of his last words. Think simple. Think innocent. I vowed silently to try and do that. Dwelling on one's past mistakes was, after all, a pretty useless occupation.

Buster stood talking at the bar and I sat down thankfully with what remained of my drink. I don't know about Stone but I was tired myself and just content to sit there, leaning my arm on the deeply carved, mahogany side table, the patina of which was made up of ancient beer stains.

'Not finished that drink yet, old lad? You're definitely letting the side down, you know.'

'Sorry, Buster.' His voice at my elbow had made me jump and I didn't really know what I was saying.

'That's all right, but we must keep up,' he said, putting the small round tray on the table. 'And I did get spares,' he went on, quickly getting outside about half a glassful. 'Thirsty work, this listening.' As always, I wondered where he managed to put it all, although to give him his due, it wasn't all he had on his mind.

'Now then,' he said eagerly, 'what did Stone have to say? And why you?' he added artfully, ever hopeful that I might let some of my own Detail slip, which would have been the quickest way to my divorce that anyone could have imagined.

But I saw no reason why I shouldn't tell him what Stone had told me – of the theories he had propounded. I did so.

'Hm. And that's it?'

'What else would there be, Buster?'

'But why you?'

'Well, it was me who approached him in the first place.'

Ron Flint, another member, was sitting close by and, overhearing our remarks, turned towards us, obviously inviting comment. I gave him his cue. 'Ron, you know Harold Stone, don't you? What's your opinion of the man?'

'I actually knew the rest of the family. Only slightly, of course. That's all anyone knew them. Father as hard as nails. Mother's head full of feathers. Poor Harold didn't stand a chance. Got out as quick as he could, though he was never the most enterprising young man. Had no direction at all. But something's certainly changed him. It's in the carriage. And the eyes. Have you seen them? Like polished pewter.'

How strange it is, I thought, how different people see different people. Which made me wonder how Harold Stone would think of Flint.

The following evening Buster was already there, drinks at the ready, determined not to be late two nights running. At my entrance, he waved across, pointing to the table, but I called at the bar anyway, to 'get spares', as Buster would have happily put it. I fetched three, for he was talking to Kevin Lowe, another member, whose wife, Wendy, together with her friend Liz Peach, were the only two female members. Like myself, Kevin didn't come in every night. We didn't all have Buster's money. Today was Tuesday and I wouldn't normally have been in, but I didn't want to miss Stone's story, of course.

I sat down and the three of us made polite enquiry after the health of each other's spouses. But there was time for little else, for Stone was beginning to speak and we all settled down to listen. After brief greetings, he got straight into his story, just giving me time to wonder whether he was anxious to be done with it.

'Even on those first innocent visits, Peking, or Beijing, as it became known under the Pinyin system of romanization, brought in by the leaders of the Cultural Revolution during the late fifties, the place proved, to me at least, a bitter disappointment. And after all I had heard and learned, it took me a while to get used to the fact. So this was the city of splendour, was it? This was the wonder of the world, of grid-like sections reflecting the harmony of nature and the universe. This was the city of walls and gates, of ancient temples and rickshaws, the city that awaited the arrival of long camel caravans. This was the city of the great Mongols, was it?

'For don't forget, gentlemen, Europeans hadn't been popular there for quite a while. Anyway, it's not much like that now. After the real trouble started, in 1949, when the Nationalists were beaten in the Civil War, all ideas of conservation seem to have been abandoned. The walls were pulled down to make room for ring roads and the old architecture was frenziedly vandalized. To deprive the mosquitoes of their habitats, all the grass was pulled up, turning the city from a green one into a brown. Neither does any bird sing freely, for they were all caught and killed because they ate too much. The only ones to be seen now are those in cages, for sale on the roadside, alongside the cigarettes.

'Now it's a place of bicycles and dust, huge tenements, with smoke and skyscrapers springing up like fungi and, rather than one of the world's ancient cities, it now looks more like one massive suburb, looking no one in the face. 'There are excuses, perhaps. But such degradation! And with it came the most terrible oppression. Mao said: "Let a hundred flowers bloom." Such innocent-sounding words, inviting open debate. But of course, the party leadership soon changed their minds, claiming that this had been a ploy to flush out the traitors, by whom they meant those who should happen to disagree with them. Hundreds of thousands were tagged as Rightists, prevented from teaching or writing. Most were intellectuals and were sentenced to long periods of hard labour in prison or distant farms, to be re-educated and having to write out long confessions. It was a time when child betrayed parent and friend betrayed friend. It was brainwashing at its worst and one of the most terrible things about it, it seemed to me, was that many of the prisoners were actually Party members.

'Steel production was to double in one year. What a bland statement that was. Families had to contribute any household goods made of iron and great amounts of quite useless steel were made in backyard furnaces. There were bad harvests and they came successively. Millions died of starvation – quickly as it is said. And one five-year plan followed another...

'To me, though, the most awesome fact of all is that had not these obscenities taken place when they did, then neither would my own minute role in the matter, with the result, I am convinced, that my mental state would have declined to the point where I would merely have drifted into uncaring obscurity. I am certain of it. And there is the perverseness of it all – the crushing of a complete and ancient culture in order to save the sanity of one man. For I believe myself to be sane, and even through the boundless infamy and scale of it all, I did

85

try and seek the truth. I observed and talked and I read...
It was in such ways that I kept my sanity.

'Over the years, I saw the situation worsen, telling myself
each time I came home that I would never go back. I
was no arch-hero, leaping about and doing great deeds.
Even as I came to the committee with my proposal, I
believe they were a little nonplussed and no wonder, for
I didn't quite know what I was about myself. But as I
didn't need to ask them for funds and as they knew, I
suspect, that I would have gone anyway, even though
things were now really getting out of hand over there,
they gave me their blessings.

'This was the time when my motives – my true motives
– must be brought into question. Who, amongst those
concerned, were the most honest? But I hadn't the energy
to do more than brush all this impatiently aside.'

Now with the usual polite excuses, Stone took a drink,
giving me time to reflect, from what he had just said,
that here was another similarity that the man shared with
Alan Parkin. They were both comfortably off. For my own
Detail, I'd had to be funded. I looked round the room
to see if Parkin was here, but he was not. Where was the
man, anyway? But Stone was now talking again, thanking
us all for our continued attention. His drink seemed to
have refreshed him anew. His manner became more lively,
an indication perhaps, that he would like to finish his
tale in this session.

'Measuring events by time alone,' he said, 'rather than
by the worst excesses, I suppose I was observer to a
comparatively small part of it all and, by the time I first
went over there, the bulk of the atrocities were over. Or
so I believed. Mao was already dead, although, as yet,
there was no tourism as such. And the pot was still
simmering. One could sense that quite easily, for although
no one man could have said with any real conviction what

was happening, there seemed little doubt that there was both economic stagnation and political repression. The so-called Gang of Four, one of whom was Mao's widow, were about to be arrested, tried and convicted, ostensibly for their part in helping to create the Cultural Revolution.

'Adding to all the confusion was the fact that there were now so many different factions, even amongst the Red Guards themselves. Each faction would lash out in all directions, obsessed only with their political enemies. For they knew only too well the penalties of failure. But the really sad part of it all, I thought – one that brought it all to its proper perspective – was that such things as normal family life, a normal childhood, had become things of the past. This was one of those things that one never seemed to read about in the international press.

'In the very uncertain aftermath, then, of these bestial times, I tried, at first, to immerse myself in my studies. I was staying with Yuan and his family in part of the Hutong, that labyrinth of small dwellings and courtyards that is the city's inheritance from the Mongols. More than this, it was a way of life.

'They were a simple people, edaphic in origin – children of the earth – knowing little of politics, and caring less. And with some success, I played the part of the student. I visited the site of Peking Man, a few miles south-west of the capital, where bones were unearthed, a couple of teeth and a cranium actually, and which are reputed to be half a million years old. Not my cup of tea really, but a thing one does.

'I went to restaurants, trying everything without too many questions, for there's a saying that the Chinese will eat anything with four legs except the table. But I did develop a taste for dumplings and for the spirit mao-tai, which is made from sorghum.

'I visited the university, of course, and I went to the

opera, all amongst an uneasy calm. Perhaps I was not to be of much help after all and I came home with mixed feelings.

'My next visit coincided with the students' demonstrations. I suddenly became rather violently ill and I dared do no other than return home, some of you recalling perhaps that, a little later on, I spent some time here at the club. Then I heard that things didn't seem to be going too badly over there, what with the free market being allowed at last and the apparent waning of interest in politics. With such things as television sets and washing machines beginning to appear in the shops, in what capacity, I asked myself, would I be returning? Idle scholar? Casual observer?

'And then my quandary was settled for me. The students began protesting again, for more democracy, a word not really in the Party manifesto. There would be trouble then – danger maybe – to rescue me from my ennui. Surely I could do something and off I went, back through Moscow this time, quietly. Strangely, too, I was eager to get there before any trouble was resolved.

'Tiananmen Square – The Square of Heavenly Peace – will, in its infamy, reside in the minds of men for as long as there is moral thought. Democracy Wall, with its huge posters, criticizing the Party as allowed, had recently been dismantled for taking the Party at its word. There were concessions – mere sops. The young, for instance, were no longer being persuaded to persecute and kill the old. Suddenly, however, the city workers, those who were naturally most affected by the fast-rising inflation, understandably joined the students in protest. And this was the situation as I found it.

'Then came the tanks, lumbering down Chang'an Avenue and, with them the crackdown, vicious and uncompromising.

'I suffered no specific illness. It was just that my mental condition chose this particular moment to betray me completely, all of Yuan's teachings disappearing as though they had never been. It came on the instant and without warning, affecting my belief that I had somehow contracted some vile and endemic disease, which, under the circumstances, was more than understandable. And I have memories of running along corridors ankle-deep in filth, of the dying screams of my fellow man and of having vile-smelling and even viler-tasting slop being forced down my throat in order to keep me alive. If there was any grain of comfort at all in my plight, it was that I was suffering all this in support of my friends. I had run with them. No one could take that away.

'And then at last I heard voices, sombre and calm around where I lay exhausted. They were the voices of my friends, speaking in Putonghua, which is the people's language in that part of the country. They were speaking of me.

'Yuan wasn't there and I tried to rouse myself from my stupor. What was I hearing? Perhaps I was mistaken and I strained every fibre to try and cut through the mist until, at last, the words sliced through my thoughts like a knife. Yuan was dead, saving me. "What a burden he's been, this man," someone was saying. "If only he had stayed at home in England. How can we say go home, persuade him that..."

'My mind would accept no more and I fainted away.'

Stone stopped speaking at last and looked round the room, his eyes reflecting his weariness. There were other things he could have said, either in bitterness or regret. But apart from thanking us for listening for so long, he forbore to make further remark. He smiled tiredly, just content is seemed, to sit there for a while, to regain his strength, his composure. No one moved and the only sound now, in the big room, was the faint rustle of the dried grasses in the fireplace, stirred by a whisper of draught from the chimney.

Long Seconds of Terror

The body was found in a ditch, midway between the Breeley Road and the dull waters of Hawkesworth Mere. It was nine days after the disappearance of the well-known local figure George Earl. The face of the victim had been shot almost completely away by a charge from a shotgun, probably a twelve bore and more than likely belonging to Earl himself and, as so often happens, a man out with a dog had made the gruesome discovery. Mr Arthur Kemp had hurried home to Norrs End, phoned the police and then made his way back to the scene. On the arrival of the police, Mr Kemp, after giving what details he could, was thanked and allowed to go. It was a damp day in mid-April and there was no sign of the weapon.

In spite of the small amount of suitable material available in the immediate area, some untidy attempt had been made to conceal the body, mainly with twigs and dead grass. There were no noticeable tyre tracks in evidence but, in any case, the road was flanked by a low stone wall, though, in places, this had broken down to nothing. The body was about twenty-five yards from the road and was thus assumed to have been carried to the spot from a vehicle, unless, of course, the killing had taken place in situ, although this was considered unlikely.

After frowning at two of the uniformed officers who were, as he put it, 'clumping about in their size elevens', Detective Chief Inspector Donald McKuen knelt down briefly beside the body. But quick as he'd been to arrive on the scene after having been informed at the station in Breeley, Doctor Alan Payne was there already and, having made his own examination, was even now removing a pair of thin rubber gloves. He was a tall, spare man with a mournful expression, this having earned him, to the lesser ranks at least, the title of Alan the Pain.

'How long, Alan? Roughly?' asked McKuen.

'A week at least. Tell you more later, of course. Nasty. Someone didn't care for the fellow,' and with this, the doctor stalked off back to his car.

Detective Sergeant Errol Curtiss didn't kneel down but he was close enough to see the expensive-looking wristwatch, still in place on the victim. The two detectives walked back to the road, leaving the rest of the team to get on with it.

McKuen looked up and down the road, first towards the nearby hamlet of Hawkesworth, with the market town of Breeley two miles or so beyond, then in the other direction towards the village of Bradern, where Earl had lived, passing the track which led to Norrs End, on the way.

They were stood roughly between Breeley and Bradern then, he thought, his mind suddenly being distracted by a movement on the low wall where a blackbird, fat in its sleekness, was busy trying to crack the shell of some small mollusc. McKuen watched it. Everything preys on something, he thought. But it was the reasons for doing so that were important.

Murder. McKuen wondered suddenly what Detective First Grade John Crowle of New York would have made of it, what his first move would have been. Having already visited England on an exchange system, staying with McKuen and his wife, Sarah, the Manhattan policeman had been McKuen's own guide on his return visit to the

States. The two had taken to each other and now kept in touch on a more or less regular basis.

But at the moment, thought McKuen, I only have Sergeant Curtiss to help me. 'Notice anything special, Errol?' he asked at last.

'Not a lot beyond the obvious, sir. Robbery obviously wasn't the motive. Or should I say common robbery? There are other things to steal besides watches. A man's identity for one thing, though that's extremely doubtful in this case.'

'Quite right, Sergeant. But who would want to kill such a man? Very well liked by all accounts. It looks as though we could be in for a hard time.'

Curtiss made no reply to this and this is what McKuen liked about Curtiss. He didn't make pointless remarks. If he either knew or suspected nothing, then that's what he said.

'Come on,' said the chief briskly. 'Let's go and have a word with this Arthur Kemp. There's something I want to ask him. Whilst things are still fresh in his mind.'

Norrs End. McKuen remembered having been there years ago, on a bike, just to see what the place looked like. He wondered whether the picture of the place still in his mind had been distorted by time, at all.

But in such a place little changed. A single row of nine houses, old and terraced but well enough maintained. Ever since his first visit he'd wondered vaguely why they were there. Surrounded by farming country, the road itself was still little more than a cart track. A further quick assessment of the place in general was enough to suggest that no one very well off lived in Norrs End.

At his knock, the door was opened by a thin woman with a pain-lined face, opening the door wide as the two made themselves known. 'Come in, officers,' she said. 'Arthur is in.'

The street door opened onto the room itself and a man sat there in front of the gas fire. He was cleaning a pair of boots, and brushes and polish rested on the newspapers that were strewn on the carpet at his feet.

'These gentlemen are from the police, Arthur,' the woman said quietly.

Arthur Kemp got up quickly, extending a hand. 'Good morning,' he said. 'I did half expect a call. Not quite so soon, perhaps.' He was a wiry-looking man and, by his colour and his movements, an active one who spent a great deal of time in the open.

'Well, the sooner we get things moving, Mr Kemp.' The chief shook hands, introducing both himself and Curtiss as he did so. 'I know you won't mind telling your story again,' he said. 'So that we can hear it first hand so to speak. As you must realize, you're an extremely important witness, especially as you acted in exactly the correct manner, if I may say so.'

Kemp smiled without embarrassment. 'Good of you to say so, Inspector. Not that I think I can be of any further help. But you'll be the best judge of that. Won't you gentlemen sit down?'

'Thank you and, as you say, you never know. The smallest detail could help.'

The easy chairs were small and upright but plenty big enough for the size of the room. Mrs Kemp had disappeared into the back and McKuen could hear the rattle of cups whilst Kemp himself hurriedly cleared the shoe-cleaning gear away, giving the chief a chance to look at a photograph on the tiny sideboard. It was in a silver frame and was of a handsome-looking couple in wedding apparel.

'Must have given you a bit of a shock, Mr Kemp. Finding a body like that.'

'Shock? I nearly passed out, I can tell you. Nell found it first, of course. She yelped and that's not like her at all. I knew something was amiss. It'll take me a while to get over that, Inspector.'

'Of course it will. Terrible experience. Tell me, did you know George Earl and that he'd been missing a while? Make any connection? We're pretty sure it's him.'

'Yes, I knew him but only by sight. We used to pass each other out walking on occasion. But we only nodded. But I ... the face, you see... No, I didn't make the connection.'

He stared into the fire and McKuen gave him a moment. Then, 'Anything else, Mr Kemp? Anything at all? Please take your time.'

'Well, I don't think the body had been there all that long. Me and Nell go that way quite often. She'd have seen it.'

'Yesterday, Mr Kemp. Did you go that way yesterday?'

'No. Let's see now. Not the day before either. Then Saturday I do the shopping. Friday. That would be it. Not that we had to pass that very spot, you understand.'

It was at this moment that Mrs Kemp limped painfully in with the tea and McKuen winced inwardly at the interruption but still managed to smile gallantly. 'Mrs Kemp, you really shouldn't have bothered. But it's very welcome all the same,' he lied. He was often offered tea in this job and almost as often, he wondered about the tradition – this offering of tea to strangers – the true motives behind it all. For not everyone was a willing host. 'You won't mind my saying so, I'm sure, Mrs Kemp, but are you a bit under the weather? I couldn't help but notice.'

'Arthritis,' the woman smiled tiredly. 'Bothers me a bit sometimes.'

'I'm sorry to hear that. I can imagine.' But he doubted that he could.

He and Curtiss helped themselves to sugar and they all sat drinking, McKuen suddenly realising how thirsty he'd been after all. And, as he had to admit to himself, it was a good cup. 'Was there anything else, Mr Kemp? Anything at all?'

The man began to shake his head and then stopped. 'There was one other thing, Inspector. It was the way the, er, body had been left. Yes. I had the idea that the whole thing had been carried out in the dark – you know, the complete darkness. In panic, like. No torch or anything. The clumsy way one of the legs...'

'Very good, Mr Kemp,' said McKuen, as the woman shuddered visibly.

The rest of the conversation was taken up with slightly wider issues such as Norrs End itself, for, after all, it was the place nearest to where the body had been found, including the tiny hamlet of Hawkesworth. Although it would normally be expected that the killer would want to hide the evidence as far away from his own habitation as possible, you could never really tell. Especially as the inference had been made that the body had been hidden in a panic.

As casually as he might, McKuen asked after the other residents of Norrs End and about Kemp himself.

Arthur Kemp, an ex-insurance man, had retired early to look after his arthritic wife, buying the smallest practical place they could find. The houses themselves, all numbered oddly and suggesting perhaps a former intention to build over the way, had been farm cottages, most of them having changed hands several times since. Two of the residents were single householders – Don Ayrton, who worked at a supermarket in Breeley, and Clement Betteridge, a motor mechanic with a small garage, also in Breeley.

Curtiss scribbled their door numbers and a few other notes but that was about it. The two policemen thanked the Kemps and left. 'A useful enough half-hour I thought,

Errol,' said McKuen as they got in the car. 'Good background stuff.'

'Yes, sir. I thought Kemp did well. Observant man.'

'I agree. Friendly to the rozzers, too. We could do with a few more like him.' McKuen turned the car round the way they had come. 'Where to now do you think, Sergeant?'

'Lunch, sir?' Sergeant Curtiss was a pink, round man who liked his food.

'All right. Let's go to The Hind.' The pub being in Breeley, McKuen could just as easily gone home for lunch, but as he had made no arrangements to do so – Sarah might even be out – and as he wanted to think about the case a bit, a sandwich would have to suffice. On these occasions he had an arrangement with his sergeant, one of them having a pint, the other one, tea. The tea person then did the driving. It was Curtiss's turn for the pint; McKuen knew that but the Sergeant could have forgotten. 'Let's see now, whose turn is it for the pint?'

'It's mine, sir.'

Pulling off the cart track onto the Breeley road, they quickly reached the crime spot and the chief stopped the car for a moment. Uniforms were still poking about and now, in the distance, they could see frogmen preparing to go into the mere itself. From this distance and dull as the day still was, the waters looked dark and forbidding.

The Hind wasn't too crowded and, having eaten his sandwich, McKuen was thinking about the case at the same time as he watched Curtiss enjoying his pint. The Sergeant was also drumming on the table with his fingers, the moment disturbing the Chief's train of thought until, in the finish, he could stand it no longer. 'Where next then, do you think, Sergeant?'

'I've been giving it some thought, sir. Mrs Earl, I suppose. Am I right, sir?' Curtiss replied still drumming on the table.

'Quite right. And what do you suppose we should say to the lady?'

'Keep it simple, sir. Something like, "I'm sorry, Mrs Earl, but I'm afraid we have some bad news. It's about your husband."'

'Right, Sergeant. There's just one thing, perhaps. Suppose after all that the body isn't that of Earl at all?' And at that, Curtiss stopped drumming at last and McKuen smiled to himself. It was nice to be petty on occasion, he thought.

Standing in its own grounds, the Earl residence was large and mature and, looked expensive to maintain. There was a gravel drive and the windows were leaded. McKuens' thoughts were running along somewhat commercial lines. Such a house, in such a location, must surely be worth somewhere in the region of... He jerked his mind back to the immediate present, to more pressing matters. Idle speculation wouldn't get them very far.

The woman, like the house, was large and handsome but, McKuen told himself, she had never been beautiful and she was, if he was right, now having a struggle to keep her weight down. His next impression was that she was the sort of woman who would make the effort. Her clothes were quietly expensive. 'Mrs Earl?'

'Yes?'

'Detective Chief Inspector McKuen and this is Detective Sergeant Curtiss. Do you think we might come in?' He held out his ID as he spoke.

'Please do. Is it about George?'

'Yes, Mrs Earl.'

The two were led through a wide, ornate hallway into a room on the right. It was bay-windowed and a middle-aged woman was wielding a duster.

'Thank you, Mrs Barnes. Will you leave us, please?' As

she said this, Mrs Earl motioned the detectives to sit down. 'Can I get you gentlemen anything?'

But rather than serious enquiry, the question was issued in that tone which betokens mere politeness and McKuen, reflecting that this was something of a variation on the tea ceremony, declined just as politely. Perhaps there would be a more genuine offer later. But as he sat down, he did take the brief opportunity of glancing round the room, noting that the furnishings were as tasteful and expensive as the woman's clothes. No surprises there. Then, with the courtesies over and with Mrs Barnes having closed the door quietly behind her, he began without further delay. 'A body has been found, Mrs Earl. Between Hawkesworth and Norrs End and we believe it to be that of your husband.'

She looked suddenly startled at the statement, looking at the Inspector with a look almost of terror. But she recovered quickly, even though her whole body seemed to momentarily sag with the effort.

'Are you all right, Mrs Earl?'

'Perfectly, thank you, Inspector. Just the finality of it all at last, perhaps...' She sat up straight, her back as rigid as the chair she occupied. 'Hardly a surprise really, I suppose,' she went on. 'It is well over a week...' Her voice trailed off to nothing.

He risked a glance at his sergeant, before going on to other details, including the watch, and Mrs Earl nodded. 'That sounds like George, all right. How was he... How did he die, Inspector?'

She was fully in command of herself once again and McKuen saw no reason for speaking other than plainly. 'Shotgun wounds, Mrs Earl. His face, er, he was shot in the face. Bit of a mess, I'm afraid.'

She got up quickly. 'Which one of you drove here, Inspector?'

McKuen blinked. 'Mrs Earl?'

'Which one?'

'I did, Mrs Earl.'

'Right.' She went to a small walnut side table, which was stood near the wall. There were glasses and a bottle of brandy with more stars on the label than can be seen in the night sky. There was also a small blue-and-white jasper vase, which McKuen would cheerfully have put in his pocket in exchange for a week's wages. He watched as Mrs Earl poured two generous shots of the star-spangled liquor and brought them back to where they were sitting, handing one to Curtiss.

'You're driving, Inspector, so your sergeant is not and I never drink alone.'

McKuen was up to most things and he was up to this one. But only just. In conscience, he couldn't appear to condone the incident. But neither did he wish to appear churlish nor upset Mrs Earl. So he did the best he could. Casting the most fragmentary glance at Curtiss, he cleared his throat and carried on with his task as though nothing had happened. 'Mrs Earl,' he said, 'tell us when you last saw your husband. As exactly as you can, if you will.'

In her turn, she glanced at Curtiss before taking a generous sip of her drink. 'Well, as you know, Inspector, it was a week last Sunday, the fourth. As to the exact time, as I said before, it was two-forty as near as I can say. He'd been to The Cockleshell, as usual. He came home, picked up his gun and went for a walk. I never saw him again. But you know all this.'

'Of course we do, Mrs Earl. We've read your original statement thoroughly. But you know how it is. Or perhaps you don't. Things are often remembered in the second telling. Important things.'

But she was looking absently at the carpet and shaking her head in doubt.

McKuen tried a different tack. 'Mrs Earl,' he said softly, 'in this job, as you may imagine, one tends to get the measure of people pretty quickly, witnesses in particular. One gets a nose for it, you might say,' he said, smiling and shrugging his shoulders. 'There are many categories of witness, of course,' he went on, 'and these, as again you can probably imagine, vary widely.' He paused, as though he was considering a rather unusual step. 'I know you won't mind me saying so,' he went on now, 'but you very much strike me as being one of the more sensible ones. In which case, would you perhaps help us to cut a few corners? Unpleasant ones, even?'

'Now it was up to her. For some witnesses, whether innocent or not, did indeed tend to bridle or even clam up altogether at any question that might suggest the least invasion of their private lives. And to be any help at all, this was almost always unavoidable. Although, as he reflected, such touchy individuals were rarely known to have happily dispensed hard liquor to the enquiring officers. 'It goes without saying, of course, that this would be in complete confidence.'

She gave a rather tired smile. 'Ask what you will, Inspector.' A movement caught McKuen's eye as she spoke, a movement more than suggestive of Curtiss bending his elbow and, just in time, he steeled himself not to look.

'The general consensus then, Mrs Earl, according to those who might be said to have known him well, is that your husband was a good man. Something of an extrovert, perhaps, but, in general, generous and well liked. A self-made man, too. Have we got it about right, do you think?'

She took a good sip of brandy and, getting up, walked to the window, looking out at the grey expanse of neglected garden. Within her reach, there was a grand piano, a Brinsmead, and, without looking, she rested a hand on

101

the instrument, stroking it lovingly. McKuen noted absently that the piano had its own carpet-free area.

She turned to face them again. 'Yes,' she said without expression. 'They would say that, wouldn't they? Of course they would. Generous men are well liked, anyone knows that, especially in such places as The Cockleshell. But a good man? A self-made man? No, Inspector, he was neither of these. It is I who have the money.'

She returned to her chair and carried on tonelessly. 'When we first met, George and I, he was full of ideas and wanted me to invest in them. Hare-brained most of them, or so they sounded to me, little as I know of business. But I'm not a stupid woman and, of course, I flatly refused. That's why we moved here. I let him have an allowance and tell what tales he liked and, to a point, the arrangement suited us both. God knows why I married him in the first place, but there it is. He had his moments of anger, too, and I think he could easily have been a violent man. Neither,' she finished softly, 'would I let him see my will.'

At this last remark, involuntary as the movement was, McKuen couldn't resist raising a quick eyebrow and Mrs Earl saw the gesture easily. 'Take what you will from the comment, Inspector. Anyway, I think that's about the essence of our lives together.' She glanced vaguely out of the window. 'I will miss him, or at least,' she said, 'I will miss what he used to be – that time when he did make the effort. For loneliness is seldom a very enviable state.'

Back in the car, the chief sat looking thoughtfully at the photograph of George Earl which his wife had given them and which had been taken in Colchester four years previously. The place was their hometown and where they'd first met.

The face staring back at McKuen reminded him of nothing so much as the old, popular image of a well-fed bookmaker. Only the check suit was missing and he could understand how, in the right surroundings, such a man would be popular, especially one free with his money. Then, thinking that perhaps there was some reason, some idea, that just maybe, he wasn't being entirely objective in the matter, he looked at his sergeant 'What do you think, Errol? What, say, would his occupation have been?'

Curtiss gave the matter some brief thought. 'Old-time music-hall artiste?' he said. 'Specializing in questionable one-liners? Butcher? Bookie?'

'Assuming that you're not just being flippant, Sergeant,' McKuen had to grin, 'I think you might have it about right. But then again,' he made an effort to be serious, 'you have to be fair. It is only a photograph after all. Just the same...'

The pair sat in silence for a moment. 'What about Mrs Earl, Errol?'

'I don't think she killed her husband, sir.'

'Nor do I. Not that we can just cross her off the list, of course.' Saying this reminded McKuen of something the New York detective had once said. 'Cross 'em off by all means, Donald. But don't rub 'em out. That way, they're always there.'

'Anything else, Errol?'

'Yes. What about the way she reacted when you mentioned where the body had been found, sir. Between Hawkesworth and Norrs End? I did wonder which place it was that affected her in the way it did. And why you didn't jump on to it.'

'You're quite right, Errol. But I thought I'd store that one up. Find out a bit more for ourselves first, perhaps. Then catch her out in some way. Maybe she didn't kill her husband but she certainly knows more than she's

5545555

saying at present and, for the moment at any rate, we are a bit short on suspects. Right. Where now, do you think?'

'Cockleshell, sir?'

'I think not. I think we really aught to save that one for during the morning, when probably there aren't so many customers to distract from whatever the landlord might have to say. What about setting up an incident room at the station? See what we might come up with?'

'If you think that's best, sir.' Pink, round Curtiss sounded – what? – Torpid? Not exactly right. Contented, that was it. The beer and the brandy. It was certainly Curtiss's day. The chief strove to think of some fitting remark on the matter, but failing in this, he started the engine.

Back at the station, a big desk was cleared and an OS map of the area was spread out and, at the side of this, a clean sheet of paper, upon which McKuen drew a small cross to represent the spot where the body had been found. Computers were all very well but they were only as good as the people who worked them. This is what he liked to tell himself on occasion but, as he well knew, this was his shortcoming, this reluctance, or inability, to keep up with all the new technology. He'd tried a couple of books, getting lost on the second page. Never mind. There were plenty of other experts knocking about. Anyway, you could carry a piece of paper with you and look at it any time.

He looked at the cross, deciding at the same time that, after all, he would like to be on his own for a short while, give some thought to everything that had happened so far. He came to decisions.

'Sergeant...' The title and the tone were delivered in this way when prompt action was required and Curtiss always responded. Like taking turns for the beer, it was part of their working repertoire. 'We need a WPC. Get Barbara Knowles if you can. Then find Walt Briscoe. He lives at Hawkesworth. Look at the roster. If he's off duty, go to his home. Quiz him about the people who live there. Put him in the picture and, unless he'd rather work on a written report, get him to knock on a few doors. He's to change shifts if he has to. After that, nose around yourself. You know the drill. The computer could help, I suppose. I want to know all you can find out about the Earls. Both of them. I want you, WPC Knowles and PC Briscoe here in the office at eight-thirty sharp in the morning. Any questions?'

'No, sir.'

'Right. Get to it.' And McKuen knew that he would do. That was another thing he liked about his sergeant. Food-loving and comfortably built he may be but he could move when he had to. And he could think for himself.

The Chief bent over his maps.

The office window was frosted and McKuen had opened it slightly to look out at the crowds scurrying home from work or struggling along with their plastic bags of shopping and their problems. Bent over the maps, his back had started to ache and he rubbed at it now, his mind flitting from one thing to another, in the familiar knowledge that this was a sign of fatigue.

He knew there were certain rules to be followed but, even so, no two people tackle any problem in exactly the same way and McKuen wondered vaguely how Tom Jade of Colchester, for instance, would have gone about this one. He knew that Jade was like himself, a mild protestor against form. What was it they used to say? 'Bookmakers wear check suits and DIs wear hats.' Not quite like that now but times change faster than mentalities. Strange, he thought, how the higher-ups in any job are always wary of change. Something to do with age, perhaps. But he quickly shied away from that thought when he reflected on his own attitude to computers. And he'd done well

105

for his age so far, he knew that. Young, slim and hatless – this dislike of headgear being the reason he'd hated uniform so much – he was a countryman with a city man's awareness. His rather rapid rise in rank was due not only to his talent for the job but also to his ability to get on with his superiors, whilst at the same time lacking any kind of subservience. His natural good manners also endeared him to many others and although all these traits may have intimated some kind of reserve – no one could ever remember seeing him lose his temper – yet he could still be an impulsive and passionate man, having been know to shout 'Yes!' to the heavens when some vicious felon had been caught.

The one thing, however, that did irk him and which he'd no time for at all, was sloppy work from whatever rank. For his own part, he stuck to the rules as far as he thought was sensible. But if he had to take a drink with some wrongdoer in order to help crack a case, then he would not hesitate to do so.

Of middle height only, he was yet handsome to a fault and there were those who averred that he could have disarmed a tiger merely by smiling at it.

When he realized that, for the last few minutes, he had been thinking of nothing but home and Sarah, McKuen, suddenly fearful that he would be interrupted, closed the window in haste, put the maps quickly away and made for the door. Briscoe, if he arrived, would be too late. As would anyone else.

Briscoe in fact missed the Chief by a whisker and, a little later, rang him at home. But the conversation was brief. McKuen could detect no particular excitement in the Constable's tone and the first chance he got he interrupted the flow. 'Don't worry about it now, Walt. See you first thing...' The last thing he wanted at the moment was a lengthy conversation on the telephone. For he was suddenly weary.

The call had cut in on Sarah's greeting. 'Guess who rang, my love,' she'd said as, smiling in apology, he'd picked up the phone.

Now, as he put the instrument down, he tried to force himself out of his near exhaustion. All he really wanted was a few minutes in the armchair before the evening meal, to try and empty his mind for a spell.

'I'll bet I know who phoned.' He said this as lightly as he could manage. 'Linda. The one with the fat Labrador.' He knew he would be wrong. Sarah wouldn't have shown such enthusiasm over such a call, probably wouldn't even have mentioned it.

'Wrong,' she sang. 'It was Warwick. To remind us about Saturday. As if we needed it.'

Damn. The name hit him right out of his lethargy. Damn. The murder had put it right out of his mind. Of course. He and Sarah were supposed to be going there at the weekend. Warwick Edwards and Sarah were brother and sister and Fawkley was McKuen's own hometown. That's where he and Sarah had wed. The two families had grown up nearly next door to each other. Damn.

She saw it in his face – knew something was wrong. 'Who was it, Donald, on the phone just now?'

He told her about the murder and her eyes kindled in shock. 'Murder? So close?'

He gathered her to him. 'Oh, it's not Jack the Ripper, my dear,' he said gently. 'Just a one-off. An argument or a grudge. Possibly even an accident.'

'Good morning, sir, Still here?' The airy greeting came from Curtiss, coming through the door to see his chief bent over the maps in exactly the same position as when he'd left him the evening before.

'Good morning, Errol,' McKuen grinned back. 'The upper ranks do have to show an example, you know.' But what he was really thinking about was how he and Sarah had spent the early part of the night. And how he was really not yet fully awake.

WPC Barbara (Babs) Knowles and PC Walter Briscoe came through the door together. 'Good morning, chaps.' McKuen did his best to sound brisk. 'Now then, Constable Briscoe first, I think. Anything, Walter?'

'No, sir. I know most of the villagers, of course, and there's no one I can remotely think of who might be implicated. Not a whisper. Doesn't necessarily mean there's nothing there. Hawkesworth can be as tight-lipped as anywhere else.'

'Right.' McKuen looked at the calendar. Wednesday the 14th. 'Not everyone will be in, I know, but get down there, Walter. Knock on doors and see if you can stir anything up. Nothing else for it. Then chase them up at work if you have to. See the duty sergeant to get someone to go with you. Any questions?'

'No, sir.' Briscoe was a large, square man with a red face and no waistline. He began to move but McKuen stopped him.

'Not just yet, Constable. You're part of the team now and you need to listen to the rest.' He turned to the WPC. Babs Knowles was sturdy and healthy-looking. She played a lot of squash and McKuen shuddered at the thought of opposing her at the game. 'Constable? You fancy the job? Murder enquiry?'

'Yes, sir,' she answered eagerly as the thought occurred to the Chief that, as far as he could recollect, it was the first time he'd used the phrase and, as far as that went, this was the first case of murder he'd ever handled. Taking a brief second to dwell on this, he then told himself he would handle it as he would any other felony. No alternative, really.

The others were waiting and he felt constrained to speak. 'OK. We'll be straining resources a bit but ... my hope is that we don't have to get too much help from other forces. Keep it in the family, eh?' he grinned. 'Now then, Sergeant,' he said, turning to Curtiss. 'Anything?'

'Not too much, sir. Just a little background stuff on the Earls. They did reside in Colchester. Met at the Repertory Company there, it seems. George actually fancied himself as an actor and Margaret, that's Mrs Earl's name, had friends there. The Rep's quite a thing there, I understand. Anyway, Margaret Preece trained as a musician. There's money in the family. When she decided to marry George, the family went wild – marrying beneath her station and all that. But she was forty and she was determined. That's why they came down here to live. To get away from all the bickering.

'There's a little on George, too. Something about a garage scam. Nothing serious as far as the law went, though, and it was years ago. He also got a few penalty points at one time, for careless driving. That's about it, sir.'

Curtiss had not once referred to his notebook and McKuen looked at him in real admiration. 'Well done, Errol.'

'Thank you, sir.'

'Right, everyone,' McKuen said now, 'gather round the master plan.' His smile at the exaggeration almost melted WPC Knowles' heart as they all huddled round the crude drawing. 'Here's where the body was found.' He stabbed away with a finger. 'The road is here and I've put all the other places in by name.' WPC Knowles read them all out. There were two of them that were quite unknown

109

to Curtiss, both houses, one on either side of the Breeley Road, close to Bradern, and neither of them too far from the Earls' house. They were marked Brace and Stowe, respectively.

'Why these two, sir?' asked Curtiss. 'There's lots of other houses in Bradern.'

'Good question, Errol. But look at the OS map here.' The Chief spread the larger map out as he spoke. Typically, it was an old one, the shiny cover long gone, but it suited the purpose well enough. 'The houses themselves aren't marked, of course,' he went on, 'but I've marked the spots with a ball-point. See? And slightly isolated from Bradern as they are and occupying the positions they do, I'm willing to bet that Earl regularly passed one or other of these houses on his jaunts. Had to, unless he simply walked across the fields or stuck to the main road, both of which are highly unlikely, don't you think?'

They all huddled closer, thinking on McKuen's words and studying the maps in silence.

'Do we know who lives there, sir?' asked Curtiss at last.

'Names only, I'm afraid.' McKuen stabbed the map again. 'Kate Brace here and Belinda and Graham Stowe here.'

'I know them all,' said Briscoe quietly. 'And now that I've thought about it, you're right, sir. Earl would have had to pass those two houses on occasion.'

The others looked up at him. 'Let's have it then, Walt,' said McKuen eagerly. But he knew Briscoe wouldn't be rushed. Although he was the older man by a piece and still only a constable, the two shared a certain familiarity, having known each other since McKuen had come here from Fawkley. McKuen had learned a lot about the area from the steady country bobby, this and other things, not the least of which was that promotion was not sought by everyone and, for those who did hanker after it, brains alone was not enough.

And he'd learned that Briscoe would not be rushed. 'Nothing special, sir,' said the Constable now, his brow creased in thought. 'Let's see now. Kate Brace. Forty or forty-five. Lives on her own. Her place is a smallholding. Pleasant woman. Came here a year or so before the Earls. I don't know where from.' McKuen nodded – let the man carry on talking. 'Belinda and Graham Stowe. They've only been here a few months. They came from the coast somewhere. Walton or Frinton. One of those places. Only young. Not been wed long. She's a nice, friendly sort, but he's a bit of a stuck-up bugger. Works in Palings Insurance in the High Street. Manager, I think.

'As for Earl. I used to see him regularly and unless he went in the other direction, away from Breeley and which he sometimes did, then he had to pass one house or the other. That's it, sir.'

And well worth waiting for, too, thought McKuen. Aloud he said, 'And that's about enough I should think, Walt. If we knew much more, we'd just about be able to solve the case without leaving the station any more.' He'd never had occasion to regret showing appreciation.

'Right, Errol.' He became brisk again. They had a lot of ground to cover. 'Take yourself off to Colchester. Follow up on that garage thing. You never know. We'll see you back here. WPC Knowles will come with me.' He looked thoughtful for a moment. 'No word from Payne yet. I wonder if Mrs Earl's been to identify the body yet – get the post-mortem going. Could ring him I suppose but you know what he's like. OK. Let's get on with it.'

It was at this moment that the phone rang. 'That could be him.' McKuen snatched up the instrument. 'McKuen. Oh, yes, sir.' He shook his head at the others as he carried on listening. 'Thank you just the same, sir,' he said at last, 'but we're managing quite well, I think. Of course we will. Goodbye, sir.'

'The ACC,' he said, putting the phone down. 'Wishing us luck. Right, let's try again, shall we? Oh and, Walter…'
'Sir?'
'Don't worry about ruffling a few feathers. Straight to me if you have any trouble. Any at all.'
Briscoe opened his mouth to reply as the phone went again.
'McKuen.' The Chief looked up quickly at the others. 'Yes, Alan. She did? Good.' He listened for a while. 'Right, Alan,' he said then and put the phone down. 'The body was that of George Earl, all right.' His tone was thoughtful. 'But that's not all. The good doctor wouldn't say what, of course. Not till he's sure. OK. Let's see if we can make it to the door this time. Beat the switchboard girl.'

Judy Trace, landlady of The Cockleshell, had a black eye or, more exactly, she'd had a black eye, the area surrounding the organ now fading in hue, no doubt through the passing of time and various assorted shades, to a sort of pale green – somewhat of a bilious colour, thought McKuen.
As many such women seem to be, she was past her best, fiftyish and tired-looking, although she still appeared to take some pride in herself – make-up carefully applied. But it was equally obvious that she wasn't in the best of moods, thus being brought to the door, especially by the police, just as she was about to begin the cleaning rounds. McKuen could hear someone on a similar chore somewhere in another room. 'It's about George Earl, Mrs Trace. Do you think you might fetch your husband? Might as well get it over in one.'
She stalked off without a word – she even managed to look hostile from the back. He motioned WPC Knowles to sit down at one of the small, round tables and did the same himself. He took a look round the room – the

'lounge'. It could have been one of a thousand others and it was not at all to his liking. All easy-wipe surfaces. All plastic and pinballs. Am I that old-fashioned? he wondered. He indulged in small talk with sturdy WPC Knowles, on how she liked the job and so on. In the comparative intimacy of the situation, she answered haltingly – almost shyly. He knew how attractive he was to women. Not all of them, of course. Not Mrs Earl, for one. Nor Judy Trace, apparently. The landlady had seen it all before – many times. He wondered about the black eye.

Ben Trace appeared, following his wife. He was a sharp-featured man, not bad-looking and, thought McKuen, a bit younger than she was, although, as he'd often understood, the women usually worked harder in this job than the men did.

The man was busy tying the cord of a robe over pyjamas and it was clear he'd pulled himself hurriedly from his bed. Sleep was still there in his eyes, but unlike his wife, there was not the slightest sign of ill-temper. Even so, there was wariness there – or perhaps it was something else.

McKuen began to rise but Trace motioned him back, sitting down himself and extending a hand. 'Ben Trace, Inspector.' He then turned to his wife, standing there behind him, her face suddenly uncertain. 'Judy.' The man blinked sleep from his eyes. 'Why don't you get us a drink? Inspector, I know you're both on duty, but won't you just have a small one?'

'Thanks, Mr Trace, but it is just a bit early and we do have rather a lot to do. This is WPC Knowles.'

Ben Trace nodded to WPC Knowles in friendly fashion whilst his wife went off to the bar, still saying nothing. She poured two liberal whiskies and, coming back, handed one to her husband before sitting down herself. Without further delay, McKuen then began with his questions and, as the minutes passed, Ben Trace passed his empty glass to his wife and she fetched two more, again without a word. The Chief had time to wonder whether all landlords drank like this. – 'Was George Earl a womanizer?' He asked the question suddenly, hoping for a possibly unguarded answer.

Judy Trace had begun to mellow under the influence of the raw spirits and she now answered on impulse. 'What man isn't, Inspector? Underneath, I mean. It's just that George was maybe a bit more, er, forward than a lot of others. Generous, too.'

'Quite.' Under McKuen's soft regard, she now smiled, even colouring up a little, landlady or not.

They were coming out of the pub and McKuen, having thanked them both, turned at the door. 'Sorry about your eye, Mrs Trace.'

In reaction to the sudden remark, she touched her eye and, quite friendly now, she turned, laughing, to her husband. But the laughter was forced, as though perhaps to cover some other emotion. 'We fight sometimes,' she said.

Ben Trace was also confused and in the absence of having anything else to do, he now came forward, although his own smile was even less successful than hers had been and the lines of vigilance were back. 'Might I ask, Inspector? Have you any suspects yet?'

It was a lame performance and Judy Trace now grabbed her husband's arm as if in comfort. But McKuen couldn't help but note that she held it rather tightly – a warning to watch what he said perhaps? 'You know better than that, Mr Trace.' He nodded in farewell. 'You know where to find me.'

Back in the car, he glanced across at WPC Knowles,

who was in uniform, and wondered how she could bear
to wear a hat for such a long period. 'Do you drive,
Constable?' he asked.

'Yes, sir.'

'Right. Let's change places.' A bottle of expensive brandy
in expensive surroundings had come into his mind's eye
– certainly a more appealing thought than whisky in a
dim pub, probably offered as some kind of sop to... No.
Perhaps he was being harsh. The drink seemed to have
been offered in good faith – casually, in fact.

But he much preferred to think of the number of stars
on the brandy bottle and the least he could do was to
protect a young WPC from the demon drink. 'Mrs Earl's
house, then. I'll give you directions.'

She fastened her seat belt and reached for the ignition.
'A moment, Constable. Don't start the car just yet,' he
said and then explained the intervention. 'Whilst your
mind is fresh, just give me your impression of the Traces.
It won't do any harm to let them see us hanging about
a bit.'

'Well, there was certainly something, sir,' she said 'Both
of them. But he wasn't quite as cute as she was. Probably
still half asleep. And she did try her best to warn him.
Something else, sir. He may have blacked her eye but you
can bet she'll pay him back tenfold.'

He thought she'd just about got it right, and said so,
before asking her to start the car. He would have given
a lot to hear what the Traces were saying just now, too.
They pulled away from the pub.

'Can you drive and talk, Constable?'

'Yes, sir.' She was enjoying the whole business.

'Right,' he said and, briefly, he gave her everything that
had happened in the case so far, then inviting her
comments.

'Just the one, sir,' she said, after thought. 'If Mrs Earl's

115

home is as big as you say it is, then that's the second place the body might have been kept. Preparatory to being dumped where it was found, sir.'

'And the first place?'

'The Cockleshell, sir.'

McKuen was delighted that she hadn't bothered to mention the possible implications of the statement. They were both obvious and speculative anyway, and he enjoyed a feeling of self-satisfaction at having specified this particular PC for the team. But they were now making the approach to the house, preventing further talk for a while.

The strains of Ravel, skilfully played, were coming through the open bay window of the lounge as, to McKuen's ring, the front door was opened by Mrs Barnes. 'Good morning, Mrs Barnes,' he smiled. 'May we come in?'

A pleasant-looking woman with a good figure, she held the door wide. 'Good morning, Inspector, and to you, miss. I'll just go and tell Mrs Earl you're here.'

They stepped inside and, closing the door behind them, she went off on her errand, the Chief noting mentally that she didn't knock on the lounge door before she went in. There was then a pause before the playing stopped, Mrs Barnes now appearing once again, to give the officers a friendly nod.

'Good morning, Mrs Earl. This is WPC Knowles. We've come unannounced, I'm afraid. I do hope we're not being a nuisance.'

'Not at all, Inspector, believe me.' She was closing the piano lid carefully. 'Please, both of you, sit down.'

McKuen thought that the woman looked tired, almost as though she hadn't slept. 'Mrs Earl,' he began, 'the main reason for our visit is to say how sorry we are. That it was indeed your husband, I mean.'

116

'Thank you, Inspector. But I think it would have been even more of a shock to discover that it was someone else.' She was sitting in the same chair she'd occupied the previous day, hands folded calmly in her lap.

He was thankful that once broached, the matter had been dealt with so easily and that now he could get down to business. 'If you are up to answering a few more questions, Mrs Earl?' She nodded and he said, 'Do you happen to know Kate Brace?'

Her brows went up. 'Yes, I do. But I don't see...' She seemed uncomfortable with the question, as though perhaps she had the idea that Kate Brace should be answering her own questions.

'Mrs Earl. As I said yesterday and, I believe, as you seemed to appreciate, cutting a few corners could expedite matters. A man has been done to death after all and when I mentioned yesterday where the body had been found, you did appear to be somewhat unsettled, shall we say?' They both knew that this was something of an understatement. 'I couldn't help wondering why, Mrs Earl. I couldn't ask you at the time, of course, as we weren't then sure who the victim was. You do see my point? And we have also since discovered that Kate Brace's house is, as likely as not, on the route that your husband took on that day. It was that way or one of two others. Naturally, we're trying to find out which.'

It was as though he hadn't said a thing and he changed tack slightly. 'I never get used to it, Mrs Earl. Never. This customary reluctance to help the police. And usually through misplaced motives. And you know as well as I do that it won't be a very difficult thing to find out anyway.'

She was looking down at one hand and nodding thoughtfully, as though trying to decide whether or not the nails needed attention. 'You're perfectly right, of course,

Inspector, and I'm sorry. I truly am. One's loyalties, tenuous though they may sometimes appear...' She looked up at McKuen just as Mrs Barnes came in, carrying a tray. 'Thank you, Mrs Barnes.'

The woman withdrew and Mrs Earl began pouring the tea. 'Help yourself to sugar, my dear,' she smiled at WPC Knowles. 'You too, Inspector. Can I get you anything else?'

The rejoinder to this which leapt to his mind went something like, 'Thank you, Mrs Earl. Since you so kindly ask on this damp morning, do you think I may have my tea laced with some of your excellent brandy over there. In fact, I don't think I'll bother with the tea at all. And WPC Knowles is driving.'

'Thank you, Mrs Earl. This'll do fine,' he said.

They all sipped tea, McKuen letting the woman choose her moment. 'Yes, Inspector,' she said at last. 'I know Kate Brace. We often talk in Bradern. She has a smallholding on the Bradern track.'

'Did your husband know her? To speak to, I mean?'

'Yes. As you know, he used to pass right by her place on his ramblings. She didn't like him, though. Wouldn't give him the time of day if she could help it. Had no time for him at all.'

'Any reason in particular?'

'They were totally different types.' She drew a deep breath. 'You also know by now what he was really like. Any presentable woman. It was his nature. And she just wasn't that sort. That's why she would never visit. I did ask her. No, Inspector,' she went on, 'the person I had on my mind yesterday was Mrs Barnes. She lives at Norrs End, but you already know that, too, don't you?'

McKuen almost dropped the expensive china cup.

'Ah,' she said, 'I see you didn't know. But you would soon have found out.' At his obvious discomfiture, she was now genuinely smiling.

'We, er, would have got round to it, naturally, Mrs Earl.' Unusually enough for him, he'd been caught completely on the hop, now being uncomfortably aware of WPC Knowles' presence. It was a bad mistake – no, an unfortunate omission. Was her expression quite neutral, he wondered? He wouldn't risk a glance. 'What about Mrs Barnes?' he managed to say.

'Well, the thing is,' Mrs Earl answered, more soberly now, 'George even began trying it on with her. Here in the house.' She looked towards the window, remembering. 'When she told me about it, I could cheerfully have killed George myself. Sorry as she was and need the money as she did, she said she'd have to leave. Eric Barnes isn't much, doesn't care for work himself, but he wouldn't have that kind of thing.'

'What does he do with his time? Do you know?'

'Well, he does have a big allotment at home. Grows just about everything. I buy produce from him. Anyway, Mrs Barnes had to tell him why she had to leave here, of course.'

'When did she come back here?'

'After George disappeared. I went to the house and persuaded her to come back. Until his return, I said. She's a lovely woman, Inspector. As much a friend as anything. On that last day, that Sunday, although you may already know this, Eric Barnes went for George. In The Cockleshell. They had to be pulled apart. George came home in a foul temper. There was a flaming row, made the worse as I wasn't brought up to that sort of thing. I told him he'd have to go.'

She stopped talking but McKuen knew there was more. There was calculation there. He could discern it in the strained attitude. He waited.

'Do you know what he said then, Inspector?' she said at last, looking from him to WPC Knowles and back again.

'He said that's what I really wanted. An excuse to be rid of him. So that Mrs Barnes and I...' Her fingers were interlaced in her lap and she twirled her thumbs slowly. Capable and educated woman she may have been but he guessed this was out of her usual sphere – this humiliation brought on by another – and she was having a struggle with it. 'In that moment I could cheerfully have...' She smiled, determined to hang on to her dignity. 'I may have said that before. It's easy to say when one thinks of George. And in my mind, I tried to make light of it. When he snatched up his gun and stamped out, I thought it might give us both a chance to cool off a bit. Difficult as he was, I thought there might yet be hope for us. But as I did say before, I never saw him again.'

As the occasion seemed to demand, there was a moment or two's silence. 'Just one more thing, Mrs Earl,' McKuen said then. 'Why did George frequent The Cockleshell as much as he did? Both The Grayling and the Gentle Ride in Bradern are at least a little closer to home.'

'Oh, that one's easy, Inspector. George said he liked the atmosphere. For atmosphere, read cheap women. And he liked the Traces. But he would, wouldn't he?'

'Did you ever go there yourself?'

'Just the once. In the early days. And as they say,' she smiled, now fully in command of herself once again, 'I never darkened their doorstep again.'

They were back in the car. He'd wanted to ask about Belinda and Graham Stowe – other things. Composed once again as she was, he knew that Mrs Earl would have been up to it. But he'd left before these questions could be asked – before he'd given vent to his own feelings and screamed. His usually calm exterior, and, come to that, his interior as well, had been pushed to the limit. He knew it was mere chance that he hadn't known that Mrs Barnes lived at Norrs End. Curtiss hadn't asked Arthur Kemp for all the names living there and neither had he himself. Where was the need? No blame there.

But the Traces. He thought grimly of what he'd say to them when next he should see them. He savoured the moment.

'Observations, Constable?'

'Well, sir. The Traces apart, nothing beyond the obvious. Nothing sinister, I thought. Strong woman but quite human. I don't think she killed her husband.'

'What about the two women?'

'Nothing at all. And certainly no kind of *ménage à trois*. I could be wrong, of course. And such things can lead to murder. And the Earl Grey was nice, sir.' WPC Knowles was really beginning to enjoy herself.

'Hm. Is that what it was?' He was thinking of the untouched bottle with the fifty stars on the label. But wanting to dwell on other things, he indicated her to the driving seat. And the tea had been nice, at that. 'Where to now, do you think, Constable?'

'The Kate Brace place, sir?' She smiled at the sound.

'The Kate Brace place, then,' he said, smiling back as, just at that moment, the sun decided to make a belated appearance. 'Tell you what, Constable,' he said. 'Let's walk it. Get the feel of the place.'

The track leading to the Brace place could be joined by going through an iron gate at the end of the Earls' garden, thus saving them from taking the car through Bradern itself. This was the way George Earl had always gone and this was in McKuen's mind as he closed the gate behind him. Which way had the man gone on that last journey of his? Right into Bradern, or left to the more immediate countryside?

Intent on visiting the smallholding first, the two turned

121

left and now, as if perhaps to throw light on their problem, the sun came out in full to guide the way.

Forty yards or so along, the track forked, the main branch leading to their intended destination whilst the lesser, right-hand one crossed the Breeley Bradern road before leading to the home of the Stowes. He couldn't really have said why he wanted to see Kate Brace first. Perhaps it was because Mrs Earl had confirmed Kate's association with the family. What he did note at this point was that, because of tall hedges, the fork could not be observed from the Earls' place. But keeping to the main track and after about another hundred yards, he stopped and shouted, 'I've got it.'

WPC Knowles had been walking along with the sun on her back and with this handsome fellow at her side, telling herself that she was actually getting paid for it. Now she jumped almost out of her wits. 'What is it you've got, sir?' she asked, happy for him anyway. Whatever it was he'd got.

' "Pavane for a Dead Princess".'

'Sir?'

'That's what Mrs Earl was playing. On the piano.'

'If you say so, sir.' He wasn't eccentric or anything, she decided. He was just not that ordinary.

They had started walking again and she stole a look at the handsome profile. Suddenly she had the idea what he would say next: 'Constable. Barbara. I want you to come with me behind those bushes. Just for a few minutes. We've got time. My wife, you know. She doesn't understand me.'

He glanced at her in his turn. 'Constable,' he said. 'You look warm. We're in the country. Why don't you remove the damned hat for a while?'

'That's all right, sir,' she said. 'We can't be far off, now.' It took a real effort to prevent herself from giggling

122

hysterically. And what on earth would Bernard have said? Bernard worked in the Co-op Bank in Breeley.

Scorning any kind of make-up, Kate Brace's face seemed to give the game away easily – reflect the outdoor life she obviously lived. With her dark hair pulled back and tucked under a bright-yellow scarf (McKuen thought it should have been a red one – no matter), she was engaged in trying to mend a broken fence, one which would never see worse days unless a match was put to it. There were chickens and ducks everywhere and one goat. And in stark contrast to the untidy confusion of the yard, the house, with its tiny windows and old as it undoubtedly was, seemed, like the woman herself, to glow with health.

On seeing the approach of visitors, she paused in her labours, to lean against the wall of an ancient byre of which most of the roof was gone. There was no sign of welcome in her glance at all and although her brow may have cleared a little when the Chief produced his ID she still didn't ask them into the house.

'It was him then, was it, Inspector?' she said, when he had explained a little. She was soft-spoken and without the faintest trace of surprise in her voice. 'Yes, of course I knew George Earl. But you'd know that, wouldn't you? Terrible thing, just the same...' and then, as though the picture of the body, lifeless and mutilated, had suddenly presented itself, she paled beneath her tan. 'Yes,' she went on, 'he did come by here on occasion. With his gun. Not that I ever heard him fire it. I think he just fancied himself as a country gent of some kind.'

'Well, someone fired the gun, so it follows that it was loaded, Mrs Brace. Is it Mrs?' He shuddered inside himself in case she said Ms. He liked the term about as much as he liked computers. To him, Ms never sounded quite, well, English. And he did think, rather unkindly perhaps, that she might be the type to revel in such a thing.

'People call me Kate. I never married.'

She was not at all a bad-looking woman and McKuen was somehow surprised at the statement. 'Would he stop for a word or two on those occasions when he did pass the house, er, Kate?' Informal as he could easily be, he was yet never quite at ease in using a witness's given name. To him, it suggested a familiarity which rarely proved to be justified by subsequent events.

'Oh, yes. He would. Made a point of it. Not that I ever once encouraged the man. I didn't like him and he knew it. But he couldn't help himself. It was his wife I felt sorry for.'

'Why was that, Kate?' But even as he said it, he knew that it was an unworthy question. And her shoulders had drooped and, although she smiled, the expression was completely without humour.

'We're wasting time, aren't we, Inspector?' she said.

He smiled back. 'Yes, I'm sorry. Of course we knew what George was like. But tell me. Did you happen to see him on that Sunday? Any glimpse of him at all?'

'As I said, he often came by. Not on that Sunday, though.' She paused – looked over the fields for a moment before her eyes came back to him. 'And I would have remembered, don't you think? After I heard about the murder? And would I not have reported it? Don't you think so, Inspector?'

'Mm.' He changed tack. 'Don't you get a little nervous at times, Kate? Here on your own, I mean?'

'No. I'm never nervous here. And I'm not on my own. I've got Bruce, you see.'

'Bruce?'

'Yes.' She raised her voice a mere fraction. 'Here, Bruce.'

Like some nervous actor awaiting his first-night cue, the dog appeared quickly round the corner of the byre and stood there, awaiting his next one. He was a Border collie

124

and, thought McKuen, didn't look that unfriendly. But when Kate then slowly raised a hand a little way towards her face, as though perhaps to ward off danger, the dog's upper lip began to crinkle. Probably just showing off, said the Chief to himself. Just showing us how white and long his fangs were.

Kate Brace raise her hand a bit further and the dog moved another step towards the visitors, the full length of his canines now gleaming hopefully. He didn't bother growling.

'All right, Bruce.' Kate dropped her hand and the dog sat down, putting his teeth away once more. 'Trained him myself,' she said, patting her knee. The dog rushed over, rubbing his muzzle on her thigh. 'Just an old silly, really,' she said.

'Of course he is,' said McKuen. 'Just an old silly. With teeth. But tell me. Why didn't we see him when we first came?'

'Probably lying down. But he knew you were here. Barked just the once when you were way up the road. He didn't care for George Earl, either. Used to watch him all the time.'

Brief as the interview had been, McKuen had hesitated in questioning her further. He could hardly begin to quiz her about her history. Where was the excuse to do so? She was, after all, only a bit player in the game. Wasn't she? And it wasn't as though she was a talker. He couldn't even make the remark that she'd 'got a nice place here'. It was a dump. A homely sort of dump maybe, but still a dump. He'd had one last try. 'Lived here long, Kate?'

'Four years,' she'd answered. And that had been it.

There was no one in at the Stowes. The two had retraced their steps as far as the spot where the track branched off and after crossing the main road, had found the house after another few hundred yards walking. His knock brought no response and the two stood looking at the place. It wasn't a place that should be here, he decided – not the sort of place that should be on its own, belonging rather to an avenue or a street. It was a pretty house, one to vie with its neighbours, not a country cottage. He thought he could picture the couple who lived there. They would be neat and tidy, like the curtains and the garden. 'Come on, Constable,' he said. 'No use hanging about.'

McKuen's Mondeo had a two-way radio, which he had never been known to use. It was crackling now and WPC Knowles remarked on it. 'That's all right, Constable,' he answered. 'It won't be for me. More likely some bored motorway man reminding a colleague that he hasn't paid his lottery money into the pool. The thing's never worked properly anyway.' He saw the use of such gadgets but not in his particular job. He also hated the metallic click it gave out between messages. It had been installed a while. Round about the last time he'd washed the car, he remembered.

The truth of the matter was that all personnel back at the station had long since ceased to try and contact him with it and at one time bets had been placed on how someone could get him to answer the thing. Someone else had suggested a carrier pigeon but the idea had never been taken up. On her own part, WPC Knowles reminded herself that no one is entirely ordinary.

'I wonder if Mrs Earl guessed where we've been,' McKuen said. They were pulling out of her drive and he'd just made the remark when he saw a flash of white in the nearside mirror. 'Stop the car, Constable,' he said. It was someone on the track and he was out of the car almost as she slammed the brakes. Previously obscured by hedge, whoever it was, was now heading in the direction of either the Brace house or else that of the Stowes. For it was doubtful that they were making back to the Breeley road itself.

He dashed to the bottom of the garden, pulled open the iron gate, and looked down the track. He was just in time to see the back of someone in the distance, someone on a bike. Running down the track to where it branched, he saw the cyclist disappearing in the direction of Kate Brace's place. He was almost certain it was a woman.

Back at the car, he told WPC Knowles, rather more breathlessly than he would have wished, what he'd seen and that the rider had, of course, come from Bradern.

'I didn't see the point in chasing after you, sir,' she said.

'Quite sensible, too. We might have finished up in a heap at the gate. Any ideas at all, Constable?'

'Could it have been Mrs Earl, sir? There's nothing to say that she's in the house now. She could have been to Bradern.'

'Mm. Now there's a thought. I wonder if she rides a bike. Even keeping watch for us to leave from way up the track and hardly giving us time to leave, so to speak.'

There was an integral garage, quite big enough to hold a bike and a car. He didn't even know whether she drove. And as WPC Knowles had remarked, they didn't even know whether or not she was still in the house. He could hardly knock on the door and ask. 'Ah, so you are at home, Mrs Earl. Thank you. It's as I was just saying to WPC Knowles. I wonder if Mrs Earl's at home.'

He asked the Constable to start the car.

* * *

As they reached Hawkesworth Mere on the way back to
Breeley, McKuen asked WPC Knowles to pull up at the
roadside. There was now no sign of a police presence at
all and even though the sun still shone, the place still
managed to maintain its aspect of bleakness.

But shine it did and Babs Knowles couldn't prevent her
thoughts from going into overdrive again. Why had he
asked her to stop the car? 'Come on, Constable ... Barbara,'
he would say in a moment. 'Let's just take a walk over
to the mere. There's something I'd like you to do if you
will. You're a damned attractive woman, you know.'

What should she say? 'Do you think we should, Inspector?
We are on duty, after all. And what about my Bernard?'

'Come on, Constable,' he said. 'I'll show you where the
body was found.' He helped her over what bit of wall
was remaining and they walked across the rough ground
to stand looking at the exact spot. But for all the inspiration
to be found there, they could have saved themselves the
trouble. McKuen looked at his watch. It said one minute
from midday. 'Come on,' he said. 'Let's go to The Hind
for a sandwich. You're driving so I'll have a pint.'

'But I'm in uniform, sir.'

'That's OK. I have an old raincoat in the boot and you
can take your hat off.'

As usual, the hour being what it was, the place was
fairly busy and they had to stand a moment or two. Then
someone stood up from a small table in the corner and
McKuen propelled her towards it. 'Sit there for a moment,
Constable, and decide what you want. My treat. I have to
go to the gents.'

In the scruffy fawn raincoat with the odd patch of oil
on the sleeve and with the collar turned up at the neck,
Barbara Knowles reminded herself of one of those itinerants
who made a living, precarious as it may seem to some,
by roaming the general countryside in large vehicles,

patronizing, on arrival, each destination's benefits office. Dog lovers all, they each appeared to have a minimum of two. What were they called, now? Space travellers? No, that wasn't quite it. No matter, she was having sandwiches and tea in a pub, with the dishiest inspector on the force. Wait till she told Bernard.

McKuen's thoughts were running along rather different lines. Unable to converse properly in the hubbub, he thought about the case. George Earl, both liked and disliked, both hailed and heartily detested. He'd been a character, all right. But murder? Jealous husband? Boyfriend? Creditor? Relative? Give it time, he thought, lifting the glass to his lips. As he did so, he made a mental note to find out, as soon as he could, which places had been searched for George Earl prior to the discovery of the body.

'Where now, sir?' They were coming out of The Hind, leaving the warmth and the noise behind them.

'Station, I think, Constable. See if anything's happening. Do you agree?'

'Yes, sir.'

As they came in, the switchboard girl handed him his messages. They carried on through to the incident room but none of the others had yet arrived. 'Right, Constable,' he said, looking at the notes. 'Let's see what we've got.'

Three of them were relevant to the case, the first one being from Curtiss, saying he expected to be back from Colchester before two.

The next one was from the lab. The shotgun had been fished out of the mere and McKuen could now pick it up anytime. 'Ah,' he said, as he ripped open the third one. This was from Alan Payne, asking McKuen to 'get down here ASAP'. 'Mm,' he said, rubbing his chin as he handed the notes to WPC Knowles. 'What do you make of that one, Constable? Not phone, but "get down here".'

But she could think of nothing. 'Right,' he said. 'Then let's get down there and find out. See what's so urgent in the good doctor's opinion. Walk it, shall we?' He knew that, at this hour of the day, it would be quicker.

'Yes, sir.' WPC Knowles was now back in uniform once more, hat firmly in place.

Breeley had a small hospital on the outskirts of town. There was a morgue and Payne had an office there. The two officers set out and as the crowds began to thin out a little, they were able to walk at a good pace. 'Any thoughts, Constable?' asked McKuen.

'Just the one, sir,' she answered. 'That old byre at Kate's place. Just the spot for hiding a body, don't you think?'

'As you say. And that's something we have to enquire about first chance we get – a list of all the places that were searched after Earl had been reported missing.'

He fell quiet again, thinking of the morning's events. During the last few hours, he'd not only been taken by surprise. He'd also been lied to, even though it was only by omission, and he had been intrigued. And the jumble of thoughts made him happy. Things were coming together. 'Frailty, Thy name is Man.' Is that how it went?

Then the sun went in and it began to drizzle. Shame they hadn't used the car after all. There was nothing like a good shower for washing the car.

'Good afternoon, Donald.' The greeting put McKuen on the alert. Payne never used the Chief's given name unless he had something up his sleeve.

'Good afternoon, Alan. You couldn't tell me over the phone?' Fat chance of that, thought McKuen even as he spoke, but he had little option but to play along. Payne would insist on having his moment.

'Well, it's simply this, Inspector.' Reverting to title, the good doctor forced himself to remain calm. 'You'll no doubt have been wondering what took me so long with the report. But I had to be sure. You see, Earl wasn't shot to death at all,' and now, he was actually smiling.

Twice already that day, McKuen had almost dropped an expensive cup and had he been holding one now, he told himself, it would have been almost a hat-trick. 'Go on, Doctor.' He thought his voice sounded steady enough.

'He was stabbed to death.' Payne was now positively beaming. 'I suppose I was a bit lucky getting on to it,' he said, trying to sound modest. 'But get on to it I did. Devilishly tricky, though.'

McKuen would have bet his last pound that there'd been no wounds on the body itself – no tears in the clothes, anyway. Unless... 'He was dressed afterwards, Alan?'

'No. He was stabbed in the eye. The left eye.'

The words 'Are you sure?' leapt to McKuen's mind, but he stopped himself in time and Payne carried on. 'With some force, too. A heavy blow all right. Just about went through to the back of the skull. Can't figure out what the weapon was exactly, though.' It was at this point that Payne would normally have said that the rest was the Chief's job, but he was enjoying himself far too much for that. 'It wasn't a knife,' he went on, 'but something thinner, round and sharp, like a fencing foil or piece of wrought-iron gate or something. Perhaps something from a piece of machinery. That's what killed the man, Inspector. Then he was shot.'

Both men were far too intelligent for either of them to ask the other a possible reason for the shooting, for both knew that this was McKuen's job. 'Good job, Alan. Anything else?'

'Just the one. The body hadn't been there above two days at the most.'

McKuen nodded. 'You're a wonder, Alan.'
The good doctor nodded in his turn.

Sergeant Curtiss was viewing the meat pie with the utmost
suspicion, for small as it was, it seemed more than anxious
to hide its contents behind a wall of thick, mottled crust
and, although he'd eaten nothing since breakfast, he had
the idea that this might be tempting providence a bit.
'You're not thinking of going for that thing head-on,
are you, Sergeant?' The voice in his ear sounding remarkably
like that of his Chief.
McKuen sat down and the two of them sat looking at
the pie, thoughtfully. Unless he were looking for someone,
the Chief never came in the canteen. 'When you're ready
then, Errol,' he said, getting to his feet.
'I'm ready now, sir.' Curtiss picked up the six hermetically
sealed biscuits, deciding to leave the pie to its own devices.
PC Briscoe had been in the incident room for ten minutes
already, writing in his book as he waited for the others.
'Hello, Walter. How're the feet?' asked McKuen as WPC
Knowles joined them all from the ladies' room.
'Warm and dusty, sir,' Briscoe was saying with his slow
smile. 'All in the line of duty, too.'
'Glad to hear it, Constable,' said the Chief, getting out
his maps and then sitting down himself. There was a
small pain behind his eyes which he hoped wouldn't get
any worse. 'Right, chaps,' he went on. 'Who first?'
'Me, sir, I think,' said Curtiss. 'It's just a trifle involved.'
'Off you go then, Errol.' McKuen was now suddenly
conscious of an unfamiliar tension and he made an effort
to relax.
Just as Curtiss was about to begin, however, there was
a discreet knock at the door. Briscoe was the closest and
he got up to answer it.

'It's Tom Swaines, from traffic, sir,' said Briscoe. 'He came with me. Wants to know if there's anything else.'

'Of course there is, Walt,' answered McKuen. 'Bring him in here.'

Briscoe said something to the young PC, who then came in, said, 'Sir,' to McKuen and, nodding to everyone else, sat down without another word.

'Right, Errol,' said McKuen.

'Well, sir, I started off in Colchester Library, looking at the back copies of the local paper in the micro files. I know there are other sources, but I thought this way would be the quickest. I knew the rough date I was after but it took a while. Reason for that was that the thing didn't make much of a splash at all. But I found it eventually and, as it turned out, there were three of them involved – one Andrew Rollinson, one Bryn Daniels and one George Earl.

'They went into business together in Colchester. Garage and used car sales. The usual thing. Rollinson and Daniels were the mechanics and Earl was to supply the cars, supposedly from auctions. They were to be done up and sold on. Well, it wasn't long before the police were on the scene.' At this point, he picked up his plastic cup from the canteen, to look doubtfully into its depths. 'Do you think Babs might make us all a decent cup of tea, sir?'

WPC Knowles jumped to her feet, grabbing for the kettle and, at the same time, angling her head so that she wouldn't miss what was being said. As this seemed to satisfy everyone, Curtiss carried on.

'It seems that the cars had been nicked. Just about all of them. But at the time, nothing could be proved and they all got away with it. The business was ruined, though, even before it got properly going. The result was that Daniels, who appears to be a rather hot-tempered chap, threatened to kill George Earl.

'A few years on, however, Daniels and Rollinson opened another garage together and this time they were more successful. A few years after that, they opened another one, here in Breeley. And both businesses are still in operation, Rollinson running the one in Colchester and Daniels the one here in Breeley. In Horley Street. And, sir, guess who works for Daniels.'

Walter Briscoe not only stood in little awe of rank. His feet were tired and he was thirsty. 'I know, Sergeant,' he said. 'The Sultan of Brunei. And he's supplying pinched oil.'

Curtiss looked hurt. 'Be serious, Walt,' he said.

'You're wrong anyway, Walter,' McKuen intervened. 'It's Clement Betteridge. From Norrs End.'

Curtiss's jaw dropped, making the kettle whistle. 'How did you know, sir?'

'Easy, Errol,' said the Chief, smiling. 'You asked us to guess, giving us the clue that we knew the individual, or of him, and as he's the only other mechanic in the case so far... Tell me. Did you go to see either Rollinson or Daniels?

'No, sir. I had the thought that they should both be seen at the same time – separately, but at the same time. Not give them chance to talk together.'

'Good thinking, Errol. Anything else?'

'Yes, sir. I called to see Inspector Jade. He'd seen it in the papers that Earl had disappeared, of course, but this morning's spread suggested that there could be a link between him and the body found at Hawkesworth. When I confirmed this, he said he would be in touch with you. Put someone on it in the meantime, he said. George Earl hadn't been a total stranger to him and, to save time, I detailed what we already knew. That's it, sir.'

'Good. I'll ring him when we've finished here. Right. That's tea I can smell. Let's get to it,' and soon, they were all drinking greedily. 'Good cup, Barbara.'

'Thank you, sir.' WPC Knowles flushed. It was the first time the Chief had used her Christian name.

'You next then, Walter,' McKuen said then. 'Anything?'

'Not a peep, sir. Me and Tom here checked everyone thoroughly. The Hawkesworth lot are as clean as a whistle, I swear it.'

'Fair enough. Finding out there's nothing gets a lot of people out of the way. Makes the rest tidier. Anything else?'

'Well, when we'd finished, we thought we'd have a look round Bradern. Spoke to one or two. Nothing. Even Jim Pearce told me to fuck off. Pardon my French, Babs, but Jim is an old acquaintance of mine and that's his way of telling me there's nothing and how annoyed he is. You see, he sometimes whispers in my ear for a couple of pints. So that's about it, sir... Oh, we did catch a glimpse of Belinda Stowe going down the track on her bike. Couldn't catch her to have a word, though.'

'Did you now?' McKuen looked at him sharply. 'What time would that be, Walt?'

'Oh, about ten to twelve, sir. Somewhere around that time. Is it important?'

'Probably not. But we caught a glimpse of her without knowing who it was. And she wasn't going home. She must have been going to see Kate Brace. Hm. Anything else?'

'No, sir.'

'Right. Constable Knowles here will now tell you all how we spent our own day. OK, Barbara?'

WPC Knowles was taken just a little by surprise but recovered quickly enough. How nicely, she thought, he said Barbara.

It had taken a while, with all possible suspects, motives and opportunities having been discussed in detail. McKuen thought they'd all acquitted themselves well and said so. What they were all waiting for now was to hear what he should next decide. He looked at his watch. It was 4.20 p.m. and it also seemed that the weather had at last made up its mind which face to show, settling for a uniform greyness. He looked down at the list again, open on the desk in front of him – the list brought in by Curtiss from next door, just two minutes ago. They were all there with times and dates, the places that had been searched before the discovery of Earl's body. Nothing unusual there. Just the usual haunts of the man – his home, Kate Brace's place and the Stowes – a cursory examination of The Cockleshell, one or two others. But not Eric Barnes' place at Norrs End. At the time, there would have been no reason for it. But it seemed most other avenues had been covered.

The others were still waiting, content to rest for a while and McKuen looked out of the window, opened for a little air. As happens so often when a case was coming to a head, as he believed this one was now doing, things were becoming conversely more complicated, bringing it home to him that the decisions were still his alone. Which officer should he send where? For much as he would have liked to see all the witnesses for himself, he knew that this was both selfish and impractical. He turned to Briscoe. 'You're sure about this Jim Pearce, Walt? The one with the nice turn of phrase? You're sure he knows nothing?'

'Certain, sir. Any family he has, never mind his grandmother, would be shopped for a drink.'

McKuen sighed. 'All these people with their little secrets,' he said. 'One of them at least has to know the one we're interested in. A man goes out to do a little rough shooting, perhaps to cool his temper, or clear his mind and then...' He rubbed the back of a forefinger along the barrel of the shotgun, up from the lab and now resting on the maps.

'May I interrupt, sir?' asked WPC Knowles.

'Certainly you may, Constable. What is it?' McKuen tried to clear his thoughts, ignore the slight headache.

'Well, sir. I've been meaning to ask. What is rough shooting, exactly?'

'Good question, Constable.' McKuen glanced briefly at the others, noting that, whilst Briscoe's satisfied smile confirmed that he knew the answer, Curtiss's pink cheeks told him that the Sergeant did not – a fact which gave the Chief a childish delight. The traffic man, Swaines, still seemed a little overawed by it all. 'Let's see now.' McKuen looked down at the shotgun again as he searched his mind. 'Rough shooting. A vague term, really. In fact, informal shooting might be a more apt description for as often as not, it's done on one's own and not on terrain managed by a gamekeeper. Unfortunately, Constable, there are a lot of idiots in the school I'm afraid, shooting at anything that moves, although I wouldn't necessarily put George Earl in that category. A thought does occur, though,' he said, suddenly uneasy. 'We don't even know whether he had a licence for the thing.'

'He did, sir,' Briscoe broke in simply, and McKuen nodded briskly in appreciation for, relieved as he was, he knew that he should have checked up on this sooner.

Briscoe was a marvel, not bothering to enlarge on the matter. It wasn't his way. But McKuen could picture the Constable, stopping Earl the first time he saw him with the gun, perhaps speaking as he ponderously dismounted his bike. 'Excuse me, sir...' And Earl was the type who would bluster.

'Listen, Constable...'

'No, sir, you listen,' and Briscoe would begin to expound on that section of the Act concerned with carrying a shotgun in a public place, whether loaded or not. 'And while we're at it, sir, may I examine your current shotgun certificate?'

Smiling at these thoughts, McKuen now took up the gun, a beautiful old thing, with hammers. 'The few cartridges found in Earl's pocket were 70mm. No. 5 shot for rabbits,' he said, 'so presumably, that's what he would usually be after. Hm. Shotguns. Can you believe it? That Act does not prescribe a minimum age at which a certificate may be granted? Not our concern at present, of course. OK, Constable?'

'Yes, sir. Thank you.'

'Right.' He put the gun in a corner. 'This is what I suggest,' he said now, coming back to the maps. 'Bright and early in the morning, Walt, you and Swaines here – ... wait, though. Not *too* early. I want you, Errol, in Colchester at the same time as Walter goes to see Daniels at his garage at, shall we say nine-thirty? Can you be at Colchester by then, Errol? To see Rollinson? In your own car again?'

'Yes, sir.'

'Right. And Walter. Try and see Betteridge at the same time. Watch him, Walt. I'm not trying to teach you your business but it is important. OK?'

'Trust me, sir. What then?'

'Go and see Graham Stowe at his office. Same thing. You know the drill. Palings Insurance in the High Street, isn't it?'

'Yes, sir.'

'Right. Then go and see Eric Barnes at Norrs End. Then come back here and wait for us. Can you manage that lot, Walter? You and PC Swaines, here?'

'Leave it with us, sir.'

'Right.' McKuen now turned to Curtiss again. 'Errol. When you've finished with Rollinson, go to the station at Colchester and wait for me there. I'll be there as soon as I can. OK?'

'Yes, sir.'

McKuen then told them all where he would be himself, before turning to WPC Knowles. 'Thanks for your help, Barbara. Would you like to go back to your beat now?' Try as she might, she couldn't help her face from dropping. 'Yes, of course, sir.' 'That is, unless you want to help me interview Belinda Stowe, perhaps? And the others?' This time, it was the blushes she couldn't help. 'Yes, sir. Thank you, sir.' I'm entitled, thought McKuen. Just now and again. 'Right,' he said, reaching for the phone. 'I'll just confirm that it's OK with PC Swaines' people. Then I'll ring Tom Jade. You lot get off home.' He looked at his watch. It was ten past five and the pain was still there behind his eyes.

The rain had stopped and McKuen was on his way home and tired as he was, the small irrelevant thoughts crowded into his mind and, as always, he let them have their way, knowing full well that in his present state, more constructive reflections were out of the question. Indeed, he had long since learned that if he went with the tide, all the little uncertainties usually faded into the background, actually acting as a kind of therapy on his weary brain. He listened now. 'McKuen, are you sure you've given the right jobs to the right people?' 'Yes, I am.' But this stuff is too practical by far. Let's be more flippant. Let's see now. 'Are you really up to the job, McKuen? Better at it than your colleagues?' Well, the examining board thought so, half listening though they may have been, what with their golf handicaps and their kids' school fees on their minds at the time. Nice to hear Tom Jade's voice again, too.

As he came in at the front door to greet Sarah, the pain behind his eyes was almost gone.

139

McKuen wouldn't have sworn to it but he was reasonably sure it was the first morning sunshine he'd woken up to for the whole of the year so far. Would it prove to be the herald of success? he wondered. But early as he was to the station, Curtiss had beaten him to it. 'Good morning, Errol. Are we ready for it?'

'Morning, sir. Ready as we'll ever be, I think.' Curtiss was already busy with reports, not having to set off for Colchester for quite a while.

Constable Briscoe came in, followed a minute or so later by WPC Knowles. McKuen decided against going over the intended procedure again and, after greetings had been exchanged, together with a quick brew-up, he and WPC Knowles set off. He didn't mind how early he was this morning. And this morning, he decided to drive the car himself, leaving Barbara Knowles to dwell on the disloyal hope that the case wouldn't be solved too quickly – that all this wouldn't come to too abrupt an end.

This time Judy Trace was distinctly nervous and gone was any sign of the annoyance that had been so evident at the early hour of their call, the last time. 'You again, Inspector.' She tried to smile as she said it but didn't quite manage it.

'As you say, Mrs Trace. Would you be kind enough to fetch your husband? I wish to speak to you both.' True to his nature, his anger of the previous day towards them both was gone. He knew officers who would have gone storming into The Cockleshell like a ... well, like an irate policeman. There were others who would have drawn the whole thing out, quietly scathing the meantime. But, for himself, he had neither the wish nor the energy for such shenanigans, being now almost completely detached in the matter and having no relish at all for what he now had to do. Indeed, even as he awaited the arrival of the landlord, he put the question to himself as to whether he should be here at all – whether the time would not have been better spent elsewhere. But he did reach the conclusion that at the very least, it was his duty to tick the Traces off for wasting police time. And you never knew, something further might slip out.

The innkeepers just stood there now, the pair of them, waiting for McKuen to speak. Neither was there any question, this time, of having a drink, and no one sat down. 'Right,' said the Chief at last. 'Let's not waste any more police time, eh? Out with it. All of it.'

It was as he'd expected. With hangdog expressions and with all the excuses for wishing to protect the good reputation of the house, they admitted their mistakes in withholding information, and so on and so forth. And again as expected, it looked as though there was to be nothing new at all but, then, with either real or assumed concern in his voice, Ben Trace haltingly revealed that Eric Barnes had stayed behind when The Cockleshell had closed for the afternoon. Together with another man, from Bradern, the three men had sat drinking, whilst Judy Trace had gone to bed for an hour. 'Just three mates drinking together, Inspector,' Trace concluded. 'They didn't even pay for their drinks.'

I'll bet they didn't, thought McKuen. Aloud, he said, 'What time did they leave?'

'About quarter past four, I should think, Inspector.'

That was about it and with a stern warning that they would more than likely be back, McKuen ushered WPC Knowles to the door. 'What do you think, Constable?' he asked when they got outside.

'Not a lot, sir,' she replied. 'I think even the tale about the black eye was probably genuine, too. Now that I got another chance to study them both. They do fight.'

141

'Hm. I suppose it puts Eric Barnes in the clear as well,' he grumbled. 'Although, of course, we don't know the exact time Earl was murdered.'

Belinda Stowe was not what McKuen had expected, a fact for which he was extremely thankful. He didn't like patterns. It was like the story that owners become to look like their dogs. Heaven forbid, and whilst Belinda Stowe should then have reflected an image brought up by what the outside of the house looked like – neat and trim and punctual – she was nothing of the sort. Tall, brown of skin and sloe-eyed and, with long, dark and wavy tresses, the word houri came to McKuen's mind, with the duster and apron doing nothing at all to dispel the image. And as he introduced both WPC Knowles and himself, she looked at him with open appraisal. 'Won't you come in, Inspector?'

'Thank you, ma'am.'

Again, the room, had it primly partnered the outside, as it should have done, needed to be of the furniture showroom variety, together with its strict colour scheme. But, like the lady of the house, this too had rebelled against such formality. Rather it was bright with pots of flowers and frothy drapes – a room in which anything smaller than a dining chair would easily be misplaced. 'Is it about the murder, Inspector?' She motioned them both to a floral settee before sitting down herself.

'It is, Mrs Stowe. We understand you knew George Earl.'

'Yes. Both by sight and reputation. I didn't like the man. Neither did my husband.'

'You know Mrs Earl?'

'Yes, and, of course, I feel sorry for her. A nice woman. Cultured. I hope to be calling on her. Indeed, I...' She stopped herself but it was too late and a slight tinge came to her cheeks.

'Mrs Stowe?'

'Yes, I have to finish it now, don't I, Inspector? What I was thinking aloud, perhaps, was what an ill-matched pair they were and, although you surely know that already, it really isn't my business. Nor up to me to say it.' She had recovered her composure completely and she smiled for the first time. And WPC Knowles, watching the woman closely, thought this was something to see.

'There was no indiscretion, Mrs Stowe. Not under the circumstances. A man has been murdered, after all. Tell me,' McKuen went on, 'did Earl pass your house on occasion?'

It was the woman's turn to admonish slightly. 'And who is playing with words now, Inspector?'

Mrs Stowe wasn't a fool and she was quite right, thought McKuen, seeing no point in further concealing the real reason for his visit. So, smiling in his turn, he said, 'Forgive me, Mrs Stowe, but some people, you understand, especially when talking to the police... Tell me, then, did you happen to see Earl pass your house on that particular day? Not that you wouldn't have already reported it, of course. But with that gun of his? Perhaps he was in the habit of stopping for a word?'

'We didn't notice that he came this way on that particular day, no. Neither did he ever stop to talk at all.' She looked a little bleak for a brief moment. 'I only ever spoke to him the once,' she then said, pointedly, 'and I believe my husband exchanged words with him the same number of times.' She smiled again, radiating the room. 'We all know what George Earl was, don't we, Inspector?'

'Hm. Quite. Mrs Stowe, how well do you know Kate Brace?'

'Very well. Why do you ask?'

'Do you visit? Reason I'm asking is that we saw her yesterday and the subject didn't come up. So many

143

questions, you understand. And we're trying to get the overall picture, that's all.'

'I see. Well then, yes, I do visit Kate. I sometimes fetch her some shopping from Bradern. I also get my eggs from her.'

'Does she visit you? Or perhaps your husband doesn't care for visitors.'

'She has been here on occasion. Graham doesn't mind but in any case, Inspector, no one tells me who I can or cannot have to the house and that includes my husband.' That was something McKuen could believe. 'But she doesn't come often,' she went on. 'She doesn't like leaving the animals.'

He stood up to go. 'Right, well, we won't take up any more of your time, Mrs Stowe. Oh, when was the last time you did see George Earl? Can you remember at all?'

She thought for a moment. 'About three weeks ago, I think.'

'Hm. And Kate Brace?'

'Er, now then.' A tiny crease appeared between her brows – a minute flaw in the smoothness of that incredible complexion. 'Er, a few days ago. Perhaps a week, Inspector.'

'Thank you, Mrs Stowe.'

'What did you think, Constable?' They were back in the car, which was protesting a little at the uneven terrain of the track. He was also wondering what would happen in the event of another car coming to meet them. With a hedge on one side and a ditch on the other, they certainly couldn't have passed each other.

'Well, I thought that I might commit murder myself, sir. For that skin and that head of hair, sir. Did you see it?'

It wasn't the particular line of thought he'd meant her

to follow, but he said, 'Yes, I saw it. Was there anything else? Concerning the case, I mean.'

'Well, I did wonder why you didn't ask her why she was lying, sir. About Kate Brace, I mean.'

Busy pulling off the track on to the Breeley road, he didn't answer straightaway. 'Good question,' he eventually said, 'and I don't really know the answer. I believe I wanted time to think about it. Funny thing is, it was the answer I was half expecting. And I still don't know why.'

'Another thing, sir. Don't you think it's a pretty isolated place to live? A woman like that? On her own all day?'

'Damn,' he said. 'I meant to broach that one. I agree with you. Still, that's the way some people seem to prefer it. Kate Brace, for instance. Anything else?'

'She is beautiful, isn't she, sir? Mrs Stowe, I mean.'

'Yes, she is. And just think of the impression she must have made on someone like our George. I'd like to have heard the only conversation he had with Graham Stowe.'

They were passing the murder spot once again and he pulled up at the side of the road, as before. WPC Knowles hadn't quite got it right the last time but, on this occasion, she felt suddenly sure what he would say. And do.

Putting his hand on her knee, he would say, 'Come on, Barbara, let's have a walk over to the mere. As you say, Mrs Stowe is a beautiful woman but give me a woman with a bit more substance. And I'll tell you what. You can keep your hat on. Even in this sunshine. What do you say?'

'Well, sir, I don't know,' she would reply, having her answer ready. 'There *is* Bernard to think about.'

McKuen nipped his lower lip between finger and thumb. 'You know, Constable,' he said, starting the car again, 'I do believe the case is coming together.'

'Yes, sir.'

The desk sergeant at Colchester told McKuen that Inspector Jade was at a meeting which was expected to last another twenty minutes or so and that Sergeant Curtiss could be found in the canteen. The Chief thanked the man and making his way to the place, looked at his watch. It was three minutes to eleven. 'No pie, Errol?' he said. 'I thought you were partial.'

The Sergeant was on his own, writing in his book. 'Not this time, sir,' he said, looking up, 'but the tea's better than it looks. Can I get you both a cup?'

'Please,' they said together, sitting down. There'd been no refreshment at Mrs Stowe's. Curtiss was soon back, however, and now faced his chief across the table. McKuen was already wondering if he'd made the right decision, looking doubtfully at the contents of the polystyrene beaker, which had come complete with its own lid. 'Good morning, Errol?' he asked then.

'Well, I did the work, sir. Shall I tell?'

'No. Let's leave it till we're all together, shall we? Write up some notes?' McKuen sighed as he said this, taking out his pen and trying to think of something he disliked more than paperwork. Beards, perhaps? Canteen tea? He picked up his polystyrene cup and in gratitude to Curtiss, took a gracious sip, before starting to write.

If George Earl had looked like a bookmaker, then Jade looked like an academic – tall, pale, ascetic-looking. But the appearance was misleading. For he was a brisk, hearty man, with a ready sense of humour and refusing to take life too seriously. Hardly surprising, then, that he wouldn't conform for the sake of it, McKuen being of the firm opinion that had Jade done so, then he would have been higher up the promotion ladder than he was. Of course, McKuen admired the man immensely.

'Sorry I wasn't here to meet you, Donald. You know how things are.'

They were all sitting in conference, Jade and McKuen, Curtiss and WPC Knowles, together with a Detective Sergeant Bill Goodall.

'Me and you both, Tom,' replied McKuen. 'Don't worry, I spent the time doing important paperwork.'

Jade grinned. 'Right, then. George Earl. The name struck a chord straight away, although I hadn't heard it for some time. Things started coming back as I thought about him – trouble with a woman, a touch of fraud and so on. Not too much to worry us though. He wasn't a real villain. He wasn't clever enough. But he was always popping up somewhere. I put Bill Goodall here on to it.' He picked up a thin file from the desk and passed it over. 'That's it, Donald. The top sheet is just a summary. Some of the cases were just civil matters but Bill put them all in. Why don't you read them out and then anyone can interrupt if necessary?'

'Right.' McKuen opened the file and, as Jade had remarked, it was only minor stuff. He read out the main points, giving dates and times. 1. Drunk and disorderly. Fined. 2. Dangerous driving, colliding with a woman. Fined. Penalty points. 3. Paternity case. Civil. Wivenhoe. Paternity denied. Daughter born. Brief history of mother with photo on back page. 4. Behaviour likely to cause a breach of the peace. Fight over a woman in a public place. (The Unicorn.) Fined. Warned that a custodial sentence was only just avoided. 5. Garage scam. Civil. Daniels. Rollinson. Earl.

'You've done well here, Sergeant,' said McKuen. 'Your name will go properly in my report, of course.'

'Thank you, sir.' Goodall was a tall, middle-aged man with a good head of beautifully dressed hair, a source of much ribald comment in the locker-room.

147

'And thanks to you, Tom,' said the Chief. 'Invaluable help.'

'Right. But aren't you going to look at the photograph?'

'Oh, I know who it's of, Tom. I hope.' But he hesitated nervously before turning the penultimate page. Then, doing so quickly, they were all looking at a photocopy of a young Kate Brace.

Much as he would have liked to relax for an hour over beer and sandwiches in the comfort of The Hind, McKuen thought the team had better get back to the station, listen to what they all had to say. Things were hotting up and, over thick cheese butties and tea brought over from the canteen (rather less palatable, he thought), the team were giving their separate accounts of the morning's efforts.

Curtiss had gone first and his tale was a simple one. Rollinson, at the garage in Colchester, had appeared faintly surprised at being interviewed by the police, although not for an instant did he try to deny his past association with Earl. In any case, he had an alibi for the whole of that Sunday afternoon, which Curtiss had checked and believed to be genuine.

Then it was Briscoe's turn, and he and his partner, Tom Swaines, had had not only a rather busier time but also one which was to provoke a little more thought. First going to the garage in Breeley, as instructed, they had interviewed Daniels. Briscoe quickly put him down as a loudmouth and not much else. Whilst Betteridge he'd also put down as an innocent one. Daniels snorted that he had an alibi, anyway, which, as yet, there'd been no time to check up on. Betteridge had no alibi.

Something which Briscoe didn't bother mentioning was that he'd promised himself that he would, on some trivial pretext, drop in a time or two on the garage. Daniels wouldn't like that at all but the Constable didn't like being put down just for doing his job.

The two policemen had then gone to see Graham Stowe at Palings Insurance and, even more so than Rollinson had done with Curtiss, the man had feigned amazement at the visit. But Briscoe had soon put the 'stuck-up bugger' straight, reminding him that a murder enquiry was afoot. 'All right,' Stowe had said, simmering down. He'd known George Earl by sight, didn't like him and had not seen him on that particular Sunday. Both he and his wife had been at home all day and no, there was no way he could prove this.

As far as McKuen knew, he'd never set eyes on the man. 'What's he like, Walt? Really?'

The country bobby rubbed his chin. 'Bit of a stuck-up bugger, sir, but I have to admit, fairly well set up, if you know what I mean. Not a bad-looking man at all.'

Thinking of Belinda Stowe, McKuen had the thought that he'd have been surprised to hear otherwise. For the rest, he had to wonder what the man had ever done to earn Walt's particular soubriquet. But grinning to himself, he forbore to ask. 'Anything else about him, Walt?'

'Well, he doesn't strike me as being a man who would act on impulse, sir. Quite the opposite. To plan a deliberate killing, now, yes. I think that might be more in his line.'

'Right. Now then, did you see Eric Barnes?'

But at Norrs End, there had been few surprises. Barnes had been on his allotment and yes, like one or two others, he'd had the odd bust-up with Earl. But risk prison for killing him? Not likely and, besides, George hadn't really been a bad sort, open-handed as he was and good company most of the time. And he couldn't help 'keeping his brains in his shorts'. That's how the man was. 'That's about it, sir,' Briscoe finished, 'except to say that I'd be very surprised to hear that Barnes was the killer, for apart from everything else, it's a big allotment. The body could have been buried anywhere on it. Why take the risk of being seen moving it?'

'Good point, Walt. Right, now then. Constable Knowles here will tell us all how we spent our own morning, including, of course, our impressions of the admirable Mrs Stowe, with whom we were both rather taken. Right, Barbara?' McKuen smiled across at her as he spoke and for some reason, her heart thumped away in her chest, reminding her to be extra tender to Bernard when next she should see him.

With frequent reference to her notes, as was right and proper, she then gave a full account, including opinions and observations, of their morning's activities, only leaving out her remarks to the Chief on Belinda Stowe's more enviable qualities.

No one seemed willing to break the silence and they were all sat quiet, waiting to hear what McKuen should say next as, in his thoughtful manner, he went to the window and opened it slightly to look at the passers-by. 'So many people,' he muttered. 'So many secrets. But no. There's no one else it could sensibly be. Otherwise...' He closed the window with a snap, came briskly back to his seat, and looked at them all in turn. 'Well done, you lot,' he said quietly. ' I think we've done it, although I must admit that Kate Brace's involvement was crucial to my line of thought. Even so, there are still some gaps. The main one is that, although I'm sure Kate is the central figure in the case, it could have been her accomplice – for accomplice she had to have – who was to commit the actual killing.' His brows came together in thought as he carefully weighed his next words.

'I know neither the real motive nor the method,' he then went on, 'and at this point, I won't speculate. But before I carry on, I would like to ask if any of you have

150

ideas of your own. But I'll tell you this. They'll have to
be pretty strong to convince me, for otherwise I intend
to arrest Kate Brace this afternoon. Now think. Does
anyone want first go?'

No one spoke. 'Right,' he went on. 'My pigeon then
but, first, who wants to make the tea?'

There was a sudden rush – a general easing of tension.
But WPC Knowles let the others do it for once. It took
a few minutes and then, settled once more, McKuen took
up his conclusions.

'We weren't that short of suspects, although most of
them would prove, I'm sure, to be entirely innocent. We
have the garage people. I know it was a while ago but
who knows – a sudden opportune meeting – old wounds
brought to life? Then, taken perhaps out of context, I
know, but then we have Kate Brace herself. You see, apart
from Mrs Earl, of course, the people mentioned so far
are the only ones in the case we know to have a past
history of association with Earl. Kate Brace, then, again
wronged long ago by the man. It must have come as
something of a shock to both of them, meeting after so
long, and one would have thought, after the first time of
seeing where she lived, that he would in common decency
have chosen a different route for his rambles. But not
our George. Kate does have the dog, of course. Quite an
animal, too, is Bruce. Another mystery to be solved. Where
was he at the time?'

McKuen paused for breath and glanced keenly at them
all. 'But let's look at the others,' he now went on. 'There's
Graham Stowe. I shouldn't imagine he was very pleased
to see Earl on a more or less regular basis, hoping to
ogle his lovely wife. You know how a thing like that can
fester and men have murdered for less. Then there are
the Traces, lurking in the background, black eye and all.
Not too likely candidates perhaps, but not out of the

question altogether... I wonder, is there possibly any more tea in that pot? Ah, thank you, Barbara.'

What he would have liked to do now, he thought, as he drained his cup, was to go home – home to his petite and desirable Sarah. But instead, he heaved a quiet sigh. 'Right,' he said, 'who else? There's Mrs Earl, of course. And Mrs Barnes and the innuendo, unlikely as the reality is in substance, of their possible relationship. Then there's Eric Barnes and there's person or persons unknown, although I think we would be in trouble should that prove to be the case.

He smiled at them all. 'Plenty to pick from, eh? Here, though, I believe, is the nub of it. The murder had to be carried out, if not by a man, then a woman aided by another party or parties. A woman alone couldn't have managed the job. I did think about Mrs Earl – motive, opportunity and so on. But that, perhaps, is where Curtiss and myself have some small advantage over you others. We two were the first to talk to her. She spoke about being without George – about the bleak future and the loneliness. Not that she tried to hide his shortcomings in any way, numerous as they were. She seemed genuine. It could all have been an act, of course, but somehow we didn't think it was. And for myself, I can't really see Mrs Barnes being involved in anything like that. I think she left Mrs Earl for the reason given – that George was beginning to bother her. Trouble with George, of course, was that he hadn't got enough to occupy his mind.

'Then there's Eric Barnes and the fight in The Cockleshell. But if he'd been intent on killing Earl, I can't see him staying behind at the pub that afternoon, drinking with Ben Trace. Then there's the manner of the actual killing. You have to think of that. It was on impulse, surely. Unpremeditated. Earl had his gun, which I believe to have been already loaded. No, the slaying was carried out by someone driven to distraction.'

McKuen looked round at them all and, except for the murmur of traffic outside, the room was quiet. And in the even tones and impeccable manners which endeared him to so many, he carried on. 'I know you chaps will forgive me if I happen to have gone over the same ground a time or two, but it has taken a bit of thinking out. Trouble was, I don't consider there was ever a strong enough motive for the killing. So, not being planned, it was the harder to spot. It was Kate Brace, though. I'm certain of it and I'm going to arrest her now. I believe her accomplice, dragged in after the deed, was Belinda Stowe, whom I believe to be the daughter of Kate Brace and George Earl.'

At this, there were one or two small gasps, but still no comments. 'Yes,' McKuen went on, 'there are still some questions to be answered. Was Graham Stowe involved? How and why was the killing done and why on that particular day? The body itself. Why was it kept so long somewhere before being moved to where it was found? And what about the dog? Where was he? But I am convinced. Belinda Stowe lied, rather stupidly I thought, about her last visit to see Kate Brace, and there's something else, a little less specific though it might be. When we were leaving the smallholding, both Kate and myself knew that I'd be back. She's basically an honest woman, you see – lying is alien to her nature. Kill Earl she may have done but she's no real criminal. Except in the eyes of the law, of course.'

He gave them a moment in which to make comment should they wish but there was none. 'Right,' he said, WPC Knowles, Sergeant Curtiss and myself will go and bring them in. Walt, you and PC Swaines go and check up on Daniels' alibi if that's at all possible. Then come back here and wait for us. Write up your reports or something. That OK, Walt?'

'Yes, sir.'

'All right with you, Constable?'

'Yes, sir. And thank you. For keeping me on the case, I mean.'

'Only fair, Constable.'

'Kate Brace. I'm here to arrest you for the murder of George Earl. You do not have to say anything. But it may harm...' As he handed her the written notice, McKuen knew by her quiet acceptance of both this and the uttered caution that he'd been right but, even so, a tiny shiver of relief ran through him. 'Would you like to tell us about it, Kate?'

She smiled without rancour, as though glad it was over. 'Do you think we might all go inside, Inspector?' she asked. 'Have a cup of tea or something?'

'Certainly, Kate. Then we have to go and pick up your accomplice, don't we?'

'Of course, but then, it's no great distance, is it?'

The inside of the house was like the outside in that it was extremely untidy – unlike it in that it was spotless. Bruce followed them in and, obviously by right, stretched out in front of the small open fire, whilst his mistress, calm and apparently resigned, put the electric kettle on. 'Perhaps the lady constable will lend a hand,' she said, 'whilst I begin my story.' WPC Knowles set about the work quietly.

The cottage suite and one old wooden chair just held them all. 'I didn't mean to kill him, of course.' Kate said, sitting down herself, opposite McKuen. 'But it was self-defence. He'd been drinking as usual and he was there, with his constant, hateful leer. He often came by, suggesting that we should "take up where we'd left off", as he loathfully put it. It was all a vicious game to him, of course, and I always ignored him completely, just as though he weren't there. But this time, it was different. Bruce wasn't there, you see. He was at Corleys, the vets. He'd had a cyst removed from the inside of his leg and was being kept in overnight to let the anaesthetic wear off properly.' She stopped stroking the dog's neck to show them the strip of white plaster, close to his chest. 'It wasn't essential that he stop in but, well, I suppose the decision was the sealing of George's fate.'

Her whole speech was becoming softer, as though she was withdrawing into herself, but at this point the kettle began to sing, causing her to blink back to reality again. WPC Knowles stood up to make the tea and amidst the quiet rattle of cups, Kate went on with her tale.

'George seemed to sense that Bruce wasn't there. "Where's the damn dog?" he sneered, coming towards me, first leaning his gun against the fence. "Here, or in the house, Kate? It makes no odds to me," he said. He was completely out of control. I panicked and I saw red, Inspector. I backed up against the byre and into the old hayfork. Then I was pointing it at him. He just laughed and made a grab for it. I shoved it at him and he actually deflected it. Into his own eye. He just stood there. He was still laughing.' She stared in front of her, unseeing. 'He collapsed in a heap. The fork was still there, leaning at an angle. I stood ... for long seconds of terror ... I was ... I ran and grabbed the gun – his gun. I put it to his face and I pulled both triggers. He stopped twitching and I wasn't terrified any more. I sat down in the mud...'

The dog appeared surprised that everyone was suddenly so quiet. He'd rather be outside anyway and he had made his point. These people didn't seem to mean harm to his mistress and he now stalked to the door to scratch at it.

Curtiss got up and opened the door softly and, just as softly, a little colour was creeping back into Kate's cheeks. 'I somehow managed to drag the body into the byre,' she said. 'I knew I would have to have help although, to do what, I didn't know. But I had to have help – involve someone else. And who would judge me for that, Inspector? I didn't want to be alone in the world and, at first, it didn't seem to matter that much that even the two of us couldn't do it. Bury the body, I mean. Then at last, the horror of what I'd done struck home. It began to threaten my sanity. It wasn't as though we were achieving anything, discovering all too soon that a body takes some burying and, half-hearted as the attempt must have been ... well, we knew, you see. And the days were going by. It was a living hell, Inspector.'

McKuen tried hard to imagine it, wondered whether the others were doing the same. Surely no one should have to go through this sort of thing. But her voice was cutting across his thoughts.

'And then, just two hours before the police arrived to search the place, we wrapped the body in plastic and dragged it to the ditch across the track.'

McKuen automatically craned his neck to look through the tiny window in the direction of the track and the ditch beyond. But the angle wasn't enough and all he could see, like a great wodge of cadmium carelessly splashed on the palette, was the great expanse of rape, stretching far into the distance. He hated the stuff, viewing it as nothing more than a vast, bilious blot on the countryside.

'I don't honestly remember whose idea it was,' Kate was saying, 'to try and sink the body in the mere. I have an old van out back you know and we went by night, of course. But we couldn't even manage that – dragging that dead weight over that rough ground in the dark, panting with our exertions whilst Earl mocked me as much as he'd ever done and we fearful that someone would come by and see the van. The plain truth of it all, Inspector, is that we just weren't up to the task.'

Not even the coals in the fire could be heard now, as Kate Brace, hands folded calmly in her lap, finished her tale. 'That's about it, Inspector, and as you said, you'll be wanting now to go and arrest my accomplice – at Norrs End.'

Facing her as he was, McKuen was not in a position to see either of his colleagues without turning his head and this he dare not do. Sitting either side of him, he would have given much to know whether one or both of them were looking at him but, try as he might, he could detect no movement. Perhaps they had leant back slightly and were looking at each other. Ah, well, he told himself, I was half right, anyway. Barnes after all, then? Betteridge? 'You might as well finish the tale in your own words, don't you think, Kate?' he said gently. 'Before we go?'

'As you wish, Inspector. Out of those who I thought would help me, I chose Arthur. You know, of course, that George once knocked Mrs Kemp down with his car. Arthur told me one day how he hated the man, being convinced that the incident was the beginning of her arthritis and how it virtually ruined the Kemps' lives whilst George got off almost scot-free.'

McKuen let his breath out very slowly. He could not have been more wrong. He had not, after all, considered every available detail. He also thought of the coincidence of the Kemps coming to live here as well as Kate Brace and, strangely, how Earl had unwittingly been the cause of their coming, all of them – Kate to find the desired isolation – the Kemps to find a smaller, more manageable house. But what he said, was, 'One thing does puzzle me, Kate. Why did Kemp "discover" the body himself, I wonder?'

'I'm sorry, Inspector, but I'm afraid you'll have to ask him that yourself. I haven't set eyes on him since that terrible night, and,' she said pointedly, 'there was no other relationship between us, no matter what anyone may think. But if I was to try and answer your question, I imagine it was due to some kind of conscience preying on his mind, eating away at his soul. He's such a gentle man and I've cursed myself a thousand times since for entangling him. Believe me, I don't think I've slept more than an hour at any one time since the beginning of the whole, horrendous affair.'

'I'm truly sorry about that, Kate. Really,' he said. Felon in law that she undoubtedly was, the words sounded trite, even to his own ears, but he could think of no more fitting comment. 'Is your daughter well, Kate?' he asked, then.

Coming as it did, the sudden change of topic caused her eyes to widen in some surprise, but she answered readily enough. 'Quite well, thank you, Inspector. She's in Germany, you know. Married to an army officer. And I'll have to let her know about all this, of course.'

No, he didn't know and he still dare not risk a glance at the others. 'One last thing, Kate,' he said. 'Why did Mrs Stowe deny she'd been to see you the other day? We knew that she had.'

She almost smiled. 'You are clever, Inspector. I mean it.'

Once again, he had to wonder if the others were looking at him. For he was certain that by now, in all decency, this further slight misjudgement, as he modestly thought of it, must be showing in his colour.

'I told her to say that,' Kate was saying. 'I didn't want her to participate in any way, not even by association. Concerned, yes, but involved, no. I thought I'd already done enough damage in that direction. Then there's Graham. He can be just a wee bit stuffy, you know. Not that that bothers Belinda. And I'll ring her now if I may. To arrange about the animals. She'll see to them. Her and others. I do have friends, Inspector.'

'Certainly, Kate.' What a problem that could have been and this time he didn't care what emotion showed on his face.

With the others busy writing, McKuen had inched the station window open to stare moodily at the passers-by. Unusual as the sentiment was for him, he couldn't shake the feeling that there'd been little satisfaction in the case's outcome. He'd done his own job, of course, done it well and the ACC had congratulated both him and his team personally. There'd be commendations. But, as he thought of different things, McKuen struggled to keep it all in perspective. Arthur Kemp, for instance. The man had practically had his coat on, waiting to be arrested, after having made what arrangements he could concerning his wife. How would she manage?

And poor Kate. What had she really done wrong? She'd broken the law, of course, but then, Earl was breaking the law when he'd been killed – attempted rape. And he was breaking the law even before this, with his loaded shotgun, carrying it in a public place without either lawful authority or reasonable excuse. Everyone broke the law at some time.

He wondered what the final charge would be. The extreme provocation was certainly sufficient to reduce it to voluntary manslaughter. Hot-blooded killings are less offensive to society than cold-blooded ones. Unfortunately, he mused, the plea of self-defence was out. Using the gun had seen to that, hardly being able to be described as using reasonable force, as required by law. But there was Earl's unsavoury character to consider.

159

McKuen heaved a sigh, hoping that the courts would be as lenient as the case surely merited. But all this was getting him nowhere and he turned back from the window, wondering whether to start on his report. But he didn't feel like it and there was all day tomorrow. He had an idea. He would let his friend in New York know about the case. That was it and, glancing at the others, who were all busy writing, he went to his desk and fished furtively in the top drawer for his sheet of instructions. In trepidation, he now went to the computer furthest away from the rest and looked once again at his paper before beginning to tap unevenly away. To him, the sound seemed to fill the office. But no one seemed to be watching and, at last, there was a final click of the button and he got to his feet. He went towards Curtiss. 'I've just sent Detective Crowle an e-mail,' he said, as casually as he could manage.

'Yes, sir.' Curtiss didn't look up.

'Do you realize, Errol,' McKuen then said, to the top of the Sergeant's head, 'that we've solved a tricky case of murder in under seventy-two hours? Of course,' he went on, 'we had a good team – Briscoe and young Swaines – WPC Knowles. Good lass, that. Imaginative,' he finished quietly, out of the earshot of the others.

'Yes, sir.' Curtiss looked up at last. 'We did well, didn't we?' He then went back to his reports, leaving the Chief to look at the top of his head again.

McKuen went to his desk and sat down. There were two pencils on his blotter but neither of them wanted sharpening. All day tomorrow for the paperwork, he thought, and then me and Sarah will be able to go to Fawkley for the weekend after all. He would be able to talk to Warwick, tell him about the case as they drank cold beer together in the Lantern Club.

Right, he thought, if Curtiss doesn't want to talk, I'll go home to my petite and desirable Sarah. Hm. Curtiss.

Let's see. He's getting married in July. I wonder if it's too early to start collecting. But for now, I'll go home.

He got to his feet, coming round the back of Curtiss's chair to peep over the Sergeant's shoulder. 'Whom, Sergeant.'

'Sir?'

'Graham Stowe, *whom* we believe to be ... not who. You see, Sergeant, "we believe" is not parenthetic. "Whom" is the object.'

'So formal, sir?'

'Why, Errol,' said McKuen, making for the door, 'it is, after all, a formal report.' It was nice to be in charge, he thought – to be petty to Curtiss now and again. Anyway, I'm entitled, he thought.

And he hadn't forgotten Mrs Earl's brandy, either.

Parkin of the Lantern Club

In the early days, Alan Parkin was the one club member I didn't care for much. Nothing specific, although I did have the idea that several others more or less had the same idea. Not that anyone mentioned it much, not even Buster Howes, and Buster talked about everybody. But there wasn't that much to say, for rather than being just quiet, Parkin seemed, well, sort of secretive. Having joined the club, after agreeing to abide by the few rules, he seemed unable to integrate in any positive way, making me often wonder why he'd bothered to join in the first place.

And then one day Alan Parkin disappeared. By the time I had finished with Morbury, he'd gone. Even Buster could find nothing out, and the committee members, as was their right under the rules, were saying nothing, although, as it turned out, they knew little themselves. All that could be found out with any degree of certainty was that he hadn't resigned, and from this, the general assumption was that he'd gone out on a Detail. What else? Even from the beginning, rumours abounded of course, but vague as they were and lacking any kind of believable development, interest, naturally enough, began to decline.

Then, out of the blue, Parkin was back. No one could remember how many weeks it was since he'd left the scene so abruptly and now he was suddenly upstairs in the big room of the club, ready to tell his story to any who might wish to hear it. As, of course, we all did.

I went up there and sat down quickly and, whilst the

others who happened to be in the club at the time, made their own entrance, I took the opportunity to study Parkin with interest. There had, as I recalled, never been anything very remarkable about him physically but now, as he sat there waiting quietly, I knew there was something different about the man, something I couldn't define, but there just the same.

But everyone was now quite settled and he began his tale without delay. 'Good evening, gentlemen. Let me begin by thanking you all for being here and also to tender my apologies for the short notice. But if I don't begin straightaway I'm sure my story would lose something in the telling.'

And then I knew what it was. It was the air of confidence – of calm assurance – as though, from being a person of little importance to most people, a nonentity almost, he was now quite aware of being the equal of anyone in the room. Indeed, his was such a finely balanced assumption, that even though this new-found confidence was definitely to be indulged in, a thing in which to revel, his words yet lacked even the slightest tinge of patronage. It was nicely done – as though he'd been addressing such groups for half his life – and even at this early stage, I found myself warming to the man.

'When I came to the committee with my suggestion,' he was now saying, 'they were kind enough to agree to a very strange deal. This was simply that they would allow me to attempt my Detail without first telling them what it was. That they would then, after I had reported completion, pass judgement on the results. And I remember being encouraged by their very first response: that this request was in fact a novelty – a first – the remark then being added that variety, after all, was what the club was supposed to be about. They were even gracious enough to thank me for reminding them of the fact.

164

'It seemed a good omen and a heartening beginning. Of course, I did have a good reason for making the request and, on hearing my story, I hope that each of you will judge me as fairly as they were to do.'

Now seemingly quite certain of his ground, Parkin paused briefly in his narrative, taking a sip of whisky and glancing at the single sheet of paper in front of him. As he did this, many of us directed our own looks at the two members of the committee present, and John Coombes and Barry Smith, as might be expected, were already nodding in confirmation of the little that had been said. Barry Smith then caught my own eye and his smile broadened slightly, no doubt at the memory of the few horrid moments we'd shared together at 15 Garland Close.

Then Parkin was talking again. 'I wasn't born Alan Parkin. Until I was eighteen, my name was Alan Moore.'

Everyone was now listening intently. 'It was a name I grew to both fear and hate,' he went on, 'perhaps the more so since the early part of my childhood was so very happy. I led a sheltered life in those days, wanting for nothing. Then, when I was eight, my parents were killed in a car crash. I was asleep in the back at the time, being wakened by the squealing of metal and, for the first time in my young life, intense pain. I had suffered a greenstick fracture of the thighbone and I was to limp for years. It often ached terribly.'

Parkin looked round at us all. 'I assure you,' he said, I have to tell you all this for, you see, this is what started my hatred of disablement. Oh, I know that many people, children in particular, often get over these things easily or, at least, try and disregard them. But I couldn't. It's the way I happened to be. Anyway, I was sent to live in Cumbria with my father's brother and his wife, my Aunt Anne. She was a lovely woman, still is in fact, and I loved her from the beginning, almost as though she were my own mother. Conversely, though, my uncle, the blood-relative, hated me from the start. It was the money. He hadn't any and, had I been poor, I'm certain he would have found some excuse not to take me in at all. He was a charmer though, or fancied himself to be. I was young then, but I have often since wondered what sort of life Anne really had.'

The sudden sound of a striking match in that quiet atmosphere made everyone jump, for apart from anything else, there is a no-smoking agreement up in the big room. Everyone turned to the sound, of course. It was Jack Billets and he was about to light his pipe. But as everyone looked round, he realized his mistake, putting the match out quickly as he muttered his apology.

'Jack Moore was a wastrel,' Parkin went on with a half-smile as he picked up the thread. 'A devil in disguise. He was a physical man, striding about and often making me go with him to the top of Beacon Point, which was near where we lived, in St Bees, not far from Whitehaven. It would do me good, he said, cure my limp, which I knew he viewed with contempt. Anne used to try and reason with him, saying that the climb always exhausted me. But he would smile at her in that hateful, condescending way that seemed so habitual to him and which I had come to fear so much. "But it'll do the boy good, Anne," he would say. But she wasn't a stupid woman and, years afterwards, from what she would say in some unguarded moment, there was just a hint, I am sure, that she harboured all the right suspicions. At the time, however, there was little she could do. What crumb of comfort she did manage to communicate, though, just about kept me sane, I think. For had they both been as bad as he was, I don't think I could have borne it. Resilience does have its limits, even in the young.'

Parkin took another sip of whisky, but this time he

didn't refer to the few notes he had. It was as though this part of the affair, at least, was etched deeply in his mind.

'Anyway,' he began again, 'one day in early spring – in fact, as I realized later, it was exactly nine months after my parents' death – my uncle again said we'd go up to Beacon Point. Of all the headland walks around the area, this one was the steepest and I'm sure the choice was deliberate. Of course, I had to go. "We won't be long, my dear," he said to Anne, and I can still see the look on her face as we set out, with my uncle striding out as usual. It wasn't long before my leg was bothering me. He was going far too fast and it was all uphill. It's a fairly heavily wooded slope and I kept catching my clothes on the lower branches and, even at this height, the ground was soft and muddy with the melted ice. "Come on, boy. We'll never get to the top at this rate," he sneered. He never did call me anything but boy. But we got almost to the summit at last, and here, for the last twenty yards or so, the place is bare of trees. Too windswept, I suppose. I shivered in the stiff breeze and, although it's a really beautiful view, especially in the summertime, this was anything but summer and I was in no mood at all to even begin to enjoy it. I was cold and hurting and wet. But all this was by no means the worst of it all, for now the whole of my discomfort was abruptly and completely overshadowed by a far stronger emotion. It was sheer fright – more than that even – I was rooted to the spot with terror.'

Parkin stopped talking and he now looked suddenly exhausted, as he must have done on that cold spring day so long ago. His former confidence, for the moment at least, was flagging more than a little, as he must be recalling the terrible memories that would no doubt lurk there until the day he died, ready perhaps, to spring out at any time. What could it be? I asked myself. How could all this happen to a mere eight-year-old? Where were the angels?

Parkin resumed his tale at last, having once again gathered his wits together. 'I'm sorry,' he said. 'What was I...? Oh, yes, my uncle ... I've always hated calling him that, by the way, but there's no altering the fact that that's what he was. Anyway, there he stood, already on the edge of the Point, rather precariously too, as even I noticed, with his back to the sea. And he was beckoning now and smiling, and had he wished, somehow, to put me on my guard, he couldn't have chosen a better expression. This was, in fact, the cause of my terror, for smiling was a mood alien to him and I could never before remember him even making the effort. I knew that he meant me harm – knew it and I could do nothing. Mesmerized, I couldn't look away. I cannot, in fact, remember having the will to do so.

'Jack Moore wasn't a man given to bouts of rage. He was far too cunning for that. "Come and look at the view, boy," he shouted. "It's wonderful," and even at this stage he couldn't bring himself to use my given name. And he was making not the least pretence of looking at the view for himself. It was one of those situations which are numbered in seconds rather than minutes, and now, unable to help myself and in the worst kind of dismay, I began to edge towards him, propelled, I am sure, by some evil force. And I could now hear the tide coming in, crashing on the shingle, fifty feet below us. I was staring into the centre of his devil's face...

'I lost my footing and the movement saved my life.'

Parkin folded one flat hand between the fingers and thumb of the other, holding them close to his chest for a moment, as if for comfort. 'As I stumbled, my uncle took an involuntary step towards me and, what was it?

The slight shift of stance? Or the added fractional impetus on that soft edge perhaps? Whatever the cause, he was gone. His eagerness and his monstrous concentration – maybe even his nerves at the terrible step he intended – whatever the cause – something had been his undoing. I went down in the slush and sobbed uncontrollably.'

The big room fell quiet and even the muted hum of the traffic outside was an intrusion.

'After what may have been ten minutes,' Parkin now went on, 'I came to. I just lay there shivering and picking absently at the turf, wet as it was.' His voice was now so low that one had to strain to catch the words. 'Just for a moment, gentlemen, look down with me at the boy and if you will, put yourself in his place and let me tell you what I think he saw.'

There wasn't the slightest note of self-pity in the tone and this was probably the reason that, for the moment at any rate, he had shifted from speaking in the first person – an appeal to the listener to join him in an entirely objective view of the situation.

'There was a lone herring gull making its raucous cry. The boy looked up and there it was, wheeling about in the sky and crying at him accusingly. By now, too, the boy was soaked to the skin and knew he would have to move. He got to his feet, stiff in both body and mind, but determined at last to look over the edge of the Point. As he got closer, however, he became terrified of going over himself, so he got down on his stomach once more and tried to peer over. The ground here was like sponge and he had to ease himself fearfully forward with his toes. He didn't know what he expected to see but, in truth, he didn't believe it could have been worse.'

Parkin's fist was seen to clench on the tabletop, his notes long forgotten.

'Jack Moore lay there on his back and he was conscious.

169

The water was already slapping around his body, with every flowing movement of the incoming tide working its way a little further up. One of his legs lay at an extremely acute angle, obviously broken. But he saw the boy straight-away and raised an arm in mute appeal. Then his broken body wriggled horribly as he tried to shout something, but the sound was carried away on the wind. The herring gull was still there and began circling lower, as though its job in life was to patrol the skies in search of wrongdoing. But then it suddenly turned, to hurry nervously out of sight, the boy wishing for all the world that he was that bird, now with nothing to do in all the world but go about its mundane business. Fascinated now by the truth, however, he could do nothing but look again at the drowning man. He lay there watching him, watching and waiting for the tide to reach him. The boy didn't know how long he waited, but he suddenly wanted the tide to hurry – to cover the man completely. But then he could bear it no longer, edging back to safety and thinking of nothing but the man's broken limbs. Then he got to his feet to make his way slowly down through the trees.'

As he said this, Parkin was nodding absently, his earlier air of confidence now just a little less apparent and who would blame him for that? 'For years after that,' he now went on, 'and although my own limp eventually disappeared altogether, I was to suffer nightmares about twisted limbs.

'Jack Moore was drowned, of course. Fifteen or twenty minutes earlier, they said, and he might have been saved. I had murdered my uncle then, although, naturally enough, no one said so. There was no mention at all of it being any other than an unfortunate accident. There was only me who knew – knew that I'd walked so slowly down through the trees, slowly and deliberately, just wanting time to pass – like Christ at Gethsemane. And as I came down, each branch seemed to catch my face accusingly,

170

each one a twisted limb, deformed with hate. And extreme youth was no shield at all. The imagination won't stretch that far, gentlemen, believe me.'

He fell quiet, rubbing the small of his back with his hands. 'I'm sorry,' he said then, 'I'm just a bit tired. Would you all mind awfully if we carried on with it tomorrow?'

We broke up in silence and I was reflecting how, speaking for myself at least, I had previously judged him, and how far this habit went in trying to mask our own shortcomings. One thing was for sure. Fate had certainly dealt the young Parkin a rough hand. And wasn't abuse like this supposed to lead to all sorts of things?

One club member had been called away on business, but on the following evening the rest of us were there, plus one or two others, and I went up early again, wanting the same seat. And Parkin looked better tonight, refreshed no doubt after his day's rest. There was something else. I was sure there was an aura of sympathy in the room – as though the telling of his trials were not only easing his own burden, but, for the moment at least, also helping the audience to put aside their own minor troubles. I'm sure this was the response he was getting, and if I could sense it, so, surely, could he. And I believe it was a sympathy he'd already earned.

Everyone settled once again, then Parkin took a final sip of his drink and began straightaway. 'Thanks for being here again, gentlemen,' he said. 'Most kind of you all. I'll get straight on. Yes, after that time on the Point, I developed, not unnaturally, I suppose, a most deep abhorrence for the cold and damp and for disabled limbs. Neither did the thing seem to diminish with time, and yet, from the time of Jack Moore's death until I grew up,

I never knew happier years. Aunt Anne blossomed and she took me everywhere – the theatre, London, the big houses. It was as though she, too, had won her freedom and, strangely, she now had part of my parents' money in trust, a thing which my uncle had never enjoyed. A mystery I have never cared to make enquiry into. All I did come across was the fact that the family solicitors had been given some discretion in the matter. But all that aside, once I got older, and apart from my education fees, I insisted she keep the lot. My aunt knew, you see. I'm sure of it, though never a word passed between us. It was as though we were both in accord to try and erase the very memory of the man from our minds. What I would have done without her, I can't begin to imagine. She's still going strong too, bless her.'

It was at this point that an oblique and unkind thought entered unbidden into my mind. How far had the relationship between the two of them really gone? I wondered. A young man and a woman, living alone in the same house. Two people thrown together, released from a common adversity. Just how old was she anyway? Even in these confidences of his, it wasn't a matter Parkin would even begin to hint at, not to a large crowd. Hardly aware of what I was really doing, I looked at his face afresh, trying to penetrate his most inner thoughts. Many are the things that will be forgiven, forgotten even, but, as it has always been, when sex raises its ugly head...

'...And I did well for myself,' Parkin was saying. 'Communications. Saw the internet coming well before the reality occurred. Seemed to get in at just the right time. But I never got over my dread – my phobia – call it what you will. In the early days, Anne did suggest a psychiatrist but you either have faith in those people or you don't and, rightly or wrongly, I couldn't bring myself to do it. Afraid of the answers he might come up with,

I suppose. I wouldn't even discuss it. Not even with her. I just wanted the good times to carry on,' I had my wicked thoughts again, 'ignore the rest, hoping it would just go away.'

Good times, eh? And to which good times was he referring exactly? I wondered, almost rubbing my hands together. This just as Parkin, suddenly feeling the need for a sip of his whisky, reached out for it and, as he did so, just about everyone else in the room reached for his own drink. It was amusing really – like some sort of ritual. And I was honestly happy for Parkin in this proof that everyone was listening so intently. And he didn't even have his odd sheet of notes this time.

'Anne's wish,' he was now saying, 'was that I should marry, or at least socialize more. I think she was afraid I might turn out to be queer or something, but I can assure you all that that at least didn't happen.'

A few people laughed and, for the first time, Parkin smiled. I was glad they were looking at him too, for anyone happening to glance in my own direction at this moment would have seen the heavy flush coming to my face, though they might, I hoped, have put this down to the heat of the room. In vain I tried to console myself by thinking that I could not, after all, have prevented thoughts, however unworthy, from coming into my head. But I knew they shouldn't have been hidden there in the first place.

'Joining the club here was a good start,' Parkin was now saying. 'I knew I would have difficulty – that I wouldn't prove to be the most popular member in town. And whilst I'm at it, wiping the slate clean so to speak, I must admit to one more thing...' Here his tone took on a note of mock conspiracy. 'Sometimes,' he said, 'when I'm alone in my bed at night, when I'm certain I'm unobserved, I do. I listen to the test scores,' and once again, as he smiled, and this even more broadly this time, the pleasant sense of humour, which, in spite of everything, seemed natural to him and which at last was finding an outlet, was coming through.

Everyone present laughed with him this time, too, and there were shouts of 'bounder!' and 'traitor!' and suddenly the whole atmosphere was much less oppressive. For it had been a sorry tale so far.

'Shall we break off and get fresh drinks, gentlemen?' Parkin even had to raise his voice a little amidst the general buzz of conversation. The break was needed, too, and there was a scraping back of chairs as we now began to realize the length of time over which the unhappy tale might stretch – that it would prove to be much more than simply a tale based mainly on an unhappy childhood.

But further morbid thought on the matter was interrupted by a fresh drink – one which I could well have done without – being slapped on the table in front of me. Buster Howes, of course. 'Drink and be merry,' he said. 'What do you think of our Alan, then?'

'Cheers, Buster,' I replied graciously. 'Yes. He may well prove worthy of joining our august ranks.' I knew this would make Buster beam even further in his already happy state. Not that I wanted to belittle his honour in any way.

'And then it happened.' Parkin was talking once again and, looking at Buster, I put a quick finger to my lips. Just as well as it happened, for the next name I heard was my own. 'It was about the time that Greene was away on his own Detail.' Parkin was looking straight across at me and I nodded back, trying to keep the pride out of my face. I'd never told my own story to the members, nor was I likely to. The tie would have to suffice and the curious would just have to wonder, Buster included. Buster especially. The committee and myself were the only ones who knew anything at all. But I was missing Parkin's story.

'... On my way to my office in South Aukley. A woman was crossing the road and a car knocked her down. Terrible. Neither did the car stop, although I did manage to get most of the number. I couldn't bring myself to help the woman, though. All I could do was to stand there, looking down at the broken body. Then I turned away and threw up. I clenched my fists in self-disgust, forcing myself to turn to her again. But I was too late. Others were there now and I dashed to my office to phone for an ambulance and the police.

'They caught the driver and he was convicted on my evidence. He'd had a previous conviction for drink driving and he got sent down. Six years. The woman was in court, still bandaged up, and she smiled at me gratefully, both her and her relatives. Me! And the judge commended me for my actions, my public spirit. I can tell you, gentlemen, I wanted the earth to open up and swallow me whole. But there it was and in that moment, I knew I would have to do something. But what?

'Then, a little more than a week later, I spotted the article in the paper, though I doubt whether I would even have read it at all had not the word disabled leapt up at me out of the page. "Fenley Association for the Disabled", it said. "Trip to Bad Ischl", wherever that was. It was as though the article had been written just for me and I studied it carefully. It was about sulphur and brine baths, and walking trips to mineral springs and things. It sounded horrible – cold and wet somehow. Not daring even to consider the matter for one moment in case I chickened out, I picked up the phone there and then, speaking to the Principal, a Mr Kiddey. A simple call, but one which was to change my life and had I known ... still...'

' "Of course, Mr Parkin." The voice at the other end sounded eager, just as though he'd been waiting for my call – ah, it's Parkin ringing. Now we have him.

175

'Or was it that I had been desperately hoping that the trip was already fully booked? In what capacity had I been wishing, or rather not wishing, to go, anyway. But there was still a way out, still time to call it off – make out I was just wanting to make a donation or something – that I hadn't given a thought about actually going on the trip myself.'

Parkin glanced at us all for a second, pleading for us to understand his problem, his dilemma at having to make up his mind on the instant. 'Kiddey was giving me so little time to think,' he said. 'As though he was playing me like a fish. "Is there any possibility of coming to see me straightaway, Mr Parkin?" he was asking. "Just for a few minutes?"

'Driving to Fenley, I was thinking furiously about what I would say to the man. I could, after all, hardly begin with the truth. "I want to go on the trip with those disabled people, Mr Kiddey. It sounds just what I want – wet, cold, and oh, yes, disabled." It wouldn't do, of course. It wouldn't do at all.

'"Good afternoon. Mr Parkin?" Kiddey was a short, rounded fresh-faced man. But his homely appearance didn't reassure me at all. He was a stranger. I couldn't confide in a stranger. Successful businessman I may be, but suddenly I had never felt more alone. This wasn't my office. It was Kiddey's. A stranger. Then, like a shaft of light, the idea struck me.'

'"That's right," I said. "I'm Parkin. Parkin of the Lantern Club." I was Parkin of the Lantern Club, and as I shook hands with the man, I was alone no more. "About the trip, Mr Kiddey. I've only just read about it and, if it's at all possible, I would like to go with them. Help out, you know. That sort of thing. At my own expense, of course. I am my own boss. No restrictions on time, or anything."

176

' "Please, Mr Parkin. Sit down." Kiddey's eyes were positively gleaming.

' "Tea?" he asked.

' "Thank you."

'Kiddey flipped a switch on the intercom and, as he did so, I saw that his arm had been crushed at some time. I looked away, feigning to look round the room. Then the door opened and a woman came in. Ample of bosom and indeterminate of age, she looked harassed, as though annoyed at being called away from whatever other duties she had and, indeed, the whole place looked as though it operated on a shoestring. But my mild interest in the lady was in no way returned. She didn't even glance in my direction.

' "Two teas, Joan, please." Kiddey settled back more comfortably in his chair. "Now then, Mr Parkin. Tell me, please."

'Joan sailed out and I took a vague second to wonder what her own disability might be. By her manner, I thought it might be a total lack of the milk of human kindness. Perhaps her legs ached, though.

' "Well, Mr Kiddey," I began, "I'm a member of a certain organization. Very private. But I can give you an address, of course. It's a bit like the Samaritans," I lied. "But we shun publicity altogether. Now and again, however, we go out into the field, mainly to see that the money finds its way to the right place. You do understand. And it happens that it's my turn. It's that simple, really. Naturally enough, too, we don't want everyone after us. But you'll want to know more about me personally, I expect. Here's my business card. Make any enquiries you wish."

'That wasn't bad, I thought, not at such short notice, as Joan came in with the tea.

' "Thank you, Joan,' said Kiddey, and the lady drifted out like an over-laden barge. Kiddey got down to business.

177

"It's very good of you, Mr Parkin," he said, handing me my tea. "Very good indeed. Obviously, we need all the help we can get." He was drumming gently on his desk with his fingers and I knew he was going to choose his next words carefully. "The thing is, Mr Parkin," he said at last, "the Austrian thing is settled already. Fully booked and ready to go."

'Immense relief and tense disappointment are not really two emotions that sit well together in the stomach and I just sat there gaping. It was like being told that the dentist had been called out just as it was your turn after forty-five minutes in the waiting room. All this tension and, so far, nothing. For something to do, I began to drink my tea. It was a good cup. But Kiddey was looking thoughtful again and, of course, I began to feel even more nervous.

' "Have you ever been sailing, Mr Parkin?" he asked suddenly. I shuddered. Perhaps I was sickening for something. But I made the effort to apply my mind to the question, or, to be more exact, the implications behind it. Firstly, no. I had never been sailing. Even on a small boating lake. I expect it could be cold and wet and, on a windy day especially, I should think the deck could even tilt a little. No, I had not been sailing. But then, I chided myself, what, after all, was I doing here? One could always surely steel oneself – concentrate on coming ashore to a nice warm bed. What was the odd day or two, anyway? Perhaps it wasn't even vital that one had actually got to be on board, just helping out ashore – transport – that sort of thing. Easier than Austria, anyway. I began to breathe more easily. I would work really hard.

' "No, Mr Kiddey," I said. "Not recently that is."

' "Well, Mr Parkin," he replied, "the thing is, we really do need someone like you. Sound in wind and limb, as they say. It is a bit basic, this one. Say no if you wish."

My heart was already going like a trip-hammer. "It's in five weeks time. Eight days' round trip or thereabouts. Sailing trip for the boys. Women, too, I believe. Portsmouth to Hamburg and back." '

Just for a moment, it seemed as though Parkin was back in Kiddey's office on that day a while back. There was that look in his eyes, rather like a man recalling an unpleasant dream – knowing that his very next words to Kiddey would commit him to the unknown. And without having the slightest inkling of what the real cost was going to be, Kiddey would thank him.

'Gentlemen,' Parkin said at last, 'when was the last time any of you saw a ventriloquist act? A good one, I mean. Because, believe me, this one was the best. Kiddey didn't even have to put his hand up the dummy's back. Mind you, the dummy himself wasn't that good. Not at first. Could do little more than just stutter. Just sat there gaping, he did. The words did manage to come out at last, though – a bit hoarsely, maybe, but none the less surely for that. "Put my name down," the dummy was screaming. Then the dummy was shouting it into my own ear. "Put my name down."

' "Are you all right, Mr Parkin?" Kiddey was asking anxiously. "You look a bit warm."

'I was drenched in sweat. How on earth would I go on when I had to face the actual situation? I gulped the rest of my tea before answering. "Oh, I'm all right, Mr Kiddey," I said then. "Been working rather hard lately, you know," and I couldn't help adding, "I expect the trip abroad is just what I need."

'Kiddey seemed satisfied with this, getting quickly onto a subject about which he would obviously appreciate some little confirmation. "Good, good," he said. 'Er, you did say something about, er, finances. We do need, well, you understand."

'The tone was diffident – even a bit embarrassed – and

179

I didn't hesitate in putting him at his ease. So I did have that small pleasure at least, certainly the only one in the business so far. "Certainly, Mr Kiddey," I said, pulling my chequebook out. And for the moment at any rate, that was it. Then I was on my way out, passing through the outer office where the competent Joan now sat battering away at an ancient Underwood. She looked up as I passed and the smile she gave transformed her face.

' "Good afternoon, Mr Parkin. Hope we'll see you again sometime." I smiled weakly in return, ashamed of my recent thoughts. Then I was shaking Kiddey's hand at the door and, in my agitation at everything, I didn't even notice whether or not it was his damaged limb.

' "You're quite sure about the oilskins and things?" he was saying. "To donate afterwards? They are rather expensive, I know. And I can go ahead and cash the cheque? Whether you go or not?" I waved an expansive hand in reply. There was certainly no condescension with this charity, I thought. "I'll be in touch with the rest of the details," he called, determined, it seemed, to give me my money's worth as I made for my car. And that, chaps, is when it really came home to me – hearing the word Detail. Believe me, the ordeal had almost begun.'

Buster Howes could hang on no longer. Polite mouthfuls were all very well in a normal situation – when one was talking and so on – but all this listening was thirsty work and the temptation of facing a full pot now proved too great to resist. There were limits, after all. Having settled his conscience then, he lifted the glass to his lips without further ado and, blissfully unaware of the general interest he now commanded, concentrated on the task in hand, which was to empty the pot in one go. But now having done this without too much effort at all, he suddenly became aware of being observed by all and sundry and in almost the same instant, everyone was smiling.

In answer, Buster now put the back of a polite fore-finger to his lips, burped just about inaudibly, and smiled back.

The business had the welcome effect of introducing a break. Parkin was up to the situation, too, blaming himself by pleading weariness, and finishing, 'Just before we break up for the night, gentlemen – ready as we all must surely be – I would like to say that I can't thank the committee members enough. As I said at the beginning, I dared tell them nothing, the reason for this being a simple one. You see, I couldn't have borne the shame of having to report failure. Whether or not you can begin to understand this, all I can say in my defence is that that was the very uncertain state I was in. That's what I meant a while back when I told Kiddey that I was Parkin of the Lantern Club. I had to tell someone that I wasn't alone in the world. Of course,' he ended with a wry smile, 'I don't for an instant suppose that I would have been inclined to thank the committee quite so warmly had they reached any decision other than the one they did.'

Everyone laughed, happy for the man and, after agreeing we would next assemble on the evening after next, we broke up for the remainder of the evening.

As usual, Alan Parkin had arrived early and this time sporting his new dark-green club tie. He was smiling a little self-consciously and, although there were a number of standard jokes about the tie, no one had ever been heard to ridicule it in any way. Five ties, after all, in as many years is not that many.

Early as Parkin was, too, this evening, it also seemed that everyone else was in similar frame of mind. Buster saw me come in and waved me across, pointing to a ready drink. But I went to the bar anyway to get two more. I spoke to Warwick Edwards, back from somewhere or other, and to several others, before I managed to get to my seat.

I put the drinks down, but there was no getting past Buster and, before I could protest, he'd poured a whisky into my beer. He opened his mouth to say something but I beat him to it. 'Yes, I know, Buster,' I said. 'It peps it up. Cheers.'

He grinned, happy already. Then I looked round again, for the place was really filling up. I waved across to Liz Peach and her friends, Wendy and Kevin Stowe. Liz and Wendy were the only two women members of the club and I remembered the occasion of their admittance. Liz was a hairdresser and, although she could be quite forthright at times, she was pleasant enough company. The two women had applied formally for membership and, on such an important matter, there'd been a general meeting. Kevin, a railway worker, had excused himself, and Warwick Edwards, in the Chair, had put the proposition forward, simply and without frills. Simply for something to say, one or two members had demurred mildly, but Warwick, in his usual manner, had put the thing in perspective.

'Gentlemen,' he said, 'the question is, membership for whom? Which people exactly would we not want in our club? Tibetans? Catholics? Homosexuals? Those under five feet six, or who happen to grow cucumbers? All that we, as your committee, ask, is that you consider your motives. The vote is up to you, of course.'

His logic was as sound as it usually was and, apart from two abstentions, the thing was carried unanimously in favour, and the ladies, happy to have made their point, accepted graciously, now coming into the club on a regular basis. But only once a week. It was, as Liz Peach was later heard to remark, a very happy day and gentlemen would always be welcome in her salon.

* * *

Now comfortably full and with everyone settled, the big room suddenly took on a quieter tone, the conversation dropping to a mere hum, and Alan Parkin, still fingering his tie, took a final bracer and began.

'Good evening, everyone, and once again, my thanks to you all for being here.' He paused for just a moment to gather his thoughts before going on. 'I arrived at Portsmouth that morning in as sombre a vein, given the circumstances, as I would have expected to be. It wasn't that I was determined to suffer, but rather that I somehow knew I would do so – a sobering thought, but I just couldn't shake it off. The day was a grey one in every sense of the word.

'I don't know how many of you are familiar at all with this particular port, the dockyard especially, but the sheer size of it, something like three hundred acres, I believe, makes it, by any standards, a big place. I had been to the place but once before, when, as a child, I'd been taken to see the *Victory*, but the memory was very hazy, hardly anything at all. However, I should imagine that, even in those days, Portsmouth would have been unsure of its future role, what with the Navy's links with the place getting ever weaker, policies being what they are. I'm sorry if I seem to be digressing a bit, but given the parlous state I was in, I know you'll be sympathetic with my feelings on that drab day. I was alone here and a stranger to the place, although, of course, everyone's a stranger at some time, even the *Victory* herself, for she was commissioned in Chatham, I believe.

'So it did seem fitting that I should be starting my journey from here, from amongst these people, these Portmuthians who have seen such troubles themselves – the thousands of them who were killed at Jutland alone and the carpet-bombing durng the Second World War. Oh, I know that my motives were different from theirs, as being rather more personal, but on that lonely morning I had to try and identify with someone, or some place.

'I couldn't find my ship. Search as I might, I could find no sign of it. I'd been given instructions, but sketchy as they'd been I'd give them little heed, believing that I would be able quite easily to find it on my own. But this was before I had any idea of the size of the place and, by now, I was getting more dispirited by the minute. Unlike Southampton, Portsmouth has no inflowing river, but it's still incredibly busy. At last, however, I managed to make my way to the Outer Camber, which is an old creek around which the place was built. It's a commercial dock now, just inside the harbour entrance, a rather sleepy-looking place with a fishing-village atmosphere.

'Then at last, by enquiry both extensive and tiring, I found the area I was after and, sure enough, there she was, the *Fulmar*. It, or she, rather, was easily the largest craft there, although this wasn't saying that much and, having just arrived from Calshot, she belonged to the Hampshire Education Authority, which explained, I suppose, what we were doing here. Not that I was much interested in any of this. I was much more concerned with my own troubles. It seemed I was in danger of disregarding the only reason I was here, which was to help myself by helping others. It was all rather disheartening.

'But a sudden relief flooded over me, for I was now in the act of attempting to cross the beams of two smaller craft in order to reach the seemingly distant deck of the *Fulmar*. It was a precarious business and the fact was that it would now have been as bad to go back as it was to go forward and, in the next instant, the matter was thankfully out of my hands – I now stood upon the gently swaying deck of the *Fulmar*. Full of misgivings though I still was, I knew that I was now totally committed. I began to feel rather pleased with myself. For in order to reach this completely alien place, had I not searched diligently and with little or no aid? Had I not successfully negotiated two heaving decks to clamber awkwardly up a rope and plank ladder to reach my goal? Perhaps I was more cut out for this sort of thing than I had at first thought. Would it not prove to be the case, in fact, that I was here under false pretences? But this thought lasted for about a second and a half. For even as I began to square my shoulders, the *Fulmar* gave a more definite movement – a warning perhaps, against my complacency.

'I've often since wondered what sort of picture I presented. An intriguing, if not comical figure. Think of it if you will – a lone, motionless individual in the middle of the deck, playing perhaps a private game of statues, or else waiting for ... what? A ghost? How silly. And I began to relax in shame but, of course, this was the moment when the villainous *Fulmar* knew that she hadn't paused in vain and, like a siren shaking out her tresses and smiling at my awaited trust, she now gave a further lurch, causing the whole deck to shudder. I grabbed at the nearest rope, which I later learned was to be called a sheet, in order to steady myself. It vibrated in my hand like a live thing. It was as though the whole world was about to take off and I hung on bravely. Not that we'd yet left harbour. I didn't feel well. I didn't feel well at all.

'This simply would not do. I had to pull myself together before I became a gibbering wreck. I was almost saying it aloud. But before I could begin bringing my iron will into play, figures started to appear, making me jump. They were coming from somewhere below – from hell. My nerves were thrumming in unison with the sheet I was holding. The figures ignored me completely but this didn't prevent me breaking out into an alarming sweat. I was the detached, unobserved onlooker in some kind of nightmare. Then I suddenly remembered deciding to keep a journal – yes, I was awake after all – responsible for my actions. Covertly then, I pulled the ballpoint and notebook from my pocket, writing the date and then just the two words, 'On board' – a brief enough beginning perhaps, but a voluntary movement at least.

'But I now had other things to think about, for I was approached and identified at last. I was given welcome and, with the drying sweat caking my body and with my nerves settling now to a more even keel, I was hustled – out of the way? – rather hurriedly below...' Parkin smiled gravely. 'Shall we break off for a minute or two, everyone? To get fresh drinks?'

The sudden request caught everyone by surprise, or almost everyone, for Buster was already off the mark. I went to him at the head of the queue, determined to pay for the drinks. 'Sit down, Buster,' I said. 'I've got a surprise for you.'

'Right,' he said, hastening off. 'Gents first, then.'

'This is good,' he was to say a little later, trying the drink. 'What is it?'

'What it is, Buster,' I replied, 'is a pint of the very best, with a double shot of the very strongest in it.'

'Well, it's good. Have you got the same?' he asked.

'I have,' I lied.

'Good. Got to keep our spirits up, you know.'

I wondered, as I often did, how long his constitution would put up with it all.

We were all nicely settled once more and Parkin resumed his story. 'I don't know why we set sail at a particular time,' he began. 'It wasn't the tides, of course, for in these deep waters, ships aren't dependent on them. But after I'd been on board for about three hours, things began to happen. I was stretched out on my bunk at the time, trying to steady my nerves for the voyage. It wasn't the ideal setting. As cabins go, I suppose it was much the same as any other on a similar vessel – functional, more or less seaworthy and carefully lacking anything which might suggest the least kind of luxury. To me, it was rather like being in a mobile shed, with no yielding surfaces and with but the minimal provision of light.

'I hadn't been in there for the whole three hours, though. I'd been advised to find my way around the ship – become familiar with my bearings and so on – and for an hour this is what I'd done. No doubt there would be certain members of the crew in whose way I hadn't stumbled, but I was sure these would be in the minority. Then having been told that a meal would be served in about an hour, when I would meet everyone properly and be given my duties, I went below for another rest, more to get out of the way than anything else, the while to brood vaguely on what the immediate future might hold.

'So there I was, making the most courageous attempt to convince myself that the experience might not after all turn out to be too horrendous, when a mighty crash overhead, resembling nothing so much as a ton of coal being dropped from a great height on to the deck above my head, threatened surely to swamp the vessel, going down with all hands. So shooting upright, a purely involuntary action, I cracked my head hard on the bunk above, so hard indeed as to make the whole vessel shiver. Then, the whole world began to move, although, in my pain, I could hear no one shouting to abandon ship, or anything. Just the same, I thought I'd better get up top.

'We were under sail. I never did find out what the crash was. I certainly didn't dare ask. People were working at ropes and things, and the best I could do, once more, was to keep well clear. So I kept as still as I could, looking up at the great spread of sail and marvelling at the power in them. How many people had had this experience? I wondered. They were so high up. But it soon began to make me feel dizzy, so I then went to the side-rail to take in the view, being suddenly reminded that I had never before seen any kind of coastline. There were the old sea forts gliding by and, though there seems to be no clear distinction between The Solent and Spithead, the names are bound to conjure up so many past and tragic events in the place's history. I freely admit to having read about them a bit in anticipation of the voyage – anything to take my mind off the real issue – but the magic was there just the same. I remembered reading about the *Sheffield* and the *Coventry*, the *Mary Rose*, and the sad case of Admiral Byng.

'Past Hayling Island then, and Langstone Harbour, although once we were past the natural shelter of the Isle of Wight, the Channel weather began to make its presence known and bringing me sharply back to the present. Not that it was really that bad, but the water was becoming a bit choppy, and here I must remind you all that I had never been to sea before – never had a foot off dry land. The thought that there has to be a first time for everything brought me no comfort at all and I began now to shiver in the brisk sou'easter, as I heard one of the crew say that it was. I went below.

'Over dinner, I was introduced in a more or less formal way to the rest of the crew or, at any rate, to those of them who weren't on duty up top. This came as another surprise to me, having the vague idea that during dinner, apart from the one brave chap to steer the ship, everyone would be there. Proof, I think, that I wasn't thinking too clearly at all. To confuse me further, I was also being given a rather sketchy idea of my own duties. This was the Captain speaking. He was the one with the peaked cap and, although he welcomed me most warmly, it gradually transpired that I was in somewhat of a unique position. For being the only paying guest aboard and also being the only crew member who'd never actually been to sea before, the implication was that my duties would not only be light but also voluntary, or, at least, extremely flexible. Rather sensibly, I think, I made little or no comment on this.

'For the rest, the meal consisted of a hot, metallic-tasting stew and strong sweet tea. It wasn't too bad and as I ate I looked at the faces there in the mess-deck, trying to remember names, a task rendered the more difficult as nearly everyone was being introduced to each other at the same time. Again I was surprised, having had the quaint idea that they would be a regular crew. An absurd notion, of course, when I considered that by far the biggest number of them must have come aboard for the first time, the same as me.

'It would have been hard to put an average age on them all. There were young collegians and middle-aged social workers. There was an ancient old salt with a beard of the same colour, and there were four women. Almost all were noticeably disabled in some way, some worse than others, although, as it turned out, I was to prove rather quickly to be the most disabled person on board. Something else. They were all incredibly jolly. Noisy too and, to my amazement, I began to get caught up in the general enthusiasm. Was it possible? I wondered. Would I be able to become part of it all, get away from my role as ... what? And what would I say back home, to the committee? That I hadn't undergone that much discomfort after all?

'Ladies and gentlemen, the idea was short-lived, believe me. For the moment, however, brief as it was, the atmosphere at that initial gathering was simply too infectious to resist. Neither was there anyone on earth, surely, like those people for laughing at each other – mocking each other's imperfections and giving each other nicknames to suit these faults. Captain James, for example, was quickly known as Coot for the fact that he was completely bald, although in respect to his rank it was always Captain Coot. Bill Crawshaw, a respected civil servant, who suffered severe curvature of the spine, became known as Dick, after Richard the Third. And it wasn't too long before I was to have my own sobriquet thrust upon me, becoming known simply as Sid, although it was a while before I found out why. When I did, it turned out that Sid was short for sidewinder, by the manner of my progression. You see, everyone else on board could walk. I never did quite acquire the skill myself. I had to run, from side to side, bumping into objects and people both, on the way. I became an added hazard to the everyday life on board ship and, one and all, the crew learnt very quickly, not only to avoid contact, but to warn others as well. "Look out, here comes Sid", became a much more regular cry than, for instance, "Hands to dinner", the latter being required but once a day, of course.'

Excusing himself, Parkin at last grabbed at his drink, taking a couple of quick swallows. I thought that he must by now be tiring, too, but after the briefest of pauses, he carried on with his tale. 'I did learn things,' he said. 'I learned that a sailing ship, in all of man's devices, is the most wonderful, the most complex, perverse, beautiful, and demanding thing of them all. I can never before remember having given the least thought to such a thing as a ship propelled in such a way – had not the slightest interest in such a thing. And I still know next to nothing about the moods – the nasty little fits of temper – which seem to be her natural birthright and of which she, and no doubt all of her sisters, take the fullest advantage. And I know even less on how one is supposed to react to

190

them. Not now, nor in the foreseeable future, one always hesitating, I suppose, to say never.

'The trouble is, you see, that the more you learn, the more there is. This was rudely brought home to me at breakfast on the first full day. I felt a bit queasy to start with, what with a not too comfortable night and with the weather now definitely taking a turn for the worse. But I thought I should make the effort at least and, feigning an interest I didn't in any way feel, I asked, in all innocence, what manner of ship the *Fulmar* was. In seaman's terms, that is. Was she a frigate, I asked, knowing that certain sailing vessels were thus called? I did know she wasn't a galleon.'

At this, one or two club members began to guffaw, but Parkin smilingly broke into their merriment. 'Before you laugh too loudly, gentlemen,' he said, 'I would ask you to kindly ask yourselves how many sailing ships you alone could identify. Apart from a dinghy, perhaps.'

Talking immediately broke out amongst themselves, but Parkin would have none of it. It seemed he wanted to get on and he quieted them with the one word. 'Topsail. Topsail-ketch, gentlemen. The answer had come without hesitation from the bearded one and I made the resolve to remember it. Sadly, however, this resolve was weakened a little by another messmate who interrupted almost as quickly.

' "Not entirely accurate," the awkward one broke in. "But near enough. She's really a schooner-ketch."

'I would rather,' Parkin went on, 'that this man had not been present. Then I could have remembered "topsail-ketch" with confidence. As it was, the two began to argue – would you believe it? – about the relative proportions of masts.'

' "And you will have noticed, shipmate," said the bearded one, tetchily, "that the *Fulmar* has square topsails."

191

' "Ah, I'm glad you brought that up," said the other. "Then you'll also have noticed..."

'It was at this point,' Parkin went on, 'that I pulled my journal furtively from my pocket and wrote "The *Fulmar* is a fine, two-masted topsail-ketch". In this way, I knew that I was certainly half right. For there were two masts, I knew that. I had counted them. And after that, I was determined that I would hereafter refer to the *Fulmar* as, simply, the ship.'

A hand came sneaking across the table, the fingers wrapping themselves quietly around my almost empty glass. I looked across at Buster and he grinned owlishly. I began to mime that I had really had my intake, but shaking his head in mock severity, as though I was rudely interrupting the proceedings, he disappeared like a wraith.

'... The weather chose this moment to become decidedly more unkind,' Parkin was saying, 'and brought my thirst for knowledge to an abrupt end. My cup began to slide alarmingly across the table and this was the last meal I was to enjoy for quite a while. What little part of it I had enjoyed, that is. And so, in some quick reluctance to engage in further conversation, I struggled manfully to my feet, intent on going about my duties, which this morning were supposed to be in the galley. I made my hazardous way there now, preceded, of course, by the many warnings of, "Look out, here comes Sid", my most annoying thought of the whole business being that all of the other crew members seemed to be enjoying it all so much.'

I sensed a movement and glanced across the table. It was as though Buster had never been away, smiling happily in my direction and edging my brimming glass towards me with one eager finger.

'And on this morning in particular,' Parkin was smiling at Buster's theatrics, 'it was certainly one occasion at least upon which they couldn't but help seeing my approach, for this time I'd managed to struggle into my special life jacket and trousers. Just to try them out as I'd early been advised to. And I was reminded of Mr Kiddey when he told me, almost in embarrassment, how much the jacket alone would cost. For my promise to him, amongst others of a financial nature, was that I would buy one, afterwards to donate it to his association.

'I well remembered his hurried explanations at my very evident surprise, telling me what was entailed in the making of such a simple-sounding garment. It was simply covered in gadgets, being double-seamed, breathable and so on. There was a drain channel, although to be quite honest, I never did quite manage to locate this little feature, although again, on reflection, I do believe that I forgot to look for it. But I did find the double-action safety hook – a handy innovation this, one which we sailors call a karabiner...' and this was one of the rare occasions when Parkin was to grin at his own humour.

'There was an upward floating flashlight unit. That's a torch. Oh, and a host of other things. Reflective microprism tape was one, as I recall. I think I wore the jacket twice. Most uncomfortable things, but a lifesaver in the right conditions, of course. Then there was the life raft to hold four people. I paid for one of those also, helping, I suppose, to assuage my conscience somewhat for undertaking the trip under false pretences. But it was a deal of money just the same and they made me an honorary member.

'So you see why I was allowed to go. Like many others, I believe, I have often heard where the heaviest seas might be found – The Horn, the Bay of Biscay and so on, but for me at least, on that day, none of this mattered a jot. For it simply could not have been worse. Like many other things, suffering is relative, and, folks, stretch your imaginations just a little if you will for a moment on some of the ways in which a person may undergo torment – the brilliant surgeon who loses a patient and a friend, immediately after a tricky four-hour operation, only to discover a little later on that the cause of death had been a faulty swab. In near despair, and anxious to make amends, he supervises every last detail of the following operation for himself. It's a complete success. Afterwards, he hears the nurses discussing the patient. "I know this man," one of them is saying. "He's a convicted wife beater, you know."

'As my delirious writhings began to take real hold, the surgeon, and others, came into my mind like avenging spectres. There was the last man on earth who had suddenly discovered the secret of writing perfect prose. There was the painter, blinded in an accident and there was the sybarite pools winner whom, on the day of his good fortune, was also informed of his inoperable tumour.

'They were all there, jeering at my anguish. How long it went on, I don't know, but there seemed to be added terror, also, in the perpetual movement and the darkness. And outside, with hardly a break in the waves, there was a horrible swell and, although I had been housed amidships, having been assured that this was far preferable to bunking in the fo'c's'le – that's the front part of the ship – I couldn't have cared less where I was, thinking that I might have done as well high up the masthead in the crow's-nest and have done with it. I knew I was supposed to be helping up on deck, but for the moment my limbs just refused to respond. Neither were the contents of my stomach sitting too well. I'd eaten some hot mess the night before and the thought had occurred to me then that the food on board always seemed to taste just about the same. Not so to the rest of the crew, though. If it happened to be lukewarm, they would say it was OK. But

194

if it was hot, which did happen on rare occasions, they would smack their lips, saying it was delicious and asking for seconds. I don't know what most of the ingredients were, but to most of the others, at any rate, it seemed to be merely a matter of temperature.

'I think it must all have been something to do with their general state of health – their collective fitness. As though to compensate a bit for their disabled limbs, although, of course, had they been unfit as well, they would never have been allowed on the trip. But all this was merely a reflection on my own sorry state, for now, even laid down, I began to feel alarmingly dizzy, this becoming steadily worse until I became certain that, surely now, the life of the ship itself must be numbered in seconds with the crew naming me as the Jonah, and with the lead weight now rolling about in my stomach helping us, in no small measure, in hastening us to the bottom.

'But I wasn't to be let off quite that easily and, just for a brief second, I recovered a little, vaguely aware once again that I should be elsewhere. I made some feeble effort to rise and in the same second I both threw up and soiled myself. The stench was unbelievable.'

Parkin had stopped talking at last, either anxious that, however briefly, we should dwell on the horrendous situation with him, or else being overcome on his own accord as he relived the thing in his mind. Whichever it was, for all the sound in the big room, it could have been empty, and, for myself, I thought that Parkin was displaying a particular brand of courage.

Then after a while, and nodding strangely a few times, he carried on speaking. 'There were options,' he said. 'And even now, with my condition becoming increasingly befuddled as it was, I managed to consider them, each one in turn. I could, for instance, have screamed for someone, anyone who might appear, to put me out of my misery as an act of kindness, as they would a dog. Or I could have made a sudden, determined rush up top to fling myself overboard, paddling as best I could, away from the ship, uncaring that someone might get into serious trouble over the business.

'And this was only the beginning of the nightmare. This at last was the lancing of the boil – the eruption – the result of the build-up of hate and uncertainty over the years, regardless of the outcome. This bout of seasickness was merely the lit fuse to it all – the detonator – and as I stared through the madness, I saw a glimpse of hell.

'Then, for the briefest moment, there was the tiniest pinprick of reasoning and I grasped at it weakly. In this mere glimmer of comprehension, I saw that last strand of dignity, which is surely there in all men, buried though it may be at various depths in the mind. And in this last fleeting thought – this last shred of reasoning – I hung on desperately, as it told me that the remedies I had considered were untenable, unworthy of serious consideration.

'What I did, after all, was to take the only way out of which I was truly capable – simply laying there prostrate and cursing everything and everyone: my long-dead uncle, the day I'd been born, that nauseous philosophy of the team spirit, the mere suggestion that such a thing as nobility had ever really existed... Throughout that hideous day I whimpered and wept, for of all the curses on the planet the one of seasickness has to be up there with the worst of them – as potent a leveller as any.

'As it took a real hold, I almost swooned away. But not totally, for this would have been too much of a blessing. Rather did I become the central figure in some dreadful sci-fi feature, as shadowy, faceless shapes began to appear throughout the day. I was too ill to care what they were

196

about. What, in fact, they had been about had been undressing me, bathing me, washing my foul clothing and forcing hot liquid down my retching throat.'

He fell quiet once again as he relived the horror, and I thought that he might justifyingly plead a lengthy break. But glancing around the room, as though asking us to bear with him, he carried on, determined it seemed, to finish his tale.

'I felt a bit better the next morning,' he began, 'and although incredibly weak, I could have shouted for joy, crawling up on deck as best I could in my newly laundered clothes. Every crew member I encountered asked if I was OK, and passed on without further fuss. But when I saw the Captain, he ordered me back to my bunk. "Get up for a bit after dinner, if you like," he said. "You're in no fit state to do more. Not yet."

'Captain Coot, née James, was right, of course, and it was also on my way below that my face went crimson with embarrassment at the sudden recollection of what had been done for me. I lay on my bunk thankfully and the near darkness was now a comfort. I dozed off. Then, at dinner time, a woman came below with some hot stew and, as far as I could tell, they were exactly the same ingredients as usual, but it was hot at least and I managed to get most of it down. She said her name was Sarah and there was something wrong with her shoulder – the result of some farming accident some years ago, she said. She asked me how I was, and then, somehow, I knew it was she who had washed my clothes. I began to stutter some kind of thanks but she cut me off midstream. "Hey," she said. "They were there and so was I and they had to be done."

'Once again, I was thankful of the gloom and, somehow, I was aware of being thankful that I was now well enough to be so. But she was well able to sense my acute discomfiture, and smilingly, she said, "Oh, don't worry too much. It wasn't me who bathed you," adding, "Not that I wouldn't have done so."

'She was now taking pleasure in the situation, saying, "I don't suppose you were much bothered at the time." She would certainly get no argument from me there.

'But by far the worst was over and much of the ensuing time was spent in counting my blessings on the fact. It was now mere ordinary discomfort until at last, even this began to fade. And I got to know some of the crew better, actually coaxing some of them, in my enforced idleness, to tell me their stories.

'They say that the best way to see Hamburg is from the water, but I had nowhere near enough recovered sufficiently to appreciate it, even finding the place a little overpowering. As the largest city in West Germany, it positively hums with activity, of course, with its ferries and its waterbuses and its huge network of canals. I had read about the place beforehand a little and, to me, Thomas Mann seemed to get it about right with his thoughts on the place – his insights into its materialism, although, again, I expect it's just a matter of mood. But even a moment's pause makes you realize that the huge brick warehouses along the front do reflect real elegance.

'Inland, though, it's different altogether. Extensively green. But I went ashore only the once, to one of the museums, the Kunsthalle, and the art collection there has to be one of the finest in the world. Just my opinion, of course. And having said all this, I was really quite content just lazing about on board ship for most of the time, fitting in willingly for any on-duty watchkeepers who wanted to be off. Not that I could ever hope to begin to repay those people. Almost everyone apart from myself, however, went off to celebrate some big occasion to do with Mendelssohn and Brahms, both of whom, it seems, had been born there. But for myself, I just wanted the thing to be over.

'There was only one incident of note on the homeward voyage. Having at last actually taken up my assigned duties, I trapped my finger in a winch. Lost a nail.'

He proudly held up his hand to show us the injured member. 'I did squeal a bit at that,' he went on, as he tapped his ragged notebook. 'It's all in the journal here. I'll be keeping this yet awhile. To keep my feet on the ground, sort of.

'And that's about it, folks. Thanks for listening and I'd like to buy you all a drink, downstairs. Just to dampen the new tie, you know. Oh, and to meet my intended. She's over there. Look. Her name's Sarah.'

Surprise for Podowski

Although the three men who sat holding their beer critically up to the light in the lounge of the Fawkley Social Club had chosen to follow the same line of work, they could in no way be described as being closely associated in their professional lives at all. For only one of the three actually lived in the area. This was PC Dennis Hayseldene, a dog handler in the East Fawkley Division who, as such, was the only one of them who could get to the club on anything like a regular basis.

Another one of the group, Detective Chief Inspector Donald McKuen, was, in fact, a native of the place, but since he'd been promoted to Breeley, a small town near Colchester, on the other side of the country, Fawkley didn't see too much of him. That was three years ago and, as he often said, he'd had little time for socializing since. Most of the major crimes in his region fell on his desk and, understaffed as he was, he was usually a busy man. So it is doubtful if he would have visited Fawkley much at all, hometown though it was, had it not been for strong family ties. His wife was sister to Warwick Edwards who was chairman of the Lantern Club, here in the building.

Even as boys together, the two had got on, and Warwick was the reason McKuen had joined the club in the first place. Not that he'd disliked cricket, the half-jovial reason why the club had been formed in the first place. For he'd actually been a spin bowler of some ability in his school's first eleven. But he had been keen to sponsor his brother-in-law's attempt at the Eiger, way back in the early days of the club.

So he came to Fawkley whenever he could, although, as he sometimes remarked, he would never have made an attempt to win one of the special ties for himself. For as he also said, Details were his everyday work – his bread and butter. Every case which dropped on his desk or wrapped itself around his shoulders was a Detail.

Detective First Grade John Crowle, based in the Yorkville district of Manhattan, was able to visit the Lantern Club even less times than McKuen and, in fact, this was only his second visit to the country. It was over a year ago now, when he'd first arrived in Colchester, to exchange police procedures and so on, that he'd first met McKuen. And although the visit had been an official one, the two had got on from the start and they now corresponded on a more or less regular basis.

But this visit of Crowle's was a holiday. Having a few days' leave due, the plan had been to bring his girlfriend, Nancy, to show her something of the country, but at almost the last minute, a rush of work had prevented her from being able to come and Crowle had decided to come on his own. After consultation with Sarah, McKuen had insisted Crowle stay with them. The American had split his holiday in two, accompanying McKuen on some of his enquiries for the first half and then hiring a car to go off on his own and see something of the country, for the second. But, on this occasion – his penultimate day before his flight back to the States – McKuen, after hurried talks on the phone with Warwick Edwards, had arranged not only a visit to the Lantern Club, but that the novel visitor should also be presented with honorary member status, complete with special tie. And Crowle, an educated man, was conscious of the honour. He also loved the old building and the seemingly casual pace of it all. 'Tell me, chaps,' he said now, his accent jarring rather grotesquely with the noun, 'tell me once more. Why are we holding our beer up to the light like this?'

'You tell him, Dennis,' said McKuen.

PC Hayseldene held his own glass solemnly up to the window again. 'Well, John,' he said, 'it's to tell if the pumps are in order – clean, you know.'

'And if they're not?'

'We complain to the landlord.'

'And what does he do?'

'Well, he examines the beer for himself, and then, depending on his mood, he empties it out and pulls you a fresh pint. I mean, you can't expect him to start cleaning the pumps in the middle of a session, can you?' As he spoke, he looked across at McKuen, who also managed to keep a straight face.

'Yeah, right.'

The old Mondeo was running well enough as McKuen drove through the night. He'd expected Crowle to doze but this was not the case. The New Yorker talked of crime and of police methods and of his colleagues back home. He talked of how he'd enjoyed his holiday and of his hopes for the future. McKuen liked the man.

Crowle sat back in his seat on the 747 at Heathrow, flight number 117, for the 7 hours 40 minutes journey to New York, waiting for his first drink. He was also thinking of what might be waiting for him when he got back, of how he'd enjoyed the last few days and of the continuance of his English pub education. As he did so, he fingered his new tie, wondering what they might say in a downtown bar should he happen to hold his brown, impatiently opened bottle up to the light for inspection. Nothing, probably. They'd just hold him down while someone sent for the wagon. Crowle then slept.

Menny Podowski paused in his labours to wipe the back of a greasy hand across a still greasier brow, pushing the ancient homburg to the back of his head in so doing. But he quickly tipped it forward again, for the night was cold and the late October darkness chilled the bones. The cold's partner in mischief, the wind howled down to the end of the wide, block-ended alley, and then, enraged, came howling back, bringing great swirls of dust, newspapers and whatever else it could dislodge from the trash cans, as it did so.

Menny had the thought that it was not such a nice night. The single yellow light at the end of the alley winked at him evilly, mocking him, just as though it had known all along that there was nothing worth a cent in the trash cans – even perhaps that it had other, far more sinister secrets. So far, the gunny sack had just five bottles in it. Five lousy bottles and an old coat hardly worth the trouble and, to add to this, the wind had now become even more determined to teach Menny a lesson for his trespass, blowing the detritus into his red eyes, like tiny knives of ice.

But Menny Podowski had known worse enemies than this and he grinned back mirthlessly at the alley sprites, daring them to do their worst as he moved to the last can. It would take more than a few fancies to stop Menny. He pushed the lid off with a crash and peered in. At last. Here was something and it seemed as though his luck had changed. It was a something pale and solid. A parcel? Books? Surprising how many people threw books away.

But the light was poor and Menny had to shove his hand in, get hold of whatever it might be. What it was,

was a hand. He was shaking hands with Death. For he knew that both the hand and its owner were dead. Unkindly though life may have treated him in these later years, Menny suddenly knew that he wasn't yet ready to loosen his hold on it, tenuous as he might have believed it to be. Inured to most kinds of hardship, this quick and ugly appearance of the Reaper at once jolted him out of his usual torpor and, before it could shoot up his arm to transfer its bony wish to his own thin body, Menny whipped his hand clear and, in the same movement, plunged it into an inside pocket for his bottle.

The carefully collected dregs of many other bottles, it wasn't the classiest of cocktails, but a huge gulp of the stuff burned his throat as effectively as the best of them. As he well knew, Death was wont to come in many guises and, in answer to the liquor, his heart began at last to resume a more even pace. What could a dead man do to him anyway? And putting away the bottle, he took a huge breath and got hold of the hand once more, searching the dead fingers carefully for rings. Nothing. His stomach now churning a bit, Menny averted his eyes and forced himself to reach further down in an even closer embrace...

Putting the watch and the fifty-five dollars in his pocket, Menny carefully replaced the now empty billfold neatly back in the inside pocket of the dead man and then put back the trash can lid. The wind howled savagely at his back as, working quickly, Menny hid his takings where even his draughty tormentor would have been hard put to find it, and then made his way to the street. He began to hurry, for, even in a city as busy as New York, loneliness is never very far away.

Menny Podowski had come down in the world and, at fifty-three, he looked ten years older, now being nothing more than a bag person. As a meatpacker, working regularly, and with a wife and an apartment in the South Bronx, he'd been doing well enough. Then a fight had broken out at work and he's lost his job. Searching around for something else, he'd come home one day to find his wife had left, taking the few bits they'd actually owned with her. He didn't blame her too much but he'd quickly given up. He couldn't quite have explained why.

The corner he now came out on was on 95th and 1st Avenue in the Upper East Side of Manhattan in the district of Yorkville. Menny's parents and their parents before them had lived here. It was the place where the Central European and German immigrants had settled early in the century. But these origins were little in evidence nowadays, the tenements being so rapidly pulled down to make room for new apartment blocks. For there's no city in the world whose inhabitants are more fond of pulling things down, simply to make room for new ones. As they're always saying, nobody's making any more land and the builders have to be kept busy.

At the present moment, however, none of this was of much concern to Menny. What he was now reflecting on was that you could still buy the best Wiener schnitzel and red cabbage here, and tomorrow he might treat himself to some with his fifty-five dollars. Or a pastry perhaps, from Kramer's. It would have to be given serious thought. Then, of course, there was the money he would get from his friends, the police.

This line of thought now forced him to change his line of direction somewhat and he made his way to the nearest precinct station. That was the thing about Manhattan. Everything was to hand. 'Is Sergeant Parkes on duty?'

The desk-man was beefy and uncompromising. 'What is it this time, Podowski? More dud info for a few bucks? The door's behind you.'

'Is Sergeant Parkes on duty?' Menny knew exactly what he dare, and dare not, say.

The desk-man, Sergeant Raines, sighed. 'No, he isn't. Detective Crowle is. Wait here,' and scowling disapprovingly, he disappeared, to return almost straightaway with a thin man who sported a pencil moustache, a man who wasn't feeling too well. For Crowle now knew that he should have come home a day earlier, rest up a day before coming on duty. But with Podowski here, he knew there was little chance of nursing himself against jet lag, no option but to get to it and he decided to play good cop and bad cop. And knowing Bill Raines, Crowle knew which part he would have to play himself. He had a sudden, wistful vision of holding an amber glass up to the light in a nice quiet room three thousand miles away and, like Sergeant Raines before him, he sighed.

'Hello, Menny. It's a cold night to be out. Time you were in Grand Central. You'll be missing the soup.' As he spoke, Crowle forced himself to crack a smile.

'I want twenty dollars. I've found a body.'

Crowle and the Sergeant exchanged quick glances. 'If you've found a body, Podowski, and you don't tell us now...' Raines was blustering and he knew it. Both policemen knew Menny, as they also knew that they would get into real hot water if they didn't get the information he obviously had as soon as possible. But the game had to be played out and Raines tried snarling. 'Now listen hard, Podowski...'

It was a one-act play and, as it had been running for quite a while, this was Menny's cue to make for the door. 'Good night, Officers.' He was word-perfect in the role.

'All right, Menny.' The pencil moustache was quivering just a little. 'The body had best still be warm, that's all.' And then Crowle made the conscious effort to relax from his fractional anger. As an intelligent man, he knew the futility of allowing emotion to take over – knew how it clouded the judgement. He then asked himself what he would have done in Menny's position, telling himself that he would have done exactly as the bag man was doing, which was just trying to get by. And Crowle's smile, when it came, was genuine enough. 'Just kidding, Menny. Who'd be warm on a night like this anyway, eh?'

'Throat slashed with something real sharp. Messy, though. About four hours ago.' The ME was already peeling off his gloves. 'I'm back to bed. Tell you more tomorrow.'

'Any good guesses, Mark?' Crowle still felt extremely unwell. And he'd always hated the night shift.

Mark Foster stood pondering for a moment or two. 'A left-hander, I would say. Just a guess, mind. And fairly tall.'

'Strong, do you think, Mark?'

'Not necessarily. But either strong or fast. Or angry. This guy was big and it was certainly no weakling who dumped him in the garbage. Unless he had help, of course. Who found him?' There was sudden surprise in Foster's voice.

'A bag man. Menny Podowski. Lucky, eh? To find the body this soon, I mean.'

'Yeah, lucky. Tell that to the stiff. G'night, John.'

Henry Hinkley had been a waiter on West 43rd in midtown Manhattan, although, according to his big toe, he was now number sixteen in the city morgue. It was 11 a.m. and John Crowle had just arrived, managing to change shifts. Detective Sergeant Sean O'Shaunessy was there to greet him. 'Why the change-over, John?' The big Sergeant was gazing down at the body.

Besides being smart, John Crowle was also ambitious.

He knew Sean would be on this one and he thought it might be a case that could get a smart cop noticed. O'Shaunessy was older, had got as far as he knew he would get. A good policeman but a convergent thinker most times. Nothing wrong with that but the Sergeant might welcome a younger man with ideas, and here he was. 'Anything to get off the graveyard shift, Sean,' which was also true. 'And I'd like to work with you on this one. If that's OK?' 'Sure, why not? If it's OK with Thorne.' They both knew it would be. Henry Thorne appreciated genuine initiative. 'And we've already got one goody,' said Sean, as they were leaving the morgue.

'And what's that, Sean?'

'You'll see. When we get back.'

Back at the station, the 'goody' was being examined by a lab technician who had the air of a man of education and position. It was always joked that Jack Dennison could tell a man's sexual preferences simply by examining a single flake of his dandruff.

'Anything, Jack?' Sean asked the man eagerly. He was the type of cop who loved visible clues. They were tangible. They had substance. And if it was there, Dennison would get it.

'There's always something, Sean,' the man replied without modesty. 'But so far, I'm afraid it's very little. No sign of prints at all. That does away with the need for the tweezers...' He passed the article over. Sean handled the thing as though it was a priceless stamp.

Crowle looked at it closely. It was a small label, light green on one side, adhesive on the other. The only other thing of note was a number 2, written on the coloured side, obviously with a black roll-ball. O'Shaunessy put it gingerly on the desk, as though terrified it might blow out of the window.

'Tell me, Sean,' said Crowle.

209

'On the underside of the left upper arm, almost in the armpit.'

Crowle whistled. 'Premeditated then?'

'Looks that way. Something else, John. Look here.' He pointed to the dead man's belongings, neatly laid out on the desk. Keys on a ring, three of them. Roll-ball, blue ink. ID. Handkerchief. Two credit cards.

'No dough, Sean. No watch.'

'That's right. And the guy was a waiter. He'd have to be a bad one not to get any tips at all.'

'Menny?'

'Who else?'

'What now then, Sean?' Crowle had to ask, the older man being the senior officer.

But O'Shaunessy far preferred being the workhorse. 'Well, what do *you* think, John?' he countered now.

'I think we should divide our labours for a time. One to find Menny. See what he has to say. The other on the small blue screen. It might tell us something.'

'I'm on my way. See you in a couple of hours.' As he often put it himself, Shaun had never gotten used to computers. He also knew where he might find Menny.

It was not a very fruitful couple of hours and at 2 p.m., back at the station, the partners were comparing notes. It didn't take long. The big detective had been unable to locate Menny, a significant point in itself, and John Crowle had been equally unsuccessful, his eyes aching from looking at the small blue screen. Nothing. The main hope had been the label, possibly part of some weirdo's MO, although, as the partners had to admit, this and the robbery just didn't seem to go together. That's why they had to find Menny Podowski.

Crowle had learned in stages that police work is about many things – information received, luck, endless footwork. But there was something else and that was the waiting.

There was always the waiting. Waiting for something to happen so that a course of action may be decided on. Waiting for someone to show. Waiting for someone to make the next move. It was often a slow process.

Over hot pastrami on rye, the two went over what little they had, after which they agreed to go and see if they could have a word with the ME, and this time they were lucky, catching Mark Foster straightaway. A stooped, grey-haired man, of rather past middle age, who still showed the strain of being hauled out of bed during the night, he turned to them with his tired smile. 'Hello, boys. I got the time of death about right. Nothing very significant there. On his way home from work, I suppose. A waiter, you said. Like I said, too, the weapon was sharp. Cut-throat razor, perhaps. I said left-handed. Either that or ambidextrous. One wound. Untidy, but deep and determined. Not frenzied, though. Everything considered, I would say premeditated.'

The partners exchanged glances, Sean then breaking in to ask the ME if he had any thoughts about the label.

'Not my field, Sean. Could even have been there by accident. Not too likely, of course.' He could tell them little more, falling now into generalization. 'The guy was healthy enough. A little overweight. Non-smoker. About forty-five, I should say.'

'Forty-seven, Mark,' said Crowle.

'Hey, right.'

They had options. It was three-fifteen and time to move. They could set out the blackboard. Or go to try and find Menny again. Or they could visit the eating house on West 53rd off 8th Avenue, the restaurant where Hinkley had worked. They could visit the crime scene again or try the SBS once more.

Possibly the one thing that didn't have priority was

211

visiting the victim's home. It had already been established that Hinkley had been married. Someone from the Welfare Division had already been dispatched and would have reported anything untoward. This small division was the Captain's idea, considering it worth the cost. The visitor was usually a woman.

In the event, they did none of these things. They had just poured coffee when Captain Thorne poked his head round the door. 'In here, you two.'

The result of this was that the rest of the shift was spent in making enquiries on older cases, the partners each going their own way. 'It's a matter of priorities,' Thorne was fond of saying. He could have been right. If all other cases were to be abandoned in favour of the latest one, seemingly urgent in following up any hot clues as it might appear, then few cases would ever get solved. A lot of it, of course, depended on the importance of the case. There was no easy way.

Common sense also came into it a good deal. The precinct had a good record, both in homicide cases and others. The Captain had instigated an extremely flexible way of working and, to implement this, the men often worked with whom they pleased or, as often happened, on their own, knowing that back-up was there quickly should they need it. If no one else was available, then the Captain would go himself.

Henry Thorne would also discuss any new ideas suggested but change for its own sake was out. He was a 34-year-old black graduate of flair and intelligence and all he wanted was results. He didn't expect to solve all of New York's crime on his own. He just wanted his precinct to have its share. He wanted his men to work as hard as he did himself and in return, he would back them to the hilt. In the main, the men not only respected him, but liked him.

212

It was 6.30 p.m. when, as arranged, the partners met at the crime scene. It was a gloomy evening and the alley looked even dirtier than Crowle remembered it – bleak and forbidding – and he shuddered, wondering to what kind of pass a man had to come to search this place at night, for the sake of ... what? He thought he could share Menny's horror and he glanced at Sean, curious as to whether the big man was similarly affected.

But Sean looked much as the lab men must have done, poking around that morning, looking for things of a more concrete nature than mere impressions. And they too, had found nothing useful to the case.

The two stood there for a while, saying little, for that was all they could see. 'Chinese?' said Sean at last.

'Sure, Sean. Nothing we can do here.'

They went to the nearest place they could find. O'Shaunessy then went home to his big Irish wife, while Crowle went to the phone to try and catch up with Nancy. Not for the first time, he wondered how she managed to put up with him and he always felt a sense of relief when she answered, as she did now.

At eight forty-five on the following morning, Crowle was watching the SBS. But there was nothing of real interest and a few minutes later Sean came in, and soon after that they were on their way to the restaurant where Hinkley had worked.

Donny's was clean, fairly big and mid-range. Donny himself was there, a fair, good-looking man with an athletic build. 'I thought you'd soon be along,' he said, when the pair had shown their badges. 'Coffee?'

'Thanks, Donny.'

They sat in the window, and Donny, who was still well this side of forty, told them about Hinkley. 'Good worker.

Quiet. Didn't say much about himself. Been here two years. Didn't drink much or anything. Quiet enough home life, I think...'

There was nothing either of the partners could spot in the interview that could be seen to be of much use and, after thanking Donny for the coffee and the information, they left.

Hinkley's home address was the next logical stop and, taking the F train to the corner of Delancy and Essex, Crowle looked round him eagerly, trying to spot any significant changes made since he had last been in the area. He always tried to store as many of these things in his mind as he could, not knowing when the knowledge might come in useful.

But there was nothing very different here from the last time. The same outdoor tables were piled high with garments and shoes of every possible description and Crowle glanced at them keenly, even suspecting that he recognized some of the clothes from when he'd last been here.

Detective O'Shaunessy took a more casual view of the place. To him, it was just the same Lower East Side with the same sagging tenements, the same dreary markets. So although both men saw the same things, they saw them in quite a different way and, as it was nothing at all to do with the case, neither man made comment on them. Had they happened to do so, however, there was one point at least upon which they would have agreed, this being how on earth these people contrived to make any kind of living. For they all appeared to be vendors.

The apartment was neat and clean, although, as Crowle reflected, there was no reason why it shouldn't be, Lower East Side or no. The woman, too, was neat and clean. Neither was she tearful, just letting them in with a quiet motion of the hand and, as Crowle did the talking,

214

O'Shaunessy glanced surreptitiously round the apartment. 'I know someone's already been, Mrs Hinkley...'

As far as they could make out, it was another wasted trip. Crowle had the thought, as they were coming away, that only door-to-door salesmen spent more time in useless talk ... *and* their journeys were usually shorter. Donny had told them as much as this. Right until the last second... On their way out, Mrs Hinkley, now staring into space, mused, 'Henry was happy with me. He'd been married before, you know.'

They didn't know and Sean started to turn back, but Crowle had recognized the signs. The woman was close to tears. The flood banks were about to burst and Crowle motioned his partner back to the door. They could find the information elsewhere. 'Would you like us to send someone, Mrs Hinkley? Welfare again, perhaps?' But Mrs Hinkley, face now buried in a handkerchief, merely shook her head.

The partners called for a bagel and cheese and then, talking of what little they had on the case, made their way back to the precinct. Things had happened. Menny Podowski was there. And there'd been another slaying.

It didn't take long to deal with Menny, any hopes that he might be of further help in the case soon being dashed. Thirty-five dollars had been found in his pockets, money which he said he'd earned, and whichever way you looked at it, thought Crowle, there couldn't be much argument there.

But there was no watch. When asked where he'd been all this time, Menny had also managed to look annoyed. 'Why?' he said. The query was a fair one. OK, so he had kept out of the way long enough for his stomach to settle down after his ordeal. And he had kept out of the way long enough to pawn the watch, and also to give the police time to find someone else to question or, as Menny liked to put it, to harass. So what? All it seemed to prove, to Menny and to everyone else, was that really the police had little else as yet to go on.

But there was another reason why he'd kept out of the way. Sly Menny had used the time thinking of other ways of coming up with something which might earn him a few more dollars. But he'd come up with nothing, although, at least, he had seemed to manage to put them rather on the defensive and, if nothing else, there was some satisfaction in that.

'Off you go then, Menny,' said Crowle at last and Sergeant Parkes decided to put his buck's worth in.

'You know the score, Podowski. No news. No dollars.' But when Menny had gone out of the door, the big Sergeant sat thinking, finally arriving at the conclusion that he'd come out of it all second best. And nodding sagely to himself didn't seem to help much, either.

Crowle was also thinking, trying to direct his thoughts into more profitable lines than those of the worthy Sergeant's but all he could come up with was that Menny was now out of the case. At least it was a hurdle jumped.

In certain situations, the passage of time seems to lessen the urgency. But with murder, it's just the reverse. Clues get trodden on and trails go cold. And this fresh murder was different. A high-flying lawyer's wife in Sutton Place had had her head bashed in. No sex. No robbery. A small, green label with a number on it had been found on the body. O'Shaunessy whistled. 'What was the number, Captain? Number one for a guess.' he said. Crowle also though this was a fair bet.

'Three,' said Thorne. 'Get down there, boys. And don't forget the kid gloves. This guy's got to be important.'

They took the Lexington subway, then walked the last part of the journey to Sutton Place. The address was a town house on the East Side and, looking at it, the partners were inclined to indulge in more whistling practice. Mason Adams looked what he was, a successful lawyer. Just at the moment, however, he was staring out of his big window at the East River. Shirt-sleeved and with his hands deep in his trouser pockets, he was obviously shocked, and deep in thought. Even big-shot lawyers aren't immune from tragedy.

Covered with a sheet, the body was in the same room and Department men moved around quietly which said a lot for the opulence of the surroundings.

The story was soon told. Household help, in the shape of a middle-aged Hispanic woman, had arrived to find the dead woman. She'd not panicked, but phoned in a nine-one-one, and then the lawyer at his offices. A heavy, bronze statuette had been used, at least one blow on each side of the head, caving the skull in. One blow would have been more than enough but the killer might not have known that. But as Mark Foster had said, when he came earlier, there wasn't really any evidence that the attack had been frenzied. Rather, determined.

The statuette lay where it had been dropped, covered in blood. The green slip of paper, perhaps with the three already on it, had then been deliberately stuck under the hair on the back of the neck.

The silver-haired attorney turned round, calm-faced. 'Terrible shock,' he said in an even voice. 'I hope you boys catch the bastard. I've told the others – there was nothing taken as far as I can tell. And I don't know of any enemies. Me perhaps. But not her. We weren't getting on that well but it was all quite civilized. We were both seeing someone else. But this. I just don't get it.'

Crowle took details of a son in Jersey, a vet, and of

the boyfriend of fifty-year-old Claire Adams. 'We'll catch whoever it was, Mr Adams. This type always gets caught. Too late for Mrs Adams, of course, and we can't say how sorry we are about that.'

The partners turned for the door, Crowle turning back on an impulse. 'How long have you lived here, Mr Adams?'

'Sixteen years. We came up here when I made it big.'

'And before that?'

'Greenwich Village. Is it important?'

'Well, something is, Mr Adams. We'll keep in touch.'

'What was all that about, John?' said O'Shaunessy, as soon as they got outside.

'Just a shot in the dark, Sean. There has to be a connection somewhere. At least I hope there is. That wasn't it, though. Hinkley lived in Brooklyn. Somewhere off Bushwick Avenue.'

'That's right, he did. But why did he cross the river? Was it to be nearer his work or was it his domestic affairs which caused the move? Not quite the same background as Claire Adams, anyway. Wait a minute though, John. We might be missing something here. Did Hinkley have any kids? Not much of a connection, I know, but...'

But Crowle was already shaking his head. 'No, Mrs Hinkley...' Then he stopped dead. 'Of course. Just because Mrs Hinkley was listed as having no kids, doesn't mean to say she didn't have step-kids. You're right, Sean. She did say he'd been married before. So much for the SBS. That didn't list any kids, either.'

'Yeah. I always said that thing doesn't beat good old legwork.' The big detective sounded pleased with himself and, in his turn, Crowle smiled inwardly, happy for his partner.

They thought their next move should be back to the precinct – check up on what they'd got, maybe report to the Captain, who may or may not make them catch up on other stuff. But happily, the good man was busy and Crowle wrote down what they had, item by item, on the blackboard:

Henry Hinkley. Waiter at Donnys, W.53rd. Married twice. Children? Present add. Orchard St L.E.S. Age 47. Murdered Yorkville. 18 Oct. Tuesday evening. Victim No. 2?

Claire Adams. Housewife. Sutton Place. Married. One child, now a vet in New Jersey. Victim's age, 50. Murdered at home. 21 Oct. Friday morning. Victim No. 3?

Crowle stared at the board, not wishing to cloud the issue by speculation, but at the same time searching his mind for some connection between the victims apart from the numbered slips.

'Nothing much yet, Sean,' he said at last as he picked up the phone. 'Let's ring Mrs Hinkley.'

He dialled and then nodded at his partner as the instrument was answered. 'Detective Crowle, Mrs Hinkley. How are you now?' There was a pause as she replied, then, 'I'm really sorry to bother you, Mrs Hinkley, but you said your husband had been married before. Tell me. Did he have any children by the marriage?'

He began scribbling on a pad, nodding at Sean again as he listened. He scribbled again and then, 'Thanks, Mrs Hinkley. Thanks very much.' He put the phone down and sat back. 'That's it, Sean. The lady sounds a bit calmer today, too. Poor woman. Hinkley did have a son. Came down yesterday to see about the funeral. Gone back home now though. He's a motor mechanic on Long Island. Queens. Should we go first thing tomorrow, Sean?'

'First thing, John.'

'It's a start, anyway,' Crowle said then, but there wasn't much conviction in the tone. Although he was quite aware of the dangers of habitual impatience in this job, he was also equally conscious of the fact that he could never quite help himself from indulging in the habit, and now, for no real reason at all, he was annoyed with himself that he couldn't yet see more possible connection in the slayings. He knew it would come, he told himself moodily as he stared at the blackboard, but then, so would Christmas.

'Come on, Sean,' he said. 'Let's go and see Claire Adams' boyfriend. We've time for that. If that's OK?'

'That's fine, John.'

But on their way out, they bumped into Henry Thorne. 'Right, boys, what have we so far then?'

Crowle explained briefly what they had, finishing, 'We're just away to see the boyfriend, Captain,' and moved quickly towards the door.

But Thorne was up to the situation. 'Hold it, boys. The paperwork? Can't wait. Not up to me, you understand.'

Crowle opened his mouth to speak but the Captain raised an imperious hand. 'Sorry, boys.'

But the partners weren't beaten yet. 'Tell you what, Captain,' said Sean quickly. 'I'll stay here and John can go. Give us a good start for tomorrow. And that Adams guy's a big shot. He could make waves.'

'I'm not bothered about that. The paperwork's important,' but as the Captain said it, he was rubbing his chin reflectively. 'OK,' he said then. 'Do as you think best,' and, shaking his head, he made for his office. 'For now!' he flung over his shoulder. Crowle winked at his partner and hurried to the outer door.

Timothy Pile was an insurance assessor, working for a large firm off 8th Avenue and, as Crowle remarked to himself, not far from the restaurant, Donny's, where Hinkley had worked. Pile was noticeably a similar type to

Mason Adams, smart and successful-looking. But just now, he looked decidedly out of sorts – almost haggard, thought Crowle.

'What can I tell you, Detective?' he said miserably, and it was, in fact, very little. He was obviously cut up by the business and the interview didn't last long. But as he was thinking that was about it, Crowle thought of one last thing.

'By the way, Mr Pile. Just to fill in the gaps. Where do you eat lunch?'

In his distress, the man showed no surprise at the question. 'Well, I'm often out of town, of course, but when I'm here I just send out for something. It's quicker. Unless I'm with a client, of course. Then we go to the Carlton. They know me there.'

'Thanks, Mr Pile.'

'Any time, Detective. Anything.'

Pretty shaken up, thought Crowle, as he left the building. There's no way he's our man. Too involved with just the one victim and, still mulling over what had been said, the Detective called for a sandwich and coffee before making his way back to the precinct to talk to Sean about it. But the big man was out, having found some excuse to leave the paperwork. Crowle had a word with Sergeant Parkes and with the phone girl but there were no messages, and so, seeing no way out of it, he sat down resignedly to try and clear some of the backlog. Thorne came through the office and, seeing Crowle doing this, smiled happily.

Arriving early next morning, Crowle sat at his desk thinking. Information was, as yet, rather thin on the ground and, in fact, there were no real clues. Two murders, so far as they knew, with just the same calling card. Nothing else. He looked up to see Sean coming in.

'Morning, Sean. Mrs Hinkley's stepson?'

'Right, John.'

On this particular morning, the chill, unseasonal wind had dropped and there was a bright, fresh sunshine. In spite of Long Island's notoriety for traffic jams, the partners really had no option but to go by car. They set out for Flushing, in Queens, with Crowle driving, making for the Midtown Tunnel with its two-and-a-half-dollar each-way toll and, as they went, Crowle filled his partner in on Pile, pointing out the man's self-despair and giving his opinion that the man was out of it.

A thought came to the big man. 'Why Hinkley's son, John? In preference to young Adams, I mean.'

'Well, Hinkley was murdered first, Sean, and as the Captain would say,' he grinned, 'first things first. Seriously, though, Sean, I should have been on to this sooner. But when Welfare said that Hinkley had no kids...'

'My fault as much as yours, John.'

'No, Sean. You let me do the running. Anyway, we're filling in the gap now. There's still no connection, of course – social background and so on. I just can't begin to fathom it out. It'll come though, Sean. It'll come.'

'Not just a nutter then, perhaps? One who bought or found some coloured slips? Picked them up from the sidewalk somewhere and didn't quite know what to use them up on? Gets high on drugs first, maybe?'

'Depressing thought, but I don't buy it, Sean. Yorkville and Sutton Place? No way. Which is another way of saying I hope to God not. Or we'll never catch the bastard.' His partner's suggestion, feasible as it was in this city, had depressed him a little and they rode in silence a while. 'Something else,' said Crowle, at last. 'We don't yet know why Hinkley was where he was when he was killed. We'll have to look into that one, Sean.'

'Already have,' came the surprising reply. 'That's where I was yesterday afternoon. While you were sat on your butt, John. Pretending to do paperwork?'

Crowle dug his partner in the ribs with his elbow.

'Oh, yes,' said Sean. 'Reason that Hinkley was where he was, was that he had an old buddy in the area who he used to visit quite often. Was due that evening but he never showed.'

'Hey, right. OK. Hm. I wonder if Donny knew of this habit of Hinkley's?'

'Sure he did. I went to see him as well. Said he assumed we knew. Covered ourselves by saying that of course we knew, but could he possibly confirm how often. He said about twice a week as far as he could remember.'

Crowle took his eyes from his driving for the briefest second to glance at the older man with a renewed respect. Was he himself, Crowle wondered, perhaps guilty of having associated Sean's age with some slight slackening of effort or even reasoning powers? He couldn't recall ever having consciously done so, so was it then possible that he was in the habit of overestimating his own qualities perhaps? If so, he knew that in this line of work, it would be a dangerous assumption. And this was as near as he could get to admitting that maybe, after all, he might not be the best detective around. Best remember that.

Crowle's mind then wandered to the general area they intended visiting and he snatched another glance at O'Shaunessy. 'Did you know, Sean, that the town of Great Neck is the West Egg of Fitzgerald's Gatsby?'

'Yes, John, knew that. Enjoyed the film version, too. Robert Redford.'

'That's right. But I think I preferred the older film. Alan Ladd. Who was that other guy in it? Ladd's pal.' Crowle screwed up his face in concentration.

'Macdonald Carey, John. It was Macdonald Carey.'

Crowle thought he'd better concentrate on his driving.

* * *

223

The neighbourhood of Flushing, in Queens, holds little interest for most New Yorkers unless they happen to have specific business there. It seems to have been increasingly taken over by the ethnic communities, although this didn't in any way prevent the partners from easily locating the garage where young Hinkley was employed.

Martin Hinkley was a thinner version of his late father. He had black hair and powerful-looking hands which, at present, were covered in motor oil. After introductions, Crowle got right down to it, the young man insisting they use his given name.

'Right, Martin,' said Crowle. 'First of all, we'd like to say how very sorry we all are and that's the truth. Then to apologize for the short notice, but you'll understand about that, of course, trying to keep on top of the case as we are.'

'That's OK, Detective.' Young Hinkley's grief seemed genuine enough. 'Have you any ideas yet?'

Crowle took a chance. 'Well, you don't strike me as a fella that'll go running to the press, Martin, so here it is. It looks like a serial killer.'

The young man's jaw dropped. 'No kidding.'

'No kidding, Martin. But quietly does it, eh?' Crowle knew that the killings had started to hit the papers but, from the little Thorne had decided to give them and omitting the numbered slips, there'd not been any headline stuff as yet. 'Tell me, Martin, did your father have any old enemies that you can think of? Even way back? Anyone at all? You know the sort of thing I mean. Business grudges? Domestic ones?'

Young Hinkley rubbed away at his dark chin, his grubby hands making it blacker than ever. 'Not a one. You see, Detective, he was such a steady sort of fella. Most times, anyway. He did go to pieces for a while when Ma left. Sort of wandered over here as I remember it. Of course,

224

it's all just a bit vague now. Then when he met his second wife, he crossed the river again. I opted to stay here and I haven't seen too much of them over the years. I did visit from time to time, of course. But I didn't know a lot about his affairs. Sorry I can't go further than that, Detective.'

Crowle was disappointed. He wasn't sure what he'd expected but it was more than this. He asked a few more questions but only in a rather desultory manner, before looking at Sean, who shook his head. 'Well, thanks anyway, Martin,' he said, 'and for what it's worth, we will catch the guy.' He remembered saying the same thing to Adams, but at the present stage of the game, Crowle wouldn't have bet on it. They didn't seem to be getting far at all. The breaks just weren't... 'By the way, Martin,' he said, on a sudden thought, 'whereabouts were you brought up? As a child?'

'Greenwich, Detective. We lived in Greenwich.'

Crowle didn't leap for joy, but he had all on not to. He made for the door of the workshop as he smiled at the young man. 'Thanks very much, Martin,' he said.

'That's it, Sean.' They were in the car, driving back. 'That's the break. It has to be. Greenwich. That's the connection.'

'Well, it had to come, John.' Sean settled himself comfortably in his seat. 'You just happened to dig in the right place. But what I couldn't figure is why you didn't question him further. About Greenwich, I mean.'

'I thought about it. But just for now, Sean, I thought we'd keep it to ourselves. We don't want to alert anybody and, as yet, we don't know who might be involved.'

'You don't suspect young Martin at all, do you, John?'

'No, I don't. Trouble is, I don't yet suspect anybody. Let's play our cards close to our chest for a while, eh, Sean?'

225

'Sure thing, John.' The older man settled himself even more comfortably in his seat, giving Crowle time to think. Crowle's mind drifted back to his long conversations on various cases with Don McKuen back in Colchester and, at last, a case with similarities came to mind. What was it McKuen had said? 'In the majority of such cases, John, look for a family connection.' Crowle wondered. Then he promised himself that at the first decent opportunity, he would write to McKuen about the case. The good DCI would appreciate that – the written word. Facsimiles and other such gadgets were OK in emergencies, he said, but they did tend to do away with the human element – the common touch. Funny race, those Brits.

The slaying of Citibank cashier Carl William Graham, in Battery Park, downtown Manhattan, was assumed to have been something of an opportunist killing – that is, until the green-coloured slip had been found on the body. Sergeant Montgomery, from the nearest precinct, had thought that all the circumstances pointed to it. It had taken place in daylight, presumably as the man was eating his lunch, and in these conditions easily approachable. But when the numbered label had been found, hurriedly stuffed under the shirt collar, Captain Thorne's station had been informed.

All this happened as the partners were returning from Queens and on their arrival Thorne told them to get down there straightaway. 'Things are hotting up, boys,' he said. 'This guy doesn't care who he hits.'

For this journey, the subway was quickest. They came out at Battery Park from one of the few booths still above ground, and then made their way to the murder scene, which wasn't too far from Castle Clinton. And still there, furiously chewing gum and dispensing instructions, Montgomery saw the pair approaching. 'Hey, Sean, you great oaf,' he shouted. 'How goes it?'

'Good to see you, too, Jim,' Sean answered. 'What's the deal?'

'Murder most foul, that's what. On my patch, too,' the Sergeant added indignantly, as though the killer should have had the forethought to choose his spot more carefully. The two Sergeants went back and, after these initial greetings, Montgomery became expansive, giving the partners all the information he could. It wasn't much. But he had found out about Graham. Fifty-three years old, the victim had been in the habit, in fine weather, of emerging from the gloomy canyons of Wall Street, to eat his lunch, take some air and perhaps watch the harbour traffic, from the pleasant environs of Battery Park. His home was in Brooklyn Heights where he lived with his wife. There were two daughters, both married.

The body had been found by one Harold Platt, a youngish barman on his break from Harry's, in Hanover Square. He'd seen an arm sticking out from the bushes.

Graham had been stabbed from the front with a folding knife. It had been driven upwards into the heart with considerable force. The knife had been left in the body, which had then been dragged behind the bushes. The green slip, crumpled a little, presumably in haste, had the number 4 on it and, on the ME's arrival, a few minutes after Montgomery, the killing had not been done more than twenty minutes.

All this was delivered with that kind of studied air, thought Crowle, that one might reserve for addressing a bunch of rookies. He also thought he saw, reflected in the Sergeant's eyes, that hitherto elusive lieutenancy which could possibly result from the quick solving of such a case. And the information was, after all, only bread-and-butter stuff.

Then Crowle pulled himself up short. He was being ungenerous, he chided himself. So far, Montgomery had done a good job. 'Have you let the barman go yet, Sergeant?' he asked.

'No. He's over there. Looks a bit shook up, of course. But he agreed to wait for you guys. And it's been quite a while now. Of course, we've let them know at Harry's.'

Crowle now really had to concede to himself that Montgomery had done as much as he could. Then his mind went off at a tangent as he hoped that it would be proved that Graham had at one time lived in Greenwich.

Harold Platt was of average build, wore thickish eye glasses and sported a rather untidy growth of hair on his upper lip. All this, thought Crowle, was perhaps somewhat in variance with the young man's hands which, though large, were not only shapely, but also finely manicured and well looked after. The hands of a pianist maybe, thought Crowle. 'Thanks for waiting, Mr Platt. Very good of you.'

'That's OK, Detective.' Platt was pale and, as Montgomery had remarked, still obviously very much affected by the whole thing. 'I don't suppose I'd be much good back at Harry's just now anyway,' he said then.

But in the second telling, thought Crowle, the barman might recall some other small incident. It sometimes happened.

But not this time. The Detective couldn't deduce another detail. As he'd already said, he sometimes came here from the bar as he had today, just for a breath of air. He'd seen the body and automatically looked round to see if there was anyone else in the vicinity. There were several people, quite close by too, some of them and in fact, some of these were still here at the scene, eager to go over their story again, to anyone who would listen.

But Crowle knew the disadvantages of clouding the issue with too much trivia. Platt's story was likely to be as useful as any and, thinking there was nothing else much of use to be gained here, the partners thanked Montgomery and left.

Brooklyn Heights. As the partners made their way back to the precinct, Crowle gave thought to the victim. The murder not having taken place in Thorne's patch, the partners wouldn't be obliged to visit the victim's wife and Crowle wasn't sorry about that. Any relevant details could be obtained elsewhere, such as how long Graham had lived there. Brooklyn Heights, Manhattan's first suburb and similar in so many ways to Greenwich with its restored brownstones and its gentrification.

Crowle had made a hobby of studying his city and he cast back in his mind, exercising it by trying to recall who'd lived there in the Heights. Whitman. Tom Paine. Auden. Yes, they were some of them, and the place attracted the Grahams of New York – to get away from the hubbub of the city for just a brief space each day, before plunging back into the maelstrom.

Christopher Street, Greenwich. Any last doubts Crowle may have had that Greenwich was the key to the whole case were now dispelled, for this was where Carl Graham proved to have lived before moving to Brooklyn. Christopher Street, eh? The end nearest to 6th Avenue. Crowle picked up the phone and dialled. 'Hello, Mr Adams? Detective Crowle here. Glad to have caught you.' He paused as the attorney enquired whether any progress had been made in the case and, having made the right noises, Crowle then asked his questions. 'Tell me, Mr Adams, whereabouts in Greenwich did you live? Barrow Street? Right. And what about Mrs Adams? Sorry to bring it all up again, but it is important. Milligan Place, you say? Right. And what was her maiden name? Chapman. Well, thanks a lot,

Mr Adams. You've been a great help. We'll keep in touch. G'bye now.'

'Just one thing, John,' said O'Shaunessy. 'Why did you ask him his wife's maiden name? We knew it was Chapman.'

'I'm not sure, Sean. I just wanted to get his reaction, I guess. But as far as I could make out, there wasn't any. He didn't pause at all. But he is a lawyer, of course. And we're still at the stage where we have to scrape all the bits off the wall.' Crowle still hadn't the faintest idea who the killer might be, but even so he knew that some kind of conclusion to the solving of the case was in sight. Had to be, for things were coming together. And this was the part he liked best, although whether or not this was a fault in his approach to the job he couldn't have said.

They couldn't wait to visit Greenwich. Even though the next day was Saturday and Crowle enquired of Sean whether he wanted a break, he knew that the big man was now as keen as he was himself. And Thorne was good like that – give and take and, should anyone disappear on private business at any time, he never balked much. The Department was based on trust. Except for the paperwork, of course. Then it was every man for himself.

Knowing the city as he did, Greenwich was one of Crowle's favourite places and he knew the Village as well as he knew every other district, perhaps even more so. Nancy, his girlfriend for over two years, lived here, at St Luke's Place, hanging on to her apartment even though prices in the area seemed to be almost spiralling out of control. She worked as a clerk, midtown, and Crowle knew they didn't see enough of each other, both of them wanting to get on in their jobs a bit first. That her qualifications were somewhat better than his own, he didn't mind a bit.

He brought his mind back to the case, knowing full well that they could have done a bit more digging before they actually came here, but, as Sean had said, it could prove to have been unnecessary anyway. They could hit lucky. So armed with what sketchy details they had, they made their way, via the 8th Avenue Line, to Washington Square.

Sean was no chatterbox and, once again, Crowle let his mind wander, in a kind of controlled therapy. Had any place in the whole of New York ever changed so much? he wondered. And what had the prevailing social conditions been here, at the time the murders had been instigated? That Greenwich was the key, Crowle would have put his last dollar on it.

Back in time even further went his musings – to the Square itself. In turns, he knew, it had been a cemetery, a site of public executions, a drug dealers' paradise – other things. He gave thought to all the famous artists and writers who'd lived here, making the mental observation as he did so that history, after all, is about people. And it's still a place of opposites, he thought, with its students, its gays, its broken-down shopfronts, its mews and its tree-lined avenues.

They called for coffee, both he and Sean smiling at one shop sign as they did so. It was called Kiss My Cookie. Then both men disappeared into the tangle of streets they were sure would give them some answers.

Milligan Place, where Claire Chapman had lived, is a good way from Mason Adams' Barrow Street, and Crowle thought that the latter might be discounted – after all, the husband hadn't been murdered.

Milligan Place is a cul-de-sac and the partners stood there, trying to decide where to start.

'Salesmen?' It was as though the woman had been waiting for them. Standing in the doorway of an old brownstone, she looked down her long nose, past her grubby apron and, from the top of three stone stops, issued her challenge.

'Police, ma'am,' said Sean, reaching for both his ID and his most winning smile, although, as it happened, neither inducement was needed at all, for as the woman gave him the once-over close-up her decision was already made. 'Come in, Sergeant,' she leered, ignoring Crowle completely and, though it was a command rather than an invitation, she was obviously having all on not to rub her hands in glee.

Crowle thought he ought to tag along anyway and, on the way in, all the partners had time for was an exchange of glances.

'Don't worry, Sean, I'll stick by you,' said Crowle with his eyes.

'You'd damn well better,' was the silent reply.

The partners sat down gingerly on the worn easy chairs. 'Just a few questions, ma'am,' said Sean, having put both ID and smile quickly away.

'Coffee?' Another command. She wasn't going to be rushed.

'Thank you, ma'am.'

The coffee was bitter and not too hot, but the men played around with it and the woman finally sat down. Her name was Mrs Parkes. 'Henry's been gone over four years, now.'

The big detective resisted the temptation to ask where. 'Sorry to hear that, Mrs Parkes. Mrs Parkes, tell me, did you happen to know a Claire Chapman who lived round here some time ago?'

It was the jackpot question first time and for the second time in almost as many minutes, the woman's eyes lit up. 'Did I know Claire Chapman? Of course I knew Claire Chapman. Everyone knew Claire. Long time ago now, though. Why, it must be...' She screwed up her eyes in concentration. 'It must be over fifteen years ago, now. Has to be. Lived right opposite me, she did.'

The partners grabbed a glance at each other. Decided to let her carry on. 'Fancy piece, our Claire,' she said then. 'Right fancy. Waitress somewhere, she was. Till she got married, that is. Married well, she did. A man from here in the Village somewhere. Businessman of some kind. What was her married name, now?'

'Adams, Mrs Parkes.'

'That's it. Adams. Moved away soon after they were married.' Her face now lit up again. 'What's our Claire been up to, anyway? Been getting herself into trouble, has she?'

'She's been getting herself murdered, Mrs Parkes.'

The woman looked up sharply and then fell silent, breathing hard. 'Why come here?' she asked at last in a soft voice.

'We have reason to believe it might have started here, Mrs Parkes. We're not entirely sure, of course. Not yet. And at this delicate stage in our enquiries, all this has to be kept in the strictest confidence, you understand. But we have to start somewhere and you look like a sensible woman. One who can keep her mouth closed.' As he said this, Sean couldn't resist sneaking a glance at his partner.

'Of course I can. Especially when it's anything as important as this.' Mrs Parkes still looked shaken up. Neither partner was insensitive to the situation but there was never really any easy way.

'Of course you can, Mrs Parkes,' Sean now went on. 'Tell me, did Claire have any enemies that you knew of? Anyone ever threaten her for any reason that you can remember?'

The woman shook her head slowly. 'No one that I can think of. Fancy piece she was, but nothing like that. There was Bill Edgar, of course. But that was such a long time ago.'

233

'Edgar?'

'Bill Edgar, yes. At the time of the suicide, you know.' Crowle took an involuntary breath but, sudden as it had taken him, he then leaned back deliberately in the old chair, tried to relax. This was it. It sometimes happened like this. Not often enough, but sometimes. He knew that just about every living adult had information tucked away in the dark recesses of their minds, events and memories almost forgotten until something jolted them out into the light.

Crowle jerked his mind back to the woman. Willingly but unknowingly, it may well be that she could crack the whole thing. Sitting there now, she was staring into space again, dreaming perhaps of the time of her youth. 'It all began with the teachers' strike, as I remember,' she said at last. 'They all went on strike, you know. A while back it was now, mind.' Crowle could remember the strike vaguely but he made no comment. Neither did Sean say anything. The woman was now doing fine and the partners didn't want to break the thread.

'It was comfortable round here then,' she went on. Used to neighbour a bit. Not nowadays, though. One of the teachers was young Evelyn. Nice young woman. Evelyn Hainsworth, her name was. Lived right here in Milligan Place. Worked at the school behind Patchin Place. The school's still there, you know. Anyway, Evelyn's husband died early on. I can't remember what of. Always worked hard, she did. Had to. And she never looked that strong. Not to me, anyway. More coffee, boys.'

Using the plural form was the first time the woman had bothered to acknowledge Crowle's existence. Not that she actually looked at him. Sean began to shake his head, but stopped himself in time. For it hadn't been a question. The woman was already on her feet.

Whether Mrs Parkes was capable of making hot coffee

was a question that was to remain unanswered. But as the partners made appreciative noises, smacking their lips over the tepid brew, the woman carried on happily with her story. 'Where was I now? Oh, yes. Young Evelyn. She had to come out on strike with the others, of course. I don't remember what the strike was about. Poor Evelyn. She did have a boyfriend, mind you, but he was away most of the time. He was in the Services. Army, I think. We didn't see him much. I told you before, didn't I? His name was Bill Edgar.

'Claire Chapman was the start of the real trouble. Her boy couldn't go to school, of course, and, being the kind of bitch she was, she blamed young Evelyn personally. Someone to pick on, you see. Someone who couldn't hit back. Used to rant and rave she did, whenever she saw Evelyn. Then, knowing what people can be like, others started picking on her, nothing serious, just tormenting her like. Harry Hinkley was one. Henry his name was really, but we all called him Harry. Lived on Gay Street somewhere. Had a lad at the school. Harry wasn't a bad man, but you know how folks can be. Poor Evelyn. She couldn't stand it. Hung herself in the house one night.

'People were horrified. Even Claire Chapman was badly shaken but, of course, it was too late by then. And that wasn't the end of it. Someone let the boyfriend know and he quickly appeared on the scene, found out what had been going on. Well, he went wild, swearing vengeance on all concerned. He came to see me. Had a list of names already – I don't know where from. All he asked me about was Claire Chapman. I didn't deny it. Why should I? Almost out of his mind, he was. But the police warned him off and away he went. I haven't seen him since that terrible time.

'The district was never quite the same after that.

Something else had died along with Evelyn.' Mrs Parkes fell silent.

Neither of the partners thought it necessary to mention Carl Graham.

Having toned down the colour, Crowle was staring at the SBS. 'The New York teachers' strike was caused by a social experiment which was to prove an utter failure. The blacks were to be given a bigger say in the education of their children, but most teachers were white and, in addition to this, a great many of these were Jewish. New York is easily the most Jewish city on earth and trouble was inevitable. In one Brooklyn area, a black administration was brought in and several teachers were suspended with the threat that they wouldn't be allowed to teach anywhere in the city. The Teachers' Union organized a strike for the opening day of term in September '68. Most went on strike for five weeks.

The whole thing was simply a confrontation between Jews and blacks...'

Not wishing to read any more, Crowle switched off the machine and sat thinking. Wondered if Edgar had changed his name. It might be a bit of a job finding him if he had. Now somehow on tenterhooks, Crowle reached nervously for the switch again. He knew that this was the moment he'd been edging towards. He fiddled with the keys, hitting the odd wrong one in his tension.

'Edgar, W.A., U.S. Army. Service Number 8743902. Rank on discharge, Sergeant. Record, exemplary. Date of discharge...' Crowle read on, his excitement mounting and, so far at least, Edgar hadn't changed his name. 'Last known address...' The address given was in New Jersey, not far from Cape May. This was it.

But suddenly, it was all too easy, too pat, and Crowle

became uneasy. A man like Bill Edgar, intelligent, an ex-Sergeant in the U.S. Army? He wouldn't be caught out like this and now feeling strangely despondent, Crowle picked up the phone to get in touch with the New Jersey police. There were other ways to get the information he wanted, but he thought this one might be the quickest. The call didn't last long. 'They're going to call back, Sean.'

They had coffee and waited. It wasn't long. Crowle put the phone down again and looked across at this partner and the tone of his voice was quite level. 'Bill Edgar, chicken farmer, was killed just over three years ago in a car accident.'

'They sure it's the same guy, John?'

'They're sure.' Crowle got up quickly, suddenly thinking of Nancy – how he would like to get away from the precinct for a while, forget the case for a time. 'I'm away, Sean. Monday, eh?'

'Monday, John.'

A small pile of finished paperwork lay on Crowle's desk, neatly placed on the left. He viewed it without satisfaction, before glancing with distaste at a pile of similar size, but unfinished – or rather, unstarted – on his right. And now restless with the idea of seeing the job through, he stood up, walked over to the blackboard and picked up the chalk. He knew he could have done the thing just as easily on the SBS but he wanted to write it down big, stand back and look at it. He wrote names, neatly and carefully, so that they would be easily readable. Menny Podowski. Donny. Mason Adams. Timothy Pile. Mrs Hinkley. Martin Hinkley. Mrs Parkes.

Crowle stood back, surprised there were so few names. Then, Sean was at his elbow. 'You've missed one, John.'

'Don't tell me, Sean.' He ran his eye down the list again. 'You don't mean Bill Edgar. He's dead, Sean.'

'Not Bill Edgar.'

'Who then? Wait. Of course. Adams' son. The vet in New Jersey. That's right. I didn't catch his name. New Jersey. Like Edgar.' Crowle was thinking furiously.

'We're on different tracks, John. I'd forgotten about young Adams, myself. No. I was thinking of Harold Platt.'

'Platt?' Crowle looked in the big man's direction but he was seeing something else. It was a bright light and his mind was racing almost painfully. He could once again see the young barman's face clearly, or what there was of it to see. That was it. The thickish eye glasses, the untidy moustache, the well-kept hands which had seemed to go so ill with the rest of him. The man had been in disguise and Crowle knew suddenly that Platt was the killer. 'That's right, Sean. And Harold Platt's the killer. Not that that's his name, of course.'

The two men stared at each other. 'He's our man, Sean, and I didn't even have his name down.' Crowle was now shaking his head as though to clear it of some nightmare.

'You sure, John?'

'Think, Sean. Think of the contradictions. The untidiness and the well-kept hands. The glasses. Did you notice how he peered? That young man doesn't wear eye glasses, Sean. No more than we do. And think of the body. Where it was found. You'd have had to trip over it to see it.' Crowle swore softly. 'Damn it, Sean. I should have seen it.'

'Well, I was there too, John, and so was Montgomery. And you've got to admit, the young fella had sand.'

'Yeah. That's what threw us, of course. Cool as ice. Killed Graham and then didn't have time to get away without being seen. And don't forget, Sean. The other passers-by didn't see anyone else. So Platt decided to make

238

himself very much in evidence – very much seen. And what better way to do that than by "discovering" the body. It all fits.'

Sean began laughing. Quietly at first but then enough to split his sides. 'Oh, dear. Oh, dear,' he managed at last.

'What is it, Sean?' asked Crowle, sourly. 'I'm sure we could all do with a laugh.'

'I was just thinking. Who's going to break the news to Thorne? Yes, Captain, we did have the man but...' The big man wiped his eyes. 'As senior man on the case, John, I've decided to delegate that task to you,' he finished.

'Yeah. You're a good friend, Sean,' Crowle said, but his own laugh was genuine enough.

'But who is he? Who is Platt?' asked Sean, settling down to business at last. 'Any ideas at all, John?'

'I don't know, but... Hey. Of course. It's just an idea, but... Do you know, Sean, I bet we've made the same damn mistake that we made with young Hinkley.' As he spoke, Crowle snatched for the phone book. But Mrs Parkes wasn't listed. 'Come on, Sean. We have to be too late, but let's try anyway,' and once again, the pair made for what they believed was the quickest route to Greenwich, Crowle explaining his idea to his partner as they went. He fretted some on the journey, too. What if Mrs Parkes was out? Shopping? Visiting a crony, perhaps? She certainly had news to impart and, even though she was under an oath of secrecy, there was surely no harm in dropping a few hints – with a promise of more to come later.

As the partners approached the house, Crowle, his whole mood lightening, decided to tease the Sergeant. 'You know, Sean,' he said seriously, 'I think you should interview Mrs Parkes on your own, while I have a nose around the street. I'm sure you'll get plenty out of her.'

'You're probably right,' Sean grinned back. 'I do have

a way with the ladies. But I think we'll conduct this one on the doorstep. We are in a hurry after all.'

'Come in, Detectives.' To Crowle's immense relief, Mrs Parkes was at home, twitching the curtains in readiness and making the detective wonder absently at what hour she did the housework.

'Perhaps next time, Mrs Parkes. We are in a dreadful hurry,' said Sean, and Crowle thought that he couldn't have put it better himself. But the mouth closed like a trap and she just stood there, holding the door open and refusing to be even partly mollified by vague promises of further visits.

Over lukewarm coffee, with Crowle wondering whether it was part of the same brew they'd had before, Sean got down to business as soon as he humanly could. 'Tell us, Mrs Parkes. We're just trying to establish the full picture. Did Evelyn Hainsworth have any children?'

At the everyday nature of the question, the disappointment appeared quickly on the woman's face. Perhaps she thought she was going to be made privy to some murkier titbit, considering her importance in the case. 'Yes. Didn't I say last time? There was a boy. Richard. About ten I think. Or a bit under. Why?' and the tone of her voice said it all.

'Like I said, Mrs Parkes. We're just trying to get all the facts together. What happened to the boy? After the tragedy, I mean?'

'Taken into care as far as I remember.'

The only thing now, was to get away as fast as they could. It was obvious that she could help them no further and, appeasing her as well as they could by further half promises, the partners left. But she was not a happy woman.

* * *

240

As they walked across the pleasant, tree-lined Square towards Harry's Bar, Crowle's mind was busy. He was mentally berating himself for not being on to this sooner. The introduction of Bill Edgar into the case had muddied the waters a little of course, and this fact made him feel a bit better. And, he supposed, once Edgar was out of the picture, he had been onto the idea of Evelyn Hainsworth's offspring quick enough. There was some comfort in that, too. And, after all, most folks had 20/20 vision after the event.

Their pace across Hanover Square in the mid-afternoon sunshine was leisurely, for there was no chance now of catching the killer – they knew that. They might as well have stayed for more nearly hot coffee at Mrs Parkes. At least that would have brought a little sunshine into somebody's life and after all, she was entitled. For she had played no small part in cracking the case. And he knew there would be no more killing.

So there was no hurry and, as it turned out, there was no Harry either but an Alan Birbeck, middle-aged, smart, and just a little harassed. 'Yes, Detectives. Harold had to leave quickly. On Friday night. Family business, he said.' The partners had expected nothing much different and they let the man carry on. 'He was only temporary anyway and not really very good at the job. Left me in a bit of a fix, though. Till I get someone else. He was honest, mind. In fact, I got the idea that he wasn't much bothered about money at all. Got the notion that he was a writer or something. You know. Doing research. Didn't say much, though. About anything.'

'Did he leave anything behind at all?' asked Crowle.

'I doubt it. But you can take a look in his cupboard in the back room if you like. I haven't had time and, anyway, he didn't actually say he wouldn't be back. He was in such a hurry, like.'

The cupboard turned out to be little more than a box and it still had the key in the door. Crowle knew there would be no prints but he opened the tiny door with a handkerchief anyway. Inside was a short, white jacket, neatly folded, a pair of glasses with rather thick lenses and a letter. The envelope said 'To the Police'.

Birbeck gaped. 'I'm sorry, fellas. I didn't know...'

'That's OK, Mr Birbeck,' said Sean. 'You weren't to know.' He didn't think it necessary to add that they hadn't known themselves until a very short while ago.

'Harold in trouble, then?'

'We're not sure. Whose are the glasses?'

'Not the foggiest. Never seen them before.'

The Sergeant nodded and, indicating that he'd finished, looked across at his partner. 'Tell us, Mr Birbeck,' said Crowle. 'Did Mr Platt have a beard, or anything?'

'Clean shaven, Detective.'

The partners thanked the man and left.

The letter was spread out on Montgomery's desk, the pair just having caught him leaving his precinct. Crowle had pulled the letter from his pocket but he let Sean do the talking. 'Shall we all read it together, Jim?' the big man asked.

'Sure thing, fellas.'

Almost illegible at times, the odds were that the handwriting had been disguised, like the man himself had been. Neither was there anything in the presentation to tell whether or not the writer had been well educated – another matter for conjecture. Nothing sure so far, then.

'Detectives,' it said, 'the killing has finished. I was only just in time too and I know that Friday was a close-run thing. I was worried there for a moment. But I got those who did for Ma. The hard part, after all this time, was finding out where they all lived. Luckily for me, they all still lived in New York. I am sorry for those they left behind. I am not a bad person and don't worry about victim number one. That was me. I changed my name. I'm a new citizen and I work regular. But I had to do something. It wasn't right, not after what they did to Ma. The authorities did nothing. For the record, I killed three people.' The letter was simply signed 'Platt'.

John Crowle had not only finished his paperwork; he had also written a long letter about the case to DCI McKuen, his friend in England. He stretched his arms out in satisfaction and looked across at Sean, wondering when he would be working with him again. O'Shaunessy was hunched across the keyboard like a terrier worrying a rat and with about as much love. His unfinished pile, for all his efforts, never seemed to get any smaller.

'I wonder where he is now:' said Crowle softly.

The big man stopped tapping straight away. 'Do you think he lives here in New York, John?' he asked, his face warm and agitated from his efforts.

'Anybody's guess. But I think not. Otherwise, I think he would have acted sooner. Remember what the letter said. The hard part was finding out where they all lived? The one I feel sorry for now, though, is Thorne. Wondering what he'll say to people like Adams. And those upstairs.'

'That's how it goes, John. That's his job.'

'Yeah.' Crowle paused. Then: 'Something else, Sean, if you think about it. Not only did we not catch the guy, but neither did we crack the case until it was all over.'

'I thought about that and there's a good reason. There was nothing to bite on. No sex motive, no baking soda crack, no greed. Just a crackpot with an addled brain and driven by hate. What real chance did we have?'

'Yeah.' The pause was lengthier this time and finally, Crowle glanced at his watch. Tuesday. 2.15 p.m. 'I've had enough today, Sean. I think I'll go and see if I can catch Nancy. Get her to leave a bit early. Treat her to a steak or something.'

'Hey, John. You could just give me a hand here with the paperwork. As a buddy?'

But Crowle was already passing through the doorway.

A little way from the centre of Marina City in Chicago, Illinois, stands the North Western Memorial Hospital and, here in reception, with her raven locks and her Latin profile, Maria Burillo was on duty. In her beauty and her starched whites, she looked almost out of place, giving the impression that the whole scene might have been a film set. And the cameras could just have started rolling as her great eyes now lit up as they flashed towards the entrance, towards the youngish man just coming through the door.

Of middle height and good looks, he approached the desk briskly.

'Good morning, Maria, you ravishing creature. How much have you missed me, then?' His tone was confident, assured.

'Oh, good morning, Dr Jacques. I haven't see you for a while. Have you been away then?' she asked archly.

'For three long weeks and there wasn't a single day went by when you weren't in my thoughts.'

'I'll bet. How was the break then? Seriously, Mark. New York, wasn't it? How was the big city?'

'Busy. And violent. The Apple's not really the place for a rest. Perhaps, after all, I should have gone elsewhere.' He was more serious now.

'Well,' said the girl, serious in her turn. 'That's all the

244

rest you're likely to get for a while, Mark. The work's piling up as always. Have you got your little knife ready?'

'I suppose so,' said the house surgeon. He held up his hands and looked at them as he spoke.

They were large, well-kept hands. And beautifully manicured.

Wendy Lowe Goes to the Dogs

It was always the same – always this last, most inaccessibly placed nut on the entire bogie frame that was the hardest one to crack. And leaning awkwardly across the deeply rusted girder as he had to, merely to locate the nut, let alone hold his chisel on it, Kevin Lowe found it impossible to swing the two-pound hammer with any real power. In this severely restricted space, it was all he could do to tap away viciously at the chisel head. Cursing didn't seem to help much, either.

But the nut began to crack at last and Kevin kept at it, ignoring as best he could the skinned knuckles which were black with grease and goodness knows what else besides. The air was stale, too, which didn't improve matters. For here, near the canal, in the last remaining railway workshop in the market town of Fawkley, nothing seemed to work properly any more. Lack of proper maintenance in the whole system was the cause, of course, and such conditions were bound to have an effect, sapping the strength, shortening the temper. And tapping away at the three-quarter nut as he was doing, Kevin's feelings in the matter were no less frustrated than any other of the 'lifters'. For this wasn't really his job, this hammer-and-chisel stuff. He was a lifter and the rest of his team was waiting. Piecework was piecework after all, and the fitters, whose job this really was, weren't going fast enough.

The nut flew off at last and Kevin knocked the bare bolt out of the frame with one more blow.

'About bloody time 'n' all.'

Of course, it had to be 'Big Mouth' Blaney, and Kevin answered by gesture alone, raising the back of a fist in Blaney's direction, with the middle finger alone being held upright. Even Blaney, stupid as he was, would get that message, and the rest of the team were already grabbing the hooks from the overhead crane, ready to clamp them under the bogie, ready for lifting. All hooks in place, a shout to the craneman above was now enough to see the bogie being lifted from the axle boxes, then swung over for agitation in the evil-smelling wash tank.

It had probably been done like this since before the turn of the century and it was all very predictable. But not for much longer. At one time, not too long ago, a good day's work had been almost as satisfying as receiving the Friday pay packet. But not any more. It had started with threats, hanging over the place like heavy skies – rumours of closure which soon erupted into the clouds of reality.

Closure was announced and was already under way, but piecemeal, like a cat playing with a mouse. For there was never any exact intimation of when the next blow would fall. Or where.

Kevin's shop was now the last one in work and, during the working day, these thoughts could never be shaken from the men's minds, taking toll on their strength like a nagging backache or a persistent creditor. And in Kevin's case, and on this particular day, the feeling continued till after knock-off. He walked towards the bike sheds, the gloomy remarks of old Arthur Reeves, walking at his side, going over his head unheeded.

Arthur's remarks had never carried much importance, changing little over the years. Grumbling had always been his pleasure, although now, as Kevin had to admit, Arthur did have the advantage of cause.

'Sorry, Arthur. What was that?'

'I'm just saying. The bastards. They don't care, y'know.'

'That's very true, Arthur,' Kevin replied absently, sinking further into his own reveries. As he walked, he looked at the brickwork on the side of the shop, stretching endlessly before him. He looked at the dust, the same dust which may well have been there for years but which, before today, he'd never really noticed. It was industrial dust, large-particled and sharp. It was of no known colour and it was dead and at this time of year, early April, clammy to the touch.

Kevin had spent years of his life in this shop. It had always had its own sounds – sung its own praises – and Kevin had been part of the percussion section, happily swinging his two-pounder. But now the place just moaned like a lost child, or like an old man worried that no one would come to his wake.

The shop was now behind them and they were passing the thirty-foot chimney, the servant of the 'fire-hole', an incinerator where the works' rubbish had always been burned. The thing had been built for this very purpose, probably never being strictly within the limits of the law. But being quite a pace from the public highway, no one had ever complained, and a good man at the job, once he'd got it properly lit, could keep it going all day with hardly any visible smoke at all.

How many more times would it be lit, Kevin wondered? How many more labourers from the shop, gladly waiting their turn to tip their laden barrows, ready for the contents to be shovelled into the firebox, would stand round the blaze, shielding faces with hands rather than back away from the blast as they regaled each other with last night's cavortings?

'Got 'er up against the back gate, I did. Better than 'er 'usband, a lot, she said. An' that's after I'd 'ad four pints an' got most of the way through a Chinese.'

Kevin smiled at the memories, his former mood lightening a little. Arthur and he were now passing the boiler house where Sam Lipton, given much less than half a chance, would take a good three-quarters of an hour to tell you why his greyhound, a bitch called Sarah, had lost her last race, just about everyone else in the sport, excepting himself, being crooked.

'G'night, Arthur.' Kevin got his bike from the rack and wheeled it past the gatehouse where Frank, the watchman, didn't even look up from his paper as the men streamed out. He hadn't done so for quite a while, now. Perhaps he's dead, Kevin said to himself, grinning at last.

An hour had passed and, at just about the time that certain people were kneeling down to face the east, Kevin was following his own conventions, studying his face in the bathroom mirror. It was now a clean and freshly-shaven face and as unprepossessing as it had ever been. He was to study each feature in turn, as though, during a day's work, he'd forgotten what he looked like. Each bit came under quick scrutiny – the forehead, curiously lined in one so young; the eyes, two, brown and intelligent; nose, shapeless and mud-coloured, as though added as an afterthought from bits left over.

Kevin went through the whole bit, although nowadays, and well before the muezzin had finished his cries from the lofty heights of the minaret, it was soon done. For of late, he couldn't bring his mind to it the same. Shame, for it had all been a pleasant game, this whiling away the minutes in this way whilst his body wound down from the day's efforts. Men did things. Some knelt down facing the east and Kevin studied his face in the bathroom mirror, whilst others no doubt engaged in their own rites – studying the racing page, perhaps. It was the order of things. But now the yards were to close and the order was changing. From the first hesitant whispers to the later certainties, history was gathering pace, and history, after all, is about people. The yards, upon whom so many depended, were to close ... had begun to do so ... had almost all.

Some men had fled quickly, anxious to get whatever spare jobs might be available elsewhere. Others, like Kevin, had hung on, though unable to say why. Perhaps each morning, the freshness of daylight had brought a frisson of hope – a sudden speck of possible reprieve. But then, as the shops had closed, one by one, this had turned, upon waking, into a daily pang of despair, and the few remaining men, as they entered the yards each morning, would wonder – would it be today? The bold statement on the shop noticeboard. Or the sly slip of paper behind each clocking-in card, skulking there in guilt until the very last second.

It had never been a luxurious existence, here in the shops, but every man shuddered at the alternatives. And in Kevin's case, his mind had wandered, and now, rather than spend the whole of his daily few minutes in studying his face in the mirror, he'd lately taken to the practice of using some of the time in counting his real blessings, listing them off on his fingers. One – Wendy and young Derek. Two – his health. Three – his friends. Four – his social life, i.e. his club and his vintage car.

'Dinner, Kevin.' The soft cry from the bottom of the stairs shattered his thoughts.

'Right, love.'

Wendy Lowe was a special kind of woman. Although but average in face and form, if there is such a thing, she could mix quite comfortably in any kind of company, easily capable of adjusting her conversation to any level

251

required, but was perhaps even more important, always quite willing to do so. And although essentially a home person, a good wife and mother, a superb cook and a competent manager of resources, she was also a very fair contralto and with her special friend, Liz Peach, enjoyed continued pleasure in the ranks of the Fawkley Amateur Operatic Society, which said body tended to lean to Gilbert and Sullivan.

But perhaps her most outstanding talent was in her ability to get on with animals. She should have been, could have been, a vet, but a domineering mother, constantly and plaintively bemoaning the death of Wendy's father when the girl was three (selfish man), had convinced her daughter, in her youth and her sympathy, that they should stay together, rather than 'run off to some big, strange place where goodness knows what went on'.

Then, still only average in appearance and quite uncaring of fashion, Wendy had met Kevin. The awakening had come and after making love one night in the unlikely precincts of the churchyard on the west side of the railway yards, Kevin had proposed and she'd accepted, making the plea that her mother should live with them.

Kevin would have none of it. He'd been to the house but once to meet the lady in question – seen her smiling complacently as she counted her pills for 'my terrible arthritis', seen her unable to take most of her attention off *Coronation Street*, but still quite confident of her loving daughter's alliance.

'No, Wendy,' he'd said. 'She'd destroy us within six months.'

And that was the moment when Wendy's intuition had leapt easily over any parental duties, innate or not. Indeed, later reflection had resulted in the conclusion that she would have been more than dismayed had Kevin reacted in any other way.

The older woman had ranted and raved, pleaded and cajoled. To no avail. Wendy wouldn't even argue the matter with her. It was a waste of mental energy. At the wedding, the woman would scarce acknowledge the existence of Kevin's parents. No one was very much worried, though. 'She'll come round, Kevin,' Wendy had said.

And eventually the woman had.

In the early days of the marriage, Wendy had also been slyly reticent in airing her considerable mental capacities in case Kevin might come to resent them in some way. Such things did happen. But not unintelligent himself, Kevin had soon become aware of what she was capable and, rather than otherwise, had revelled in the fact – proud to have such a wife and more than willing to leave all major domestic decisions in her hands whilst he went to work.

A pattern was quickly established and any remaining doubts Wendy may have had as to her real reasons for marrying Kevin were soon cast aside. She quickly came to adore her husband, mud-coloured nose and all. The marriage had bloomed.

'Wendy, that was superb,' he said. 'What was it?' Kevin wiped his mouth with his napkin, as expected. They always had napkins at dinner. Much better than using the back of your hand, much more civilised, and, in fact, it was now quite a while since he'd even had to think about it.

'Did you really like it, my dear?'

'As I said, Wendy, it was superb. Not that it would be easy to surpass yourself.'

In the privacy of their home, he liked to talk like this – express his constant appreciation. Both of them knew that it was a little flowery and they both loved it. She smiled at him fondly and got up to serve dessert. 'Well,' she said, 'it was smoked-trout fishcakes with lemon. What about you, Derek? Do you like it? Are you almost ready for dessert?'

The nine-year-old was still stuffing his mouth. He tried, not too successfully, to say, 'Yes, Mum', which was all he could manage and which in its brevity anyway could have meant 'yes, he did like the fishcakes' or 'yes, he was almost ready for dessert'. Or perhaps it meant something else.

'How many times have I told you, Derek? That you don't necessarily have to stuff your mouth in order to enjoy your food?' Had he dared, it was a statement Derek might have contested. 'And your father agrees. Don't you, Kevin?'

'Your mother's right, son,' Kevin said primly. 'You know it's not good manners.'

Now just about able to answer at last, the boy said, 'Sorry, Mum. It was that nice, though.'

Serving dessert, a pear and almond tart, Wendy didn't say anything else. For she was now mentally busy in going through the whole meal calorie-wise. She'd already done it once, but now she went over it a bit more carefully, knowing that it had been a good bit over the top and, although she refused to make a big thing over the issue generally, she would remember to balance the meal slightly on the morrow, a little less mouth-watering though it might prove to be.

But for today the boy could hardly wait. And Wendy, thinking back to when he'd been born, just eight months after the wedding, couldn't resist stroking his hair. Eight months, and Wendy's mother, having already learned her lesson, had only dared sniff. Just the same, there was no denying that the woman had quickly come to idolize the boy, having him to stay with her often and showering on him the affection that she seemed to have withheld from her daughter.

After Derek, no other children had come along and neither parent had worried about this unduly. They enjoyed a decent standard of living and Wendy would say that there was no such thing as an only child, providing that the parents spent plenty of time with the one that was there. This was why she had never even considered going out to work full-time and, always being aware of the situation, often wondered if the boy was really happy, once broaching the matter with Kevin, who'd tried his utmost to look wise. 'He seems OK, love,' had been Kevin's contribution at last.

Her dessert as yet untouched, Wendy looked wistfully out of the window. She was never quite sure.

She returned her glance to the boy once more and Derek, caught unawares again with bulging cheeks and misinterpreting the look from his mother, could do no more than smile and nod as convincingly as he could.

Wendy relented, appearing to be thinking of other things, until at last: 'What is it tonight then, Derek?' and having chosen her moment, he was able to answer quite clearly.

'Football with Tom and the rest, Mum.'

'Homework?'

'Yes, Mum.'

'In for half-eight then. You know that, don't you?'

'Yes, Mum.'

His mother nodded, the lull in the conversation allowing Derek to transfer, once more, a generous portion of pear and almond tart to his mouth. Wendy had been about to enquire about the content of his homework, but seeing that she had misjudged the timing by about half a second, she decided not to be so unkind. Then, a knock on the front door precluded any further thought on the matter. 'That'll be Carol Jacques,' she said, jumping up from the table. 'Calling for Buffer. She's a bit late.'

She went to the door and Kevin heard the two talking. '...Stuck in the traffic...'

Buffer was a schnauzer, one of four dogs Wendy looked after in the yard whilst their owners went to work. Listening to the two women talking, Kevin was reminded of the time when it had first started. Liz Peach was a hairdresser with her own business and, although the place was open all day, she only usually went in herself in the afternoons. Wendy had worked at the checkouts in the supermarket at the time, mornings only. Liz had asked her if she would like to take care of her dog in the afternoons, take it for walks and so on. The dog got bored in the shop and Liz would pay her well. Then one day soon afterwards, Liz had asked if she would consider taking more dogs, for customers who worked. They would pay well, but it was all day. Wendy said she would talk it over with Kevin.

Looking wise, Kevin had listened without comment. 'What about the problems, love?' he'd asked at last.

'Yes, Kevin. I've already given thought to those.'

Kevin had sighed with relief, for the remark meant that not only had his wife thought about them but had also decided on exactly what action to take and merely awaited Kevin's assent to the venture. So he'd nodded at last in a thoughtful way and also, to give her his full backing, he had said, 'Right then, my dear,' in a profound undertone, just as though he were still pondering the issue.

Most of the requirements had been settled easily. Kevin had put a rug at the open end of the garage in case of rain. The dogs could sit in there in comfort.

The immediate neighbours had been consulted. Joe Bratton was an old man with an old man's problems. Wendy did a bit of shopping for him and he'd seemed surprised when asked if he would mind a few dogs next door. 'Eh? Oh, no, Wendy. Stick 'em in my yard if you like. Keep the cats off my cabbages.' Joe cackled at his own joke, never having been known to disturb his tiny plot with anything more suggestive of action than an old deckchair. On the other side, Herbert Clarkson and Molly had said, 'Not at all, Wendy. Keep the tinkers away, eh?'

Just the same, Wendy was more than aware of what good neighbours she had. But after four months there was still the one thing outstanding. The council. Like the good citizen she was, Wendy had called in. But to her amazement, there hadn't even been a form to fill in – either in isolation or in the more familiar triplicate. It appeared that no one got a form on the first visit. But the young lady in the moleskin trouser suit had assured her that the matter would be passed on to the relevant department. 'Yes, Mrs Lowe,' the girl had said, tapping her lips with alternative fingers so that Wendy would be able to admire the purple nail varnish which may well have been the colour of the month. 'I'll see to it personally.' Who else? thought Wendy, but aloud she said her thanks and left. And the girl had been true to her word, for a mere nine weeks later, with incredible efficiency, a form had indeed dropped on the front mat.

Ah, thought Wendy, and what would life be without forms? '... A business on the premises...' Yes, this was the right form, and she started at the beginning. 'It has been brought to our notice...' Wendy did bridle a bit at that, but she duly filled the thing in and posted it back the same day.

Since then, nothing. Not a word. She had remarked on the matter to Liz. 'Ah, yes' that lady answered. 'They're probably working on the usual philosophy of "if it's not broken, then don't fix it".'

But Wendy knew that the present carry-on was living on borrowed time – that the form had to reach the right department eventually, and then, if she knew anything about it at all, the wheels would begin to grind. But as there was nothing further she could do herself, she put the matter from her mind.

Kevin heard Carol Jacques' car start up as she and her schnauzer made for home. It wouldn't now be long before he would be seeing Graham Ogden. Alternating the weeks, they would spend Monday evenings in either one garage or the other, working on that person's vintage car. They were both men who worked happiest with their hands and as they also enjoyed each other's company, there were very few missed Mondays.

It was Kevin's car tonight and he glanced at the clock. Twenty minutes to go and, as he didn't even have to walk the few doors to Graham's, he picked up the paper. He could hear Wendy in the kitchen, washing the pots. Every other working day, he would insist on doing the pots but, on Mondays, she always made him sit down for this few minutes after dinner. 'After your first shift in the yards, love,' she would say.

He could also hear her doing a flask. She usually brought coffee to the garage but a flask meant there was something on telly she wanted to watch without interruption. Kevin wondered what it was tonight and he turned idly to the telly page. Yes, there it was. John Thaw, Wendy liked John Thaw.

Stood in the doorway of the garage waiting for Graham, Kevin was in no hurry, quite content to stare at the 1937 Singer saloon which, all those years ago now, had been little more than a pile of rust. He recalled being rather alarmingly dismayed when, at the auction, Graham had said it could be restored. They'd brought it home in a borrowed furniture van, as they had Graham's Lanchester and, for weeks, Kevin had still been nowhere near convinced. But since then, the car had undergone several major operations. Countless minor ones too, and today it had really started to assume its proper identity and Kevin's joy had grown with its progress. Not that the job was anywhere near finished, but the body now shone with pride and, apart from the transmission and one or two other mysteries, the internal organs positively pulsed with health. But there was still some welding to do, as well as some bits of tapping out. Things of small account and, in his mind, Kevin cast these aside, dwelling rather on the motor's specifications.

For the period, he knew that the car had a roomy body with a twelve-horsepower unit to pull it along at a very respectable seventy. Overhead valve with . . . Kevin's thoughts were suddenly interrupted by the faint smell of pooch wafting up to his nostrils, causing him to sidestep his ponderings. It wasn't really an unpleasant smell and he knew that Wendy took the dogs out every afternoon. What a woman she was, he thought, as he pushed the doors open as wide as they would go. For the schnauzer was only the runt of the bunch. There was a standard poodle, a German shepherd, and one of those leggy, hairy things of which Kevin could never remember the name.

Wendy would take them out religiously for an hour, rain or shine, locking the garage carefully and herding the brutes together. Kevin remembered having been with her twice, as he was getting over a flu cold. If any of the dogs happened to forget itself enough as to growl at herself or, indeed, either at one of its companions or a passer-by, she would tap the animal smartly across the nose with a rolled-up newspaper she carried. Any droppings were picked up with a plastic bread bag.

The back gate clicked open and he heard the crunch of Graham's welding barrow on the yard. He heard him negotiate the thing smartly round the old family Cortina, for which, since the arrival of the dogs, there was no room in the garage, big as it was.

'Good evening, Graham.'

'Good evening, young man.'

At thirty-three, Kevin was the junior by three years, but the greeting was always the same. For in most things, Graham was a man of habit.

'And how are we this evening, then,' said Kevin.

'Not too warm,' Graham answered. 'Chilly on those building sites just now.' He was a good-looking man, not as stocky as Kevin, but a good two inches taller. And he was fast losing the black hair on his handsome head. A joiner by trade, he had to take work where he could get it, especially nowadays. But he hated the building sites. The materials they gave him to work with were hardly of top quality and, in fact, the timber was, on occasion, almost green, and Graham knew that on several of the jobs it would soon warp. The workmen would get the blame for this, of course, like a concert pianist being asked to perform on a faulty instrument.

But Graham Ogden had a family to keep and so there weren't too many options.

Both he and Kevin Lowe had been teammates, playing football for the Fawkley Clerks, and the two of them, each recognizing the basic honesty of the other, had become firm friends, this being cemented in the mutual interest in old cars. Bangers, really. And staunch Methodist though he was, even being accused by some of his teammates of being a bit stuffy – by which was meant that he wouldn't get roaring drunk, even after a home win – it was he who had proved the most venturesome of the two, being the first to actually buy the real challenge, the vintage Lanchester, at the auctions.

Goggle-eyed, Kevin had been with him and, as he looked

at the pile of junk, he said the first thing that came into his mind. 'Graham,' he said, 'it's a pile of junk,' and that, he thought on reflection, was no exaggeration at all.

From that day on, however, Kevin's admiration of his friend had never ceased to grow. The man was clever, honest and tolerant and, as Kevin knew, there weren't too many like that around. They had finished playing for the team together, making way for younger men and spending their energies on the cars instead.

'Right. Let's get inside, then.' Kevin helped to push the welding bottles in, before pulling the garage doors together and lighting the big paraffin stove. Then, before starting work, they stood looking at the clean lines of the Singer for a while, each busy with his own thoughts. But these were very similar in content, for they were reminding themselves of the hours they had spent, on the new skills they had been bound to acquire. Having gazed critically at each part of the car, these parts now coalesced into the whole, and it was now more than a car. It was a bond between the two men. For neither of them would really have wished to work on such a project alone.

They worked for an hour after that and then sat down to share the flask, having to wave a hand in front of their faces to try and clear the air a little, which was blue and acrid from the fumes of the welding. The paraffin stove had long since been turned off. The job had gone well tonight and they talked as they rested. But Kevin's mind was only partly on the conversation. For he was wondering how long all this could last. He would hate to have to give it up but, in the present climate, there were no guarantees. Once he was finished in the yards, he might even have to work shifts, should he be lucky enough to get a job at all.

The two stood up together, ready for the final stint of the evening, but though he tried not to show it, Kevin was now a little depressed. For this was all very pleasant.

'G'night, Arthur.' Tonight Kevin couldn't wait to get rid of the old man. For his rambling was getting worse, Kevin was sure of it. And you can't close your ears. You can close your mouth, thought Kevin, and your eyes, but not your ears. Mother Nature had slipped up somewhere. Perhaps she hadn't had to contend with Arthur, though. And Kevin wanted to think.

But as he dashed for his bike, he was gracious enough to wonder just how unhappy Arthur's life really was. Strange. All these years and he didn't know the man at all. But grabbing now at his bike, he was suddenly reminded of the weight swinging against his back, for wrapped in newspaper in his lunch bag was one of Graham's headlamps, newly coated in the chrome shop. Two pounds Kevin had slipped the man and the lamp now shone like the morning sea. He hoped the watchman wouldn't notice the bulge and start asking awkward questions, but as he rode past the gatehouse on one pedal – for no one was allowed to ride in the yards – he saw that he needn't have bothered. For Frank was still dead.

But then, behind the newspaper, Kevin saw a finger twitch. Some stage of rigor mortis, thought Kevin. Then he tried to imagine what job Frank might apply for, once the yards were finally closed. Artist's model, perhaps. For the man could certainly keep still. But just as he was congratulating himself on his ready wit, Kevin quickly pulled himself up short. For this isn't why he'd wanted to get rid of Arthur. He had to get down to it. The time for pondering was over, for when the chop finally came, as it soon must, what would he do? He must think.

He stopped outside the works and turned his bike round, facing the gatehouse. As though he was waiting for someone.

'G'night, Kev.'

'G'night, Henry.'

The works looked tired, as though ready for the night's rest and, aided by the last wisps of smoke from the fire-hole, some of the buildings already shimmered in the evening's haze.

'Night, Kevin.'

'G'night, Richard.'

Without reason, Kevin's mind wandered again, his thoughts turning to Big Mouth Blaney. What was the man's real name, anyway? Bernard, that was it. In a way, thought Kevin, Blaney was lucky. He would probably settle into the sloth of redundancy as he had always settled in... No. Kevin stopped himself with an effort. Blaney worked hard, as all the team had to. What would such a man do in enforced idleness? Kevin realized with a shock that he couldn't remember the last time they had exchanged a friendly word. He determined there and then that he would make the overture tomorrow. Before it was too late.

'Night, Kevin.'

'Night, Dez.'

Then his problem was solved. Of course it was, and he turned his bike round and made for home. Wendy. Of course, she was cleverer than he was. More insight. Some time in the near future, as they were sat together, over dinner perhaps, or in bed, she would say, 'Has notice been served yet, love?' Knowing, of course, that it hadn't.

'Not yet, love, no.'

'Well, love. Have you any ideas? What you might do, I mean?'

'Nothing definite, my petal, no.'

'Well, I've been thinking,' she would say, and this is the moment when Kevin would inwardly rejoice, for inevitably, when Wendy said she'd been thinking, the problem would have been already solved.

* * *

263

Kevin pedalled harder, for having hung about in thought outside the gatehouse, he was a bit late. And it wasn't much later, when, after evening prayers, when certain people were already getting to their feet, Kevin was hurriedly examining the hue of his nose in the bathroom mirror. Tuesday was one of his nights at the Lantern Club and he always looked forward to the cold beer. Wendy and Liz Peach were also members, but they only came with him on Thursdays, while Derek stayed with a school pal. Liz sometimes also brought a current boy-friend along, but they didn't last long. She valued her independence too highly. But she was a good friend to Wendy.

Kevin hurried along, for apart from these two evenings at the Lantern Club, and seeing Graham on Mondays and going on the odd car rally or to watch the Fawkley Clerks on a Saturday, he spent the rest of his spare time with his family, either watching telly or, if there was nothing much on, playing Scrabble. He used to lift weights at the local club on Fridays, but it had decided to go upmarket, putting the subs up and buying all kinds of fancy machines. It was now known as a fitness club, ladies welcome, and, in fact, Kevin had left as Liz Peach had joined. She made no secret of the fact that this is where she picked most of her boyfriends up. At least, this is how Kevin put it. But only to himself.

'What particular small expression of complete approval did I use to describe last night's dinner, my love?' said Kevin as he put down his knife and fork.

'I think it was "superb",' Wendy smiled.

'Well, tonight's creation was absolutely exquisite. What was it, my dear?'

'It was spinach roulade with cheese and mushroom

filling,' she said, running over in her mind once again the number of calories involved.

'What did you think, Derek?' said Kevin then, turning to the youngster. 'Oh, sorry, son. Not your time for talking, I see.' The parents looked at each other and, for once, decided to retreat in good order.

Kevin glanced at the clock before getting up to go into the kitchen. It was his turn to wash the pots, then he would have half an hour with the paper before getting ready for the club. Whistling, he began to draw water, when Wendy came in and grabbed the tea towel, ready to pick up the first plate.

This was unusual, for when it was his turn, it was his turn. The whole job. Something was in the air. When it was his turn, she always read the paper and asked Derek about school. Kevin said nothing.

'Any word at work yet, love?' She made the opening gambit as she took the first plate from the rack.

'Not yet, love, no.'

'Well, I've been thinking...'

And so have I, my love, and what I've been thinking is that I'm married to a mind-reader. He put another plate in the rack, smiling in what he hoped was a noncommittal way. Had she found him a job somewhere? He couldn't think what else it might be.

'I've been to Pettit's Farm. Liz came with me.'

'Eh?'

'Pettit's Farm. Liz and me. We went for a look round.'

Yes, he thought. I heard that bit. You and Liz went for a look round Pettit's Farm. He could picture the place in his mind's eye. Three acres of weeds, or perhaps just a bit less. Hardly big enough to be called a smallholding nowadays, let alone a farm, with a ruin of a place in the middle of it – a place where the kids played, those who knew it wasn't haunted, and where the bats nested (did bats have nests?) he wondered.

How long had it been now since old Pettit had died? Eighteen months? And it had been a dump even then. It had been a farm, in the past. But the land behind what now remained had long been converted into golf links and an electricity substation ... other things, too. The place was on the eastern boundary of the town and the developers, in the frantic way that developers do, had applied to build executive-type housing on the remainder. But the council would do no more than deliberate. And the more frantic the developers became, the more the council deliberated. For councillors are not, as a rule, frantic people. There was talk of green belts, preservation orders, other things. And did Fawkley need more housing? Besides all this, there were other things to attend to. Mrs Lowe, for instance. Could the woman keep dogs in the backyard? Drat the woman. Where did people usually keep dogs? Better leave the matter for now. All of it.

'...Then we went to Roundie's.' Wendy was saying.

'Roundie's?' Kevin thought he ought to keep slipping in the odd word.

'Yes, the agents on the High Street.'

He already knew what Roundie's was. It was the estate agents and his stomach suddenly gave a jerk.

'Guess what they said, Kevin.'

'Give us a clue, love,' he said, trying to keep the tremor out of his voice. But this didn't stop him from suddenly going weak at the knees. She wanted to look after dogs on the place. No need to guess. What else could it be? A picture came into his mind, a picture of packs of dogs, baying and barking, with Wendy stood in the middle of them and smiling fondly at them all.

'Well, it was old man Roundie himself,' Wendy said and then went on to give Kevin an account of what had been said.

'Of course the place is for sale, Mrs Lowe.' Roundie

had been surprised that anyone, considering all the restrictions attached to the place, could still be found to express an interest in it. And being on the books for so long, a place like this wasn't good for business. 'You see,' he went on glumly, 'there are no dwelling houses to be built on the place, no caravans, either permanent or otherwise, are to be allowed, and...' and here, he'd consulted some papers, '... the old farmhouse still has a preservation order on it. Who could possibly want to buy...' Suddenly realizing what he was saying to a possible client, he pulled himself up short. 'Of course, Mrs Lowe,' he said, the old glint coming back to his eye, 'the potential of the...'

It was at this point that Wendy had interrupted the old man's flow. 'How much is the place, Mr Roundie?'

'Not as much as it was, Mrs Lowe. Not nearly as much,' and eagerly, he'd written the amount on a slip of paper, the very same slip of paper that Wendy was now holding in front of Kevin's eye.

Kevin whistled. He didn't usually whistle at bits of paper, but he whistled at this one. Or rather, at the amount written on it. Seventy thousand. For a piece of waste ground. 'You want to look after dogs there, don't you, Wendy?' he said.

She was smiling, happy at his quick grasp of things. 'Not a bad idea, at that,' she said. 'And just think. We can grow all our own cabbages.' She was to use this argument often.

There's a thing, he thought. Aloud, he said, 'Just tell me one thing, Wendy, love. Where's the money coming from?'

'Well, some of it will come from the sale of this place, don't you think?'

Kevin stood very still. 'Wendy. You don't mean...?'

'It's a solid place, Kevin. Liz and me have been. It wants a bit of work, I know, but Liz and me...'

Thinking back on the conversation after several days, Kevin tried to recall her exact words. He knew it was the sort of project that Liz would enthuse about, but he could have sworn his wife had said that the place wanted a bit of work. Maybe, in her enthusiasm, she hadn't seen the roof. This was entirely possible, of course, as there wasn't any. None to speak of, anyway. Just a few lofty corners, rustling with movement.

Then it came to him and the mystery was solved. Wendy knew very well what state the place was in and he could now imagine the conversation between her and Liz. 'Kevin could never do this place up, Liz. Just look at the state of it.'

'Of course, he couldn't. Not on his own. But with help... Graham Ogden for one. He's a joiner. And there must be others.'

'I wonder,' Wendy would answer, thinking furiously. 'After all, he would do the same for them,' and that detail being dealt with, they would then have gone on to other things, like the colour scheme for the curtains and so on.

Whenever he saw Kevin, Manny Paxton always said the same thing. 'Hello, Kev. Anytime, y'know.' The grandson of a tinker, he'd worked alongside Kevin in the workshops for a year or two before deciding to try going it alone. The place was like a prison to him, he'd said. But, what he'd also said, long afterwards, was that he never would have made it without Kevin's help. He'd bought the lease to an old bakery in Back Street, aptly named too in those days – junk shops mainly and the odd betting shop, but an integral part of any town.

But the bakery would never produce the staff of life again, complete capitulation being evident in the broken machinery and tired ovens, the mantle of the half-inch layer of dust and mouse droppings a mere signature to the place's demise.

But none of this had deterred Manny. 'DIY, Kev. There's money in it,' he'd said. 'Got the lease for a song, I did.'

'And it wasn't too high up in the charts, either, by the look of it, Manny. Just look at the place.'

'It does look a bit untidy at that. Give us a hand, Kev?'

Week after back-breaking week they'd stuck at it. And time was of the essence for Manny. He'd got three cheery brats already, as well as being well overdrawn at the bank. But he'd never wavered, neither him nor Norah, his fat and lusty wife. And this is what Kevin had always believed had kept Manny going, this unquenchable enthusiasm of the couple's. Doubt was never entertained. It was simply a matter of when, not if.

It was done at last. Kevin, exhausted, had given his 'hand' and the place was clean, full of tiles and, as Manny remarked, every tool for screwing – he'd dug Kevin heavily in the ribs as he said this – sawing, hammering and planning. There was every colour of paint under the sun – every size of timber.

Manny had never suggested any kind of partnership – never even mentioned the word. He wanted to make it on his own and he'd done so. Since then, long after the last juice-head had left the area, long after the last broken needle had been swept from the street, the whole area had been redeveloped, now almost enjoying High Street status. But Manny had never forgotten what Kevin had done. 'I owe y' Kev. Anytime.'

'Bloody 'ell,' said Manny. Rain was falling gently from the skies onto the upturned faces of the three men and Manny was expressing his views, not on the weather, but rather on the hole in the roof which was allowing its admittance.

Manny swore often, admitting as much to the Father

on the rare occasions that he made the effort to pay him a visit. Manny had long been converted to the true faith by his fat and cosy wife, Norah, and he didn't mind a bit.

'Quite, Manny.' Graham, on the other hand, never swore, for happy in his beliefs as a Methodist, he didn't indulge in the habit, not even on the building sites. But this didn't prevent him from not only responding politely to Manny's remark, but also to agreeing in full with its sentiments. For as they stood on either side of Kevin, in the centre of Pettit's farmhouse, there was no argument that the place was a desolation. And Graham glanced at Kevin now, although in truth his own heart soared within him. What a challenge! Tackling this place would be akin to the time when they'd first bought the Lanchester. But he nursed the secret like a miser and thus his mood being a quiet one; it was not infectious. 'What do you think, Kevin?' was what he did say. For as he gazed up at the dark skies, the young man's thoughts were hidden.

'Well,' said Kevin at last, 'Wendy did say that the place was in need of attention.' Or words to that effect, he thought.

'Do you really mean to live here then, Kev?' said Manny.

'Well, of course, I'd really like to know what the two of you think, first,' answered Kevin.

And that's a noncommittal answer if ever I heard one, thought Manny. But he didn't swear again. What he did do, in his genuine affection for Kevin, was rather to assert the practical side of his nature. 'Come on then,' he said, pulling paper and pencil from his pocket. 'Let's get started.'

With Manny taking notes, the three then wandered round the place, poking about in the corners and marvelling at the amount of dirt and rubble that can accumulate unaided in any one spot. A tape measure was then produced, Manny asking Kevin to hold one end, then showing his notes to the others. It was nicely done, thought Kevin, for really the notes were mainly directed at Graham, who quite often made suggestions in his quiet voice as he pointed at Manny's scribblings.

But a point was now reached when Kevin decided that something in his mind had to be said. 'About prices, Manny,' he began, but Manny raised a quick hand.

'Please, Kev,' he said. 'Let's start from the right end.'

But what this meant exactly, Kevin didn't quite know.

Constable Dennis Hayseldene of the East Fawkley Division, sitting in the comfort of the lounge of the Social Club, in the High Street, lifted his pint to his lips, to down nearly half the contents in one appreciative draught. 'Good pint, this, girls,' he said to Liz Peach and her friend, Wendy Lowe, sitting opposite. The women were paying their customary Thursday evening visit to the place. 'Kevin not in yet?' Dennis put his glass carefully on the beer mat.

'Not yet, Dennis.' Wendy lifted her own, smaller glass. 'He'll be along shortly, I expect. Depends how far on they are with a particular job. They're on with the doors just now, I believe.'

'What're you going to call the place then? When it's up and running, I mean.'

'What else, Dennis?' Liz butted in. 'Wendy's Kennels, of course,' and then, 'Are you OK, Dennis?' For at the mention of kennels, a sudden veil of concern had spread over the policeman's features.

But at Liz's question, he tried to brighten up a bit. 'Oh, I'm all right,' he said. 'It was just the mention of kennels, that's all. It's Bruce. I've got to lose him. I'm just about sure, anyway.'

'Lose him?' Both Liz and Wendy knew that Bruce was Dennis's police dog.

271

'Afraid so.'

Liz stood up. 'Tell you what, Dennis,' she said. 'Let me get us all a drink. You tell Wendy all about it. She's the expert. But no gossip. Not till I get back. That is, unless you want to repeat it all again,' and off she went to the bar. And obedient to Liz's commands, Dennis indulged in small talk.

'How long have you had Pettits now then, Wendy?' he asked.

'Fourteen weeks to the day. And if I'd known everything that was involved, well, we'd still have gone for it. Kevin was a bit unsure to start with, what with the yards closing and all, but strangely, once he really thought about it, I think this is what finally made him go for it a hundred per cent. Keep him busy till he got something else.'

'Of course. But you said something about problems.'

'Problems? You wouldn't believe the half of it, Dennis. The council, for instance. What do they do all day in that place. Do you know?...'

A small, round tray with a pint and two halves was slapped on the table, interrupting Wendy's flow, and Liz sat down. 'She's telling you about the council, Dennis, isn't she?'

The policeman grinned. 'Heard it all before have you, Liz?'

Then Liz herself was interrupted as Kevin arrived, looking hot and with his hand round a glass. 'You OK for drinks?'

'OK, Kevin. Liz's treat,' said Dennis, lifting his glass. You look warm.'

'Just out of the bath,' said Kevin. 'But we got the doors on.' And they talked about the farmhouse for a brief while. But then, in deference to Dennis's problem, Wendy quickly got back to it.

'Listen now, Kevin. Dennis has something to tell us.

272

Come on, Dennis.' She knew how attached to the animal he was.

'Well, as I was saying, I'm pretty sure Bruce'll have to go.' The unhappiness, obviously so near the surface, welled up again in his voice.

'Go? Go where?' said Kevin, at once sorry for the man. As though he'd been wrestling with the problem for a while, Dennis shook his head slowly. 'As to that, Kevin, I don't know,' he answered. 'Either back to school, or, well ... it's the Super's decision. The dog's been naughty, you see.' He looked round at the others, gathering his thoughts and, as no one said anything, he carried on. 'Nearly twelve months I've had that dog and never a minute's trouble until three weeks ago. Then he started taking off – coming back after a day or two. I managed to cover for him only the once. Then I had to report it. For my own sake. Last time out, as I was chastizing him, he bit me. Not seriously, but what's the odds? Can't have that, of course.'

He fell silent, to look expectedly at Wendy.

'Well, I can't help, Dennis. Not if the matter's settled.' She couldn't think what else to say, sorry as she felt for him.

'Well,' he came back quickly, 'it's really in abeyance, I suppose. It's not really the sort of problem the Super's used to having to deal with – hopes the thing might sort itself out, like. It won't, though.'

'Right then, Dennis,' she said. 'Let's get to it. How old is the dog?'

'About twenty months. And I helped to train him.'

'Hm. No problem there then. What about his health? I know Alsatians are prone to certain things, hip trouble and so on. I don't want to waste time stating the obvious, Dennis, but we may as well start from scratch.'

'Take my word for it, Wendy. There's nothing wrong

with him physically. The dogs have regular check-ups and
I give him his daily brushing and so on. No, he's as fit
as a young dog should be.'

'Right. No one else handles him, of course?'

'That's right. He lives with me and Jane. And young
Rita, of course. They're his family.'

'Does the girl fuss him a lot?'

'No. Bruce knows he really just has the one master.'

'OK. Did you know, Dennis, that some dogs are born
vicious? Not many, but some.'

'I have heard that, but it's pretty rare, isn't it? I do watch
him carefully, living with the family as he does. I have to.
He's a big dog. But it's only me he's nipped. So far.'

'What about his love life then?'

'I know the difference, Wendy. Believe me.'

She looked down at her glass, in thought. 'May I see
the dog, Dennis?' she said then.

'Of course,' he said, suddenly heartened.

The small kitchen, here in Quarry Street, was crowded
– the dining room full to bursting and, for Wendy at
least, it was to be the last social occasion to be held here,
in the old house. In the last few days, she'd also catered
for others, neighbours and so on, but now was the moment
when any remaining regrets at leaving the place would
have to be stifled and laid to rest.

For Wendy, however, it wasn't too bad, and the usual
traumas of house-moving had been kept to a minimum
– lightly borne indeed – for sensitive and intelligent though
she might be, she was also something of a fatalist and
so, for her, the more important decisions in life had
already been mapped out, their course unalterable. As it
was, she could to a large extent ignore the more obvious
difficulties – dispense with the usual irritants such as

logic and caution. But not totally, and, as she guiltily admitted to herself, most of the residue was placed in her faith in Kevin.

Kevin would have been alarmed to hear it. For he, in his turn, leaned most heavily on her. As it was, all he was now concerned about was a few regrets. For the hardest part was over and at last, this evening, he realized how soon it would be before they were to leave Quarry Street for good. For ever. They'd been happy here. He loved the house, the garage, the whole carry-on.

He tried to comfort himself for, when it was all said and done, it was the people in one's life who were paramount – they who made a home.

He looked round the room. Besides his family, all the people who really mattered were here – Graham and Doris Ogden, Manny and Norah Paxton. Quite a religious gathering, he thought slyly. Catholics, Methodists, and for himself? He put himself down as a casual.

Then there was Liz, of course, standing in the background for once, ready to help Wendy. Mustn't forget Liz. She'd certainly done her part and he smiled to himself at the recollection of what Wendy had told him in bed one night. They'd been having worrying little troubles from the council about what they could and could not do at the farmhouse. It seemed that the relevant forms, duly filled in, had reached the right departments at last, with all the niggling results.

Wendy had mentioned it to Liz. 'Leave it with me,' Liz had replied without hesitation. I know Alec Kennedy.'

Alec Kennedy, with the thinning hair and the little paunch, was the chairman of the council and, almost overnight, the little problems had disappeared. As Kevin reflected, it was a well-known fact that Liz was acquainted with quite a few men with thinning hair and little paunches. Mustn't forget Liz, then.

Even so, and although he may have been blissfully unaware of the fact, he had, over the weeks, had a much rougher passage than his wife. The real worry had been his. Lack of proper funds had only been the half of it and, without Graham and Manny, he knew that a dream was all it would have remained. A tinker's grandson and a worker in wood had never ceased, over the weeks, to make him feel humble. They had been men inspired. 'You should just see them, love,' he'd said to Wendy on many occasions as he came home in the evenings, tired after his exertions.

'Tell me, Kevin,' she'd said.

And he'd done so. With a wink and a nod, he said, Manny had brought doors, renovated and solid. Graham had rubbed his fingers over them, saying that these were something like doors, different to the rubbish they supplied on the sites – green timber which would blunt his tools in an hour. 'So although Graham might not be in the habit of cursing,' Kevin had finished laughingly, 'he certainly makes up for it by grumbling.'

And Wendy would laugh with him, and now at last the dream was taking on shape, was beginning to be wrapped in substance. And here in Quarry Street, in the crowded kitchen, Kevin breathed in deeply, for the main dish was a favourite of his. As many were. It was baked ham with cider and apricots, its steaming aroma diffusing like a heady perfume to all parts of the room.

There was a chocolate and cherry terrine and there were chocolate biscuits with brazil-nut fillings. The wine was a dry Australian Shiraz. And for Doris Ogden, thin and jolly, but who didn't eat meat, Wendy had done a Roquefort and walnut salad. Doris had had the grace to apologize in advance and possibly, of course, in anticipation, for being such a nuisance, but Wendy, with her usual aplomb, had waved the apologies aside. 'Nonsense, Doris,' she'd said. 'If you don't eat meat, you don't eat meat. No trouble at all.'

It was the answer Doris had hoped for and she had become even more jolly, for Wendy's prowess in the kitchen was no secret at all.

Long finished eating and as a kind of floor show to settle the meal, the company sat watching young Derek, gaping in awe as, for a grand finale, he speared the last potato. 'Well-mannered lad, though I do say so myself,' said Kevin. 'Never talks during meal times.'

Wendy Lowe came round the side of the smart semi-detached in Oakland Road where Dennis Hayseldene lived with his wife, Jane, and their ten-year-old daughter, Rita.

The day was a grey one, the air damp and heavy, but this didn't prevent Wendy from catching her breath at the riot of colour that greeted her as she got round the back. She'd always thought about gardening but there were no gardens in Quarry Street. It was an omission she meant to correct as soon as they moved to the farmhouse. And having no preconceived ideas, she couldn't imagine one she would have liked more than the one here. But untrained eye or not, she knew this wasn't a show garden. Far from it, for there were too many things in need of obvious attention. There were lupins going to seed and the hostas had holes in their leaves where the slugs had been feeding. There were flowers that needed pulling up and there were others that were too closely packed and in want of thinning out. Still others were too tall for the ones behind them and many other such golden rules had been ignored.

There was a broken arbour, one upon which Dennis was later to remark, to the effect that he intended fixing it sometime. There were a hundred other faults – a thousand inconsistencies. And Wendy loved it all. To her, the overall effect was simple pleasure, like creating a new dish in the kitchen, or making quiet love with Kevin, just as they were about to fall asleep in the blackness of midnight. And she just stood there, drinking it all in as a kind of therapy from these busy times.

And now she thought of a conversation she'd had with Kevin recently about such things and how she wished he were here now, to see this garden for himself – give him also a moment's respite. 'Just think, love,' she'd said again. 'All those cabbages.' Why cabbages, she didn't know. Perhaps their very prosaicness represented plenty and freedom from worry.

For answer, he'd smiled, then looked through the back kitchen window at the garage. He thought of the Singer. Was it really all over? And just at that moment, with the worries crowding in on him just a little, the idea of growing cabbages, either his own or anyone else's, hadn't seemed to hold very much appeal. But in spite of everything, he knew that one part of him had never been happier. For it really was the most exciting time. He thought of Graham, running the ball of a thumb needlessly across the razor-sharp blade of the plane before taking up a door to balance between his knees, to take off the thinnest wafer here, the merest whisper there, before looking up confidently into Kevin's face.

"That should do it, Kevin,' he would say. 'We don't want too much off. We don't want any draughts now, do we?'

Then Manny had arrived in a lorry, having been away for a while. 'These took some finding,' he said. They were roof tiles, old and solid, made of clay and fitting the shell of the farmhouse perfectly.

'They look expensive, Manny.' Kevin remembered saying it. For answer, Manny had winked in the usual way, digging Kevin in the ribs to knock the worries right out of him.

But now, happy as he was, the worries had begun to

sneak back. Mustn't worry Wendy with them though. 'Cabbages?' he'd said, forcing the enthusiasm into his voice. 'Great, love.'

Seeing Dennis, Wendy's reverie was broken. He had his back to her and was sitting on an old sack, cleaning boots, when without warning he got stiffly to his feet and turned round. 'Hello, Wendy.'

'Dennis. You've got good ears.'

'Not me. Bruce,' he said and she could now see the dog, a little further off, ears erect.

Then after the usual greetings, she said, 'It's a beautiful garden, Dennis. It must take a lot of your time.'

'Well, not so much mine. It's mostly down to Jane.' He was rubbing the small of his back from the awkward position he'd been sitting in and, here in the garden, he wore a crisp white shirt and jeans – a tall, sturdy man.

'Ah,' said Wendy, 'and what are those, over on that trellis there?'

'Them's espaliers, for pears. But listen, Wendy. You're here in a professional capacity, after all. Let's talk about money.'

'All right,' she said, equally direct. 'Here it is, Dennis. Should I manage nothing useful at all, I will want nothing. But if I should happen to make some useful contribution, or even manage to solve the thing altogether, then Jane can pay me.'

'Jane?'

'Yes. In seedlings. And advice.'

'Listen, Wendy. Solve this problem in any way at all, and we'll both pay you. How's that?' Then he suddenly looked beyond her and she turned round.

'Jane.' Wendy knew her slightly, only seeing her when she came to the Social Club with Dennis.

Jane Hayseldene was a confident, handsome woman with the blackest hair Wendy had ever seen. Genuine, too, according to Liz.

'Hello, Wendy,' she said. 'I couldn't help overhearing you admiring the garden. It's never anywhere near finished, of course, but as soon as this sad business is over with Bruce, I'll give you a guided tour if you like.'

'There's nothing I'd like better but, as you say, I know what a worrying time it is for you all.'

'Yes.' A crease of worry had appeared between the dark eyes. 'Dennis says you may be able to help in some way. We're really attached to the dog, naturally. These things happen, of course.'

'Well, I'll certainly do what I can. I don't yet know what,' said Wendy. There was no point in trying to be more specific.

'Right. Can I get you anything at all? A drink?'

'No, really. Thanks just the same.' Pressed for time as she was, Wendy wouldn't be tempted.

'Well, if you're sure.' Nodding in a friendly way, Jane turned to go. 'See you next time, then.' She went back indoors, sensibly getting out of the way.

'Bruce. Come here, boy.' Dennis didn't raise his voice, but the dog came forward without hesitation on his running lead. But he hadn't come forward at all on Wendy's arrival. Seen by Dennis alone, he'd merely lifted his head from his paws in enquiry. Wendy thought he would have barked, but it was obviously the routine not to do so. But now, at Dennis's call, he'd trotted up. He was certainly a healthy-looking brute, she thought, as she eyed the great black muzzle and the bright eyes. 'He didn't bark at all, Dennis,' she said. 'That's right, is it?'

'That's right. Only when the house is empty. Or at night.'

'Hm.' She sat on the ground, tucking her skirt round

her knees. Only rarely did she wear trousers, and then only for rough work at home, saying that she hadn't really the figure for them.

So there she sat in her skirt, legs tucked in at the side, but being careful not to look the dog in the eyes. Instead, she glanced here and there, moving her hands gently about her face. Then after a while, she said, 'I'm going to offer him my hand, Dennis. But I won't touch him. Will you keep as still as you are now?'

Dennis looked uneasy. 'I'm not so sure.'

'It's all right. Just keep still,' and she offered the dog a flat palm, being careful to hold it below the level of his head and withdrawing it almost immediately. As she did so, the dog wrinkled his nose in warning. Then, almost straightaway, she did it twice more, before finally getting to her feet. As she did this, the animal straightened his own front legs even more, but leaving his bottom on the ground, and moved his tail just once to either side, causing a faint arc of dust in the garden path.

'What do you make of all that, Wendy? Anything at all?' The anxiety was there in Dennis's tone.

'Something, yes. I'm not quite certain what. Not yet. But I can tell you something for nothing. The dog isn't naturally vicious.' She stood for a moment, thinking. 'What's the time factor?' she said then. 'How long have we got? Any idea at all?'

'None. No idea, that is. It's up to the dog. If he takes off again, or bites somebody else, well, them's the sort of things...'

'Well, look,' she said briskly, for there was nothing else she could do here just now, 'I have things to do. It'll take me a couple of days at least. Let's keep our fingers crossed. I'll try and make it back here by Thursday,' and having taken her leave of him and asking him to say goodbye to Jane for her, she made for the side of the house.

281

'Don't go empty-handed, Wendy.' It was as though Jane had been waiting for her, coming out of the house with a plastic bag. 'I haven't had time to cut flowers, of course, but I'm sure you'll enjoy this just as well.'

Wendy looked in the bag. It was a round-headed cabbage. 'It's a Stonehead,' Jane went on. 'Nothing to do with Dennis, though,' and they both laughed.

'What's this underneath?' asked Wendy, peering.

'A few peas. They're Giant Strides. Again, nothing to do with the great man,' and laughing again, Wendy thanked her warmly.

Any tension in regard to the reason for her visit was thus totally eased. 'I'll be growing my own soon, of course,' she said.

'I know you will, my dear.'

Wendy's last thought as she hurried off was that the woman certainly had beautiful hair.

Beverly Porter looked back at her reflection with an expression somewhere between distaste and amusement. For at fifty-three, or, as she told everyone else, fast approaching forty-eight, she didn't like these big, well-lit mirrors in Liz Peach's salon. 'What do you think, Liz?' she said.

'Well,' Liz replied, getting hold of the lank locks, as though she was sorting string for the bazaar, 'I've told you before, Beverly, you've got that kind of hair. But don't worry, Bev, we'll do you up as good as new. It's just that your hair will never be your best feature.'

'What will?' said Beverly, and they both laughed out. In fact, Liz always thought that Beverly Porter tended to underrate herself. She didn't look much over fifty-something at that and when she covered her neck with a high jersey or blouse, which she usually did, she didn't look that bad.

If only the woman would accept herself as she was. She had decent features and knew how to apply make-up. It was the sallow complexion and the hair that kept her from being quite attractive. For her age, of course.

Liz got started and Beverly said, 'Guess where we're going for the hols in a few weeks.'

'Tell me.' She knew that Beverly and her husband, George, had already been just about everywhere.

'Tresco.'

'Really. I prefer Asda, myself.' They laughed out again. 'Seriously though, Bev. Where the devil's Tresco?'

'Scilly Isles. George's turn to pick and that's where he wants to go. For the plants, apparently. There are thousands of exotic plants there. Not much else, though, and it's only a tiny place, so we're only going for four days, thank God. Trouble is, we can't take Jack and Suky, of course. And we didn't think much of the last kennels they were in. Nothing we could say much about, mind, but the dogs didn't seem to have had much exercise.'

Jack and Suky were the two Afghan hounds that the Porters doted on.

'Hm. You should have mentioned it earlier. A pity, that,' said Liz thoughtfully 'A friend of mine is just opening new kennels. No frills, but she usually sees to all the animals herself. In fact,' she laughed, 'they usually leave the place in better condition than when they came. Something else, though she doesn't talk about it a lot. She actually advises on some of the town's police dogs. Not that she would thank me for repeating all this, of course.'

'Well?' Beverly shot out. 'Why earlier?'

'Well, she's pretty well booked up, I know that.'

'For me, Liz?'

'Well, you are a valued client. I'll see what I can do. Wendy is rather expensive, mind.' But at this, Beverly waved a deprecatory hand. George Porter had a successful computer business. The only one in Fawkley.

Liz Peach hadn't a lot of female friends, usually preferring the company of men, but she knew Wendy Lowe's worth very well.

Even though he was stood on the top platform of the stepladder, Kevin could only just reach the hole in the ceiling, high as the ceilings were in the farmhouse. He just managed to poke the end of the flex through to Roy 'Midnight' Marsden, a mate of Manny's and, the electrician on the job.

Roy was only one of the people Kevin had met for the first time in the past few weeks and naturally he'd enquired after the man's nickname, which turned out to have been earned from his novel hobby of taking his wife, Carol, for a late-night spin on the back of his motor bike. Upon being asked by the curious, as happened on occasion, why he went this late, he would say that it was for the peace and quiet, setting both Carol and himself up for bed.

In the peace and quiet of the late evening then, the old HRD would be heard roaring down the road. 'Ah, Midnight Marsden,' they would mutter from the comfort of the fireside. 'Early tonight. It's only just on half eleven.'

So 'Midnight' it was, although as often happens, the habit of abbreviation would win the day and many people simply called him Roy, for short.

On such a mundane job as feeding flex through a hole in the ceiling, Kevin had time to think of these things. Roy, for instance. Tall, spare and academic-looking, surely no one had ever looked more like a college professor. Apart from his work and his midnight jaunts, he would spend the rest of his spare time 'under the bonnet' of his ancient bike, dismantling it religiously and completely every six months or so just to 'keep it in trim'.

He was also a very patriotic man, often remarking that no one had ever been able to make bikes quite like the British. 'You do know, don't you,' he would say, 'that there's a good British bike for every letter of the alphabet?' And he would go through them – 'Ariel. BSA. Calthorpe...' It was no mere party trick, either. For he could also tell you where every one of them had been made, their best-selling models and so on.

He'd also been to see the Lanchester and the Singer, heard what had been done to them and, from then on, regarded Kevin and Graham as kindred spirits – men worth talking to.

Roy. Manny. Graham. Kevin knew what he owed them. It was people like these who made life worth living. 'Come on, Kevin. Feed it through.'

'Sorry, Roy.' The train of thought was broken and Kevin's mind went on to something else – the last day at work some three weeks ago. In company with the rest of the workforce, he had passed through the gates for the last time. Frank was still reading his paper and would be doing so too for quite a while yet. But he would be on his own in the place, with only echoes for company. The team had exchanged maudlin vows, swearing to meet on a certain day in a certain pub in town, every year hence – an oath that each of them knew that none of them would keep. Most of them in fact, Kevin knew, would really be thinking of little but the loss of their livelihoods. No blame there. Kevin himself could hardly wait for a few weeks to pass – in the hope that the memories would begin to fade. He already had a new job, not a good one and only part-time, making deliveries for Manny. But it was a start.

And he had so much more. This place. It was beginning to look like something he'd never even dreamed of owning. He looked down at the floor, remembering the old, broken flagstones. Men had come and taken them up with a machine, digging a foot of damp earth out in the process and replacing it all with joists and planks, planks which now had the sheen of a new chestnut.

After some discussion, the fancy cast-iron surround of the fireplace had been left in, buffed up and then blackleaded. A Georgian hob grate and a fender had appeared and Kevin had shuddered at the cost of it all, but now, whenever he should bring the matter up, Manny would say, 'You're right, Kevin, and don't worry – I'll be knocking it all off your wages.'

'I'm called little Buttercup, dear little Buttercup, though I could never tell why.' The words revolved around the inside of Wendy's head time and again. She could never remember feeling quite so tired and *Pinafore* had sneaked up on her until suddenly, it was next week – six nights at the Fawkley Civic. Had she only been part of the chorus, it wouldn't have been so bad, knowing that even should she decide to pull out, pleading something or other, the society wouldn't suffer too much. As it was...

What else had she got to do? She went over the things in her mind as she walked towards the library. She'd already been to see Dennis and the dog again. That's what was really in her thoughts now – the reason for visiting the library.

Then there was the packing-up. She'd started that a while ago, but there was only so much that could be done before the actual day came. Then there were the journeys to and from the building society and the council, and there was Warwick Edwards to see again.

If only she could get at least one of the jobs completed – lighten the load a little.

'Hello, Wendy.' Jackie Smart, the librarian, was in one of the aisles, putting books back. Since the cutbacks, she now only had one part-timer. 'How long now?'

'Good morning, Jackie. Soon I hope. We do have someone interested in Quarry Street. But what a job.'

'I can imagine.'

Wendy passed on to where the dog books were, not needing to ask the Dewey numbers nowadays, even being able to tell at a glance which of the books, if any, had been taken out.

She spread the three biggest of them on the small, round table and, sitting down, got to work. Sitting there for forty-five minutes, or thereabouts, she then put the books back quickly. 'I wonder,' she said to herself.

The object of these musings was a certain Cy Moulson and, coming to a swift decision, she went to phone Liz, hoping that she was still at home. Liz answered the phone straightaway. 'Liz. It's me. I want to go out and see Cy Moulson. I thought you might like to come along.'

'Certainly I would. Gives me an excuse to leave this dusting. We'll go in my car. Where are you?'

'Library.'

'Right. Hang on there. Be outside though. Ten minutes.'

'Are you sure? I don't want to pull you away from the dusting.'

'Ten minutes.'

'Come in, Dennis. Sit down. How's Jane?' Superintendent Leonard Pinder, being the age that he was and having always refused to enter into any kind of politics, would never get any higher in the ranks, but he still did the job in the best way that he knew how. He was also still very much in touch with the man on the beat, never fudging real issues. He would listen with patience to all suggestions, never pouring scorn on those with whom he disagreed, even though they might be below him in rank.

Normally quite phlegmatic, the thing that was quickest to rouse him to anger was prevarication of any kind, rightly considering it an insult to his intelligence.

In his present troubles, Dennis Hayseldene was thankful that this was the man in charge of the issue, knowing that this man would share the problem rather than trying to pass it on.

'Now then, Dennis, tell me.'

For the tenth time since he'd set out from home, Dennis tried to remember exactly what Jane had said. 'Don't forget, my dear, to try and remember your aitches, and don't say "them" rather than "those". He is your boss, after all. And remember that whatever happens, I love you.'

Dennis was happy with all of this, giving the Super an exact account of everything that had happened since they had last met. He outlined both his own and Wendy Lowe's involvement up until the present time, ending with the dog's behaviour since the last serious incident. He didn't add any unnecessary details or opinions, and neither would he do so unless asked, for so far this was a formal meeting.

Pinder sat thinking. An ordinary enough looking man, perhaps his most unusual feature was a shock of grizzled hair, and Dennis concentrated on this unseeingly as he waited. He didn't feel that calm himself, for to him heavy issues were in the balance.

'You're closer to the thing than me, Dennis. Tell me what you think.' Pinder was anxious to get the thing right.

'Well, sir. By all accounts, Wendy Lowe is a clever woman. Not strictly professional in the advisory sense, but I think we should give her a chance. Unless Bruce gets up to anything else, of course.'

'Hm. Right. We'll leave it at that, then. Give the lady a chance to come up with something. These dogs cost a mint to train. We should make every effort. OK, Dennis?'

'OK by me, sir.'

'Right. Oh, and by the way, Dennis,' said Pinder, as he got to his feet. 'What about the Sergeant's stripes. Heard anything lately at all?'

'Any time now, sir, I hope,' said Dennis as he stood up to go. The Constable was patting himself on the back. As far as he could remember, all his aitches had been in place and he knew he hadn't said 'them' once. In any context.

But the Super hadn't finished. 'Good,' he said. 'Oh, and just remind me, Dennis,' the tone now impish, 'About Bruce. What laws are we talking about here?'

'Well, sir.' The Constable creased his brow in thought. 'Not the Control of Dogs Order, '92. That's 1992, of course. But we coppers are excused that one. Under Section E. Er, we're more concerned with the Road Traffic Act, '88. Section 25, I think.'

'27, Dennis. What else?'

Dennis racked his brain.

'Take your time, Dennis. As you would at an exam.'

'Er I have it, sir. Dog's Act, '71?'

'Correct. That's 1871, of course. And Dangerous Dogs, 1991. Read them up, Dennis.'

'I will, sir. And thank you.'

Cyril Moulson was an ex-engine driver who, having seen what was coming, had taken early retirement, then taking both his wife Esther and himself off to live in a large rambling place 'in the middle of nowhere', as Liz was later to put it, although, in fact, it was only just over three miles from Fawkley.

Wendy had first bumped into him at a dog show at the Drill Hall and had seen him two or three times since. Whenever there was a live show, whether it was dogs, cats or small animals, she would see him there and they would talk. She'd always thought that he had some interesting theories and he'd invited her to come and see his circus, as he put it, at any time. But she'd never got round to it, never quite seeming to have the time. Until now. She had his phone number but this was at home. 'His number's at home, Liz. Shall we ring him, do you think? See if he's in?'

'Let's not bother. If he's out, we'll leave a message. Did you notice I was two or three minutes late?'

'What of it?'

'Well, guess who I've been talking to?'

'Er, let me see. One of your old boyfriends?'

Liz looked shocked. 'Wendy. I've no old boyfriends. The odd middle-aged one, perhaps.'

'Right. I give up.'

'David Clyde.'

'Who?'

'David Clyde. You remember him. Young. Worked at the building society. Disappeared from the scene rather suddenly. Don't you remember?'

'Of course,' Wendy shouted. 'That's right. Fancy seeing him. What did he have to say for himself, then?'

'Very little. Got the itch to travel a bit, he said. All a bit vague, I thought.'

'Well, what was he doing back here? Did he say?'

'Said he had to see Warwick Edwards. Then he was off again, he said. But he didn't say where to.'

'Hm. I wonder if Buster Howes knows anything. No good asking Warwick. Anyway, I must tell Kevin. They both played for the same football team.'

* * *

Rather than circus, Wendy thought menagerie might have been a better word. Or chicken farm. The place seemed to be covered in them. No particular breed, colour or size, just lots of them. There was one dog, a handsome fawn mongrel, asleep in the sun. Not a guard dog, though, thought Wendy, for, as the car pulled up in the dust of the drive, it didn't even look up. A sudden scuffling behind some bushes could have been anything but, before remark could be made on it, both women saw Cy. He was sat in a deck-chair, feeding a rabbit which, as soon as the car drew up, bolted.

Cy looked round. 'Wendy. At last. Come and sit down.'

Wendy introduced Liz, then said, 'Where's the rabbit gone?'

'Home, I expect. He's wild.'

'But he was only four feet away from you.'

'Nearest I can get him to come.'

Then a woman appeared at the door of the house. She was small and bird-like. Perhaps she was the mother of all the chickens, thought Liz, while Wendy was wondering whether this was the front or the back of the house.

'We've got visitors, Esther,' shouted Cy. 'Can we have some tea, do you think?' Esther clucked back inside. 'Come on, girls, sit down. Just a social visit, is it?'

Wendy smiled as she and Liz sat down on a cast-iron bench with 'Winsford Station' written on the back. 'I've been meaning to come and see you for quite a while, Cy, but just as it happens something else has come up.' It was the best she could do and then she told him everything about Bruce, including the fact that she'd reached a possible conclusion. Then just as she was finishing her tale, the lady of the house appeared with the tea.

Esther Moulson turned out to be a bright, intelligent woman, jovial and a good hostess, serving the tea in good china and chatting inconsequentially as the occasion demanded, giving Cy the chance to think. He brooded for a while, turning the facts over in his mind.

A wet nose was shoved into Wendy's hand. It was the mongrel, having woken up at last. 'That's Judy,' said Esther. 'She's old.'

A Border collie came round the side of the house and he was limping. 'That's Ben,' said Esther. 'He's not ours but he trapped his foot and we're looking after him for a while.'

'I've got a Ben,' said Liz. 'In the car. I'll just fetch him if I may.' She got up and went to the car and, although she'd left the window open, the Welsh terrier jumped out eagerly. The two Bens went towards each other, Liz having been assured that the collie wasn't a bully. They touched noses, sniffed at each other in various parts, keeping the best bits till last, then settled down in the sun. Judy had already gone to sleep again.

Wendy and Liz sat drinking tea, enjoying the moment and talking to Esther. Sitting in her own rather decrepit deck-chair, the little woman looked smaller than ever.

The bees droned past them all, suspiciously taking their time in the heat of the morning and then Cy looked up at last. 'What conclusion did you come up with, then?' he asked of Wendy.

She took a folded paper from her pocket. 'Do me a favour, Cy,' she said. 'I've written it down here, but please, tell me what you think before I pass it over?'

And entering into the spirit of the thing, he did so.

For at least two evenings at the Civic, every single seat had been booked and Wendy played her Mrs Cripps with gusto. *H.M.S. Pinafore* got the usual decent reviews in the *Fawkley Courier* and on Saturday night, after the last curtain call, there'd been the usual party. Liz, as she did on

292

occasion, had taken a drop too much and Wendy had to get her home in the Ford, leaving Liz's Audi to its own devices in the Civic car park.

Wendy's burden was also easing in other ways. Warwick Edwards had nearly completed all the legal bits regarding the mortgage and the council had given the go-ahead for certain things to be done to the farmhouse. 'Good job,' Kevin had said. 'Most of them have been done for weeks.'

There was the one sour note. The buyers for the house in Quarry Street, unable to get a big enough loan, had been forced to give back word. Liz had told Wendy not to worry, but not in the trite way usually employed for the phrase. 'Don't worry, Wendy. I mean it,' she'd said and, as usual, Wendy took her at her word and with this, perhaps the biggest relief of all was that the business with Bruce was settled. The business, with all its uncertainties, had been a constant drain on her time.

After all her thought and research, as well as her constant soul-searching, she had come to the belief that Bruce was one of those not too rare animals, police dogs or no, that just don't take to the regime of constant orders. It could happen to any breed and, being subjected to the strict training he'd undergone from a puppy, Bruce's true nature had only just begun to assert itself. And fancy medical terms apart, he was a big fellow and potentially dangerous.

Wendy had written the gist of all this on the paper, but before having it passed over to him, Cyril Moulson had said, 'An unfortunate combination of laziness and jealousy. Inherent, I would say. It happens. Bruce wants treating like one of the family, which, as a police dog, isn't possible.'

The solution had been Cy's, too. 'There are two options,' he'd gone on. 'The first one is that the dog has to be away from the family for a short while, somewhere just lazing about. Then back to the family but as a pet only. No police work. That would do it, I think.'

'And the second option, Cy?'

'He has to be destroyed.'

At this, Liz had been seen to shudder and Wendy herself had felt a leaden weight in her stomach. But even though Cy had never set eyes on the dog, she was sure he'd got it right.

Neither did Dennis Hayseldene argue when Wendy saw him later, rather looking relieved that some convictions had been reached. The Super would have to have the last word, of course.

'Ay, ay. We've had visitors.' The matter-of-fact way in which Manny said it, suggested that he wasn't that unused to such a thing. 'Bastards,' he went on, without the slightest trace of rancour in his voice. 'It'll be them from the North Side.'

It was early morning and Manny was looking at the disarray of building materials, strewn around the farmhouse. Kevin had to admit to himself that he wouldn't have noticed anything amiss. Manny must have noticed such a thing automatically. It must be the business he was in. 'What's missing, Manny?'

'Some of them best bricks and a couple of shovels. Nothing much. But they'll be back, of course. An' it'll be the concrete mixer next. Now that they've got the lie of the land. We'll have to take turns camping out here till you move in, Kev.'

'No need,' said Kevin. 'Leave it to me.' He said this at the same time as he had the unkind thought that Manny wouldn't have made a bad thief himself. Not that he quite knew why.

Graham, who'd arrived in time to catch most of the conversation but who'd made no comment at all, was now seen to heave a sigh of relief. He knew that working full-time and helping out here, was just about all he could manage.

Kevin's next stop was Dennis Hayseldene's house, or rather, halfway down Oakland Road, just as Dennis was catching the early forenoon shift. It took only a couple of sentences to tell the Constable what had happened. 'Give us a hand, Dennis?' Kevin ended. 'I'll stay with you.'

'No need,' said Dennis. 'I'll take Bruce. He loves the quiet.' And as it turned out, Dennis only had to wait until the second evening. Having been on duty most of the afternoon, he had just begun to doze, when the dog, resting beside him in the dark, gave him warning, just the faintest of low rumblings in the throat, as though annoyed at having his rest disturbed.

Now afraid that the dog would bark too soon, Dennis reached out in the dark to feel the hairs rising on the back of the animal's neck. But there was now a slight problem. Kevin had given him a key to the house but, as it was a warm night, Dennis was stretched out on an ancient deck-chair, which, as he now disturbed the ancient canvas, began to creak alarmingly.

A big man, the policeman now knew with absolute certainty that, should he make any sudden moves, then the rotten fabric would give way in a second. The humour of the situation now forced him to work hard to suppress a giggle. He lay there, hanging on to the nape of Bruce's neck, scarce daring to twitch a muscle, his body beginning to ache with the tension.

Then at last, to his great relief, he began to make out two moving shapes in the gloom. Another half-minute and he switched on his torch, at the same time telling Bruce to 'speak'.

'Stand still,' he shouted then.

* * *

'You should have been there, Kevin,' Dennis said later. 'I even considered asking them to help me out of the chair. Not that I really had the chance. Poor lads. I think they may even have outrun the dog. I wouldn't let him go, of course. In any case, he might even have nipped one of them. Anyway, think of the paperwork. Have you ever seen one of them forms, Kevin?'

Kevin shook his head.

'Just a couple of lads out of work, I expect, judging by the old, broken barrow they left behind,' Dennis went on. 'I went round the place again last night but they won't be back. But let me know if there's any more bother.'

It was Bruce's last foray in the job for which he had been so painstakingly trained. Three days later he went to stay with the Moulsons, and the way he'd settled down to the quiet life had been almost laughable. Cy said he thought a week or ten days would be just about right before the dog was taken back home. As a pet.

There was good news. Superintendent Pinder had persuaded the authorities concerned, to write the dog off. Dennis wouldn't be having another, what with his stripes being due at any time. And the job now being over, he asked Wendy what he owed her, but she was to settle for the quiet publicity and the huge supply of plants and vegetables Jane brought to the farmhouse. Unfinished and untidy as the place still was, Jane was still so obviously impressed by the place as to give Wendy a curious and hitherto unknown pleasure, a feeling she was to think about for a while.

When Dennis was later to ask Cy what he owed him, the answer was, 'A bag of dog biscuits and one of corn, Dennis. And bring the dog to see us now and again.'

Sadly, on the same day that Bruce first went to the

Moulsons, the old mongrel, Judy, was to pass on to even more bone-strewn pastures.

A tell-tale tin of Glade stood on the window sill and there was a faint scent of lavender in the air. And although the aerosol undoubtedly jarred with its rather more conservative surroundings – as though a pink, plastic duck had been tossed into the punchbowl at an ambassador's reception – it is unlikely whether any of the occupants of the room was even aware of its presence. For the four of them were each engaged in various shades of private thought.

It was five-thirty on a mid-August evening and, outside, a blackbird was intent on giving the small group a mighty welcome – an overture of promise. But for now at least, the liquid notes, as with the essence of lavender, went unheeded.

This was easily the biggest room in the farmhouse and they stood in the centre of it – Wendy, Kevin, Derek, and young Tom, Derek's schoolboy friend, although exactly what young Tom was doing here, neither adult had thought to ask.

All four of them searched their surroundings with moving eyes and some casual observer would easily have been excused for thinking that perhaps they were searching for an escaped fly. But in these unfamiliar settings, rather were they taking in the grand dimensions of the place, especially when compared to the modest measurements of Quarry Street.

It was to be Derek who would be the first to speak, and this to comment childlike on the obvious size of the place. 'It's big. What do you reckon, Tom?'

'It's big all right,' Tom answered and, with this particular topic of conversation thus being exhausted, the boys now wandered off, leaving the silence to reign once again in the big room.

As his gaze flicked from ceiling to floor and back again, then to sweep the walls and the fireplace, Kevin's thoughts, as he basked in achievement, were in the stratosphere. To say this was the same building he had almost despaired over all those weeks ago was only partly true. For of the original shell, filled nearly to the brim with filth, there was no evidence at all. All the grime, all the fears that surely the job was too big, that the desolation was too complete to be overcome, had now been blown away on the winds of reality. Magic had touched the place.

He stood with Wendy now, in the very spot he'd stood when the place was bad enough to quell the stoutest heart. Then, when the work had actually started, when Manny had taken the very first measurements, Kevin had asked that she didn't come again. 'Not till we get somewhere with the place, eh, love?'

And even then, when Graham and Manny had really been convinced that the job might be possible after all, a miracle in itself, the transition from mere enthusiasm to real conviction had been a slow one. For always at the back of his mind, and not too far at the back at that, was the knowledge of his own undoubted limitations, and he was only thankful that over the weeks he'd resisted the temptation to ask Wendy to share the burden and let her complete faith in him remain intact.

Then came the time when the light began to break at last, Manny whistling his way through every annoying setback and Graham easing the financial burden a little by saying that he had suddenly found out where he could get a fair price for both the Singer and the Lanchester. Their work on them was done and, apart from the hours of labour they had lovingly spent, the money was nearly all profit. 'And we can always buy another couple of heaps of rust later on,' he'd laughed.

Kevin was to dwell quite a while on what Graham had said – and on his friend's true motives.

Then his thoughts came back to the house, to all the effort, and he wanted the moment to last. What hadn't been replaced altogether in the building had been either sanded, scoured, or waxed. The bottom half of this room had been panelled in... But he would go no further. He wanted to picture the house as a whole. The garden and the outside walls. There were four large kennels finished already; others started, with a concrete and posted run joining them together. There was ... his thoughts soared on. And all without worrying Wendy.

Leaving the Glade behind but taking her tape measure with her, for she had insisted on paying for every new curtain in the farmhouse, Liz Peach had tactfully left the family to enjoy the moment alone and, for once, Wendy was thankful of this. For her cheeks, besides being ablush with pleasure, were also tinted with shame. She was busy warring with her conscience, knowing that she could no longer hide behind her fatalism.

Like so many people before her, she had dreamt often of her dream house, even down to the last detail and, just as she knew she would have chosen Jane Hayseldene's garden, she now knew that she would have chosen this house – the house she had acquired under false pretences.

She struggled to hold back the tears. She'd known perfectly well at the time that Kevin was no master of all trades, as she didn't know what sort of effort, if any, that Graham Ogden would be prepared to put in. And she had hardly been aware of Manny Paxton's existence. Oh, she knew soon after the men had started work but, by then, her dishonesty had been established.

And it was no good blaming Liz. Back on that first

day, when the two of them were stood on this very spot amidst the rubble, when Liz had enthused about the place so much, Wendy knew very well that she'd let herself be carried along – that she didn't really need any coaxing at all.

She tried to think of other things – of the fact that if they were to do the farmhouse any justice at all, then they would gradually have to buy furniture worthy of the place. The only thing really worth much back in Quarry Street was the Kilmarnock chest in mahogany, given her and Kevin by her mother on the day that Derek had been born. Wendy now looked at the space in the big room where she thought it might go best.

But in spite of her efforts, the guilt came flooding back and she glanced sideways at Kevin – at the mud-coloured nose in profile. What was it she'd said to him at the time? 'The place does need doing up a bit, love?' Something like that.

What had he really thought? she wondered. When he'd first set eyes on the place. Had he thought she must have considered him to be some kind of genius or, bright, intelligent woman though she was, was it that she just had no real comprehension of what was involved?

She mused on, on whether she would ever admit the truth to him – some night in bed perhaps, in the darkness. But she doubted it. Some things were better left unsaid. But how she loved this man. 'What colour curtains do you think, love?' she asked.

'That repast was simply out of this world, my love,' said Kevin in his old way. 'What was it?'

It was the first proper meal at the farmhouse. 'It was chicken roast with cinnamon and rosemary,' smiled Wendy as she counted the calories in her head.

'Well, it was exquisite. What did you think, boys? Oh, sorry, boys.' As a treat, young Tom was there at Derek's side, both boys being equally engrossed.

The pudding was cherry cheesecake and, as Kevin finished, he sat back and sighed. The last few days had been hard. 'You work too hard, love,' he said now. 'We both need a break. What about the Fawkley Social? Tomorrow night?'

She was about to object mildly, say they couldn't really afford it. But she stopped herself. Of course they needed a break. It would soon be a rare-enough occurrence anyway, this being able to go out together, once the kennels started filling up. People had already started to enquire about holidays.

She jumped up to phone Tom's parents, just to make sure that Derek could stay there for the following evening. It was a fancy new phone and only the second time she'd used it.

There was bustle and noise in the big room upstairs in the Fawkley Social Club. It was Thursday and members of the Lantern Club were there in good numbers. When Wendy came in with Liz, Kevin was already there, sitting with Dennis Hayseldene and Jane. And as Kevin jumped up to get the newcomers a drink, there was a slight and momentary hush in the room – an air of expectancy – as though everyone had suddenly run out of things to say. Even Buster Howes, already quite happy as he sat with Derek Greene and one or two others, fell quiet for a brief second.

Then the moment was passed and everyone was talking again. Kevin returned with the drinks just as Wendy was whispering to the other two women. Liz was nodding and smiling but Jane Hayseldene had formed an 'O' of surprise

301

with her mouth. Kevin had the thought that her hair looked as black as ever as, amid the hubbub, Dennis's face was contorted with effort as he tried, unsuccessfully, to hear what the women were on about.

Kevin sat back in his chair, thankful to ease his bones for a while, and Dennis, giving up his attempt to eavesdrop, began to talk, with the subject quickly coming round to the farmhouse. 'Glad to be in then, I expect, Kevin?'

'I'll say so. I'd forgotten how bad moving can be. It's been a bit of a push all right. But it's over now, thank God. We've had some other good news, as well. Warwick Edwards told us yesterday that we'd got a firm offer for Quarry Street.'

'I'm glad to 'ear it. It's them ... those, sort of problems that go to make the thing so much worse than it should be.'

Kevin smiled to himself, recalling the time when Dennis first told them of the trouble he was having with Bruce, speaking so slowly in his near grief as to pronounce every aitch with care. What a change in the man, now. Kevin was certain, too, that the big man had put on weight. But if he knew anything at all about Jane Hayseldene, she would soon be counting the calories, now that the trouble was over. One thought ran into another and he was reminded of what Wendy had said about when Jane had first visited the farmhouse – how impressed she had seemed and how Wendy had been so pleased, a nice kind of pride and, of course, an unspoken credit to Kevin.

'What about those two mates of yours?' Dennis was now saying carefully. 'I never see them in the club here. They do take a pint, I suppose?'

'Well, Graham's not strictly teetotal I believe, but he certainly doesn't go out drinking as such. But Manny likes a drink. Uses a pub near his shop. Green Dragon. They've a parrot on the bar, y'know.'

'Eh?'

Kevin laughed. 'That's what Manny always says. "Green Dragon. They've a parrot on the bar, y'know".'

'Ah. And what would he say, do you think, should the bird have the misfortune to die, then?'

'Oh, I don't know, Dennis. Something like, "Green Dragon. But the parrot's dead"?'

Now both of them were laughing. 'Or maybe,' said Dennis, ' "Brown Cow. But only since the parrot died." '

Both of these men had been under considerable, personal strain for the past few weeks and, as their problems had been resolved at almost exactly the same time, this light-veined conversation was a way of letting the tension drain out of them, whether or not they were aware of it. Perhaps, too, they were each of them unaware of the fact that between remarks, they made independent efforts, but without success, to catch an inkling of what the women were saying.

'But joking apart, Kevin,' Dennis said at last, 'you certainly seem to have a couple of good mates there, all right. However would you have managed without them?'

'Well, of course, the simple truth is that I wouldn't. And I'll never be able to even begin to repay either of them. And they're such experts. You should just see the place, Dennis. In the daylight, I mean,' he laughed. 'Tell you what. Why don't you bring the family? Bruce as well. Before the house-warming proper, I mean. Just let us know when.'

'I'd like that. I'll warn you now though, Kevin, while we're on about it. It's young Rita. She's mad about dogs. Can't wait to see the kennels. With some girls, it's horses, but with her, it's dogs. Keeps on hinting about a part-time job with Wendy. What do you think?'

'Right. Well. I'll talk to . . .' But Kevin got no further, for as he reached for his drink, and, to his surprise, a note was suddenly shoved into his hand from the direction of the women. It was Wendy and she looked at him across the table, before putting her other hand briefly over the one of his which now held the note. Then he saw that both Liz and Jane were also looking at him and, perplexed, he could do nothing but smile back weakly. Wendy then withdrew her hands and the women now resumed talking amongst themselves.

Kevin looked back at Dennis, who was not only looking puzzled but also now slightly annoyed at being kept in the dark about the whole business.

'Scuse me, Dennis,' said Kevin lamely as he opened the note.

'My dear,' it read. 'I am pregnant. I just thought I would let you know. You may tell Dennis. W.'

Mouth now wide open, Kevin shot a glance across at the women but they were talking casually together. Too casually, he thought. He looked back at Dennis who by now was definitely becoming pink-cheeked. And I don't blame him, thought Kevin, and, unable to speak himself, he shoved the note across. The man snatched it avidly and read it at a glance. Then, at last, a slow smile beginning to spread across his face, he too looked across at the instigators.

In their little charade of innocence and in the full knowledge that its effect on the two men was all they could have wished, the three at last looked back across the table – the cats who had just had the cream. Dennis raised an accusing forefinger, or perhaps he was merely going to point at Kevin's mouth, which was still open. 'Kevin,' he began but, in his turn, he too got no further, for there was a sudden ringing sound in the room, urgent and shrill. It was Warwick Edwards, tapping his glass for quiet. And it came straightaway.

* * *

Whether engaged in climbing the Eiger, or in his chambers conferring with a client, or here at a meeting of the Lantern Club, the man always managed to give the same impression which was that of a gentleman – calm and debonair. And as far as everyone in that room was concerned, the picture was a true one, giving presence to any gathering. He had dignity without too much convention and, now smiling round the room, he began speaking. 'Ladies and gentlemen, good evening. You all know what we're about in the club, but I'll remind you just the same. We're about unusual things, are we not?'

Kevin's breathing had now started to return to normal and after a covert glance at Wendy, who also happened to be looking across at him, he forced himself to listen to Warwick.

'And quite a few weeks ago, Dennis Hayseldene came to the committee with his idea – another first, fellow members, for it was not on his own behalf. It was on another's.'

No one was seen to stir at this point and it was anyone's guess who already knew what, although Kevin now recalled the unusual pause in the general proceedings when he'd first come in that evening. 'Wendy is pregnant. I am going to be...' No, no. Must concentrate on what is being said. Listen to Warwick.

'Most of you now know of Dennis's problem, of course. It was to do with his dog and how he was having trouble with it. He told the committee about seeking the advice of Wendy Lowe, one of our lady members and also a local and acknowledged expert on animals.'

As one, the entire assemblage turned to look at Wendy. Her suspicions having been aroused, she was already blushing prettily and she looked at Liz and Jane. Yes, they knew something, she could tell. And Kevin was thinking, 'What shall we say to Derek? About the baby?'

'So amidst his own troubles, Dennis put forward the suggestion that, should Wendy prove successful, some award might be made.' And now it was Dennis's turn to come under quick scrutiny and, in his turn, he also coloured up a little, though perhaps not quite so prettily as Wendy.

'And as you all now know, Wendy, with a little outside help, did manage to solve the problem. Therefore,' and Warwick now reached under the small, round table to produce a package the size of a small shoebox, 'and as ladies don't usually wear ties, we designed a little something else. Let's hope she likes it,' and coming forward as he spoke, he gave her the box, kissed her resoundingly on both cheeks and returned to his seat.

Slightly embarrassed, she smiled round the room and opened the thing quickly. It was a square of pure silk with a dark-green background scattered with tiny gold lanterns. She lifted it up for them all to see, happy in the murmurs of approval. But Buster Howes, in his present happy state, wasn't at all satisfied with this muted reception. 'Speech,' he shouted. 'Speech, Wendy,' and the cry was taken up, genuine enough but still with some reserve, for, after all, it was supposed to be a solemn enough occasion.

Wendy stood up and thespian though she was, she was still quite nervous, unrehearsed as it all was. But her voice, when she did begin, was clear enough. 'Lovely surprise, my friends, and thank you for the honour it bears.'

There was a little clapping at this and she went on, 'I must say that, just lately, I have been extremely fortunate. This scarf is my fourth blessing. I'll tell you all what they are if I may.' As she spoke, she put the scarf around her neck. 'The main blessing is my family and my friends, both present and absent. I won't name them. They know who they are and, without them, we wouldn't easily, if at all, have managed another blessing, that of Pettit's farmhouse. Our dream home. So thank you all once again. Most sincerely. And you all know where we are. Anytime,' and now, amidst loud applause, she made to sit down.

But Buster was on cue. 'That's only three,' he shouted.

'What's that, Buster?' said Wendy, getting to her feet once more.

'Four blessings, you said. You gave us only three,' and at this, there was a lull in the proceedings.

'Did I?' she said. 'Oh. Oh, yes of course. Didn't I mention it? It's about Kevin. He's going to be a father again, you know.'

And that's when the real applause began.